CRISIS

A bestselling author for many years, Dr. Robin Cook is currently on leave from the Massachusetts Eye and Ear Infirmary. He lives and works in Florida.

Also by Robin Cook

ROBIN COOK

CRISIS

PAN BOOKS

First published 2006 by G. P. Putnam's Sons,
a member of Penguin Group (USA) Inc, New York

First published in Great Britain 2006 by Macmillan

This edition published 2007 by Pan Books
an imprint of Pan Macmillan Ltd
Pan Macmillan, 20 New Wharf Road, London N1 9RR
Basingstoke and Oxford
Associated companies throughout the world
www.panmacmillan.com

ISBN 978-0-330-44552-8

3 5 7 9 8 6 4

A CIP catalogue record for this book is available from
the British Library.

Typeset by Intype Libra Ltd
Printed and bound in Great Britain by
Mackays of Chatham plc, Chatham, Kent

ACKNOWLEDGMENTS

As usual in writing my fact-based novels, I've had to rely on friends and acquaintances to answer my innumerable pesky questions. It was especially important for *Crisis*, since the story line bridges medicine and law. Although I thank everyone who was graciously willing to help, those whom I would particularly like to cite are (in alphabetical order):

John W. Bresnahan, investigator, Division of Professional Licensure, Commonwealth of Massachusetts

Jean R. Cook, psychologist

Joe Cox, J.D., LL.M., tax and estate-planning attorney

Rose Doherty, academician

Mark Flomenbaum, M.D., Ph.D., Chief Medical Examiner, Commonwealth of Massachusetts

Peter C. Knight, J.D., malpractice attorney

Angelo MacDonald, J.D., criminal law attorney, former prosecutor

Gerald D. McLellan, J.D., family law attorney, former judge

Charles Wetli, M.D., Chief Medical Examiner, Suffolk County, New York

*This book is dedicated to the contemporary medical
professionalism as promulgated by the Physician
Charter, in hope that it takes root and flourishes. . . .
Make way, Hippocrates!*

The laws of conscience,
which we say are born of nature,
are born of custom.

—MONTAIGNE

PROLOGUE

SEPTEMBER 8, 2005

Autumn is a glorious season, despite its frequent use as a metaphor for approaching death and dying. Nowhere is its invigorating ambience and riotous color more apparent than in the northeastern United States. Even in early September the hot, hazy, humid days of the New England summer are progressively replaced by crystalline days with cool, clear, dry air and azure skies. September 8, 2005, was a case in point. Not a cloud marred the translucent sky from Maine to New Jersey, and within the macadam maze of downtown Boston and the concrete grid of New York City, the temperature was a comfortable seventy-seven degrees Fahrenheit.

As the day drew to a close, two doctors coincidently and reluctantly fumbled to pull their ringing cell phones from their belt clips in their respective cities. Neither was happy about the intrusion. Each was fearful that the melodic ring would herald a crisis that would require their professional attention and presence. An inopportune interruption, as both individuals were anticipating interesting personal evening activities.

Unfortunately, the doctors' intuitions were correct, since both calls were to give credence to autumn's metaphorical reputation. The call in Boston concerned someone about to die with the acute onset of chest pain, profound weakness, and difficulty breathing, while the one in New York was about someone recently but clearly already dead. Both situations were emergencies for the respective physicians, necessitating that they put their private plans on hold. What the doctors didn't know was that one of the calls would initiate a sequence of events that would seriously impact them both, put both in jeopardy, and turn them into bitter enemies, and the other call would ultimately put a different spin on the first!

BOSTON, MASSACHUSETTS
7:10 p.m.

Dr. Craig Bowman let his arms dangle at his sides for a moment to relieve his aching forearm muscles. He had been standing in front of the mirror that was attached to the backside of the closet door, struggling to tie a black formal bow tie. He'd worn a tuxedo at most a half a dozen times in his life, the first time at his high-school prom and the last time when he got married, and on all of those previous occasions, he'd been satisfied to snap on a pre-tied model that came with the rented tux. But now, in his reincarnation of himself, he wanted the genuine article. He'd bought himself a brand-new tuxedo and wasn't about to settle for a fake tie. The trouble was, he really didn't know how to tie it and had been embarrassed to ask the salesclerk. At the time, he hadn't been worried since he figured it would somehow be similar to tying his shoes.

Sadly, it was proving to be a lot different, and he had been attempting to tie the blasted thing for a good ten minutes. Luckily, Leona, his new and dynamite secretary-cum–file clerk and even newer companion, had been preoccupied with her makeup in the bathroom. Worst case, he'd have to ask her if she knew how to do it. Craig really didn't want to do that. They hadn't been seeing each other socially that long, and Craig preferred that she maintain her apparent belief in his sophistication, fearing he'd otherwise never hear the end of it. Leona had what his matronly receptionist-secretary and his nurse called a "mouth." Tactfulness wasn't her strong suit.

Craig shot a quick glance in Leona's direction. The door to the bathroom was ajar, and she was doing her eyes, but all he could see was a side view of her curvaceous twenty-three-year-old derriere covered with a lustrous pink silk crepe. She was on her tiptoes, leaning over the sink to get closer to the mirror. A fleeting, self-satisfied smile passed over Craig's face as he thought of them walking down the aisle of Symphony Hall that evening, which was why they were getting decked out in their finery. Compensating for being a "mouth," Leona was a "looker," especially in the low-cut dress that they had recently bought at Neiman Marcus. He was sure she was going to turn some heads and that he'd be dodging some envious looks from fellow forty-five-year-old men. Craig realized such feelings were rather juvenile, to say the least, but he'd not felt them since that first time he'd worn a tuxedo, and he was going to enjoy it.

Craig's smile faltered when the question occurred to him whether any of his and his wife's friends might be there in the audience. His goal certainly wasn't to humiliate anyone or hurt anyone's feelings. Yet he doubted he'd see any acquaintances, because he and his wife had never gone to the symphony, nor had any of their few friends, who were mostly overworked physicians like himself. Taking advantage of the city's cultural life hadn't been part of their particular suburban lifestyle, thanks to the hours a typical practice of medicine demanded.

Craig had been separated from Alexis now for six months, so it wasn't unreasonable to have a companion. He didn't think it was an age issue. As long as he was with an adult woman of a reasonable, postcollege age, it shouldn't matter. After all, being seen out and about with a date was going to happen sooner or later, as active as he'd become. In addition to regular attendance at the symphony, he'd become a regular at a new gym, as well as at the theater, the ballet, and a number of other activities and social gatherings that normal educated people participated in in a world-class city. Since Alexis had consistently refused to go along with his new persona right from its inception, he now felt he was justified to accompany whomever he wanted. He wasn't going to be held back from becoming the person he aspired to be. He'd even joined the Museum of Fine Arts and was looking forward to exhibition openings, despite never having ever been to one. He'd had to sacrifice enjoying such cultural activities during the arduous and isolating effort of becoming a doctor—particularly, becoming the best doctor he could be—which meant that for ten years of his adult life, he was absent from the hospital only to sleep. And then once he'd finished his specialty training in internal medicine and hung out his proverbial shingle, he'd had even less time for personal pursuits of any kind, including, unfortunately, much family life. He'd become the archetypal, intellectually provincial workaholic with no time for anyone but his patients. But all that was changing, and regrets and guilt, particularly about family issues, had to be put on hold. The new Dr. Craig Bowman had left behind the lockstep, hurried, unfulfilling, and uncultured workaday life. He knew that some people might call his situation a midlife crisis, but he had a different name for it. He called it a rebirth or, more accurately, an awakening.

Over the previous year, Craig had become committed to—even obsessed with—transforming himself into a more interesting, happier, well-rounded, better person and, because of it, a better doctor. On the desk of his in-town apartment was a pile of catalogues from various local universities, including Harvard. He intended to take classes in humanities: maybe one or two a semester to make up for lost time. And best of all, thanks to his makeover, he'd been able to return to his beloved research, which had completely fallen by the wayside once he'd started practice. What had started out in medical school as a remunerative job doing scut work for a professor studying sodium channels in muscle and nerve cells had turned into a passion when he was elevated to the level of a fellow researcher. Craig had even coauthored several scientific papers to great acclaim while he'd been a medical student and then resident. Now he was back at the bench, able to spend two afternoons a week in the lab, and he loved it. Leona called him a Renaissance man, and although he knew the description was premature, he thought that with a couple of years of effort, he might come close.

The origin of Craig's metamorphosis had been rather sudden and had taken him by complete surprise. Just over a year previously, and quite serendipitously, his professional life and practice had changed dramatically with the double benefit of significantly raising his income as well as his job satisfaction. All at once it had become

possible for him truly to practice the kind of medicine
he'd learned in medical school, where patients' needs
eclipsed the arcane rules of their insurance coverage.
Suddenly, Craig could spend an hour with someone if
the patient's situation required it. Appropriately, it had
become his decision. In one fell swoop, he'd been freed
of the dual scourge of falling reimbursements and rising
costs that had forced him to squeeze more and more
patients into his busy day. To get paid, he no longer had
to fight with insurance personnel who were often medi-
cally ignorant. He'd even started making house calls
when it was in the patient's best interest, an action that
had been unthinkable in his former life.

The change had been a dream come true. When the
offer had unexpectedly come over the transom, he'd told
his would-be benefactor and now partner that he'd have
to think about it. How could he have been so stupid not
to agree on the spot? What if he had missed the opportunity to grab the brass ring? Everything was better, save
for the family problem, but the root of that issue was
how submerged he'd been from day one in his former
professional situation. Ultimately, it had been his fault,
which he freely admitted. He had let the exigencies of
current medical practice dictate and limit his life. But
now he certainly wasn't drowning, so maybe the family
difficulties could be resolved in the future, given enough
time. Maybe Alexis could be convinced how much better
all their lives could be. Meanwhile, he resolved to enjoy
bettering himself. For the first time in his life, Craig had
free time and money in the bank.

With an end of the bow tie in each hand, Craig was
about to try tying it again when his cell phone rang. His
face fell. He glanced at his watch. It was ten after seven.

The symphony was to start at eight thirty. His eyes switched to the caller ID. The name was Stanhope.

"Damn!" Craig blurted with emphasis. He flipped open his phone, put it to his ear, and said hello.

"Doctor Bowman!" a refined voice said. "I'm calling about Patience. She's worse. In fact, this time I think she's really sick."

"What seems to be the problem, Jordan?" Craig asked as he turned to glance back into the bathroom. Leona had heard the phone and was looking at him. He mouthed the name *Stanhope,* and Leona nodded. She knew what that meant, and Craig could tell from her expression that she had the same fear he had—namely, that their evening was now in jeopardy. If they arrived at the symphony too late, they'd have to wait for the intermission to sit down, which meant forgoing the fun and excitement of the entrance, which both had been keenly anticipating.

"I don't know," Jordan said. "She appears unnaturally weak. She doesn't even seem to be able to sit up."

"Besides weakness, what are her symptoms?"

"I think we should call an ambulance and go to the hospital. She's greatly perturbed, and she's got me concerned."

"Jordan, if you are concerned, then I am, too," Craig said soothingly. "What are her symptoms? I mean, I was just there at your home this morning dealing with her usual medley of complaints. Is it something different or what?" Patience Stanhope was one of less than a half-dozen patients that Craig labeled "problem patients," but she was the worst of the group. Every doctor had had them, in every kind of practice, and found them tedious at best and maddening at worst. They were the patients who persisted day in and day out with a litany of complaints that were, for the most part, completely psychosomatic or totally phantom and that could rarely be helped by any therapy, including alternative medicine. Craig had tried everything with such patients, to no avail. They were generally depressed, demanding, frustrating, and time-consuming, and now with the Internet, quite creative with their professed symptoms and desire for lengthy conversations and hand-holding. In his previous practice, after ascertaining their hypochondriasis beyond a reasonable doubt, Craig would arrange to see them as infrequently as possible, mostly by shunting them off to the nurse practitioner or to the nurse or, rarely, to a sub-specialist if he could get them to go, particularly to see a psychiatrist. But in Craig's current practice setup, he was limited in his ability to resort to such ruses, meaning the "problem patients" were the only bugbears of his new practice. Representing only three percent of his patient base, as reported by the accountant, they consumed more than fifteen percent of his time. Patience was the prime example. He had been seeing her at least once a week over the last eight months and, more often than not, in the evening or at night. As Craig frequently quipped to his staff, she was trying his patience. The comment never failed to get a laugh.

"This is far different," Jordan said. "It's entirely dissimilar to her complaints last evening and morning."

"How so?" Craig asked. "Can you give me some specifics?" He wanted to be as certain as possible about what was going on with Patience, forcing himself to remember that hypochondriacs occasionally actually got sick. The problem with dealing with such patients was that they lowered one's index of suspicion. It was like the allegory of the shepherd boy crying wolf.

"The pain is in a different location."

"Okay, that's a start," Craig said. He shrugged for Leona's benefit and motioned for her to hurry. If the current problem was what he thought, he wanted to take Leona along on the house call. "How is the pain different?"

"The pain this morning was in her rectum and the lower part of her belly."

"I remember!" Craig said. How could he forget? Bloating, gas, and problems with elimination described in disgustingly exquisite detail were the usual complaints. "Where is it now?"

"She says it's in her chest. She's never complained of pain in her chest before."

"That's not quite true, Jordan. Last month there were several episodes of chest pain. That's why I gave her a stress test."

"You're right! I forgot about that. I can't keep up with all her symptoms."

You and me both, Craig wanted to say, but he held his tongue.

"I think she should go to the hospital," Jordan repeated. "I believe she's having some difficulty breathing and even talking. Earlier, she managed to tell me she had a headache and was sick to her stomach."

"Nausea is one of her common afflictions," Craig interjected. "So is the headache."

"But this time she threw up a little. She also said she felt like she was floating in the air and kind of numb."

"Those are new ones!"

"I'm telling you, this is altogether different."

"Is the pain visceral and crushing, or is it sharp and intermittent like a cramp?"

"I can't say."

"Could you ask her? It may be important."

"Okay, hold the line!"

Craig could hear Jordan drop the receiver. Leona came out of the bathroom. She was ready. To Craig, she looked like she belonged on the cover of a magazine. He indicated as much by giving her a thumbs-up. She smiled and mouthed: "What's happening?"

Craig shrugged, keeping the cell phone pressed to his ear but twisting it away from his mouth. "Looks like I'm going to have to make a house call."

Leona nodded, then questioned: "Are you having trouble with your tie?"

Craig reluctantly nodded.

"Let's see what I can do," Leona suggested.

Craig raised his chin to give her more room to work as Jordan came back on the line. "She says the pain is terrible. She says it's all of those words you used."

Craig nodded. That sounded like the Patience he was all too familiar with. No help there. "Does the pain radiate anywhere, like to her arm or neck or any other place?"

"Oh my word! I don't know. Should I ask her?"

"Please," Craig replied.

After a few deft maneuvers, Leona pulled on the looped ends of the bow tie and tightened the knot she had made. After a minor adjustment, she stepped back. "Not bad, even if I say so myself," she declared.

Craig looked at himself in the mirror and had to agree. She had made it look easy.

Jordan's voice came over the phone. "She says it's just

in her chest. Are you thinking she's experiencing a heart attack, doctor?"

"It has to be ruled out, Jordan," Craig said. "Remember, I told you she had some mild changes on her stress test, which is why I advised more investigation of her cardiac status, even though she was not inclined."

"I do remember now that you mention it. But whatever the current affliction, I believe it's progressing. I believe she even appears rather blue."

"Okay, Jordan, I'll be right there. But one other quick question: Did she take any of those antidepressant pills I left this morning?"

"Is that important?"

"It could be. Although it doesn't sound like she is having a drug reaction, we have to keep it in mind. It was a new medication for her. That's why I told her not to start until tonight when she went to bed, just in case they made her dizzy or anything."

"I have no idea if she did or not. She has a lot of medication she got from Dr. Cohen."

Craig nodded. He knew very well that Patience's medicine cabinet looked like a miniature pharmacy. Dr. Ethan Cohen was a much more liberal prescriber of medication than Craig, and he had originally been Patience's physician. It had been Dr. Cohen who had offered Craig the opportunity to join his practice, but he was currently Craig's partner more in theory than in fact. The man was having his own health issues and was on an extended leave that might end up being permanent. Craig had inherited his entire current roster of problem patients from his absent partner. To Craig's delight, none of his problem patients from his previous practice had decided to pay the required fee to switch to the new practice.

"Listen, Jordan," Craig said. "I'm on my way, but make an effort to find the small vial of sample pills I gave Patience this morning so we can count them."

"I will give it my best effort," Jordan said.

Craig flipped his phone shut. He looked at Leona. "I've definitely got to make a house call. Do you mind coming with me? If it turns out to be a false alarm, we can go directly to the concert and still make the entrée. Their house is not that far from Symphony Hall."

"Fine by me," Leona said cheerfully.

While pulling on his tuxedo jacket, Craig went quickly to his front closet. From the top shelf, he got his black bag and snapped it open. It had been a gift from his mother when he'd graduated from medical school. At the time it had meant a mountain to Craig because he had an idea of how long his mom had to have squirreled money away without his father knowing to afford it. It was a sizable, old-fashioned doctor's bag made of black leather with brass hardware. In his former practice, Craig had never used it since he didn't make house calls. But over the last year he'd used it a lot.

Craig tossed a bunch of supplies he thought he might need into the bag, including a bedside assay kit for myocardial infarction or heart attack biomarkers. Science had advanced since he'd been a resident. Back then it could take days to get the results back from the lab. Now he could do it at the bedside. The assay wasn't quantitative, but that didn't matter. It was proof of the diagnosis that was important. Also from the top shelf he pulled down his portable ECG machine, which he handed to Leona.

When Craig had formally separated from Alexis, he had found an apartment on Beacon Hill in the center of

Boston. It was a fourth-floor walk-up duplex on Revere Street with good sunlight, a deck, and a view over the Charles River to Cambridge. The Hill was central to the city and fulfilled Craig's needs superbly, especially since he could walk to several good restaurants and the theater district. The only minor inconvenience was the parking problem. He had to rent a space in a garage on Charles Street, a five-minute walk away.

"What are the chances we can get away in time for the concert?" Leona asked when they were on their way in Craig's new Porsche, speeding westward on Storrow Drive.

Craig had to raise his voice against the whine of the engine. "Jordan seems to think this might be legit. That's what scares me. Living with Patience, he knows her better than anybody."

"How can he live with her? She's such a pain in the ass, and he seems like quite a refined gentleman." Leona had observed the Stanhopes in the office on a couple of occasions.

"I imagine there are benefits. I have a sense she is the one with the money, but who knows. People's private lives are never what they seem, including my own, until recently." He gave Leona's thigh a squeeze.

"I don't know how you have such patience with such people," Leona marveled. "No pun intended."

"It's a struggle, and between you and me, I can't stand them. Luckily, they are a distinct minority. I was trained to take care of sick people. Hypochondriacs to me are the same as malingerers. If I had wanted to be a psychiatrist, I would have studied psychiatry."

"When we get there, should I wait in the car?"

"It's up to you," Craig said. "I don't know how long

I'll be. Sometimes she corners me for an hour. I think you should come in. It would be boring to sit in the car."

"It will be interesting to see how they live."

"Hardly the average couple."

The Stanhopes lived in a massive, three-story, Georgian-style brick house on a sizable wooded lot near the Chestnut Hill Country Club in an upscale area of Brighton, Massachusetts. Craig entered the circular drive and pulled up to the front of the building. He knew the route all too well. Jordan had the door open as they mounted the three steps. Craig had the black bag; Leona carried the ECG machine.

"She is upstairs in her bedroom," Jordan said quickly. He was a tall, meticulous man dressed in a dark green velvet smoking jacket. If he marveled at Craig and Leona's formal attire, he didn't let on. He held out a small plastic vial and dropped it in Craig's hand before turning on his heel.

It was the free sample bottle of Zoloft Craig had given Patience that morning. Craig could see immediately that one of the six pills was missing. Obviously, she had started the medication earlier than Craig had suggested. He pocketed the vial and started after Jordan. "Do you mind if my secretary comes along?" Craig called out. "She can possibly lend me a hand." Leona had demonstrated a few times in the office her willingness to help out. Craig had been impressed by her initiative and commitment from the start, long before he thought of asking her to a social event. He was equally impressed that she was taking night courses at Bunker Hill Community College in Charlestown, with the idea of eventually getting some sort of medical degree as a technician or nurse. For him, it added to her appeal.

"Not at all," Jordan responded over his shoulder, waving for them to follow. He had started up the main staircase that skirted the Palladian window above the front door.

"Separate bedrooms," Leona whispered to Craig as they hurried after Jordan. "It kind of defeats the purpose. I thought that was only in old movies."

Craig didn't respond. They quickly descended a long carpeted hallway and entered the feminine master suite upholstered in a square mile of blue silk. Patience, her eyelids heavy, was lying in a king-size bed, semi-propped up with overstuffed pillows. A servant in a demure French maid's outfit straightened up. She had been holding a moist cloth against Patience's forehead.

With a quick glance at Patience and without saying a word, Craig rushed over to the woman, dropped the bag on the bed next to her, and felt for a pulse. He snapped open the bag and pulled out his blood-pressure cuff and stethoscope. As he wrapped the cuff around Patience's right arm, he barked to Jordan: "Call an ambulance!"

With only a slight elevation of his eyebrows to indicate he had heard, Jordan went to the nightstand phone and dialed 911. He gave the servant woman a wave of dismissal.

"Good Lord!" Craig murmured as he tore off the cuff. He snapped the pillows from behind Patience's body and her torso fell back onto the bed like a rag doll. He yanked down the covers and pulled open her negligee, then listened briefly to her thorax with his stethoscope before motioning to Leona to give him the ECG machine. Jordan could be heard speaking with the 911 operator. Craig fumbled to unsnarl the ECG leads and quickly attached them with a bit of conducting jelly.

"Is she going to be all right?" Leona asked in a whisper.

"Who the hell knows," Craig answered. "She's cyanotic, for Christ's sake."

"What's cyanotic?"

"There's not enough oxygen in her blood. I don't know if it's because her heart isn't pumping enough or she's not breathing enough. It's one or the other or both."

Craig concentrated on the ECG machine as it spewed out a tracing. There were only little blips, widely spaced. Craig tore off the output strip and took a quick, closer glance at it before jamming it into his jacket pocket. He then snapped the leads off Patience's extremities.

Jordan hung up the phone. "The ambulance is on its way."

Craig merely nodded as he rapidly rummaged in his bag and pulled out an Ambu breathing bag. He placed the mask over Patience's nose and mouth and compressed the bag. Her chest rose easily, suggesting good ventilation.

"Could you do this?" Craig asked Leona as he continued to ventilate Patience.

"I guess so," Leona said hesitantly. She squeezed between Craig and the headboard and took over the assisted breathing.

Craig showed her how to maintain a seal and keep Patience's head back. He then glanced at Patience's pupils. They were widely dilated and unreactive. It wasn't a good sign. With the stethoscope, he checked Patience's breath sounds. She was being aerated well.

Back in his black bag, Craig pulled out the assay kit for testing for the biomarkers associated with a heart attack. He tore open the box and pulled out one of the plastic devices. He used a small, heparinized syringe to get some blood from a major vein, shook it, and then put six drops into the sample area. He then held the device under the light.

"Well, that's positive," he said after a moment. He then haphazardly tossed everything back into his bag.

"What is positive?" Jordan asked.

"Her blood is positive for myoglobin and troponin," Craig said. "In layman's terms, it means she's had a heart attack." With his stethoscope, Craig ascertained that Leona was ventilating Patience appropriately.

"So your initial impression was correct," Jordan commented.

"Hardly," Craig said. "I'm afraid I have to say, she is in a very bad situation."

"I was trying to communicate as much on the phone," Jordan said stiffly. "But at the moment, I was referring to the heart attack."

"She is worse off than you led me to believe," Craig said as he got out some epinephrine and atropine, along with a small bottle of intravenous fluid.

"I beg your pardon. I was quite clear she was progressively getting worse."

"You said she was having a little trouble breathing. Actually, she was hardly breathing at all when we got here. You could have let me know that. You said you believed she was rather blue, whereas I find her totally cyanotic." Craig deftly started an intravenous infusion. He taped the needle in place and gave the epinephrine and atropine. He hung the small IV bottle from the lampshade with a small S hook he had made for that specific purpose.

"I was doing the best I could to communicate to you, doctor."

"I appreciate that," Craig said, holding up his hands in a conciliatory gesture. "I'm sorry. I don't mean to be critical. I'm just concerned about your wife. What we need to do now is get her to the hospital as quickly as we can. She needs to be ventilated with oxygen, and she needs a cardiac pacer. On top of that, I'm certain she is acidotic and must be treated for it."

The undulating sound of the approaching ambulance could be heard in the distance. Jordan left to go downstairs to let in the emergency technicians and direct them up to Patience's room.

"Is she going to make it?" Leona asked as she continued compressing the Ambu bag. "She doesn't look quite as blue to me."

"You're doing a great job with that breathing bag," Craig responded. "But I'm not optimistic, since her pupils haven't come down, and she's so flaccid. But we'll know better when we get her over to Newton Memorial Hospital, get some blood work, get her on a respirator and a pacer. Would you mind driving my car? I want to ride in the ambulance in case she arrests. If she needs CPR, I want to do the chest compressions."

The EMTs were an efficient team. It was a man and a woman who obviously had worked together for some time, since they anticipated each other's moves. They swiftly moved Patience to a gurney, brought her downstairs, and loaded her into the ambulance. Within just a few minutes of their arrival at the Stanhope residence, they were back on the road. Recognizing a true emergency, they had the siren screaming and the woman drove accordingly. En route, the male EMT phoned ahead to Newton Memorial to advise them of what to expect.

Patience's heart was still beating, but barely, when they arrived. A staff cardiologist whom Craig knew well had been summoned, and she met them on the unloading dock. Patience was rolled inside with dispatch, and an entire team began to work on her. Craig told the cardiologist what he could, including the results of the biomarker assay confirming the diagnosis of myocardial infarction, or heart attack.

As Craig had anticipated, Patience was first put on a respirator with one hundred percent oxygen followed by an external pacemaker. Unfortunately, it was quickly confirmed that she then had the problem of PEA, or pulseless electrical activity, meaning the pacemaker was creating an image on the electrocardiogram but the heart was not responding with any beats. One of the residents climbed up onto the table to start chest compressions. Blood work came back and the blood gases were not bad, but the acid level was close to the highest the cardiologist had ever seen.

Craig and the cardiologist looked at each other. Both knew from experience that PEA had a dismal outcome with a hospital inpatient, even when caught quickly. The situation with Patience was far worse, since she had come in by ambulance.

After several hours of attempting all possible efforts to get the heart to respond, the cardiologist took Craig aside. Craig was dressed in his formal shirt, complete with bow tie still in place. Blood spatter adorned the upper part of his right arm, and his tuxedo jacket hung on a spare IV pole against the wall.

"It must have been extensive cardiac muscle damage,"

the cardiologist said. "It's the only way to explain all the conduction abnormalities and the PEA. Things might well have been different if we had been able to start on her a bit sooner. From your description of the time course, I imagine the size of the initial infarct significantly grew."

Craig nodded. He looked back at the team that was still doing cardiopulmonary resuscitation on Patience's slim frame. Ironically, her color had returned to near normal with the oxygen and the chest compressions. Unfortunately, they had run out of things to try.

"Did she have a history of cardiovascular disease?"

"She had an equivocal stress test a few months ago," Craig said. "It was suggestive of a mild problem, but the patient refused any follow-up studies."

"To her detriment," the cardiologist said. "Unfortunately, her pupils have never come down, suggesting anoxic brain damage. With that in mind, what do you want to do? It's your call."

Craig took in a deep breath and let it out noisily as a reflection of his discouragement. "I think we should stop."

"I agree one hundred percent," the cardiologist said. She gave Craig's shoulder a reassuring squeeze, then walked back to the table to tell the team it was over.

Craig got his tuxedo jacket and walked over to the ER desk to sign the paperwork indicating the patient was deceased and that the cause was cardiac arrest following myocardial infarction. Then he went out into the emergency room waiting area. Leona was seated among the sick, the injured, and their families. She was flipping through an old magazine. Dressed as she was, she appeared to Craig like a nugget of gold among nondescript gravel. Her eyes rose up as he approached. He could tell she read his expression.

"No luck?" she said.

Craig shook his head. He scanned the waiting area. "Where is Jordan Stanhope?"

"He left over an hour ago."

"Really? Why? What did he say?"

"He said he preferred to be at home, where he would await your call. He said something about hospitals depressing him."

Craig gave a short laugh. "I guess that's consistent. I always thought of him as a rather cold, odd duck who was just going through the motions with his wife."

Leona tossed aside the magazine and followed Craig out into the night. He thought about saying something philosophical about life to Leona but changed his mind. He didn't think she'd understand, and he was worried he wouldn't be able to explain it. Neither spoke until they got to the car.

"Do you want me to drive?" Leona asked.

Craig shook his head, opened the passenger door for Leona, then walked around and climbed in behind the wheel. He didn't start the car immediately. "We obviously missed the concert," he said, staring out through the windshield.

"To say the least," Leona said. "It's after ten. What would you like to do?"

Craig didn't have any idea. But he knew he had to call Jordan Stanhope and wasn't looking forward to it.

"Losing a patient must be the hardest thing about being a doctor," Leona said.

"Sometimes it's dealing with the survivors," Craig

responded, without any idea how prophetic his comment would turn out to be.

NEW YORK, NEW YORK
7:10 p.m.

Dr. Jack Stapleton had been sitting in his cramped office on the fifth floor of the Office of the Chief Medical Examiner for more hours than he was willing to admit. His office mate, Dr. Chet McGovern, had deserted him just after four when Chet left for his workout at his posh Midtown gym. As was often the case, he'd badgered Jack to come along with glowing tales of the newest batch of nubile female members in his body-sculpting class with their skintight outfits that left nothing to the imagination, but Jack had begged off with his customary rejoinder that he preferred being a participant rather than an observer when it came to sports. He couldn't believe that Chet could still laugh at what had become such a hackneyed comeback.

At five o'clock Dr. Laurie Montgomery, Jack's colleague and soul mate, had poked her head in to say she was heading home to shower and change for the romantic rendezvous Jack had arranged for the two of them that evening at their favorite New York restaurant, Elio's, where they had had a number of memorable dinners over the years. She had suggested he come along to freshen up as well, but he again begged off, saying he was swamped with work and he'd meet her at the restaurant at eight. Unlike Chet, she didn't try to change his mind. From her perspective, it was such a rare event for Jack to be so resourceful on a weeknight that she wanted to bend over backward in hopes of encouraging such behavior. His usual evening plans included a death-defying dash home on his mountain bike, a strenuous run on the neighborhood basketball court with his neighborhood buddies, a quick salad at one of the Columbus Avenue restaurants around nine, followed soon after by a mute collapse into bed.

Despite what he had said, Jack didn't have that much to do and had been scrounging around to keep himself busy, particularly over the last hour. Even before he had sat down at his desk, he had been reasonably caught up with all his outstanding autopsy cases. The reason he was forcing himself to labor this particular afternoon was to keep his mind occupied in a vain attempt to control the anxiety he felt about his secret plans for the evening. The process of submerging himself in either his work or strenuous athletic activity had been his balm and salvation for more than fourteen years, so he wasn't about to abandon the ruse now. Unfortunately, his contrived work wasn't holding his interest, especially since he was running out of things to do. His mind was beginning to wander into forbidden areas, which began to torment him into having second thoughts about the evening's plans. It was at that moment that his cell phone came to life. He glanced at his watch. There was less than an hour to go before D-day. He felt his pulse accelerate. A phone call at that moment was an inauspicious sign. Since the chances of it being Laurie were nil, the chances were huge that it was someone who could throw the evening's schedule out of whack.

Pulling the phone from his belt clip, Jack eyed the LCD screen. Just as he feared, it was Allen Eisenberg. Allen was one of the pathology residents who was being paid by the Office of the Chief Medical Examiner to cover routine problems after hours, which the forensic investigator on duty thought needed the attention of a medical doctor. If the problem was beyond the pathology resident's comfort zone, then the medical examiner on call had to be contacted. Tonight, it was Jack.

"Sorry to have to call you, Dr. Stapleton," Allen said, his voice whiny and grating.

"What's the problem?"

"It's a suicide, sir."

"Okay, so what's the question? Can't you guys handle it?" Jack didn't know Allen very well, but he knew Steve Marriott, the evening forensic investigator, who was experienced.

"It's a high-profile case, sir. The deceased is the wife or girlfriend of an Iranian diplomat. He's been screaming at everyone and threatening to call the Iranian Ambassador. Mr. Marriott called me for backup, but I feel like I'm in over my head."

Jack didn't respond. It was inevitable: He would have to visit the scene. Such high-profile cases invariably took on political implications, which was the part of Jack's job that he detested. He had no idea if he'd be able to make the site visit and still get to the restaurant by eight, which only added to his anxiety.

"Are you still there, Dr. Stapleton?"

"Last time I looked," Jack retorted.

"I thought maybe we'd been cut off," Allen said. "Anyway, the location is apartment fifty-four-J in the United Nations Towers on Forty-seventh Street."

"Has the body been moved or touched?" Jack pulled on his brown corduroy jacket, unconsciously patting the square object in its right pocket.

"Not by me or the forensics investigator."

"What about by the police?" Jack started down the hallway toward the elevators. The hall was deserted.

"I don't believe so, but I didn't ask yet."

"What about by the husband or boyfriend?"

"You should ask the police. The detective in charge is standing next to me, and he wants to talk with you."

"Put him on!"

"Hey, buddy!" a loud voice said, forcing Jack to pull the phone away from his ear. "Get your ass over here!"

Jack recognized the gravelly voice as that of his friend of ten years, Detective Lieutenant Lou Soldano of the homicide division of the New York City Police Department. Jack had known Lou almost as long as he had known Laurie. It had been Laurie who had introduced them.

"I might have known you'd be behind this!" Jack lamented. "I hope you remember that we're supposed to be at Elio's at eight."

"Hey, I don't schedule this crap. It happens when it happens."

"What are you doing at a suicide? You guys think it might not be?"

"Hell, no! It's a suicide, all right, with a contact gunshot wound to the right temple. My presence is a special request from my beloved captain in appreciation of the parties involved and how much flak they are potentially capable of producing. Are you coming or what?"

"I'm on my way. Has the body been moved or touched?"

"Not by us."

"Who is that yelling in the background?"

"That's the diplomat husband or boyfriend. We have

yet to figure that out. He's a little squirt, but he's feisty and makes me appreciate the silent, grieving type. He's been yelling at us since we got here, trying to boss us around like he's Napoleon."

"What's his problem?" Jack asked.

"He wants us to cover his naked wife or girlfriend, and he's madder than hell because we insist on not disturbing the scene until you guys finish checking it out."

"Hold on!" Jack said. "Are you telling me the woman's naked?"

"Naked as a jaybird. And to top it off, she doesn't even have any pubic hair. She's shaved like a cue ball, which—"

"Lou!" Jack interrupted. "It wasn't a suicide!"

"Excuse me?" Lou questioned with disbelief. "Are you trying to tell me you can tell this was a homicide without even seeing the scene?"

"I'll look at the scene, but yes, I'm telling you it wasn't a suicide. Was there a note?"

"Supposedly, but it's in Farsi. So I don't know what it says. The diplomat says it's a suicide note."

"It wasn't a suicide, Lou," Jack repeated. The elevator arrived. He boarded but kept the door from closing. He didn't want to lose the connection with Lou. "I'll even put a fiver on it. I've never heard of a case of a woman committing suicide in the nude. It just doesn't happen."

"You're joking!"

"No, I'm not. The thought is that's not the way women suicide victims want to be found. You'd better act accordingly and get your crime-scene people there. And you know the feisty diplomat husband or whatever he is has got to be your number-one suspect. Don't let him disappear into the Iranian mission. You might not see him again."

The elevator door closed as Jack flipped his phone shut. He hoped there wasn't a deeper meaning behind the interruption of the evening's plans. Jack's true bête noire was the fear that death stalked the people he loved, making him complicit when they died. He looked at his watch. It was now twenty after seven. "Damn!" he said out loud and slapped the elevator door a few times with the palms of his hands in frustration. Maybe he should rethink the whole idea.

With rapidity born of repetition, Jack got his mountain bike from the area of the morgue where the Potter's Field coffins were stored, unlocked it, put on his helmet, and wheeled it out onto the 30th Street loading dock. Between the mortuary vans, he climbed on and cycled out into the street. At the corner, he turned right onto First Avenue.

Once he was on the bike, Jack's anxieties melted away. Standing up, he put muscle into his pumping and the bike shot forward, rapidly picking up speed. Rush-hour traffic had abated to a degree, and the cars, taxis, buses, and trucks were moving at a good clip. Jack was not able to keep up, but it was close. Once he had achieved his cruising speed, he settled back onto the seat and shifted into a higher gear. From his daily bike riding and basketball playing, he was in tip-top shape.

The evening was glorious, with a golden glow suffusing the cityscape. Individual skyscrapers stood out sharply against the blue sky, the hue of which was deepening with every passing minute. Jack streaked past the New York University Medical Center on his right and, a little further north, the UN General Assembly complex.

When he could, Jack moved to his left so that he was able to turn onto 47th Street, which was one-way, conveniently heading east.

The UN Towers was a few doors up from First Avenue. Sheathed in glass and marble, the structure soared up an impressive sixty-some-odd stories into the evening sky. Directly in front of the awning that stretched from its entrance to the street were several New York City squad cars with their lights flashing. Hardened New Yorkers walked by without a glance. There was also a battered Chevy Malibu double-parked next to one of the squad cars. Jack recognized it as Lou's. In front of the Malibu was a Health and Human Services mortuary van.

As Jack locked his bike to a no-parking signpost, his anxieties returned. The ride had been too short to have any lasting effect. It was now seven thirty. He flashed his medical examiner's badge to the uniformed doorman and was directed to the fifty-fourth floor.

Up in apartment 54J, things had quieted considerably. When Jack walked in, Lou Soldano, Allen Eisenberg, Steve Marriott, and a number of uniformed officers were sitting around the living room as if it were a doctor's waiting room.

"What gives?" Jack asked. Silence reigned. There wasn't even any conversation.

"We're waiting on you and the crime-scene people," Lou said as he got to his feet. The others followed suit. Instead of Lou's signature rumpled and slightly disheveled attire, he was wearing a neatly pressed shirt buttoned to the neck, a subdued new tie, and a tasteful although not terribly well-fitted glen plaid sport jacket that was too small for his stocky frame. Lou was a seasoned detective, having been in the organized-crime unit for six years before moving over to homicide, where he'd been for more than a decade, and he looked the part.

"I have to say you look pretty spiffy," Jack commented. Even Lou's closely cropped hair looked recently brushed, and his famous five o'clock shadow was nowhere to be seen.

"This is as good as it gets," Lou commented, lifting his arms as if flexing his biceps for effect. "In celebration of your dinner party, I snuck home and changed. What's the occasion, by the way?"

"Where's the diplomat?" Jack asked, ignoring Lou's question. He glanced into the kitchen and a room that was used as a dining room. Except for the living room, the apartment seemed empty.

"He's flown the coop," Lou said. "He stormed out of here just after I hung up with you, threatening all of us with dire consequences."

"You shouldn't have let him go," Jack said.

"What was I supposed to do?" Lou complained. "I didn't have an arrest warrant."

"Couldn't you have held him for questioning until I got over here?"

"Listen, the captain sent me on this case to keep things simple and not to rock the boat. Holding that guy at this stage would be rocking the boat big-time."

"Okay!" Jack said. "That's your problem, not mine. Let's see the body."

Lou gestured toward the open bedroom door.

"Do you have an ID on the woman yet?" Jack asked.

"Not yet. The building supervisor says she'd only been here less than a month and didn't speak much English."

Jack took in the scene before homing in on the body.
There was a slight butcher-shop odor. The décor read
designer. The walls and carpet were all black; the ceiling
mirrored; and the curtains, clutter of knickknacks, and
furniture all white, including the bed linens. As Lou had
explained, the corpse was completely naked, lying supine
across the bed with the feet dangling over the bed's left
side. Although darkly complected in life, she was now
ashen against the sheet except for some bruising about
the face, including a black eye. Her arms were splayed
out to the sides with the palms up. An automatic pistol
was loosely held in her right hand, with her index finger
inside the trigger guard. Her head was turned slightly
toward the left. Her eyes were open. High on the right
temple was evidence of an entrance gunshot wound.
Behind the head on the white sheet was a large bloodstain. Extending away from the victim to her left was
some blood spatter, along with bits of tissue.

"Some of these Middle Eastern guys can be brutal
with their women," Jack said.

"So I've heard," Lou said. "Is that bruising and black
eye from the bullet wound?"

"I doubt it," Jack said. Then he turned back to Steve
and Allen. "Have our pictures been taken of the body?"

"Yes, they have," Steve Marriott called from over near
the door.

Jack pulled on a pair of latex rubber gloves and carefully separated the woman's dark, almost black hair to
expose the entrance wound. There was a distinct stellate
form to the lesion, indicating that the muzzle of the gun
had been in contact with the victim when it had dis-
charged.

Carefully, Jack rolled the woman's head to the side to

look at the exit wound. It was low down below the left ear. He straightened up. "Well, that's more evidence," he said.

"Evidence of what?" Lou asked.

"That this wasn't a suicide," Jack said. "The bullet traveled from above on an angle downward. That's not the way people shoot themselves." Jack formed a gun with his right hand and placed the tip of his index finger as the hypothetical muzzle next to his temple. The plane of the finger was parallel with the floor. "When people shoot themselves, the track of the bullet is generally almost horizontal or maybe slightly upward, never downwards. This was a homicide staged to look like a suicide."

"Thanks a lot," Lou grumbled. "I was hoping your deduction about her being naked would prove to be wrong."

"Sorry," Jack said.

"Any idea how long she's been dead?"

"Not yet, but a wild guess would say not that long. Anybody hear a gunshot? That would be more accurate."

"Unfortunately, no," Lou said.

"Lieutenant!" one of the uniformed policemen called out from the doorway. "The crime-scene boys have arrived."

"Tell them to get their butts in here," Lou responded over his shoulder. Then, to Jack, he asked: "Are you done or what?"

"I'm done. We'll have more information for you in the morning. I'll be sure to do the post myself."

"In that case, I'll try to make it, too." Over the years, Lou had learned to appreciate how much information could be gleaned from victims of homicide during an autopsy.

"All right then," Jack said, snapping off the gloves. "I'm out of here." He glanced at his watch. He wasn't late yet, but he was going to be. It was seven fifty-two. It was going to take him more than eight minutes to get to the restaurant. He looked at Lou, who was bending over to examine a small tear in the sheet several feet away from the body in the direction of the headboard. "What do you have?"

"What do you think of this? Think it might be where the slug penetrated the mattress?"

Jack leaned over to examine the centimeter-long, linear defect. He nodded. "That would be my guess. There's a tiny bit of bloodstain along the edges."

Lou straightened up as the crime-scene technicians carried in their equipment. Lou mentioned getting the slug, and the technicians assured him they'd do their best.

"Are you going to be able to get away from here at some reasonable time?" Jack inquired.

Lou shrugged. "No reason why I can't leave with you. With the diplomat out of the picture, there's no reason for me to hang around. I'll give you a lift."

"I've got my bike," Jack said.

"So? Put it in my car. You'll get there sooner. Besides, it's safer than that bike of yours. I can't believe Laurie still lets you ride that thing around the city, particularly when you guys see so many of those messengers who get flattened."

"I'm careful," Jack said.

"My ass you're careful," Lou responded. "I've seen you streaking around the city on more than one occasion."

Jack debated what to do. He wanted to ride the bike for its calming effect and also because he couldn't stand the odor of the fifty billion cigarettes that had been smoked in Lou's Chevy, but he had to admit that with Lou driving, the car would be quicker, and the hour was fast approaching. "All right," he said reluctantly.

"My goodness gracious, a spark of maturity," Lou said. He took out his keys and tossed them to Jack. "While you're dealing with the bike, I'll have a word with my boys to make sure they are squared away."

Ten minutes later, Lou was driving north on Park Avenue, which he claimed would be the fastest route uptown. Jack's bike was in the backseat with both wheels removed. Jack had insisted that all four windows be rolled down, which made the interior of the car breezy but bearable, despite the overflowing ashtray.

"You seem kind of wired," Lou said as they skirted Grand Central station on the elevated roadway.

"I'm worried about being late."

"Worst case, we'll be fifteen minutes late. In my book, that's not late."

Jack glanced out the passenger-side window. Lou was right. Fifteen minutes fell into the appropriate time frame, but it didn't make him feel any less anxious.

"So, what's the occasion? You never said."

"Does there have to be an occasion?" Jack responded.

"All right already," Lou said, casting a quick glance in Jack's direction. His friend was acting out of character, but Lou let it drop. Something was up, but he wasn't about to push it.

They parked in a no-parking tow zone a few steps away from the restaurant's entrance. Lou tossed his police vehicle card onto the dashboard.

"You think this is going to be safe?" Jack questioned. "I don't want my bike getting towed along with your vehicle."

"They're not going to tow my car!" Lou said with conviction.

The two men walked into Elio's and entered the fray. The place was packed, particularly around the bar near the front door.

"Everybody is back from the Hamptons," Lou explained, practically yelling to be heard over the general din of voices and laughter.

Jack nodded, excused himself to those in front of him, and squeezed sideways deeper into the restaurant. People juggled their drinks as he brushed by. He was looking for the hostess, who he remembered as a soft-spoken, willowy woman with a kind smile. Before he could find her, someone tapped insistently on his shoulder. When he turned he found himself looking directly into Laurie's blue-green eyes. Jack could tell she had taken her "freshening up" quite seriously. Her luxurious auburn hair had been let out of her restrained, work-aday French braid and cascaded to her shoulders. She was dressed in one of his favorite outfits: a white, high-collared, Victorian-style ruffled blouse with a honey-brown velvet jacket. In the half-light of the restaurant, her skin glowed as if illuminated from within.

To Jack she looked terrific, but there was a problem. Instead of the warm, fuzzy, happy expression he was expecting, she appeared more like amber and ice. Laurie seldom bothered to conceal her emotions. Jack knew something was wrong.

He apologized for being late, explaining how he'd been called out on a case, where he'd met Lou. Reaching behind him, Jack pulled Lou into their sphere of conversation. Lou and Laurie exchanged several cheek-to-cheek air kisses. Laurie responded by reaching behind her and drawing forward Warren Wilson and his longtime girlfriend, Natalie Adams. Warren was an intimidatingly well-muscled African American with whom Jack played basketball almost nightly. As a consequence, they had become close friends.

After greetings were exchanged, Jack yelled that he would find the hostess to inquire about their table. As he began pushing his way toward the hostess stand again, he sensed that Laurie was right behind him.

Jack stopped at the hostess's podium. Just beyond there was a clear buffer zone that separated the people dining from those standing around the bar. Jack caught sight of the hostess in the process of seating a dinner party. He turned back to Laurie to see if her expression had changed subsequent to his apology for being late.

"You weren't late," Laurie said, as if reading his mind. Although the comment was exonerating, the tone wasn't. "We had just got here a few minutes before you and Lou. It actually was good timing."

Jack studied Laurie's face. From the set of her jaw and the compression of her lips, it was clear she was still irritated, but he had no idea what was troubling her. "You look out of sorts. Is there something I should know?"

"I expected a romantic dinner," Laurie said. Her tone was now more wistful than angry. "You never told me you were inviting a horde."

"Warren, Natalie, and Lou are hardly a horde," Jack responded. "They are our best friends."

"Well, you could have and should have told me," Laurie responded. It didn't take long for her irritation to resurface. "I was obviously reading more into the evening than you intended."

Jack looked off for a moment to control his own emotions. After the anxiety and ambivalence he'd expended planning the evening, he was unprepared for negativism even if it was understandable. Obviously, he'd inadvertently hurt Laurie's feelings while being so absorbed in his own. The fact that she was counting on the two of them being alone hadn't even occurred to him.

"Don't roll your eyes at me!" Laurie snapped. "You could have been more communicative about what you had in mind for the evening. You know that I don't mind any time you want to go out with Warren and Lou."

Jack looked off in the other direction and bit his tongue to keep from lashing back. Luckily, he knew that if he did, the evening could well become unsalvageable. He took a deep breath, resolved to eat crow, and then locked eyes with Laurie. "I'm sorry," he said with all the sincerity he could muster under the circumstances. "It didn't occur to me you would take offense with it being sort of a dinner party. I should have been more up-front. To be honest, I invited the others for support."

Laurie's eyebrows pulled together in obvious confusion. "What kind of support? I don't understand."

"At the moment, it would be hard to explain," Jack said. "Could you give me a little slack for like a half-hour?"

"I suppose," Laurie said, still confused. "But I can't imagine what you mean by *support*. Yet I do appreciate your apology."

"Thank you," Jack said. He breathed out forcefully before looking back into the depths of the restaurant. "Now, where's that hostess and where's our table?"

It took another twenty minutes before the group was

seated toward the rear of the dining room. By then, Laurie had seemingly forgotten her earlier pique and was acting as if she was enjoying herself, with easy laughter and animated conversation, although Jack felt she was avoiding looking at him. She was seated to his immediate right, so all he could see was her sculpted profile.

To Jack and Laurie's delight, the same handlebar-mustached waiter who'd waited on them during their prior dinners at Elio's appeared at their table. Most of those previous meals had been delightful, although some had been less so, yet still unforgettable. The last dinner, a year previously, had been in the latter category, and it had marked the nadir of their relationship, occurring during a monthlong break from living together. It had been at that dinner that Laurie had revealed to Jack that she was pregnant, and Jack had had the insensitivity of flippantly asking who the father was. Although Jack and Laurie had subsequently patched up their relationship, the pregnancy had had to be terminated in short order. It had been a tubal ectopic pregnancy necessitating emergency surgery to save Laurie's life.

Seemingly on his own initiative, although actually on Jack's prior request, the waiter proceeded to distribute long-stemmed flutes. He then opened a bottle of champagne. The group cheered at the sonorous pop of the cork. The waiter then quickly filled everyone's glass.

"Hey, man," Warren said, holding up his bubbly. "To friendship."

Everyone followed suit, except Jack, who instead held up an empty hand. "If you don't mind, I'd like to say something right off the bat. You've all wondered why I've invited you here tonight, particularly Laurie. The fact of the matter is that I needed your support to go through with something I've wanted to do for some time, but have had trouble marshaling the courage. With that in mind, I'd like to make a toast that's rather selfish."

Jack thrust his hand into the side pocket of his jacket. With a struggle, he managed to extract a small, square box made of distinctive, shiny robin's-egg-blue paper and tied with a silver bow. He placed it on the table in front of Laurie and then lifted his glass. "I'd like to make a toast to Laurie and myself."

"All right!" Lou said happily and with emphasis. "To you guys." He raised his glass. The others did the same, except for Laurie.

"To you guys," Warren repeated.

"Here, here!" Natalie said.

Everyone took a drink, except Laurie, who was transfixed by the box in front of her. She thought she knew what was happening, but she couldn't believe it. She fought against her emotional side, which threatened to bubble to the surface.

"You're not going to participate in the toast?" Jack questioned her. Her immobility aroused an unwelcome doubt as to what he had thought her reaction would be. All of a sudden, he questioned what he would say and do if she refused.

With some difficulty, Laurie pulled her eyes away from the carefully wrapped box and locked onto Jack's. She thought she knew what was inside the tiny package but was afraid to admit it. She'd been wrong too many times in the past. As much as she loved Jack, she knew he labored under the strain of psychological baggage. There was no doubt he'd been severely traumatized by tragedy prior to their having met, and she had acclimatized herself to the chance he might never get over it.

"Hey, come on!" Lou urged. "What the hell is it? Open it up."

"Yeah, come on, Laurie," Warren urged.

"Am I supposed to open it now?" Laurie questioned. Her eyes were still locked onto Jack's.

"That was the general idea," Jack said. "Of course, if you prefer, you can wait a couple more years. I don't mean to put any pressure on you."

Laurie smiled. Occasionally, she found Jack's sarcasm humorous. With trembling fingers, she removed first the tie and then the wrapping from the package. Everyone but Jack leaned forward with anticipation. The underlying box was covered with black crushed velvet. With the trepidation that Jack might be playing an elaborate and inappropriate trick on her, she snapped open the box. Gleaming back at her was a Tiffany solitaire diamond. It sparkled with what appeared to be an inner light.

She turned the box around so the others could see while she shut her eyes and fought against tears. Such emotionalism was a personality trait she despised in herself, although under the present circumstances, even she could understand it. She and Jack had been dating for almost a decade and living with each other on and off for years. She'd wanted to marry, and she had been convinced he felt similarly.

There were a series of oohs and ahhs from Lou, Warren, and Natalie.

"Well?" Jack questioned Laurie.

Laurie struggled to get herself under control. She used a knuckle to wipe away a tear from each eye. She looked up at Jack and made an instantaneous decision to turn the tables on him and pretend she didn't know what he was implying. It was something Jack could very well have done. After all these years, she wanted to hear him actually say what the engagement ring implied. "Well what?" she questioned.

"It's an engagement ring!" Jack said with a short, self-conscious laugh.

"I know what it is," Laurie responded. "But what does it mean?" She was pleased. Putting pressure on Jack had the benefit of keeping her own emotions in check. A slight smile even appeared at the corners of her mouth as she watched him squirm.

"Be specific, you ass!" Lou barked at Jack. "Pop the question!"

Jack realized what Laurie had done, and a smile came to his face as well. "All right, all right!" he said, quieting Lou. "Laurie, my love, despite the danger in the past that has befallen those I love and hold dear and my fear such danger could extend to you, would you marry me?"

"That's more like it!" Lou said, holding his glass again in the air. "I propose a toast to Jack's proposal."

This time everyone drank.

"Well?" Jack repeated, redirecting attention to Laurie.

Laurie thought for a moment before answering. "I know your fears and understand their origin. I just don't share them. Be that as it may, I fully accept the risk, whether real or imagined. If something is to happen to me, it will be my fault entirely. With that caveat, yes, I would love to marry you."

Everyone cheered as Jack and Laurie exchanged a self-conscious kiss and awkward hug. Laurie then took the ring from the box and tried it on. She extended her hand to look at it. "It fits perfectly. It's exquisite!"

"I borrowed one of your rings for a day to be sure of the size," Jack admitted.

"Not the biggest rock in the world," Lou said. "Did it come with a magnifying glass?"

Jack threw his napkin at Lou, who caught it before it wrapped around his face.

"Your best friends are always honest." Lou laughed. He handed the napkin back.

"It's a perfect size," Laurie said. "I don't like jewelry to be gaudy."

"You got your wish," Lou added. "No one is going to call it gaudy."

"When will the big day be?" Natalie asked.

Jack looked at Laurie. "Obviously, we haven't talked about it, but I think I'll leave it up to Laurie."

"Really?" Laurie questioned.

"Really," Jack answered.

"Then I'd like to talk to my mom about the timing. She's let me know on many an occasion in the past that she'd like me to have my wedding at the Riverside Church. I know that was where she had wanted to be married herself, but it didn't happen. If it's all right, I'd like her to have a say as to the timing and the place."

"Fine by me," Jack said. "Now where's that waiter? I need some more champagne."

(one month later)
BOSTON, MASSACHUSETTS
October 7, 2005
4:45 p.m.

It had been a great workout. Craig Bowman had used the weight room for a half-hour to tone up and stretch. Then he'd gotten into a series of competitive, pickup, three-on-three basketball games. By pure luck, he'd managed to be teamed up with two talented players. For well over an hour, he and his teammates had not lost and had given up the court only from sheer exhaustion. After the basketball, Craig had indulged himself with a massage followed by a steam and shower.

Now, as Craig stood in front of the mirror in the VIP section of the Sports Club/LA men's locker room and regarded himself critically, he had to admit he looked better than he had in years. He'd lost twenty-two pounds and an inch from his waist since he'd joined the club six months ago. Perhaps even more apparent was the disappearance of the pudgy sallowness of his cheeks. In its place was a healthy, rosy glow. As an attempt to appear more contemporary, he'd let his sandy-colored hair grow out a bit, and then had it styled at a salon such that he now brushed it back on both sides rather than parting it on the left as he'd done for as long as he could remember. From his perspective, the overall change was so remarkable that had he seen himself a year ago he wouldn't have recognized himself. He surely was no longer the stodgy, bromidic doctor.

Craig's current routine was to come to the club three times a week: Monday, Wednesday, and Friday. Of the three days, Friday was the best, since it was the least crowded and afforded the psychological stimulus of the weekend stretching out in front of him with all its promise. As a standing policy, he'd decided to close the office at noon on Fridays and take calls with his cell phone. That way, Leona could come with him to work out. As a present for her as well as himself, he'd sprung for a second membership.

Several weeks previously, Leona had moved in with him at his Beacon Hill home. She'd decided on her own that it was ridiculous for her to pay for an apartment in Somerville when she was staying with him every night. Craig initially had been miffed about the move, because there had been no discussion and it had been presented as a fait accompli. To him it seemed coercive just when he was reveling in his new freedom. But, after a few days, he had adjusted. He had forgotten the power of eroticism. Also, he rationalized that the living arrangement could be reversed with ease if the need arose.

Craig's final preparation was to slip on his new Brioni jacket. After shrugging his shoulders a few times to settle it into place, he glanced back into the mirror. Turning his head from side to side to view himself from slightly different angles, he briefly entertained the idea of studying acting instead of art. The notion brought a smile to his face. He knew his imagination was running wild yet the thought was not completely preposterous. As well as things were going, he couldn't help feel that the world was his oyster.

When Craig was fully dressed, he checked his cell phone for messages. He was in the clear. The plan was to head back to the apartment, relax with a glass of wine and the newest *New England Journal of Medicine* for an hour or so, then on to the Museum of Fine Arts to check out the current exhibition, and finally go to dinner at a new, trendy restaurant in the Back Bay.

Whistling under his breath, Craig walked from the locker room out into the main lobby of the club. To his left was the sign-in desk, while to his right down a corridor past the bank of elevators were the bar and restaurant. Muted music could be heard from the general area. Although the athletic facilities were generally

not crowded on Friday afternoons, happy hour at the bar
was another story and was just beginning to gear up.

Craig checked his watch. He'd timed things perfectly.
It was quarter to five: the exact time he'd agreed to meet
Leona. Although they came to the club and left together,
while they were there, they each did their own thing.
Leona was currently into the stair machine, Pilates, and
yoga, none of which thrilled Craig.

A quick visual sweep of the sitting area confirmed that
Leona had yet to emerge from the women's side. Craig
wasn't surprised. Along with a relative lack of reserve,
punctuality was not one of her strong points. He took a
seat, perfectly content to watch the parade of attractive
people coming and going. Six months ago, in a similar
circumstance he would have felt like the odd man out.
Now he felt entirely at ease, but no sooner had he gotten
comfortable than Leona appeared, coming through the
women's locker room door.

Just as he had critically regarded himself a few minutes earlier, Craig gave Leona a quick once-over. The
workouts were benefiting her as well, though, due to her
comparative youth, she'd been firm, rosy-cheeked, and
shapely from the start. As she drew near, he could appreciate that she was an attractive as well as a high-spirited
and headstrong young woman. Her main handicap from
Craig's perspective was her Revere, Massachusetts,
accent and syntax. Particularly grating was her tendency
to pronounce every word ending in an "er" as if it ended
in a short but harsh "a." Believing he had her interests
at heart, Craig had tried to call her attention to her habit
with the hope of getting her to change, but she'd reacted
angrily, venomously accusing him of being an Ivy League
elitist. So Craig had wisely given up. Over time, his ear

had acclimated to a degree, and in the heat of the night he really didn't care whether she had an accent.

"How was your workout?" Craig asked, getting to his feet.

"Terrific," Leona responded. "Better than usual."

Craig winced. The accent on *terrific* was on the first syllable instead of the second, and *better* came out as "beddah." As they walked to the elevator, he resisted the urge to comment by tuning her out. While she carried on about her workout and why he should try both Pilates and yoga, he contentedly mused about the upcoming evening and what a pleasant day it had been so far. That morning at the office he'd seen twelve patients: not too many and not too few. There had been no rushing frantically from one exam room to another, which was the usual course of events at his old practice.

Over the months he and Marlene, his matronly main secretary and receptionist, had developed a system of scheduling patients according to each patient's need, based on the diagnosis and the individual's personality. The shortest visits were fifteen minutes for rapid, return-visit checkups with compliant and knowledgeable patients, and the longest was one and a half hours. The hour-plus visits were generally for new patients with known and serious medical problems. Healthy new patients were scheduled from forty-five minutes to one hour, depending on age and seriousness of the complaints. If an unexpected problem developed during the course of the day, such as an unscheduled patient needing to be seen or Craig having to go over to the hospital, which hadn't happened that day, Marlene would call the upcoming patients to reschedule if possible and appropriate.

As a consequence, it was rare for people to wait in Craig's office, and equally rare for him to suffer the anxiety of being behind and trying to catch up. It was a civilized way to practice medicine and far better for everyone. Nowadays, Craig actually liked going to the office. It was the kind of medicine he'd imagined when he'd dreamed of becoming a doctor. The only slight bugaboo in what was otherwise a near-perfect situation was that it had not been possible to keep all aspects of his relationship with Leona a secret. Suspicions were rampant and made worse by Leona's youth and willfulness. Consequently, Craig had to weather an undercurrent of disapproval from Marlene and his nurse, Darlene, as well as observe their resentful and passive-aggressive behavior toward Leona.

"You're not listening to me!" Leona complained irritably. She leaned forward to glare at Craig. Both had been facing the elevator doors as they descended to the parking garage.

"Of course I am," Craig lied. He smiled, but Leona's mercurial petulance wasn't assuaged.

The elevator doors opened on the valet-parking floor, and Leona stalked out to join a half-dozen people waiting for their vehicles. Craig followed a few steps behind. Relatively wide swings of emotion were a trait of Leona's that Craig was not fond of, but they were generally quick if he just ignored them. Had he slipped a few minutes earlier up in the lobby and called attention to her accent, it would have been a different story. The previous and only time he'd made such a comment had caused a two-day snit.

Craig gave his parking stub to one of the attendants.

"Red Porsche coming right up, Dr. Bowman," the

attendant said while touching the peak of his cap with his index finger in a form of salute. He sprinted away.

Craig smiled inwardly. He was proud that he had what he considered the sexiest car in the garage and the antithesis of the Volvo station wagon he'd had in his previous life. Craig imagined that those waiting around him for their cars would be duly impressed. The parking attendants obviously were impressed, as evidenced by their always parking his vehicle close to the valet stand.

"If I seem a little distant," Craig whispered to Leona, "it's because I'm looking forward to our evening: all of it." He winked suggestively.

Leona regarded him with one eyebrow raised, indicating she was only partially placated. The reality was that she demanded full attention a hundred percent of the time.

At the same moment that Craig heard the familiar whine and roar of his car engine starting somewhere nearby, he also heard his name called out from behind him. What caught his attention particularly was that his middle initial, M, had been included. Few people knew his middle initial, and fewer still knew that it stood for Mason, his mother's maiden name. Craig turned, expecting to see a patient or perhaps a colleague or an old schoolmate. Instead, he saw a stranger approach. The man was a handsome African American, quick-moving, intelligent-appearing, and approximately Craig's age. For a moment, Craig thought he was a teammate from that afternoon's three-on-three basketball marathon who wanted to gloat anew over that afternoon's victories.

"Doctor Craig M. Bowman?" the man questioned again as he stepped directly up to Craig.

"Yes?" Craig said with a questioning nod. He was still trying to place the individual. He wasn't one of the basketball players. Nor was he a patient or a schoolmate. Craig tried to associate him with the hospital, but he couldn't.

The man responded by placing a large, sealed envelope in Craig's hand. Craig looked at it. His name along with his middle initial was typed on the front. Before Craig could respond, the man turned on his heel and managed to catch the elevator he'd arrived in before the doors had had a chance to close. The man was gone. The transaction had taken only seconds.

"What'd you get?" Leona asked.

"I haven't the slightest idea," Craig said. He looked back down at the envelope and got his first inkling of trouble. Printed in the upper corner was: Superior Court, Suffolk County, Massachusetts.

"Well?" Leona questioned. "Aren't you going to open it?"

"I'm not sure I want to," Craig said, although he knew he would have to sooner or later. Craig's eyes scanned the people grouped around him, waiting for their cars. A number were curiously looking at him after having witnessed the encounter.

As the valet pulled Craig's Porsche up to the stand and got out, holding the driver's-side door ajar, Craig worked his thumb under the envelope's flap and tore it open. He could feel his pulse quicken as he pulled out the contents. He was holding a dog-eared sheaf of papers stapled together.

"Well?" Leona repeated with concern. She could see Craig's exercise-induced ruddiness perceptibly fade.

Craig's eyes lifted and locked onto Leona's. They

reflected an intensity Leona had not seen. She couldn't tell if it was from confusion or disbelief, yet it was clearly shock. For a few beats, Craig seemed paralyzed. He didn't even breathe.

"Hello?" Leona called questioningly. "Anybody home?" She waved a hand in front of Craig's marmoreal face. A furtive glance told her that they had become the object of everyone's attention.

As if he were waking from a petit mal seizure, Craig's pupils narrowed and color rapidly re-suffused his face. His hands began to reflexively crumple the papers before rationality intervened.

"I've been served," Craig croaked in a whisper. "The bastard is suing me!" He straightened the papers and rapidly flipped through them.

"Who is suing?"

"Stanhope! Jordan Stanhope!"

"What for?"

"Medical malpractice and wrongful death. This is outrageous!"

"Concerning Patience Stanhope?"

"Who else?" Craig demanded viciously through clenched teeth.

"Hey, I'm not the enemy," Leona said, raising her hands in mock defense.

"I cannot believe this! This is an outrage!" Craig shuffled through the papers again, as if perhaps he'd misread them.

Leona glanced over to the valets. A second attendant had opened the passenger door for her. The first was still holding open the driver's-side door. Leona looked back at Craig. "What do you want to do, Craigie?" she whispered insistently. "We can't stand here forever." *Forever* came out as "forevah."

"Shut up!" Craig barked. Her accent grated against his raw nerves.

Leona let out a suppressed, mockingly aggrieved laugh, then warned: "Don't you dare talk to me like that!"

As if waking a second time and becoming aware that all eyes were on them, Craig apologized under his breath, then added: "I need a drink."

"Okay," Leona agreed, still miffed. "Where? Here or at home?"

"Here!" Craig snapped. He turned and headed back to the elevators.

With an apologetic smile and shrug for the benefit of the valets, Leona followed Craig. When she got to him, he was repeatedly punching the elevator button with a knuckle. "You have to calm down," she told him. She looked back at the group. People quickly averted their gaze to pretend they had not been watching.

"It's easy for you to say to calm down," Craig shot back. "You're not the one being sued. And getting served like this in public is goddamn humiliating."

Leona didn't try to make conversation again until they were seated at a small but tall table apart as much as possible from the happy-hour crowd. The chairs were barstools with low backs, which accounted for the table height. Craig had a double scotch, which was hardly customary for him. Normally, he drank sparingly for fear of being called professionally at any given hour. Leona had a glass of white wine. She could tell from how he shakily handled his drink that his mind-set had transformed yet again. He'd gone from the initial shocked disbelief to anger and now to anxiety, all within the fifteen minutes since he'd been handed the summons and the complaint.

"I've never seen you so upset," Leona offered. Although she didn't quite know what to say, she felt she needed to say something. She was never good at silence unless it was on her terms as a purposeful pout.

"Of course I'm upset," Craig snapped. As he raised his drink, he was shaking enough to cause the ice to clink repeatedly against the glass. When he got it to his lips, he managed to slosh scotch over the rim. "Shit," he said as he put the glass back down and shook the scotch from his hand. He then used the cocktail napkin to wipe his lips and chin. "I cannot believe this oddball bastard Jordan Stanhope would do this to me, especially after all the time and energy I've squandered on his hypochondriacal, clingy excuse for a wife. I hated that woman."

Craig hesitated for a moment, then added: "I suppose I shouldn't be telling you this. It's the kind of thing doctors don't talk about."

"I think you should talk about it, seeing how upset you are."

"The truth is that Patience Stanhope drove me crazy with her disgusting rehash over and over of every damn bowel movement she ever had, and that was on top of the graphic descriptions of greenish-yellow, gloppy phlegm she coughed up on a daily basis and even saved to show me. It was pathetic. She drove everybody crazy, including Jordan and even herself, for Christ's sake."

Leona nodded. Although psychology was not one of

her strengths, she felt it was important to let Craig rail on.

"I can't tell you how many times over the last year I had to drive out there after work or even in the middle of the night to that huge house of theirs to hold her hand and listen to her carry on. And for what? She rarely followed through with anything I suggested, including stopping her smoking. She smoked like a fiend, no matter what I said."

"Really?" Leona questioned, unable to contain herself. "She carried on about coughing up phlegm and continued to smoke?"

"Don't you remember how her bedroom reeked of cigarette smoke?"

"Not really," Leona said with a shake of her head. "I was too taken by the situation to smell anything."

"She smoked like there was no tomorrow, one cigarette after another, going through several packs a day. And that was just a part of it. I'm telling you, she was the poster woman for all the noncompliant patients of the world, especially concerning medication. She demanded prescriptions and then took the drugs or didn't take them according to her whim."

"Did you have any idea why she didn't follow orders?"

"Probably because she liked being sick. It gave her something to do. That's the long and short of it. She was a waste of time for me, for her husband, even for herself. Her passing was a blessing for everyone. She didn't have a life."

Craig had calmed down enough to take a drink of his scotch without spilling any.

"I remember from the few times I had contact with

her in the office, she seemed like a piece of work," Leona said placatingly.

"That's the understatement of the year," Craig grumbled. "She was an entitled bitch with some inherited money, meaning she expected me to hold her hand and listen to her complaints ad nauseam. I struggled through four years of college, four years of medical school, five years of residency, board certification, and authored a handful of scientific papers, and all she wanted was for me to hold her hand. That was it, and if I held it for fifteen minutes, she wanted thirty, and if I gave her thirty, she wanted forty-five, and if I refused, she became sulky and hostile."

"Maybe she was lonely," Leona suggested.

"Whose side are you on?" Craig demanded angrily. He slapped his drink down onto the table, clanking the ice cubes. "She was a pain in the ass."

"Geez, relax already!" Leona urged. She glanced around self-consciously and was relieved to see that no one was paying them the slightest attention.

"Just don't start playing devil's advocate," Craig snapped. "I'm not in the mood."

"I'm only trying to get you to calm down."

"How can I calm down? This is a disaster. I've worked all my life to be the best doctor. Hell, I'm still working at it. And now this!" Craig angrily slapped the envelope containing the legal papers.

"But isn't this the reason you pay the malpractice insurance you complain about?"

Craig eyed Leona with exasperation. "I don't think you understand. This screwball Stanhope is publicly defaming me by demanding his, quote, day in court. The process is the problem. It's bad no matter what happens. I'm helpless, a victim. And if you go to trial, who knows how it will turn out. There are no guarantees, even in my situation, where I've been bending over backward for my patients, particularly Patience Stanhope, making house calls for crying out loud. And the idea it would be a trial by my peers? That's a bad joke. File clerks, plumbers, and retired schoolteachers have no idea what it's like being a doctor like me, getting up in the middle of the night to hold hypochondriacs' hands. Jesus H. Christ!"

"Can't you tell them? Make it part of your testimony."

Craig rolled his eyes with exasperation. There were occasions when Leona drove him batty. It was the downside of spending time with someone so young and inexperienced.

"Why does he think there was malpractice?" Leona asked.

Craig looked off at the normal, beautiful people around the bar, obviously enjoying the evening with their happy banter. The juxtaposition made him feel worse. Maybe coming up to the public bar was a bad idea. The thought went through his mind that perhaps becoming one of them through his cultural endeavors was really beyond his grasp. Medicine and its current problems, including the malpractice mess, had him ensnared.

"What malpractice was there supposed to have been?" Leona asked, rephrasing her question.

Craig threw up his hands. "Listen, bright eyes! It's generic on the complaint, saying something about me not using the skill and care in making a diagnosis and treatment that a reasonable, competent doctor would employ in the same circumstance . . . blah blah blah. It's all bullshit. The long and short is that there was a bad outcome, meaning Patience Stanhope died. A personal injury-malpractice lawyer will just go from there and be creative. Those guys can always find something that some asshole, courthouse-whore doctor will say should have been done differently."

"Bright eyes!" Leona snapped back. "Don't be condescending to me!"

"Okay, I'm sorry," Craig said. He took a deep breath. "Obviously, I'm out of sorts."

"What's a courthouse-whore doctor?"

"It's a doctor who hires himself or herself out to be a, quote, expert and who will say whatever the plaintiff attorney wants him to say. It used to be hard to find doctors to testify against doctors, but not anymore. There are some worthless bastards that make a living doing it."

"That's terrible."

"It's the least of it," Craig said. He shook his head dejectedly. "It's mighty hypocritical that this screwball Jordan Stanhope is suing me when he didn't even stay around at the hospital while I was struggling to revive his pathetic wife. Hell, on a number of occasions he confided with me that his wife was a hopeless hypochondriac and that he couldn't keep all her symptoms straight. He was even apologetic when she'd have him call and insist I come to the house at three in the morning because she thought she was dying. That really happened on more than one occasion. Usually, the house calls were in the evenings, forcing me to interrupt what I was doing. But even then, Jordan would always thank me, so he knew what kind of effort it was, coming out there for no good reason. The woman was a disaster. Everyone is better off with her out of the picture, including Jordan Stanhope, yet he is suing me and claiming damages of five million dollars for loss of consortium. What a cruel joke." Craig shook his head dejectedly.

"What's consortium?"

"What someone is supposed to get from a spouse. You know: company, affection, assistance, and sex."

"I don't think they were having much sex. They had separate bedrooms!"

"You probably have that right. I can't imagine he'd want to or even be able to have sex with that miserable hag."

"Do you think the reason he's suing you might have something to do with you criticizing him that night? He did seem to take offense."

Craig nodded a few times. Leona had a point. With glass in hand, he slipped off the barstool and returned to the bar for a refill. As he waited among the happy revelers, he thought about Leona's idea and wondered if she was correct. He remembered regretting what he had said to Jordan when he'd gotten into Patience's bedroom and saw how bad off she was. His comment had just popped out of his mouth in the stress of the circumstances and how surprised he'd been. At the time, he'd thought his hasty apology had been sufficient, but maybe not. If not, he was going to regret the incident even more.

With a second double scotch, Craig worked his way back to the table and got himself onto his barstool. He moved slowly, as if his legs weighed a hundred pounds apiece. To Leona he seemed to have made yet another transition. He now appeared depressed, his mouth slack and his eyes droopy.

"This is a disaster," Craig managed with a sigh. He

stared down into his scotch, his arms folded on the table. "This could be the end of everything, just when things are going so well."

"How can it be the end of everything?" Leona asked, trying to be lively. "What are you supposed to do now that you have been served?"

Craig didn't answer. He didn't even move. Leona couldn't even see him breathing.

"Shouldn't you get a lawyer?" Leona persisted. She leaned forward in an attempt to look up into Craig's face.

"The insurance company is supposed to defend me," Craig responded in a flat voice.

"Well, there you go. Why not call them?"

Craig raised his eyes and met Leona's. He nodded a few times as he gave Leona's suggestion consideration. It was almost five thirty on a Friday night, yet the insurance company might have someone on call. It was worth a try. He could use the reassurance that he was at least doing something. A big part of his anxiety was from the helplessness he felt in the face of such an overwhelming, disembodied threat.

With newly found urgency, Craig snapped his cell phone from its clip on his belt. Using klutzy fingers, he scrolled through his address book. Like a beacon in a dark night, the name and cell phone number of his insurance agent popped into view. Craig made the call.

It ended up requiring several calls, including having to leave his name and number in an emergency voicemail, but within a quarter of an hour, Craig was able to tell his story to a real person with an authoritative voice who acted calmly knowledgeable. His name was Arthur Marshall, the sound of which Craig found curiously reassuring.

"Since this is your first brush with this kind of event,"
Arthur was saying, "and since we know from experience
how uniquely unsettling it is, I think it is important for
you to understand that for us it is all too common. In
other words, we are experienced in dealing with malpractice litigation, and we will give your case all the attention
it deserves. Meanwhile, I want to emphasize that you
should not take it personally."

"How else can I take it?" Craig complained. "It's calling into question my life's work. It's putting everything
in jeopardy."

"That is a common feeling for someone like yourself
and entirely understandable. But trust me, it is not like
that! It is not a reflection of your dedication and life's
work. More often than not, it is a fishing expedition in
hopes of a financial windfall despite the plaintiff attorney's claims to the contrary. Everyone familiar with
medicine knows that less-than-perfect outcomes, even
involving honest mistakes, are not malpractice, and the
judge will so advise the jury if this action were to go to
a trial. But remember! The vast majority of such cases do
not go to trial, or if they do, the vast majority are won
by the defense. Here in Massachusetts, by statute your
claim must go before a tribunal, and with the facts you've
given me, it probably will stop there."

Craig's pulse had come down to a nearly normal
level. "You're wise to have contacted us so early in the
course of this unfortunate affair, Dr. Bowman. In short
order, we will assign a skilled, experienced attorney to
the case, and for that we will need to get the summons
and the complaint ASAP. You are required to answer
within thirty days of service."

"I can messenger this material on Monday."

"That will be perfect. Meanwhile, let me suggest you begin to refresh your mind about the case, particularly by getting your records together. It's something that has to be done, and it will give you the feeling you are doing something constructive to protect yourself. From our experience, we know that is important."

Craig found himself nodding in agreement.

"In regard to your records, Dr. Bowman, I must warn you not to change them in any way or form. That means do not change a misspelled word or an obvious grammatical error or something you might feel is sloppy. Do not change any dates. In short, do not change a thing. Do you understand?"

"Absolutely."

"Good! Of those malpractice cases found for the plaintiff, a sizable number involved some editing of the records, even if the editing was entirely inconsequential. Any alteration is a recipe for disaster, since it impugns your integrity and truthfulness. I hope I'm making myself clear."

"Perfectly clear. Thank you, Mr. Marshall. I'm feeling a bit better."

"And indeed you should, doctor. Rest assured, we will be giving your case our full attention since all of us want to bring it to a speedy, successful conclusion so that you can get back to what you do best: taking care of your patients."

"I'd like nothing better."

"We are at your service, Dr. Bowman. One last issue, of which I'm sure you are already cognizant. Do not . . . I repeat . . . do not discuss this matter with anyone except your spouse and the attorney we assign! This extends to all colleagues, acquaintances, and even close friends. This is very important."

Craig looked guiltily across the table at Leona, realizing how much he'd been inappropriately babbling. "Close friends?" Craig questioned. "That means possibly having to forgo emotional support."

"We recognize that, but the downside is worse."

"And what exactly is the downside?" He wasn't sure how much of the incoming conversation Leona could hear. She was watching him intently.

"Because friends and colleagues are discoverable. Plaintiff attorneys can and do, if it serves their interests, force friends, even close friends, and colleagues to be witnesses, often to great effect."

"I'll keep that in mind," Craig said. "Thank you for your admonitions, Mr. Marshall." Craig's pulse had quickened again. Being honest with himself, he had to admit that he really didn't know Leona beyond her youthful and understandable self-centeredness. Having been so talkative added to his anxiety.

"And thank you, Dr. Bowman. We will be in touch as soon as we get the summons and the complaint. Try to relax and go about your life."

"I'll try," Craig said without a lot of conviction. He knew he was going to be living under a dark cloud until all was settled. What he didn't know was how dark it was going to get. In the meantime, he vowed to avoid calling attention to Leona's accent. He was smart enough to know that what he had confided about his feelings toward Patience Stanhope would not play well in a court of law.

NEW YORK CITY, NEW YORK
October 7, 2005
4:45 p.m.

Jack Stapleton turned his attention to the heart and the lungs. In front of him spread out on the autopsy table was the naked, gutted remains of a white, fifty-seven-year-old female. The victim's head was propped up on a wooden block, and her unseeing eyes stared blankly at the overhead fluorescent lights. Up until that point in the postmortem, there had been little pathology save for a rather large, apparently asymptomatic uterine fibroid. Specifically, there had been nothing as yet to account for the death of an apparently healthy woman who had collapsed in Bloomingdale's. Miguel Sanchez, the evening mortuary technician who'd come in at 3:00 p.m. to start his day, was assisting. While Jack prepared to examine the heart and lungs, Miguel was busy at the sink, washing out the intestines.

By merely palpating the surface of the lungs, Jack's experienced hands perceived an abnormal resistance. The tissue was firmer than usual, which was consistent with the organ's weight being higher than normal. With a knife that looked like a garden-variety butcher knife, Jack made multiple slices into the lung. Again, there was the suggestion of more resistance than he would expect. Lifting the lung, he examined the cut surfaces, which reflected the organ's consistency. The lung appeared denser than normal, and he was confident that the microscopic would show fibrosis. The question was . . . why were the lungs fibrotic?

Turning his attention to the heart, Jack picked up

toothed forceps and a pair of small, blunt-nosed scissors. Just when he was about to begin work on the muscular organ, the door to the hallway opened. Jack hesitated as a figure appeared and approached. It took only a moment for him to recognize Laurie despite the light reflecting off her plastic face mask.

"I was wondering where you were," Laurie said with a hint of exasperation. She was dressed in full-body disposable Tyvek protective gear, as were Jack and Miguel. It was a standing order by Dr. Calvin Washington, the deputy chief medical examiner, to wear such an outfit for protection against potential infectious agents when in the autopsy room. One never knew what kind of microbes might be encountered, especially in an autopsy room as busy as the one in New York City.

"Wondering where I was suggests you were looking for me."

"Brilliant deduction," Laurie said. She glanced down at the ghostly pale human shell on the table. "This was the last place I thought to look for you. Why such a late post?"

"You know me," Jack quipped. "I have no restraint whatsoever when an opportunity to have fun knocks on my door."

"Anything interesting?" Laurie said, immune to Jack's sarcastic humor. She reached out and touched the surface of the cut lung with her gloved index finger.

"Not yet, but I think I'm about to hit pay dirt. You can see that the lung appears fibrotic. I believe the heart's going to tell us why."

"What's the background of the case?"

"The victim was given the price of a pair of Jimmy Choo shoes in Bloomie's and arrested."

"Very funny."

"Seriously, she did arrest in Bloomingdale's. Of course, I don't know what she was doing. Apparently, the store staff and a Good Samaritan doctor who happened to be on the scene attended to her immediately. They started CPR, and it was continued in the ambulance all the way over to the Manhattan General. When the body arrived over here at the OCME, the head doc in the ER called to give me the story. He said that no matter what they did in the ER, they couldn't get so much as a single beat out of the heart, even with a pacemaker. As chagrined as they were that the patient was so uncooperative as to not revive, he was hoping we could shed some light in case there was something else that could have been done. I was impressed with his interest and initiative, and since that is the kind of professional behavior we should be encouraging, I told him I'd do the case straight off and get right back to him."

"Very commendable and industrious on your part," Laurie said. "Of course, doing an autopsy at this hour, you're making the rest of us look like slackers."

"If it looks like a duck, quacks like a duck, it's a duck!"

"Okay, wise guy! I'm not going to try to compete with your repartee. Let's see what you got! You've got my interest, so go for it."

Jack bent over, quickly but carefully traced the major coronary arteries, and then proceeded to open them. Suddenly, he straightened up. "Well, lookie here!" he said. He picked up the heart and held it so Laurie could see more easily. He pointed with the tip of his forceps.

"Good grief," Laurie exclaimed. "That might be the most dramatic narrowing of the main trunk of the posterior descending artery I've ever seen. And it looks developmental, not atheromatous."

"That would be my take as well, and it probably explains the unresponsive heart. A sudden, even transient, blockage would have caused a massive heart attack involving parts of the conduction system. I imagine the entire posterior side of the heart was involved in the infarction. But as dramatic as it is, it doesn't explain the pulmonary changes."

"Why don't you open the heart?"

"That was exactly my intention."

Exchanging the scissors and forceps for the butcher knife, Jack made a series of cuts into the heart's chambers. "Voila!" he said, leaning out of the way so Laurie could see the splayed organ.

"There you go: a damaged, incompetent mitral valve!"

"A very incompetent mitral valve. This woman was a walking time bomb waiting to explode. It's amazing she didn't have symptoms from either the coronary narrowing or the valve to drive her to a physician. It's also too bad. Both problems were surgically correctable."

"Fear often makes some people sadly stoic."

"You've got that right," Jack said as he started taking samples for microscopic examination. He put them into appropriately labeled bottles. "You still haven't told me why you were looking for me."

"An hour ago I got some news. We now have a wedding date. I was eager to run it by you, because I have to get back to them as soon as possible."

Jack paused in what he was doing. Even Miguel at the sink stopped rinsing out the intestines.

"This is a curious environment for such an announcement," Jack said.

Laurie shrugged. "It's where I found you. I was hoping to call back this afternoon before the weekend."

Jack briefly glanced over at Miguel. "What's the date?"

"June ninth at one thirty. What do you think?"

Jack chuckled. "What am I supposed to think? It seems a long time off now that we have finally decided to go through with it. I was kind of thinking about next Tuesday."

Laurie laughed. The sound was muffled by her plastic face screen, which briefly fogged up. "That's a sweet thing to say. But the reality is that my mother has always anticipated a June wedding. I personally think June is a great month because the weather should be good, not only for the wedding but also for a honeymoon."

"Then it's okay with me," Jack said, casting a second quick look in Miguel's direction. It was bothering him that Miguel was just standing there, not moving and obviously listening.

"There is only one problem. June is so popular for weddings that the Riverside Church is already booked for all the Saturdays in the month. Can you imagine, eight months in advance. Anyway, June ninth is a Friday. Does that bother you?"

"Friday, Saturday—it doesn't matter to me. I'm easy."

"Fabulous. Actually, I'd prefer Saturday because it's traditional and easier for guests, but the reality is that the option's not available."

"Hey, Miguel!" Jack called. "How about finishing with those intestines. Let's not make it your life's work."

"I'm all done, Dr. Stapleton. I'm just waiting for you to come on over and take a peek."

"Oh!" Jack said simply, mildly embarrassed for assuming the tech was eavesdropping. Then to Laurie he said, "Sorry, but I have to keep this show on the road."

"No problem," Laurie said. She trailed after him over to the sink.

Miguel handed over the intestines, which had been opened throughout their length and then thoroughly rinsed to expose the mucosal surface.

"There's something else I found out today," Laurie said. "And I wanted to share it with you."

"Go ahead," Jack said as he methodically began to examine the digestive system, starting from the esophagus and working southward.

"You know, I've never felt particularly comfortable in your apartment, mainly because the building is a pigsty." Jack lived in a fourth-floor walk-up unit in a dilapidated building on 106th Street just opposite the neighborhood playground he had paid to have completely reconditioned. Stemming from a persistent belief that he didn't deserve to be comfortable, he lived significantly below his means. Laurie's presence, however, had altered the equation.

"I don't mean to hurt your feelings about this," Laurie continued. "But with the wedding coming up, we have to give some thought to our living situation. So I took the liberty of looking into who actually owns the property, which the supposed management company where you send your checks was reluctant to divulge. Anyway, I found out who owns it and contacted them to see if they would be interested in selling. Guess what? They are, as long as it's purchased in its 'as is' condition.

I think that raises some interesting possibilities. What do you think?"

Jack had stopped examining the guts in his hands as Laurie spoke, and he now turned to her. "Wedding plans over the autopsy table, and now hearth-and-home issues over the intestinal sink. Don't you think this might not be the best place for this discussion?"

"I just learned about this minutes ago, and I was excited to tell you so you could start mulling it over."

"Terrific," Jack said, suppressing an almost irresistible urge to be more sarcastic. "Mission accomplished. But what do you say to the idea we discuss buying and, I assume, renovating a house over a glass of wine and an arugula salad in a slightly more appropriate setting?"

"That's a marvelous idea," Laurie said happily. "See you back at the apartment."

With that said, Laurie turned on her heels and was gone.

Jack continued to stare at the door to the hall for several beats after it had closed behind her.

"It's great you guys are getting married," Miguel said to break the silence.

"Thank you. It's not a secret, but it's not common knowledge, either. I hope you can respect that."

"No problem, Dr. Stapleton. But I have to tell you from experience that getting married changes everything."

"How right you are," Jack said. He knew that from experience as well.

CHAPTER ONE

"All rise," the uniformed court officer called out as he emerged from the judge's chambers. He was holding a white staff.

Directly behind the bailiff appeared the judge, swathed in flowing black robes. He was a heavyset African American with pendulous jowls, graying, kinky hair, and a mustache. His dark, intense eyes cast a quick glance around his fiefdom as he mounted the two steps up to the bench with a forceful, deliberate gait. Reaching his chair, he turned to face the room, framed by the American flag to his right and the Massachusetts state flag to his left, both capped by eagles. With a reputation of fairness and sound knowledge of the law, but a quick temper, he was the embodiment of steadfast authority. Enhancing his stature, a concentrated band of bright morning sunlight penetrated the edge of the shades that were pulled down over the metal mullioned windows and cascaded over his head and shoulders, giving his outline a golden glow like that of a pagan god in a classical painting.

"Hear ye, hear ye, hear ye," the court officer continued in his baritone, Boston-accented voice. "All persons having anything to do before the honorable justices of the Superior Court now sitting at Boston and in the County of Suffolk draw near, give your attendance, and you shall be heard. God save the Commonwealth of Massachusetts. Be seated!"

Reminiscent of the effect of the conclusion of the national anthem at a sporting event, the bailiff's final command initiated a murmur of voices as everyone in Courtroom 314 took their seats. While the judge rearranged the papers and water pitcher before him, the clerk sitting at a desk directly below the bench called out, "The estate of Patience Stanhope et al. versus Dr. Craig Bowman. The Honorable Justice Marvin Davidson presiding."

With a studied motion, the judge snapped open an eyeglasses case and slipped on his rimless reading spectacles, positioning them low on his nose. He then looked over the tops at the plaintiff's table and said, "Will counsels identify themselves for the record." In contrast to the bailiff, he had no accent, and his voice was in the bass range.

"Anthony Fasano, Your Honor," the plaintiff's attorney said quickly with an accent not too dissimilar to the bailiff's as he rose from his chair to a half-standing position as if supporting a heavy weight on his shoulders. "But most people call me Tony." He gestured first to his right. "I'm here on behalf of the plaintiff, Mr. Jordan Stanhope." He then gestured to his left. "Next to me is my able colleague, Ms. Renee Relf." He then quickly regained his seat as if he was too shy to be in the spotlight.

Judge Davidson's eyes moved laterally to the defense table.

"Randolph Bingham, Your Honor," the defense

attorney said. In contrast to the plaintiff's attorney, he spoke slowly, emphasizing each syllable in a mellifluous voice. "I'm representing Dr. Craig Bowman, and I'm accompanied by Mr. Mark Cavendish."

"And I can assume you people are ready to get under way," Judge Davidson said.

Tony merely nodded in assent, whereas Randolph again rose to his feet. "There are some housekeeping motions before the court," he said.

The judge glared at Randolph for a beat to suggest he didn't like or need to be reminded of preliminary motions. Looking down, he touched his index finger to his tongue before searching through the pages in his hands. The way he moved suggested he was vexed, as if Randolph's comment had awakened the renowned disdain he had for lawyers in general. He cleared his throat before saying, "Motions for dismissal denied. It is also the court's feeling that none of the proposed witnesses or evidence is either too graphic or too complex for the jury's ability to consider it. Consequently, all motions in limine denied." He raised his eyes and again glowered at Randolph as if saying "Take that," before switching his gaze to the court officer. "Bring in the venire! We have work to do." He was also known as a judge who liked to move things along.

As if on cue, an expectant murmur arose again from the spectators beyond the bar. But they didn't have long to converse. The clerk rapidly pulled sixteen names from the jury hopper, and the court officer went to fetch the people selected from the jury pool. Within minutes, the sixteen were escorted into the room and sworn to begin the voir dire. The assemblage was visibly disparate, and almost equally divided between the sexes. Although the majority was Caucasian, other minorities were represented. Approximately three-quarters were dressed appropriately and respectfully, with half of them businessmen or businesswomen. The rest were attired in a mixture of T-shirts, sweatshirts, jeans, sandals, and hip-hop clothes, some of which had to be continuously hiked up to keep them from falling off. A few of the experienced venirepersons had brought reading material, mostly newspapers and magazines, although one late-middle-aged woman had a hardcover book. Some were awed by the surroundings, others brazenly dismissive, as the group filed into the jury box area and took their seats.

Judge Davidson gave a short introduction, during which he thanked the prospective jurors for their service and told them how important it was, since they were to be finders of fact. He briefly described the selection process despite knowing they had already been apprised of the same in the jury room. He then began asking a series of questions to determine suitability, with the hope of weeding out those jurors with particular bias that might prejudice them against either the plaintiff or the defendant. The goal was, he insisted, that justice be served.

"Justice, my ass!" Craig Bowman said to himself. He took a deep breath and shifted in his seat. He had not been aware of how tense he'd been. He lifted his hands, which had been coiled into fists in his lap, and placed them on the table, leaning forward on his forearms. He opened his fingers and fully extended them, feeling more than hearing snapping from his complaining joints. He was dressed in one of his most conservative gray suits, white shirt, and tie, all on specific orders of his attorney, Randolph Bingham, seated to his immediate right.

Also on specific orders from his attorney, Craig kept his facial expression neutral, as difficult as that was in such a humiliating circumstance. He had been instructed to act dignified, respectful (whatever that meant), and humble. He was to guard against appearing arrogant and angry. Not appearing angry was the difficult part, since he was furious at the whole affair. He was also instructed to engage the jurors, to look them in the eyes, to consider them as acquaintances and friends. Craig laughed derisively to himself as his eyes scanned the prospective jurors. The idea that they were his peers was a sad joke. His eyes stopped on a waiflike female with blonde, stringy hair that was all but hiding her pale pixie face. She was dressed in an oversized Patriots sweatshirt, the arms of which were so long that only the tips of her fingers were visible as she continuously parted her hair in front of her face, pulling it to the sides in order to see.

Craig sighed. The last eight months had been pure hell. When he'd been served with the summons the previous autumn, he'd guessed the affair was going to be bad, but it had been worse than he'd ever imagined. First there had been the interrogatories poking into every recess of his life. As bad as the interrogatories were, the depositions were worse.

Leaning forward, Craig looked over at the plaintiff's table and eyed Tony Fasano. Craig had disliked a few people in his life, but he had never hated anyone as much as he'd come to hate Tony Fasano. Even the way Tony looked and dressed, in his trendy gray suits, black shirts, black ties, and clunky gold jewelry added to his loathing. To Craig, Tony Fasano, appearing like a sleazy mafioso understudy, was the tawdry stereotype of the modern-day personal-injury, ambulance-chasing lawyer out to make a buck over someone else's misfortune by squeezing millions out of rich, reluctant insurance companies. To Craig's disgust, Tony even had a website bragging as much, and the fact that he might ruin a doctor's life in the process made no difference in the world.

Craig's eyes switched to Randolph's aristocratic profile as the man concentrated on the voir dire proceeding. Randolph had a slightly hooked, high-bridged nose not too dissimilar to Tony's, but the effect was altogether different. Whereas Tony looked at you from beneath his dark, bushy eyebrows, his nose directed downward partially covering a cruel smirk on his lips, Randolph held his nose straight out in front, maybe slightly elevated, and regarded those around him with what could be considered by some to be mild disdain. And in contrast to Tony's full lips, which he wetted frequently with his tongue as he talked, Randolph's mouth was a thin, precise line, nearly lipless, and when he talked, a tongue was all but invisible. In short, Randolph was the epitome of the seasoned and restrained Boston Brahmin, while Tony was the youthful and exuberant playground entertainer and bully. At first Craig had been pleased with the contrast, but now, looking at the prospective jurors, he couldn't help but wonder if Tony's persona would make more of a connection and have more influence. This new concern added to Craig's unease.

And there was plenty of reason for unease. Randolph's reassurances notwithstanding, the case was not going well. Of particular note, it had been in essence already found for the plaintiff by the statutory Massachusetts tribunal, which had ruled after hearing testimony that there was sufficient, properly substantiated evidence of possible negligence to allow the case to go to trial. As a corollary to this finding, there was no need for the claimant, Jordan Stanhope, to post a bond.

The day that Craig had learned this news was the blackest for him of the whole pretrial period, and unbeknownst to anyone, he had for the first time in his life considered the idea of suicide. Of course, Randolph had offered the same pabulum that Craig had been given initially; namely, that he should not take the minor defeat personally. Yet how could he not take the finding personally, since it had been rendered by a judge, a lawyer, and a physician colleague? These were not high-school dropouts or stultified blue-collar laborers; they were professionals, and the fact that they thought he had committed malpractice, meaning he had rendered care that was substandard, was a mortal blow to Craig's sense of honor and personal integrity. He had literally devoted his entire life to becoming the best doctor he could be, and he had succeeded, as evidenced by stellar grades in medical school, by stellar evaluations during the course of his residency at one of the most coveted institutions in the country, and even by the offer to become part of his current practice from a celebrated and widely renowned clinician. Yet these professionals were calling him a tortfeasor. In a very real sense, the entire image of his self-worth and self-esteem had been undermined and was now on the line.

There had been other events besides the tribunal's ruling that had seriously clouded the horizon. Back at the beginning, even before the interrogatories had been completed, Randolph had strenuously advised that Craig make every effort to reconcile with his wife, Alexis, give up his in-town, recreational apartment (as Randolph had referred to it), and move back to the Newton family home. It had been Randolph's strong feeling that Craig's relatively new, self-indulgent (as he called it) lifestyle would not sit well with a jury. Willing to listen to experienced advice although chafing at the dependency it represented, Craig had followed the recommendations to the letter. He'd been pleased and thankful that Alexis had been willing to allow him to return, albeit to sleep in the guest room, and she'd been graciously supportive as evidenced by her sitting at that very moment in the spectator section. Reflexively, Craig twisted around and caught Alexis's eye. She was dressed in a casually professional style for her work as a psychologist at the Boston Memorial Hospital, with a white blouse and blue cardigan sweater. Craig managed a crooked smile, and she acknowledged it with one of her own.

Craig redirected his attention to the voir dire. The judge was castigating a frumpy accountant who was intent on being excused for hardship. The man had claimed clients couldn't do without him for a week's trial, which was how long the judge estimated the proceeding would take considering the witness list, which was mostly the plaintiff attorney's list. Judge Davidson was merciless as he told the gentleman what he thought of his sense of civic responsibility but then dismissed him. A replacement was called and sworn and the process continued.

Thanks to Alexis's personal generosity, which Craig attributed primarily to her maturity and secondarily to her training as a psychologist, things had gone reasonably well at home over the last eight months. Craig knew it could have been intolerable if Alexis had chosen to

behave as he probably would have if the situation had
been reversed. From his current vantage point, Craig was
able to view his so-called "awakening" as a juvenile
attempt to be someone he wasn't. He was born to be
a doctor, which was an encompassing calling, and not a
Brahmin socialite. In fact, he'd been given his first doctor
kit by his doting mother when he was four, and he could
remember administering to his mother and older brother
with a precocious seriousness that foreshadowed his clinical talent. Although in college and even the first years of
medical school he'd felt his calling was basic medical
research, he would later realize he had an inherent gift
for clinical diagnosis, which impressed his superiors, and
thereby pleased him as well. By the time he graduated
from medical school, he knew he was to be a clinician
with an interest in research, not vice versa.

Although Alexis and his two younger daughters—
Meghan, eleven, and Christina, ten—had been forgiving
and seemingly understanding, Tracy had been another
story. At age fifteen and in the throes of adolescence, she
had been overtly and persistently unable to forgive Craig
for abandoning the family for six months. Perhaps associated, there had been some unfortunate episodes of
rebelliousness with disturbing drug use, open violation
of curfews, and even sneaking out of the house at night.
Alexis was concerned, but since she had an open communication with the girl, she was reasonably confident
that Tracy would come around. Alexis urged Craig not
to interfere under the circumstances. Craig was happy to
oblige, since he would have had no idea how to handle
the situation under the best of circumstances and was
intellectually and emotionally preoccupied with his own
disaster.

Judge Davidson struck two potential jurors for cause. One was openly hostile to insurance companies and thought they were ripping off the country: ergo sayonara. Another had a cousin who'd been in Craig's former practice and had heard Craig was a wonderful doctor. Several other juror prospects were dismissed when the counselors began using some of their peremptory challenges, including a well-dressed businessman by Tony and a young African-American male dressed in elaborate hip-hop gear by Randolph. Four more veniremen were called from the jury pool and sworn. The questions continued.

Having to deal with Tracy's resentment had hurt Craig, but it was nothing compared to the problems he had with Leona. As the spurned lover, she became vindictive, especially when she found herself having to find another apartment. Her poor attitude disrupted the office, and Craig was caught between a rock and a hard place. He couldn't fire her for fear of a sexual discrimination suit on top of his malpractice problem, so he had to deal with her as best as he could. Why she didn't quit on her own, he had no idea, since it was open warfare between her and the duo Marlene and Darlene. Every day there was a new crisis with both Marlene and Darlene threatening to quit. But Craig couldn't let them, since he needed them more than ever. As handicapped as he was emotionally and physically from the lawsuit, he found practicing medicine almost impossible. He couldn't concentrate, and he saw every patient as a potential litigant. Almost from the day he'd been served, he suffered recurrent bouts of anxiety, which aggravated his hypervigilant digestive system, causing heartburn and diarrhea. Compounding everything was the insomnia,

forcing him to use sleeping pills and making him feel
sodden instead of refreshed when he awoke. All in all, he
was a mess. The only good part was that he didn't regain
the weight he had lost from going to the gym, thanks to
his lack of appetite. On the other hand, he did regain his
previously sallow, pudgy face, which was now made
worse by sunken eyes lined with dark circles.

As baneful as Leona's behavior was in the office in
terms of complicating Craig's life, it was trumped by her
effect on the malpractice suit. The first hint of trouble
occurred when she appeared on Tony Fasano's witness
list. How bad it was going to prove to be became evident at her deposition, which was a painful affair for
Craig, as he was forced to witness the depth of her
resentment, ultimately humiliating him with her scoffing
description of his lack of male prowess.

Prior to the deposition, Craig had confessed to Randolph the details of his affair with Leona so Randolph
would know what to expect and what questions to ask.
He'd also warned how irresponsibly talkative he'd been
about his feelings toward the deceased the night he'd
been served, but he might as well have saved his breath.
Whether it was from spite or just a good memory, Leona
had recalled most everything Craig had said about
Patience Stanhope, including his hating the woman, calling her an entitled hypochondriacal bitch, and his
assertion that her passing was a blessing for everyone.
After such revelations, even Randolph's perennial optimism about the suit's ultimate outcome had taken a
serious hit. When he and Craig left Fasano's second-floor
office on Hanover Street in Boston's North End, Randolph was even more taciturn and constrained than
usual.

"She's not going to help my case, is she?" Craig had asked, vainly hoping that his fears were unfounded.

"I hope this is the only surprise you have for me," Randolph had answered. "Your glibness has succeeded in making this an uphill struggle. Please reassure me you haven't spoken in a similar regrettable fashion to anyone else."

"I haven't."

"Thank God!"

As they had climbed into Randolph's waiting car, Craig had acknowledged to himself that he despised Randolph's superior attitude, although later he came to understand that what he hated was the dependency that bound him to the lawyer. Craig had always been his own man, struggling single-handedly against the obstacles he'd faced, until now. Now he couldn't do it alone. He needed Randolph, and as a consequence, Craig's feelings toward the defense attorney went back and forth during the pretrial months, depending on how the affair unfolded.

Craig became aware of a huff of displeasure from Randolph as Tony used his last preemptory strike to remove a nattily dressed nursing-home administrator. Randolph's elegant finger tapped with displeasure against his yellow legal pad. Seemingly in retribution, Randolph then struck the waif in the oversized sweatshirt. Two more individuals were then called from the jury pool and sworn, and the questions continued.

Leaning over toward his lawyer, Craig asked in a whisper what he needed to do to use the restroom. His hypervigilant colon was responding to his anxiety. Randolph assured him it wasn't a problem and that he should just indicate the need as he was now doing. Craig nodded and pushed back his chair. It was humiliating to sense all eyes upon him as he exited the bar through the gate. The only person he acknowledged was Alexis. With everyone else he avoided eye contact.

The men's room was old-fashioned and reeked of stale urine. Craig wasted no time getting into a stall to avoid any contact with several suspicious-looking unshaven men loitering by the sinks and conversing in hushed voices. With its graffitied walls, its marble mosaic floor in disrepair, and the disagreeable odor, the men's room seemed symbolic of Craig's current life, and with his digestive system behaving as it was, he was afraid he'd be making frequent visits to its unpleasant surroundings during the course of the trial.

With a piece of toilet paper, he wiped the seat. After he'd sat down, he thought again of Leona's deposition, and although it had been possibly the worst deposition in regard to its potential impact on the case's outcome, it hadn't been the worst from a purely emotional point of view. That dubious honor belonged to both his own deposition and those of Tony Fasano's experts. To Craig's dismay, Tony had had no trouble getting local area experts to agree to testify, and the lineup was impressive. All were people he knew and admired and who knew him. First to be deposed was the cardiologist who'd helped with the resuscitation attempt. Her name was Dr. Madeline Mardy. Second was Dr. William Tard-off, chief of cardiology at Newton Memorial Hospital, and third, and most distressing for Craig, was Dr. Herman Brown, chief of cardiology at Boston Memorial Hospital and chair of cardiology at Harvard Medical School. All three testified that the first minutes after a heart attack were the most crucial in terms of survival.

They also concurred that it was common knowledge that it was absolutely key to get the patient to a hospital facility as expeditiously as possible and that any delay was unconscionable. Although all were dismissive of the idea of making a house call in the face of a suspected myocardial infarction, Randolph made all of them state that they believed Craig did not know for certain the patient's diagnosis before arriving at her bedside. Randolph had also gotten two of the three to state on the record that they were impressed by Craig's willingness to make a house call no matter what the diagnosis.

Randolph had not been as troubled by the experts' depositions as Craig, and took them in stride. The reason they bothered Craig so much was that the doctors were respected colleagues. Craig took their willingness to testify for the plaintiff as an overt criticism of his reputation as a physician. This was especially true for Dr. Herman Brown, whom Craig had had as a preceptor in medical school and as an attending during his residency. It was Dr. Brown's criticism and disapproval that cut Craig to the quick, especially since Craig had gotten such approbation from the same individual when Craig had been a student. To make matters worse, Craig had been unable to get any local colleague to testify on his behalf.

As upsetting as Craig found the experts' depositions, his own deposition had been far more disturbing. He'd even judged it the single most irksome and distressing experience in his life to date, especially since Tony Fasano had stretched the session out for two grueling days like a kind of filibuster. Randolph had to a degree anticipated Craig's difficulties and had tried to coach him. He'd advised Craig to hesitate after a question in case an objection was appropriate, to think for a moment about the ramifications of a question before answering, to take his time answering, to avoid offering anything not asked, and above all not to appear arrogant, and not to get into an argument. He'd said he couldn't be more specific, since he'd never opposed Tony Fasano in the past, mainly because it was apparently Tony's first foray into the malpractice arena from his usual personal-injury specialty.

The deposition had taken place in Randolph's posh 50 State Street office with its stunning view over Boston Harbor. Initially, Tony had been reasonable, not quite pleasant but certainly not confrontational. That was the playground entertainer persona. He'd even persisted in cracking a few off-the-record jokes, although only the court reporter had giggled. But the entertainer persona soon disappeared, to be replaced by the bully. As he began to hammer and accuse, about Craig's professional and private life in humiliating detail, Craig's weak defenses began to crumble. Randolph objected when he could, even tried to suggest recess at several junctures, but Craig had gotten to the point where he would not hear of it. Despite being warned against anger, Craig had gotten angry, very angry, and then proceeded to violate all of Randolph's admonitions and ignore all recommendations. The worst exchange happened in the early afternoon of the second day. Even though Randolph had again warned Craig about losing control during lunch and Craig had promised to follow his advice, Craig quickly fell into the same trap under the onslaught of Tony's preposterous allegations.

"Wait a second!" Craig had snapped. "Let me tell you something."

"Please," Tony had retorted. "I'm all ears."

"I've made some mistakes in my professional life. All

doctors have. But Patience Stanhope was not one of them! No way!"

"Really?" Tony had questioned superciliously. "What do you mean by 'mistakes'?"

"I think it wise if we take a break here," Randolph had said, trying to intervene.

"I don't need a goddamned break," Craig shouted. "I want this asshole to understand just for a second what it's like to be a doctor: to be the one right there in the front-line trenches with sick people as well as hypochondriacs."

"But our goal is not to educate Mr. Fasano," Randolph had said. "It doesn't matter what he believes."

"Mistakes are when you do something stupid," Craig had said, ignoring Randolph and leaning forward to get his face closer to Tony's, "like cutting a corner when you're exhausted and have ten more patients to see, or forgetting to order a test when you know it's indicated because you had an intervening emergency."

"Or like making a stupid house call instead of meeting a seriously ill patient who was struggling to breathe at the hospital so you could get to the symphony on time?"

The sound of the outer men's room door slamming brought Craig back to the present. Hoping his lower intestine would stay quiescent for the rest of the morning, he finished up, pulled on his suit jacket, and went out to wash his hands. As he did so, he looked at himself in the mirror. He winced at his reflection. His appearance now was markedly worse than it had been before he started at the gym, and he didn't see much chance for improvement in the near future with the trial just getting under way. It was going to be a long,

stressful week, especially considering his disastrous performance at his deposition. Immediately after the
debacle, he hadn't needed Randolph to tell him how mis-
erably he'd performed, although Randolph was gracious
enough merely to suggest that they needed to practice
prior to his testifying at the trial. Before Craig had left
Randolph's office that day, Craig had pulled Randolph
aside and looked him in the eye. "There is something I
want you to know," he'd said insistently. "I have made
mistakes, as I told Fasano, even though I've tried my
damnedest to be a good doctor. But I didn't make a mistake with Patience Stanhope. There was no negligence."

"I know," Randolph had said. "Believe me, I understand your frustration and your pain, and I promise you
no matter what, I'll do my best to convince the jury of
the same."

Back in the courtroom, Craig regained his seat. The
voir dire had been completed and the jury impaneled.
Judge Davidson was giving them some initial instructions, including making certain their cell phones were off
and explaining the civil procedure they were about to
witness. He told them that they and they alone were to
be the triers of fact in the case, meaning they would be
deciding the factual issues. At the end of the trial, he said
he would charge them with the appropriate points of law,
which was his bailiwick. He thanked them again for their
service before looking over his spectacles at Tony Fasano.

"Plaintiff ready?" Judge Davidson asked. He had
already told the jury that the proceedings would start
with the plaintiff attorney making his opening statement.

"One moment, Your Honor," Tony said. He leaned
over and conversed in a whisper with his assistant, Ms.

Relf. She nodded while she listened, and then handed him a stack of note cards.

During the brief delay, Craig tried to begin engaging the jury as Randolph had recommended by regarding each in turn, hoping for eye contact. As he did so he hoped that his expression did not reflect his inner thoughts. For him the concept that this disparate, mixed bag of laypeople represented his peers seemed ludicrous at best. There was a nonchalant firefighter in a spotless white T-shirt with bulging muscles. There was a clutch of housewives who appeared to be electrified about the whole experience. There was a blue-haired retired schoolteacher who looked like everybody's image of a grandmother. An overweight plumber's assistant in jeans and dirty T-shirt had one foot propped up on the front rail of the jury box. Next to him, in sharp contrast, was a well-dressed young man with a scarlet pocket square spilling out of the breast pocket of a tan linen jacket. A prim female nurse of Asian extraction was next, with her hands folded in her lap. Next were two struggling small-businessmen in polyester suits who clearly looked bored, as well as irritated at having been coerced into their civic duty. A considerably more well-to-do stockbroker was in the back row, directly behind the businessmen.

Craig felt a mounting despair as his eyes went from each individual juror to the next. Except for the Asian nurse, none were willing to make eye contact even briefly. He couldn't help but feel that there was little chance any of these people, save for the nurse, could have any idea of what it was like being a doctor in today's world. And when he combined that realization with his performance during his deposition, and with Leona's expected testimony and the plaintiff's experts' testimony, chances for a successful

outcome seemed distant at best. It was all very depressing, yet a fitting end to a horrid eight months of anxiety,
grief, isolation, and insomnia, engendered by his constant
mental replaying of the whole affair. Craig was aware that
the experience had affected him deeply, robbing him of
his self-confidence, his sense of justice, his self-esteem,
even his passion for practicing medicine. As he sat there
looking at the jurors, he wondered, irrespective of the
outcome, if he would ever be able to be the doctor he had
once been.

CHAPTER TWO

Tony Fasano gripped the edges of the podium as if he were at the controls of a mammoth video game. His pomaded, slicked-back hair had an impressive sheen. The large diamond in his gold ring flashed as it caught the sunlight. His gold-nugget cuff links were in full view. Despite his relatively short stature, his boxy build gave him a formidable appearance and his robust, swarthy complexion gave him a look of health despite the court-room's sallow-colored walls.

After hiking a tasseled loafer onto the podium's brass rail, he began his opening statement: "Ladies and gen-tlemen of the jury, I want to express my personal appreciation of your service to allow my client, Jordan Stanhope, his day in court."

Tony paused to glance back at Jordan, who remained impassive and motionless, as if he were a mannequin. He was dressed impeccably in a dark suit with a sawtooth white handkerchief peeking out of his breast pocket. His manicured hands were folded in front of him, his coun-tenance expressionless.

Facing around, Tony regained eye contact with the jurors. His face assumed the expression of the bereft. "Mr. Stanhope has been in deep mourning, barely able to function after the regrettable, unexpected passing nine months ago of his lovely, dutiful wife and life's companion, Patience Stanhope. It was a tragedy that needn't have happened, and it wouldn't have happened except for the disgraceful negligence and malpractice of my opposing counsel's client, Dr. Craig M. Bowman."

Craig reflexively stiffened. Randolph's fingers promptly wrapped themselves around Craig's forearm, and he leaned toward the doctor. "Control yourself!" he whispered.

"How can that bastard say that?" Craig whispered back. "I thought that was what this trial is about."

"It is indeed. He's permitted to state the allegation. I do admit he's being inflammatory. Regrettably, that is his reputed style."

"Now," Tony said, pointing ceilingward with an extended index finger, "before I provide you good folks with a road map of how I will substantiate what I've just said, I'd like to make a confession about myself. I didn't go to Harvard like my esteemed opposing colleague. I'm just a city boy from the North End, and sometimes I don't talk that great."

The plumber's assistant laughed openly, and the two polyester suits cracked smiles despite their apparent pique.

"But I try," Tony added. "And if you're a little nervous about being here, understand that I am, too."

Three of the housewives and the retired schoolteacher smiled at Tony's unexpected admission.

"Now, I'm going to be up-front with you good people," Tony continued. "Just like I've been with my client. I've not done a lot of malpractice work. In fact, this is my first case."

The muscular firefighter now smiled and nodded approval of Tony's candor.

"So you might be asking yourself: Why did this wop take the case? I'll tell you why: to protect you and me and my kids from the likes of Dr. Bowman."

Mild expressions of surprise registered on most of the jurors' faces as Randolph rose up to his full, patrician height. "Your Honor, I must object. Counsel is being inflammatory."

Judge Davidson regarded Tony over the tops of his glasses with a mixture of irritation and surprise. "Your comments are pushing the limits of courtroom decorum. This is an arena for verbal combat, but established rites and rules are to be followed, especially in my courtroom. Do I make myself clear?"

Tony raised both beefy hands above his head in supplication. "Absolutely, and I apologize to the court. The problem is, occasionally my emotions get the better of me, and this is one of those cases."

"Your Honor . . ." Randolph complained, but he didn't finish. The judge waved for him to sit while ordering Tony to proceed with appropriate propriety.

"This is fast becoming a circus," Randolph whispered as he took his seat. "Tony Fasano is a clown, but a deviously clever clown."

Craig regarded the attorney. It was the first time he'd seen a crack in the man's glacial aplomb. And his comment was disturbing. There was a definite element of reluctant admiration.

After a brief glance at his cards in the crook of the lectern's top, Tony returned to his opening statement: "Some of you might wonder why cases like this aren't settled by learned judges and accordingly question why you have to interrupt your lives. I'll tell you why. Because you have more common sense than judges." Tony pointed at each juror in term. He had their full attention. "It's true. With all due respect, Your Honor," Tony said, looking up at the judge. "Your memory banks are jammed full of laws and statutes and all sorts of legal mumbo jumbo, whereas these people"—he redirected his attention to the jury—"are capable of seeing the facts. In my book this is an absolute maxim. If I ever get into trouble, I want a jury. Why? Because you people, with your common sense and your intuitional ability, can see through the legal haze and tell where the truth lies."

Several of the jurors were now nodding agreement, and Craig felt his pulse quicken and a cramp grip his lower bowels. His fear about Tony connecting with the jury was seemingly already coming to pass. It was indicative of the whole sorry affair. Just when he felt things couldn't get any worse, they did.

"What I'm going to do," Tony continued, gesticulating with his right hand, "is to prove to you four basic points. Number one: By the doctor's own employees, I am going to show that Dr. Bowman owed a duty to the deceased. Number two: With the testimony of three recognized experts from three of our own area's renowned institutions, I will show you what a reasonable doctor would do in the circumstance the deceased found herself in the evening of the eighth of September, 2005. Number three: With the testimony of the plaintiff, of one of the doctor's employees, and of one of the experts who happened to be involved in the actual case, I will show you how Dr. Bowman negligently failed to act as a reasonable doctor would have acted. And number four:

how Dr. Bowman's conduct was the proximate cause of
the patient's sad death. That's it in a nutshell."

Perspiration appeared on Craig's forehead, and his
throat felt suddenly dry; he needed to use the restroom,
but he didn't dare. He poured himself some water from
a pitcher in front of him with an embarrassingly shaky
hand and took a drink.

"Now we are back on terra firma," Randolph whispered. He obviously was not as moved as Craig, which
was some consolation. But Craig knew there was more.

"What I have just outlined," Tony continued, "is the
core of a garden-variety case of medical malpractice. It's
what the fancy, expensive lawyers like my opponent like
to call the 'prima facie' case. I call it the core, or the guts.
A lot of lawyers, like a lot of doctors, have a fondness to
use words nobody understands, particularly Latin words.
But this isn't a garden-variety case. It's much worse, and
that's why I feel so strongly about it. Now, the defense
is going to want you to believe, and they have witnesses
to suggest, that Dr. Bowman is this great, compassionate, charitable doctor with a picture-perfect nuclear
family, but the reality is far different."

"Objection!" Randolph said. "Dr. Bowman's private
life is not an issue. Counsel is trying to impugn my client."

Judge Davidson stared down at Tony after taking
off his reading glasses. "You are straying afield here,
son. Is the direction you are taking relevant to this
specific allegation of medical negligence?"

"Absolutely, Your Honor. It is key."

"You and your client's case are going to be in a lot of
hot water if it is not. Objection overruled. Proceed."

"Thank you, Your Honor," Tony said before recon-
necting with the jurors. "On the night of the eighth of

September, 2005, when Patience Stanhope was to meet her untimely end, Dr. Craig Bowman was not snuggled in his cozy, posh Newton home with his darling family. Oh, no! You will learn by a witness who was his employee and girlfriend that he was with her in his in-town love nest."

"Objection!" Randolph said with uncharacteristic forcefulness. "Inflammatory and hearsay. I cannot allow this type of language."

Craig felt blood rush to his face. He wanted to turn and connect with Alexis, but he couldn't get himself to do it, not with the humiliation he was experiencing.

"Sustained! Counsel, stick to the facts without inflammatory embellishments until the witness testifies."

"Of course, Your Honor. It is just hard to rein in my emotion."

"You'll be in contempt if you don't."

"Understood," Tony said. He looked back at the jurors. "What you will hear testimony to is that Dr. Bowman's lifestyle had changed dramatically."

"Objection," Randolph said. "Private life, lifestyle—none of this has relevance to the issue at hand. This is a medical malpractice trial."

"Good lord!" Judge Davidson exclaimed with frustration. "Counsels, approach the bench!"

Both Randolph and Tony dutifully went to the side of the judge's box, out of earshot of everyone in the courtroom and, most important, beyond the range of both the court reporter and the jury.

"At this rate, this trial is going to take a year, for Christ's sake," Judge Davidson groused. "My entire month's schedule will have to be trashed."

"I cannot allow this farce to continue," Randolph complained. "It's prejudicial to my client."

"I keep losing my train of thought with these interruptions," Tony grumbled.

"Pipe down! I don't want to hear any more pissing and moaning out of either one of you. Mr. Fasano, give me some justification for this excursion from the relevant medical facts!"

"It was the doctor's decision to go to the deceased's home on a house call instead of agreeing to the plaintiff's request to take his wife directly to the hospital even though, as the doctor himself will testify, he suspected a heart attack."

"So what?" Judge Davidson questioned. "I assume the doctor responded to the emergency without undue delay."

"We're willing to stipulate that, but Dr. Bowman didn't make house calls before he had his midlife crisis, or 'awakening,' as he calls it, and before he moved into town with his lover. My experts will all testify that the delay caused by making the house call was critical in Patience Stanhope's death."

Judge Davidson ruminated on this. As he did so, he absently rolled his lower lip into his mouth such that his mustache reached halfway down his chin.

"Provider lifestyle and mindset are not the issues in medical malpractice," Randolph asserted. "Legally, the question is simply whether there was a deviation from the standard of care, causing a compensable injury."

"Generally you are right, but I believe Mr. Fasano has a valid point, provided subsequent testimony supports it. Can you say that's unequivocally the case?"

"To the letter," Tony said with assurance.

"Then it will be up to the jury to decide. Objection overruled. You may proceed, Mr. Fasano, but I warn you again about inflammatory language."

"Thank you, Your Honor."

Randolph returned to his seat, ostensibly annoyed. "We're going to have to weather the storm," he said. "The judge is allowing Fasano unusual discretion. On the positive side, it will add fodder for the appeal if there is ultimately a finding for the plaintiff."

Craig nodded, but the fact that Randolph, for the first time, was voicing the possibility of a negative outcome added to Craig's growing despondency and pessimism.

"Now, where the devil was I?" Tony said after regaining the podium. He shuffled through his note cards briefly, adjusted the sleeves of his silk jacket so that his shirt cuffs presented just enough and his clunky gold watch was just visible. He raised his eyes. "In the third grade, I learned I was terrible speaking in front of groups, and it hasn't changed much, so I hope you give me a little slack."

A number of the jurors smiled and nodded in sympathy.

"We will present testimony that Dr. Bowman's professional life changed dramatically almost two years ago. Prior to that, he had essentially a traditional fee-for-service practice. Then he switched. He joined and has essentially taken over a successful concierge practice."

"Objection!" Randolph said. "This trial is not about style of practice."

Judge Davidson sighed with frustration. "Mr. Fasano, is Dr. Bowman's style of practice germane to the issue we discussed at the sidebar?"

"Absolutely, Your Honor."

"Objection overruled. Proceed."

"Now," Tony said, engaging the jury, "I'm looking at a number of faces here that look a little blank when I mention the term *concierge medicine.* And you know why? Because there are a lot of people who don't know what it is, including me before I took on this case. It's also called *retainer medicine,* meaning those patients who want to be included in the practice have to cough up some big bucks up front each and every year. And we're talking about some big money with some of these practices, upwards of twenty thousand dollars a head per year! Now, Dr. Bowman and his mostly retired partner, Dr. Ethan Cohen, don't charge that much, but they charge a lot. As you can well imagine, this style of practice can only exist in wealthy, sophisticated areas like some of our major cities and posh locales like Palm Beach or Naples, Florida, or Aspen, Colorado."

"Objection!" Randolph said. "Your Honor, concierge medicine is not on trial here."

"I disagree, Your Honor," Tony said looking up at the judge. "In a way, concierge medicine is on trial."

"Then relate it to the case, counselor," Judge Davidson said irritably. "Objection overruled."

Tony looked back at the jurors. "Now, what do people in a concierge practice get for all this up-front moola besides getting kicked out of the practice and abandoned if they don't come up with the dough? You'll hear testimony for what they supposedly get. It's going to include guaranteed twenty-four-seven access to their doctor, with the availability of the doctor's cell phone numbers and e-mail address, and a no-wait guarantee for their appointments, both of which I personally think people should get without having to fork over retainer fees. But most important of all in relation to this current case, they get the possibility of house calls when appropriate and convenient."

Tony paused for a moment to let his comments sink in. "During the trial, you will hear direct testimony that on the evening of September eighth, 2005, Dr. Bowman had tickets to the symphony for himself and his live-in girlfriend while his wife and darling daughters were moping at home. With him currently back in the family manse, I'd love to have the doctor's wife as a witness, but I can't because of spousal confidentiality. She must be a saint."

"Objection," Randolph said, "for the very reason cited."

"Sustained."

"You will also hear testimony," Tony continued with hardly a break, "that the known standard of care when a heart attack is suspected is to get the patient to the hospital immediately in order to initiate treatment. And when I say immediately, I'm not exaggerating because minutes, maybe seconds, count between life and death. You will hear testimony that despite my client's pleading to take his stricken wife to meet Dr. Bowman where she could be treated, Dr. Bowman insisted he make a house call. And why did he make the house call? You will hear testimony that it was important because if Patience Stanhope did not have a heart attack, even though from his own testimony you will hear that he suspected it, if she didn't, then he would be able to get to the symphony on time to drive up in his new red Porsche, walk in and be admired for his culture and for the young, attractive woman he had on his arm. And therein, my friends, lies—or lays, I'm never sure which—the medical negligence and malpractice. For in his own vanity, Dr. Bowman violated the standard of care that dictates a heart attack victim get to a treatment facility absolutely as soon as possible.

"Now, you will hear some different interpretation of these facts from the efforts of my more polished and experienced colleague. But I am confident that you people will see the truth as I believe the Massachusetts tribunal did when they heard this case and recommended it for trial."

"Objection!" Randolph called out, leaping to his feet. "And move to strike and request the court to admonish counsel. The tribunal's findings are not admissible: Beeler versus Downey, Massachusetts Supreme Judicial Court."

"Sustained!" Judge Davidson snapped. "Defense counsel is correct, Mr. Fasano."

"I'm sorry, Your Honor," Tony said. He stepped over to the plaintiff's table and took a paper offered by Ms. Relf. "I have here a copy of Massachusetts Laws, Chapter two thirty-one, section sixty B, saying the panel's findings and testimony before the panel are admissible."

"That was overturned by the case cited," Judge Davidson said. He looked down at the court reporter. "Remove the reference to the tribunal from the record."

"Yes, sir," the court reporter said.

Judge Davidson then engaged the jury. "You are directed to disregard Mr. Fasano's comment about the Massachusetts Tribunal, and you are instructed that it will play no role whatsoever in your responsibility as triers of fact. Am I understood?"

The jury all nodded sheepishly.

The judge glanced down at Tony. "Inexperience is not an excuse for not knowing the law. I trust there will be no more slipups of this sort, or I will be forced to declare a mistrial."

"I will try my best," Tony said. He returned to the podium slab-footed. He took a moment to gather his thoughts, then looked up at the jury. "I am confident, as I said, that you will see the truth and find that Dr. Bowman's negligence caused the death of my client's lovely wife. You will be then asked to award damages for the care, guidance, support, counsel, and companionship that Patience Stanhope would be providing today to my client if she had lived.

"So thank you for your attention, and I apologize to you as I did to the judge for my inexperience in this particular arena of law, and I look forward to addressing you again at the conclusion of the trial. Thank you."

Gathering his cards from the lectern, Tony retreated back to the plaintiff's table and immediately launched into a hushed but intense conversation with his assistant. He was flaunting the paper she had recently handed him.

With a sigh of relief that Tony had finished, Judge Davidson glanced at his watch before looking down at Randolph. "Does the defense counsel wish to make an opening statement at this juncture of the proceedings, or after the plaintiff's case in chief?"

"Most definitely now, Your Honor," Randolph replied.

"Very well, but first we will take a lunch recess." He smartly smacked the gavel. "Court's adjourned until one thirty. Jurors are instructed not to discuss the case with anyone or among themselves."

"All rise," the court officer called out like a town crier as the judge got to his feet.

CHAPTER THREE

BOSTON, MASSACHUSETTS
Monday, June 5, 2006
12:05 P.M.

Although most everyone else began to file out of the courtroom's gallery, Alexis Stapleton Bowman did not move. She was watching her husband, who'd sunk back into his chair like a deflated balloon the moment the paneled door to the judge's chamber closed. Randolph was leaning over him and speaking in a hushed tone. He had a hand on Craig's shoulder. Randolph's paralegal, Mark Cavendish, was standing on the other side of Craig, gathering up papers, a laptop, and other odds and ends, and slipping them into an open briefcase. Alexis had the impression Randolph was trying to talk Craig into something, and she debated whether to intervene or wait. For the moment, she decided that it was best to wait. Instead, she watched the plaintiff, Jordan Stanhope, come through the gate in the bar. His face was neutral, his demeanor aloof, his dress conservative and expensive. Alexis watched as he wordlessly found a young woman who matched his behavior and attire like two peas in a pod.

As a hospital-based psychologist, Alexis had been to numerous trials, testifying in various capacities although mostly as an expert witness. From her experience, she knew that they were anxious affairs for everyone, particularly for doctors being sued for malpractice, and especially for her husband, whom she knew was in a markedly vulnerable state. Craig's trial was the culmination of an especially difficult two years, and a lot was riding on the outcome. Thanks to her training and her ability to be objective, even about personal affairs, she knew Craig's vulnerabilities as well as his strengths. Unfortunately, in the current crisis she was aware that vulnerability trumped the strengths such that if he did not prevail in this very public questioning of his abilities as a doctor, she doubted he'd be able to pull together his life, which had splintered even prior to the lawsuit with a rather typical midlife crisis. Craig was first and foremost a doctor. His patients came first. She'd known that fact from the beginning of their relationship and had accepted it, even admired it, for she knew that being a doctor, particularly a good doctor, was in her estimation—and she had a lot of firsthand knowledge from working in a major hospital—one of the toughest, most demanding, and unrelenting jobs in the world.

The problem was that there was a good chance, at least on the first go-round, as Randolph had confided to her, that the case could be lost despite there having been no malpractice. In her heart of hearts, Alexis was sure of that from hearing the story and because she knew that Craig always put his patients first, even in those situations where it involved some inconvenience and even if it was three o'clock in the morning. In this instance, it was the double whammy of the malpractice claim and the midlife adjustment disorder that complicated the situation. The fact that they did occur together did not surprise Alexis. She hadn't seen many physicians in her practice, because seeking help, particularly psychological help, was generally not in the physician's nature. They were givers of care, not recipients. In this regard, Craig was a prime example. She had strongly suggested he seek therapy, especially considering his reaction to Leona's deposition and to the deposition of the plaintiff's experts, and she could have easily arranged it, but he had steadfastly refused. He'd even reacted angrily when she made the suggestion again a week later, when it was apparent he was becoming progressively more depressed.

As Alexis was continuing to debate whether to approach Craig and Randolph or stay where she was, she became aware of another person who'd stayed behind in the gallery after the mass exodus. What caught her attention were his clothes, which were almost identical to the plaintiff's attorney's in style, color, and cut. The similarity of dress as well as their equivalently bricklike habitus and dark hair gave them the superficial appearance of twins as long as they weren't together, because the man in the spectator area was at least one and a half times the size of Tony Fasano. He also differed by being less swarthy, and in contrast to Tony's baby-bottom facial skin, he had the regrettable sequela of severe teenage acne. The residual scarring on his cheekbones was deep enough to appear like that of a burn.

At that moment, Tony Fasano broke off his conversation with his assistant, grabbed his ostrich briefcase, and stormed through the gate into the gallery on his way out of the courtroom. It was obvious he was chagrined about the error regarding the tribunal ruling. Alexis wondered why he was overreacting, since his opening statement from her viewpoint had been regrettably effective and was undoubtedly the reason Craig was brooding. Tony's assistant sheepishly followed her boss. Without even a sideward glance or the slightest hesitation in his step, Tony called out, "Franco," while gesturing for the man dressed like himself to follow. Franco obediently did so. A moment later, they all had disappeared through the heavy double doors to the hall, which clanged shut with jarring finality.

Alexis glanced back toward her husband. He'd not moved, but Randolph was now looking in her direction. When he caught her eye, he waved for her to come join them. With an explicit invitation, she was happy to oblige. When she got there, Craig's face looked as down-trodden as she'd assumed from his posture.

"You must talk to him!" Randolph ordered, venturing from his studied, patrician self-possession with a hint of exasperation. "He cannot continue to behave in this despondent, defeated manner. In my experience, juries have special antennae. I'm convinced they can sense a litigant's mind-set and decide the case accordingly."

"Are you saying the jury could decide against Craig purely because he's depressed?"

"That's exactly what I'm saying. You have to tell him to buck up! If he continues to comport himself in this negative fashion, there is the risk they will assume he's guilty of the alleged malpractice. I'm not suggesting they won't listen to the testimony or consider the evidence, but they'll do so only with the thought of possibly negating their initial impression. Such behavior turns a neutral jury into a prejudicial one and switches the burden of proof from the plaintiff, where it should be, to us, the defense."

Alexis looked down at Craig, who was now massaging his temples while cradling his head in his hands, elbows on the table. His eyes were closed. He was breathing through an open, slack mouth. Getting him to buck up was a tall order. He'd been in and out of depression for most of the eight-month pretrial period. The only reason he'd acted "up" at all that morning and in the days immediately leading to the trial was the prospect of getting the trial over with. Now that the trial had started, it was obvious that the reality of the possible outcome had set in. Being depressed was not an unreasonable response.

"Why don't we all go to lunch, and we can talk," Alexis suggested.

"Mr. Cavendish and I will have to skip lunch," Randolph said. "I need to plan my opening statement."

"You haven't planned it before now?" Alexis questioned with obvious surprise.

"Of course I'd planned it," Randolph said testily. "But thanks to Judge Davidson allowing Mr. Fasano such discretion in his opening statement, I must alter mine."

"I was surprised by the plaintiff's opening statement," Alexis admitted.

"And indeed you should have been. It was nothing more than an attempt at character assassination or guilt by association, since they obviously have no evidence of actual medical negligence. The only good part is that Judge Davidson is already providing us with grounds for an appeal if needed, especially with Mr. Fasano's cheap trick of introducing the tribunal's finding."

"You don't think that was an honest mistake?"

"Hardly," Randolph scoffed. "I've had some of his cases researched. He's a plaintiff's attorney of the most despicable variety. The man has no conscience, not that I suspect one in his chosen field of specialty."

Alexis wasn't so certain. Having watched the attorney harangue his associate, if it were a charade, it was on Oscar level.

"I'm supposed to buck up, and you're already talking about an appeal?" Craig sighed, speaking for the first time since Alexis had arrived.

"One must prepare for all eventualities," Randolph said.

"Why don't you run along and do your preparation," Alexis said to Randolph. "Dr. Bowman and I will talk."

"Excellent!" Randolph said crisply. He was relieved to be freed. He motioned to his assistant to leave. "We'll see you back here in a timely fashion. Judge Davidson is, among his other less desirable traits, at least prompt, and he expects others to be likewise."

Alexis watched Randolph and Mark make their way through the courtroom and disappear out into the hallway before looking back down at Craig. He was watching her gloomily. She took Randolph's seat. "How about you and I have some lunch?" she said.

"The last thing in the world I'd like to do at this moment is eat."

"Then let's go outside. Let's get out of this magisterial environment."

Craig didn't answer, but he did stand. Alexis led the way out of the bar area, through the spectator section, and out into the hallway and to the elevator lobby. There were small groups of people milling about, with some locked in furtive conversation. The courthouse oozed an aura of contention from every nook and cranny. Craig and Alexis didn't talk as they took the elevator down and walked out into a bright, sunny day. Spring had finally come to Boston. In sharp contrast to the oppressive, seedy courthouse interior, there was hope and promise in the air.

After crossing a small, bricked courtyard wedged between the courthouse and one of Boston's Government Center's crescent-shaped buildings, Craig and Alexis descended a short flight of stairs. Crossing the busy four lanes of Cambridge Street took some effort, but they were soon able to stroll out onto the expansive esplanade fronting Boston City Hall. The square was crowded with people fleeing their confining offices for a little sun and fresh air. There were a few fruit stalls doing brisk business.

Without any particular destination, the couple found themselves near the entrance to the Boston T. They sat on a granite parapet, angled to face each other.

"There's no way I can tell you to buck up," Alexis said. "You're only going to buck up if you want to buck up."

"As if I didn't know that already."

"But I can listen. Maybe you should just tell me how you feel."

"Oh, whooptie do! Always the therapist ready to help the mentally ill. Tell me how you feel!" Craig echoed mockingly. "How gallant!"

"Let's not be hostile, Craig, I believe in you. I'm on your side in this legal affair."

Craig stared off for a moment, watching two kids winging a Frisbee back and forth. He sighed, then looked back at Alexis. "I'm sorry. I know you are on my side, letting me come back like a dog with his tail between his legs and pretty much no questions asked. I appreciate it. Really, I do."

"You're the best doctor I know, and I know a lot of

doctors. I also have some insight into what you are going through, which ironically has something to do with your being such a superb physician. It makes you more vulnerable. But that aside, you and I have some issues. That's obvious, and there will be questions. But not now. There will be time for dealing with our relationship, but we have to get you through this ugly affair first."

"Thank you," Craig said simply and sincerely. Then his lower jaw began to tremble. Fighting off tears, he rubbed his eyes with the balls of his fingers. It took a few moments, but when he felt he had himself under control, he looked back at Alexis. His eyes were watery and red. He ran a nervous hand through his hair. "The problem is this ugly affair keeps getting worse. I'm afraid I'm going to lose the case. Hell, when I think back on my social behavior back then when this happened, I'm embarrassed. And knowing that it's all going to come out publicly is a disgrace for both of us and a dishonor for you."

"Is the airing of your social behavior a big point of what's depressing you?"

"It's a part, but not the biggest part. The biggest humiliation is going to be the jury telling the world I practice substandard medicine. If that happens, I'm not sure I'll be able to practice anymore. I'm having a hard time as it is. I'm seeing everybody as another litigant, and every patient encounter a possible malpractice case. It's a nightmare."

"I think it's understandable."

"If I can't practice medicine, what else can I do? I don't know anything else. All I ever wanted to be is a doctor."

"You could do your research full-time. You've always had a conflict between research and clinical medicine."

"I suppose that's an idea. But I'm afraid I might lose my passion for medicine in general."

"So it's pretty clear you have to do everything in your power to win. Randolph says you have to pull yourself together."

"Oh, Randolph, good grief!" Craig complained. He looked off in the middle distance. "I don't know about him. Having seen Mr. Fasano's performance this morning, I don't think Randolph is the right lawyer. He's going to connect with that jury like oil and water, whereas Fasano already has them eating out of his hands."

"If you feel that way, can you request another attorney from the insurance company?"

"I don't know. I guess."

"But the question would be, Is it wise at this late juncture?"

"Who knows?" Craig questioned wistfully. "Who knows."

"Well, let's deal with what we have. Let's hear Randolph's opening statement. In the meantime, we have to think of a way to spruce you up appearance-wise."

"That's easier said than done. Do you have any ideas?"

"Just telling you to buck up is not going to work, but what about concentrating on your innocence? Think about that for the moment. You were presented with the seriousness of Patience Stanhope's condition; you did everything humanly possible. You even rode in the ambulance so you could be there if she arrested. My God, Craig! Concentrate on that and your dedication to medicine in general and project it. Fill the whole damn courtroom! How could you be more responsible? What do you say?"

Craig chuckled dubiously in the face of Alexis's sudden enthusiasm. "Let me make sure I understand. You're talking about me focusing on my innocence and broadcasting it to the jury?"

"You heard Randolph. He's had a lot of experience with juries, and he's convinced they have special senses about people's mind-set. I say you try to connect with them. God knows it can't hurt."

Craig exhaled forcibly. He was hardly confident but didn't have the energy to fight Alexis's zeal. "Okay," he said, "I'll try it."

"Good. And another thing. Try to tap into your physician's ability to compartmentalize. I've seen you do it time and time again in your practice. While you're thinking about how grand a doctor you are and how you gave your professional best with Patience Stanhope, don't think of anything else. Be focused."

Craig merely nodded and broke off eye contact with Alexis.

"You're not convinced, are you?"

Craig shook his head. He gazed up at the boxy, post-modern Boston City Hall building that dominated the esplanade like a crusader castle. Its brooding, distressed bulkiness seemed to him like a metaphor for the bureaucratic morass that ensnared him. It took effort to pull his eyes away and look back at his wife. "The worst thing about this mess is that I feel so helpless. I'm totally dependent on my assigned insurance company attorney. Every other hurdle in my life called for more effort on my part, and it was always the additional effort that saved the day. Now it seems like the more effort I make, the deeper I sink."

"Concentrating on your innocence like I'm suggesting takes effort. Compartmentalizing takes effort also." Alexis thought it ironic that what Craig was voicing was exactly how people in general felt about illness and their dependency on doctors.

Craig nodded. "I don't mind making an effort. I said I'll try to connect with the jury. I just wish there was something else. Something more tangible."

"Well, there is one other thing that passed through my mind."

"Oh? What?"

"I've thought about calling my brother, Jack, and seeing if he would come up from New York and help."

"Oh, that would be helpful," Craig said sarcastically. "He won't come. You guys haven't been close over the years, and, besides, he never liked me."

"Jack has had understandable difficulty with us being blessed with three wonderful daughters when he tragically lost both of his. It's painful for him."

"Maybe, but it doesn't explain his dislike of me."

"Why do you say that? Did he ever say he didn't like you?"

Craig looked at Alexis for a beat. He'd cornered himself and couldn't think of a way out. Jack Stapleton had never said anything specific; it was just a feeling Craig had had.

"I'm sorry you think Jack doesn't like you. The reality is, he admires you, and he told me so specifically."

"Really?" Craig was taken aback, convinced that Jack's assessment was the opposite.

"Yes, Jack did say you were the kind of student in

medical school and residency that he avoided. You are one of those people who read all the suggested reading, somehow knew all the trivial facts, and could quote at length from the latest issue of *The New England Journal of Medicine*. He admitted that awe did breed a certain contempt, but it was actually inwardly directed, meaning he wished he could have dedicated himself as much as you did."

"That's very flattering. It really is. I had no idea! But I wonder if he feels the same after my midlife crisis. And even if he were to come, what possible help could he provide? In fact, crying on his shoulder might make me feel worse than I do now, if that's possible."

"In Jack's second career as a medical examiner, he's had a lot of courtroom experience. He travels all over as an expert witness for the New York ME's office. He's told me he enjoys it. He strikes me as very inventive, although on the negative side, an inveterate risk-taker. As despondent as you are about how things are going, maybe his impromptu inventiveness could be helpful."

"I truly can't see how."

"I can't either, and I suppose that's why I hadn't suggested it before."

"Well, he's your brother. I'll leave that decision up to you."

"I'll think about it," Alexis said. Then she checked her watch. "We don't have a lot of time. Are you sure you don't want to grab something to eat?"

"You know, now that I've gotten out of that courtroom, my stomach has been growling. I could use a quick sandwich."

After they stood up, Craig enveloped his wife in a sustained hug. He truly appreciated her support and felt even more embarrassed about his behavior prior to his legal problems. She was right about his ability to compartmentalize. He'd totally separated his professional life and his family life and put far too much emphasis on the professional. He prayed he'd have a chance to balance the two.

CHAPTER FOUR

"All rise," the court officer called.

Judge Marvin Davidson whisked out of his chambers with a swirl of black robes at the exact moment the second hand of the wall-mounted, institutional clock swept past the number twelve.

The sun had moved in its diurnal trajectory, and some of the shades over the story-tall windows above the six-foot-high oak paneling had been raised. A bit of cityscape could be seen, as well as a tiny patch of blue sky.

"Be seated," the court officer called out after the judge had done so.

"I trust you all had a refreshing bite to eat," the judge said to the jury. Most jurors nodded.

"And as I instructed, I trust no one talked about the case in any capacity." All the jurors shook their heads in agreement.

"Good. Now you will hear the opening statement by the defense. Mr. Bingham."

Randolph took his time standing up, walking to the podium, and placing his notes on the angled surface. He then adjusted his dark blue suit jacket and the cuffs of his white shirt. He stood ramrod-straight, using every inch of his six-foot-plus height while his long-fingered hands gently enveloped the lectern's sides. Every single silver hair on his scalp knew its assigned place and had been snipped to a predetermined length. His necktie, with its sprinkling of Harvard *veritas* shields set in a crimson field, was tied to perfection. He was the picture of inbred, refined elegance and stood out in the middle of the shabby courtroom like a prince in a brothel.

From Craig's perspective, he couldn't help but be impressed, and for a few moments he'd gone back to thinking that the contrast with Tony Fasano might be favorable. Randolph was the father figure, the president, the diplomat. Who wouldn't want to trust him? But then Craig's eyes moved to the jury and went from the muscular fireman to the plumber's assistant and on to the inconvenienced businessmen. Every face reflected a reflex ennui that was the opposite of their reaction to Tony Fasano, and even before Randolph opened his mouth, Craig's brief flash of optimism disappeared like a drop of water on a sizzling fry pan.

Yet this rapid flip-flop realization wasn't all bad. It gave validation to Alexis's advice about mind-set, so Craig closed his eyes and conjured up the image of Patience Stanhope in her bed when he and Leona charged into the woman's bedroom. He thought about how shocked he'd been by her cyanosis, how quickly he'd reacted, and everything he'd done from that moment until it was apparent she was not going to be resuscitated. Over the course of the last eight months he'd gone over the sequence numerous times, and although on a few other cases over the years, he could second-guess himself and believe he should have done something slightly different, with Patience Stanhope he'd done everything absolutely by the book. He was confident that if he were confronted with the same situation that very day, he would not do anything differently. There had been no negligence. Of that he was absolutely certain.

"Ladies and gentlemen of the jury," Randolph said slowly and precisely. "You have heard a unique opening statement from someone who admits he has had no experience in trying medical malpractice cases. It was a tour de force with clever, initial self-deprecations which made you smile. I didn't smile because I saw the ploy for what it was. I will not debase you with such oratory tricks. I will merely speak the truth, which I'm certain you will come to understand when you hear the testimony that the defense will present. In contrast to the opposing attorney, I have had more than thirty years defending our good doctors and hospitals, and in all the trials I have participated in I have never heard an opening statement quite like Mr. Fasano's, which in many ways was an unfair character assassination of my client, Dr. Craig Bowman."

"Objection," Tony shouted, leaping to his feet. "Argumentative and inflammatory."

"Your Honor," Randolph interjected. With annoyance, he made a small, dismissive gesture with one hand toward Tony as if shooing away gnats. "May I approach the bench?"

"By all means," Judge Davidson snapped in return. He waved for the attorneys to come to the sidebar.

Randolph strode up to the side of the judge's bench with Tony fast on his heels. "Your Honor, Mr. Fasano was allowed wide discretion in his opening statement. I expect the same courtesy."

"I only described what I intend to substantiate with

witnesses, which is what an opening statement is supposed to prove. And you, Mr. Bingham, objected about
every ten seconds, interrupting my train of thought."

"Good God!" Judge Davidson complained. "This
isn't a murder-one trial," the judge said. "It's a medical
malpractice trial. We're not even through the opening
statements and you're at each other's throats. At this
rate, we'll be here for months." He allowed what he
said to sink in for a beat. "Let this be a warning to you
both. I want to move things along. Hear me? Each of
you is experienced enough to know what is appropriate
and what the other will tolerate, so rein yourselves
in and stick to the facts.

"Now to the objection at hand. Mr. Bingham, what's
good for the goose is good for the gander. You did object
to Mr. Fasano being inflammatory. He has every right to
object to you doing the same. Mr. Fasano, it is true you
were given wide discretion, and God help you and your
client if your testimony doesn't support your allegations.
Mr. Bingham will be allowed the same discretion. Do I
make myself clear?"

Both attorneys dutifully nodded.

"Fine! Let's continue."

Randolph returned to the podium. Fasano sat back
down at the plaintiff's table.

"Objection sustained," Judge Davidson said for the
court reporter's benefit. "Continue."

"Ladies and gentlemen of the jury," Randolph said,
"motivation is not usually part of medical malpractice proceedings. What is normally at issue is whether the standard
of care has been met such that the doctor possessed and
used that degree of learning and skill in treating the
patient's condition that a reasonably competent doctor

would employ in the same circumstance. You will note
that in his opening statement, Mr. Fasano said nothing
about his experts suggesting that Dr. Bowman did not use
his learning and skill appropriately. Instead, Mr. Fasano
must bring in the concept of motivation to get his allegation of negligence to be substantive. And the reason for
this, as our experts will testify, is that from the instant Dr.
Bowman knew the gravity of Patience Stanhope's condition, he acted with commendable speed and skill, and did
everything possible to save the patient's life."

Alexis found herself nodding in agreement as she listened to Randolph. She liked what she was hearing and
thought he was doing a good job. Her eyes switched to
Craig. He was at least sitting up straight. She wished she
could see his face from where she was sitting, but it was
impossible. Her eyes then went to the jury and her evaluation of Randolph's performance began to erode.
There was something about the jurors' posture that was
different from when Tony Fasano was speaking. They
seemed too relaxed, as if Randolph wasn't sufficiently
engaging their attention. Then, as if to confirm her fears,
the plumbing assistant gave a long, sustained yawn,
which spread through most of the others.

"The burden of proof lies with the plaintiff," Randolph continued. "It is the defense's job to rebut the
plaintiff's allegation and the testimony of the plaintiff's
witnesses. Since Mr. Fasano had indicated that motivation is his key stratagem, we, the defense, must adjust
accordingly and present with our witnesses an affir-
mation of Dr. Bowman's commitment and sacrifice
throughout his entire life, beginning with a doctor kit
given to him at age four, to be the best doctor and to
practice the best medicine."

"Objection," Tony said. "Dr. Bowman's commitment and sacrifice during his training has no bearing
on the particular case at hand."

"Mr. Bingham," Judge Davidson asked. "Will your
witnesses' testimony relate Dr. Bowman's commitment
and sacrifice to Patience Stanhope?"

"Absolutely, Your Honor."

"Objection overruled," Judge Davidson said. "Proceed."

"But before I outline how we plan to present our
case, I'd like to say a word about Dr. Bowman's practice. Mr. Fasano described it as 'concierge medicine'
and suggested the term had a pejorative connotation."

Alexis glanced back at the jury. She was concerned
about Randolph's syntax and wondered how many of the
jurors could relate to the words *connotation* and *pejorative,* and, of those who could, how many would think
they were pretentious. What she saw was not encouraging: The jury looked like wax figures.

"However," Randolph said, raising one of his long,
manicured fingers into the air as though he was lectur-
ing a group of naughty children. "The meaning of the
word *concierge* in its usual sense is help or service, with
no negative connotation whatsoever. And indeed that is
the reason it has been associated with retainer medicine,
which requires a small, up-front fee. You will hear testimony from a number of physicians that the rationale for
such a practice format is to spend more time with the
patient during appointments and during referrals so
the patient enjoys the kind of medicine all of us laypeople would like to experience. You will hear testimony
that the kind of medicine practiced in a concierge
practice is the kind of medicine all doctors learn during

medical school. You will also hear that its origins have come from the economic bind in traditional-practice settings that forces physicians to crowd more and more patients in a given hour to keep revenues above costs. Let me give you some examples."

It was reflex rather than conscious thought that propelled Alexis to a standing position in reaction to Randolph's foray into dull medical economics. Excusing herself, she moved laterally along the churchlike pew toward the central aisle. Her eyes briefly met those of the man who was dressed identically to Tony Fasano. He was sitting in the aisle seat directly across as Alexis exited her row. His expression and unblinking stare unnerved her but then immediately dropped out of her consciousness. She headed to the door to the hall and opened it, trying to be as quiet as possible. Unfortunately, the heavy door made a click heard all around the courtroom. Momentarily mortified, she stepped out into the hall and then walked out into the large elevator lobby. Sitting on a leather-covered bench, she rummaged in her shoulder bag for her cell phone and turned it on.

Realizing she had poor reception, she took the elevator down to the ground floor and walked back out into the sunlight. After being indoors, she had to squint. To avoid the smog of cigarette smoke from the nicotine addicts sprinkled around the courthouse entrance, she walked a distance until she was by herself. Leaning on a railing with her bag over her shoulder and tucked safely under her arm, she scrolled through her phone's electronic address book until she came to her older brother's entries. Since it was after two in the afternoon, she used his work number at the Chief Medical Examiner's Office in New York City.

As the call went through, Alexis tried to remember exactly when the last occasion had been that she'd called and talked with Jack. She couldn't remember but knew it had to have been months, maybe as much as half a year ago, as much as she'd been consumed by her family's disarray. Yet even prior to that there'd been only intermittent, haphazard contact, which was unfortunate because she and Jack had been extremely close as children. Life had not been easy for Jack, specifically fifteen years previously when his wife and two daughters, aged ten and eleven, had been killed in a commuter plane crash. They had been on their way home to Champaign, Illinois, after having visited Jack in Chicago, where he was retraining in forensic pathology. When Jack moved east to New York City, ten years previously, Alexis had been hopeful they would see a lot of each other. But it hadn't happened because of what she'd said to Craig earlier. Jack was still struggling to get over his tragedy, and Alexis's children were a painful reminder. Alexis's oldest daughter, Tracy, had been born one month after Jack's tragic loss.

"This better be important, Soldano," Jack said without so much as a hello after answering the phone. "I'm not getting anything done."

"Jack, it's Alexis."

"Alexis! Sorry! I thought it was my NYPD detective friend. He's just called me several times on his cell from his car but keeps getting cut off."

"Is it a call you need to take? I can call you back."

"No, I can talk to him later. I know what he wants, which we don't have yet. We have him well trained, so he's enamored with the power of forensics but he wants results overnight. What's up? It's good to hear from you. I never expected it would be you at this hour."

"I'm sorry I'm calling while you're at work. Is this a good time to chat, apart from your detective friend trying to get ahold of you?"

"Well, to be honest, I do have a waiting room full of patients. But I suppose they can wait since they're all dead."

Alexis giggled. Jack's new humorously sarcastic persona, which she'd experienced only a few times, was a marked change from his prior self. He'd always had a sense of humor, but in the past it was more subtle and frankly rather dry.

"Is everything okay up there in Beantown? It's not like you to call during the day. Where are you, at work at the hospital?"

"Actually, I'm not. You know, I'm embarrassed to say I can't remember the last time we spoke."

"It was about eight months ago. You called me to tell me Craig had come back home. As I recall, I wasn't all that optimistic about things working out and said so. Craig has always struck me as not much of a family man. I remember saying he was someone who made a great physician but not much of a father or husband. I'm sorry if that hurt your feelings."

"Your comments surprised me, but you didn't hurt my feelings."

"When I didn't hear back from you, I thought I had."

You could have called me if you'd thought as much, Alexis thought but did not say. Instead, she said, "Since you asked, things are not so good up here in Beantown."

"I'm sorry to hear that. I hope my prophecy hasn't come to pass."

"No, Craig is still at home. I don't think I mentioned last time we talked that Craig has been sued for malpractice."

"No, you didn't mention that tidbit. Was this after he'd come back or before?"

"It's been a difficult time for all of us," Alexis said, ignoring Jack's question.

"I can imagine. What's hard to imagine is him getting sued with as much of himself as he directs toward his patients. Then again, in the current medical-legal malpractice environment, everybody is at risk."

"The trial has just started today."

"Well, wish him good luck. Knowing his need to be number one in the class, I imagine he's taken what amounts to public censure pretty hard."

"That's an understatement. Being sued for malpractice is difficult for all doctors, but for Craig it is especially tough in terms of his self-esteem. He put all his eggs in one basket. The last eight months have been pure hell for him."

"How has it been for you and the girls?"

"It's not been easy, but we have been managing, except perhaps for Tracy. Age fifteen can be a tough time, and this added stress has made it worse. She can't quite come to grips with forgiving Craig for walking out on us when he did and carrying on with one of his secretaries. Her image of men has taken a beating. Meghan and Christina have taken it more or less in stride. As you know, Craig never had the time to involve himself too much in their lives."

"Are things okay between you and Craig? Are things back to normal?"

"Our relationship has been in a holding pattern, with

him sleeping in the guest room until this malpractice mess has been resolved. I'm enough of a realist to know his plate is pretty full at the moment. It's brimming, in fact, which is why I'm calling."

There was a pause. Alexis took a breath.

"If you need some money, it's not a problem," Jack offered.

"No, money is not an issue. The problem is that there is a good chance Craig will lose the case. And with the public censure, as you called it, I think there is a good chance he'll fall apart, meaning, in the vernacular, a nervous breakdown. And if that happens, I really don't see reconciliation happening. I think it would be a tragedy for Craig, for me, and for the girls."

"So you still love him?"

"That's a difficult question. Put it this way: He's the father of my daughters. I know he hasn't been the best father socially, not the best husband in a traditional storybook sense, but he's been a wonderful provider, he's always acted in a caring way. I fervently believe he loves us as much as he can. He's a doctor's doctor. Medicine is his mistress. In a real way, Craig is a victim of a system that pushed him to excel and to compete from the moment he decided to become a doctor. There's always been another test and another challenge. He's insatiable for professional approbation. Traditional social successes don't have the same import for him. I knew this was the case when I met him, and I knew it when I married him."

"Did you think he was going to change?"

"Not really. I have to say I admired him for his dedication and sacrifice, and I still do. Maybe that says something about me, but that's beside the point at the moment."

"I'm not going to argue with you about any of this. I've pretty much felt the same about Craig's personality, having gone through the same training system and felt the same pressure myself. I just couldn't have put it into words as well as you have. But that's probably because, as a psychologist, this is your area of expertise."

"It is. Personality disorders have been my bread and butter. I knew before Craig and I married that he had a lot of narcissistic traits. Now it might even have risen to be a disorder, since it's made aspects of his life dysfunctional. The trouble is, I've been unable to convince him to see someone professionally, which isn't surprising since narcissistic people in general have trouble admitting any deficiencies."

"Nor do they like to ask for help, since they see dependency as a sign of weakness," Jack said. "I've been down that road myself. Most physicians have at least a touch of narcissism."

"Well, Craig has a lot more than a touch, which is why he's finding this current problem so overwhelming."

"I'm sorry to hear all this, Alexis, but those dead patients of mine are starting to get restive. I don't want them to walk out without having been seen. Could I call you back this evening?"

"I'm sorry to be blabbing," Alexis said quickly. "But I have a favor to ask: a rather big favor."

"Oh?" Jack said.

"Would you be willing to fly up here and see if you could help?"

Jack gave a short laugh. "Help? How could I help?"

"You've mentioned in the past how often you testify

at trials. With all that experience in the courtroom, you could help us. The insurance company lawyer assigned to represent Craig is experienced and seems competent, but he's not relating to the jurors. Craig and I have talked about asking for another lawyer but have no way of judging if that would be wise or not. The bottom line is that we are desperate and pessimistic."

"The vast majority of my courtroom appearances have been in criminal proceedings, not civil."

"I don't think that matters."

"In the one malpractice case I was involved in, I was on the side of the plaintiff."

"I don't think that matters, either. You are inventive, Jack. You think outside the box. We need a small miracle here. That's what my intuition is telling me."

"Alexis, I don't see how I could possibly help. I'm not a lawyer. I'm not good around lawyers. I don't even like lawyers."

"Jack, when we were younger, you always helped me. You're still my big brother. I need you now. As I said, I'm desperate. Even if it turns out to be more psychological support than actual, I would be so thankful if you'd come. Jack, I haven't pushed you to come to visit us since you've been here on the East Coast. I know it was hard for you. I know you have some avoidant traits, and that seeing our daughters and me, too, reminded you of your terrible loss."

"Was it that obvious?"

"It was the only explanation. And I'd seen some evidence of that kind of behavior back when we were kids. It was always easier for you to avoid an emotional situation than confront it. Anyway, I've respected that, but now I'm asking you to put it aside and come up here for me, for my daughters, and for Craig."

"How long is the trial supposed to take?"

"Most of the week is the general consensus."

"The last time we talked, there was something new in my life I didn't tell you. I'm getting married."

"Jack! That's wonderful news. Why didn't you mention it?"

"It didn't seem right after you told me the latest about your marriage situation."

"It wouldn't have mattered. Do I know her?"

"You met her the one and only time you visited me here at work. Laurie Montgomery. We're colleagues. She's also a medical examiner."

Alexis felt a shiver of distaste descend her spine. She'd never visited a morgue before visiting Jack's place of work. Even though he'd emphasized that the building was a medical examiner's office and that the morgue was merely a small part of a larger whole, she hadn't found the distinction convincing. To her it was a place of death, plain and simple, and the building looked and smelled as such. "I'm pleased for you," she said while she vaguely wondered what her brother and his potential wife might talk about over a routine breakfast. "What makes me particularly happy for you is that you've managed to process your grief about Marilyn and your girls and move on. I think that's terrific."

"I don't think one ever gets completely over such grief. But thank you!"

"When is the wedding?"

"This Friday afternoon."

"Oh my goodness. I'm sorry to be asking for a favor at such a critical time."

"It's not your fault, that's for certain, but it does complicate things, yet it doesn't preclude it, either. I'm not the one making all the plans for the wedding. My job was the honeymoon, and that's all been arranged."

"Does that mean you'll come?"

"I'll come unless you hear back from me in the next hour or so, but I'd better come sooner rather than later so I can get back here. Otherwise, Laurie might start thinking I'm trying to get out of it."

"I'd be happy to speak with her to explain the situation."

"No need. Here's the plan. I'll come up on the shuttle late this afternoon or early evening after work. Obviously, I have to talk with Laurie and the deputy director, as well as clean up a few things here in my office. After I check into a hotel, I'll call your house. What I'll need is a complete case file: all the depositions, description or copies of any evidence, and if you can, any testimony."

"You're not staying at a hotel!" Alexis said with resolve. "Absolutely not. You have to stay at the house. We have plenty of room. I need to talk with you in person, and it would be best for the girls. Please, Jack."

There was a pause.

"Are you still there?" Alexis questioned.

"Yeah, I'm still here."

"Since you are making the effort to come up, I want you at the house. I really do. It will be good for everyone, although that might be selfish rationalization, meaning I know it will be good for me."

"All right," Jack said with a touch of reluctance in his voice.

"There's not been any testimony at the trial as of yet.

The defense is giving its opening statement as we speak. The trial is very much still at the beginning."

"The more material you can give me about the case, the greater the chance I might be able to come up with some suggestion."

"I'll see what I can do about getting the opening statement of the plaintiff."

"Well, then, I guess I'll see you later."

"Thanks, Jack. It's starting to seem like old times knowing that you're coming."

Alexis ended the call and slipped her phone back into her bag. When all was said and done, even if Jack didn't actually help, she was glad he was coming. He would provide the kind of emotional support only a family member could offer. She headed back through security and took the elevator to the third floor. As she entered the courtroom and allowed the heavy door to close as quietly as possible behind her, she could hear that Randolph was still describing the deleterious effect current-day medical economics was having on the practice of medicine. Choosing to sit as close as possible to the jury, she could see by their glazed eyes that they were no more engaged than when she had left. Alexis was even more pleased that Jack was coming. It gave her the sense that she was doing something.

CHAPTER FIVE

For a few minutes after hanging up with his sister, Jack
sat at his desk and drummed his fingers on its metallic
surface. He hadn't been completely up-front with her.
Her assessment of why he'd avoided visiting her had
been on the money, which he hadn't really acknowledged. Worse yet, he hadn't admitted it was still the case.
In fact, it might even be worse now, since Meghan and
Christina, Alexis's two youngest, were currently about
the same ages as his late daughters, Tamara and Lydia.
Yet he was caught in an emotional bind, considering how
close he and Alexis had been back in Indiana. He was five
years her senior, and the age difference was just enough
for his role to be somewhat parental yet close enough to
also be solidly brotherly. That circumstance, plus guilt
from having avoided Alexis for the entire ten years he'd
been in New York, made it impossible not to respond to
her pleas in her hour of need. Unfortunately, it wasn't
going to be easy.

He stood up and for a brief moment debated whom
he should talk to first. His first inclination was Laurie,
although he was hardly excited about the prospect, since
she was clearly uptight about the wedding plans; her
mother was driving her crazy and she was, in turn, driv-

ing Jack crazy. Consequently, he thought perhaps speaking first to Calvin Washington, the deputy chief, made more sense. Calvin was the one who would have to give Jack permission to take time off from the OCME. For even a briefer moment, the hope that Calvin would say no to additional leave passed through his mind, since both Jack and Laurie were already scheduled for two weeks' vacation starting Friday. Being denied leave to go to Boston would certainly solve his issues of guilt toward Alexis and reluctance to confront Alexis's daughters, and the need to bring up the idea with Laurie. Yet such a convenient excuse was not going to come to pass.

Calvin wouldn't say no; a family emergency was never turned down.

But before he'd even logged off his computer, rationality prevailed. Intuitively, he knew he should at least try to talk with Laurie first, since if he didn't and she found out that he hadn't tried, there'd be hell to pay, as close as it was to the wedding date. With that idea in mind, he walked down the hall toward Laurie's office.

There was another reason Jack was not excited about the proposed trip to Boston, and that was because Craig Bowman was far from his favorite person. Jack had tolerated him for Alexis's benefit, but it had never been easy. From day one when Jack had just met the man, he'd recognized the type. There'd been several similar personalities in Jack's medical school, all of whom had been at the very top of his class. They were the type of individuals who made it a point to smother anyone with an avalanche of journal article citations supposedly confirming their viewpoint whenever they got into a medical discussion. If that had been the only problem, Jack could have lived with it, but unfortunately, Craig's opinionated ways were also sprinkled with an irritating degree of arrogance, grandiosity, and entitlement. But even that Jack could have found bearable if he'd been able to occasionally steer the conversation with Craig away from medicine. But he never could. Craig was interested only in medicine, science, and his patients. He wasn't interested in politics or culture or even sports. He didn't have time.

As Jack closed in on Laurie's office door, he audibly harrumphed when his mind recalled Alexis suggesting he had avoidant traits in his personality. The nerve! He thought for a moment and then smiled at his reaction. With a flash of clairvoyance, he knew she was right and that Laurie would wholeheartedly agree. In many ways, such a reaction was evidence of his narcissism, which he had admitted to Alexis.

Jack poked his head into Laurie's office, but her desk chair was empty. Riva Mehta, Laurie's darkly complected, silky-voiced officemate, was at her desk and on the phone. She glanced up at Jack with her onyx eyes.

Jack pantomimed by pointing toward Laurie's chair while raising his eyebrows questioningly. Riva responded by pointing downward and mouthing "in the pit" without taking the telephone receiver from her ear.

With a nod of understanding that Laurie was down in the autopsy room, undoubtedly doing a late case, Jack reversed course and headed for the elevators. Now if Laurie found out he'd gone to Calvin first, he'd have an explanation.

As per usual, he found Dr. Calvin Washington in his office next to the chief's. In contrast with the chief's, it was tiny and practically filled with metal filing cabinets, his desk, and a couple of straight-backed chairs. There was barely room for Calvin's two-hundred-fifty-pound frame to squeeze past his desk and lower itself into his desk chair. It was Calvin's job to run the medical examiner's office on a daily basis, which was not an easy job considering there were more than a dozen medical examiners and over twenty thousand cases per year resulting in almost ten thousand autopsies. On a daily basis there were on average two homicides and two drug overdoses. The OCME was a busy place, and Calvin oversaw all the pesky details.

"What's the problem now?" Calvin demanded in his basso profundo voice. In the beginning, Jack had been relatively intimidated by the man's muscular bulk and stormy temperament. As the years passed, the two had grown to have a wary respect for each other. Jack knew Calvin's bark was worse than his bite.

Jack didn't go into details. He merely said he had a family emergency in Boston that required his presence.

Calvin regarded Jack through his wire-rimmed progressive lenses. "I didn't know you had family in Boston. I thought you were from somewhere out there in the Midwest."

"It's a sister," Jack said simply.

"Will you be back in time for your vacation?" Calvin asked.

Jack smiled. He knew Calvin well enough to know that he was making a stab at humor. "I'll try my darnedest."

"How many days are we looking at?"

"Can't say for certain, but I'm hoping just one."

"Well, keep me informed," Calvin said. "Does Laurie know about this sudden development?" Over the years

Jack had come to realize that Calvin had assumed an almost parental attachment to Laurie.

"Not yet, but she's at the top of my list. Actually, she's the only one on my list."

"All right! Get outta here. I've got work to do."

After thanking the deputy chief, who acknowledged him with a wave of dismissal, Jack walked out of the admin area and took the stairs down to the autopsy floor. He waved hello to the mortuary tech in the mortuary office and to the head of security in the security office. A waft of what New York City residents call fresh air came in from the open loading dock looking out to 30th Street. Turning to the right, he walked down the stained, bare concrete flooring past the big walk-in cooler and past the individual refrigerated compartments. Reaching the autopsy room, he glanced inside through the wire-mesh window. There were two figures in full protective gear in the process of cleaning up. A single body with a sutured autopsy incision was on the nearest table. It was obvious the case was over.

Jack cracked the door and called out to ask if anyone knew the whereabouts of Dr. Montgomery. One of the occupants said she'd left five minutes ago. Cursing under his breath, Jack retraced his steps and took the elevator back up to the fifth floor. As he rode, he wondered if there was any way to present the situation that would be easier for Laurie. His intuition told him she wasn't going to be happy with this new development, with as much pressure as her mother was putting on her about Friday's proceedings.

He found her in her office, arranging things on her desktop. It was apparent she'd just arrived. Riva was still on the phone and ignored them both.

"What a nice surprise," Laurie said brightly.

"I hope so," Jack said. He leaned his butt against the edge of Laurie's desk and looked down at her. There was no other chair. Not only did the medical examiners have to share offices in the outdated OCME facility, but the offices were small to begin with. Two desks and two file cabinets filled the room.

Laurie's questioning blue-green eyes stared back at Jack without blinking. Her hair was piled on top of her head and held in place with a faux-tortoiseshell clip. A few wisps of hair curled down in front of her face. "What do you mean 'I hope so'? What in heaven's name are you going to tell me?" She was wary.

"I just had a call from my sister, Alexis."

"That's nice. Is she all right? I've wondered why you two don't stay more in touch, especially since she and her husband have been having their difficulties. Are they still together?"

"She's fine, and yes they are together. The call was about him. He's going through a difficult time. He's being tried for malpractice."

"That's too bad, especially since you said he was such a good doctor. I hate to hear that kind of story with what we medical examiners know of the doctors who ought to be sued."

"The bad doctors are much more risk-management-oriented to make up for what they lack in skill and know-how."

"What gives, Jack? I know you didn't come in here to discuss the malpractice crisis. I'm sure of that."

"Apparently, my brother-in-law's case is not going well, at least according to Alexis, and with the extent of his ego investment in being a doctor, she believes he'll decompensate if he loses. Furthermore, she believes that if that happens, the marriage and family will fall apart. If Alexis didn't have a Ph.D. in psychology, I might not give all this much credence, but since she does, I have to assume it's on the money."

Laurie cocked her head a few degrees to the side to view Jack from a slightly different angle. "You're obviously leading up to something, which I have a feeling I'm going to find upsetting."

"Alexis has pleaded with me to rush up to Boston and try to help."

"What on earth could you do?"

"Probably just hold her hand. I was as skeptical as you are and said so, but she practically begged me to come. To be honest, she tapped into my mother lode of guilt."

"Oh, Jack," Laurie murmured plaintively. She took a deep breath and let it out. "How long will you be away?"

"I'm hoping only a day. That's what I told Calvin." Then Jack quickly added, "I came here to your office first to talk to you, then stopped in Calvin's office on the way down to the pit when I found out that's where you were."

Laurie nodded. She glanced down at her desktop and played with an errant paper clip. It was obvious she was torn between Jack's sister's need and her own. "I don't have to remind you this is Monday afternoon and our wedding is set for one thirty on Friday."

"I know, but you and your mom are doing all the work. The honeymoon was my job, and it's all arranged."

"What about Warren?"

"As far as I know, in his words, he's cool, but I'll check." Jack had had trouble deciding who was going to be the best man, Warren or Lou. Ultimately, it had come to drawing straws, and Warren had won. Other than Warren and Lou, the only people Jack had invited to the affair were his office mate, Dr. Chet McGovern, and a smattering of his neighborhood basketball buddies. He'd specifically avoided inviting family for a multitude of reasons.

"And you?"

"I'm ready."

"Should I be worried about you going up to Boston and confronting your sister's daughters? You've told me in the past that was a problem for you. How old are they now?"

"Fifteen, eleven, and ten."

"Weren't your two daughters eleven and ten?"

"They were."

"From what you've shared with me over the years about how your mind works, I'm worried that you might be set back from having to relate to them. Where are you staying?"

"At the house! Alexis insisted."

"I don't care if she insisted. Are you comfortable staying there? If you're not, listen to yourself and stay in a hotel. I don't want you to be set back over this and possibly decide not to go through with the wedding. There's a chance your going up there could open old wounds."

"You know me too well. I've thought about everything you've said. My sense is that giving serious thought to the risk rather than ignoring it is a healthy sign! Alexis accused me of harboring avoidant traits in my personality."

"As if I wasn't aware of that, considering how long it's taken you to feel comfortable marrying me."

"Let's not get nasty," Jack said with a smile. He waited to be sure she understood he was joking, because what she had said was true. For a number of years, Jack's guilt and grief made him feel it was inappropriate for him to be happy. He'd even felt it should have been he who died, not Marilyn and the girls.

"It would be small of me to try to talk you out of going," Laurie continued in a serious voice. "But I wouldn't be honest if I didn't tell you I'm not happy about it, both from a selfish point of view and for what it could do to your mind-set. We're getting married on Friday. Don't call me from Boston and suggest that it be postponed. If you do, it would be a cancellation, not a postponement. I hope you don't take that as an unreasonable threat. After all this time, it's how I feel. With that said, do what you have to do."

"Thank you. I understand how you feel, and for good reason. It's been a slow road to normalcy for me in a lot of respects."

"When exactly are you going?"

Jack glanced at his watch. It was close to four p.m. "Right now, I guess. I'll cycle back to the apartment, grab a few things, then head out to the airport." Currently, he and Laurie were living on the first floor of Jack's old building on 106th Street. They had moved down from the fourth floor because the building was under renovation. Jack and Laurie had bought it seven months previously and had made the mistake of trying to live in it while the work was being done.

"Will you call me tonight when you get settled?"

"Absolutely."

Laurie stood up and they hugged.

Jack didn't waste time. After cleaning up a few odds

and ends on his desk, he descended to the basement floor and got his mountain bike from where he stored it. With his helmet and bicycle gloves on and a clip on his right trouser leg, he peddled up 30th Street and then headed north on First Avenue.

As usual, once he was on the bike, Jack's problems faded. The exercise and the attendant exhilaration took him to another world, especially during his diagonal transit of Central Park. Like a verdant jewel plopped in the middle of the concrete city, the park afforded a transcendent experience. By the time he popped back out onto Central Park West at 106th Street, the tension that his conversation with Laurie had caused was gone. It had been worked out of his system by the otherworldliness of the park's flower-filled interior.

Just opposite his building, Jack pulled up at the edge of the neighborhood playground. Warren and Flash were on the basketball court, shooting baskets in anticipation of one of the neighborhood's fast, furious, and highly competitive evening games. Jack opened the gate in the high chain-link fence and wheeled his bicycle into the playground.

"Hey, man," Warren called out. "You've come early. You running tonight, or what? If you are, get your ass out here cause it's going to be a party tonight." Warren's impressively muscled, youthful body was completely hidden beneath his oversized hip-hop outfit. Flash was older, with a full beard that was beginning to gray prematurely. His biggest asset other than his jump shot was his mouth. He could argue any point and get most people to agree. Together they made an almost undefeatable team.

After brief hugs and ritualized handshakes, Jack told

Warren he couldn't play because he had to go to Boston for a couple of nights.

"Beantown!" Warren remarked. "There's a brother up there who's cool and plays hoops. I could give him a buzz and let him know you're in the neighborhood."

"That would be terrific," Jack said. He'd not thought about taking his gear, but a bit of exercise might be just what the doctor ordered if things got emotionally dicey.

"I'll give him your cell and leave his on your voice-mail."

"Fine," Jack said. "Listen! Is everything okay with your tux for Friday?"

"Not a problem. We're picking it up Thursday."

"Great," Jack said. "Maybe I'll see you guys Wednesday night. I could use a run or two before the big day."

"We'll be here, doc," Warren said. He snapped the ball from a startled Flash and drilled a long three-pointer.

CHAPTER SIX

BOSTON, MASSACHUSETTS
Monday, June 5, 2006
7:35 P.M.

Jack deplaned from the six thirty Delta Shuttle and allowed the clutch of people to carry him along. He assumed they knew where they were going. In short order, he found himself curbside of the Delta terminal, and within five minutes the Hertz rent-a-car bus pulled up. Jack boarded.

He'd not been in Boston for some time, and thanks to the interminable construction of the airport, he didn't recognize a thing. As the bus wended its way among the various terminals, he wondered what kind of welcome he was going to find when he arrived at the Bowman homestead. The only person he could count on being hospitable was Alexis. As far as the others, he had no idea of what to expect, particularly Craig. And even Alexis he'd not seen in person for more than a year, which was going to make it somewhat awkward. The last time he'd seen her had been in New York City, where she'd come solo to attend a professional psychology meeting.

Jack sighed. He didn't want to be there in Boston, especially since he knew his chances of accomplishing anything were minimal, other than to pat his sister on the back and commiserate with her, and also since his going had upset Laurie. He was confident Laurie would get over it, but she had already been under stress from her mother for the previous few weeks. The irony was that she was supposed to enjoy the wedding ceremony as well as the lead-up to it. Instead, it had become more of a burden. Jack had had to bite his tongue on several occasions when he'd been tempted to tell her she should have assumed as much. If it had been up to Jack, they would have scheduled a small, private affair with just a few friends. From his cynical perspective, the reality of major social events never lived up to romantic expectation.

Jack and his fellow passengers were eventually dropped off at the Hertz facility and without too much stress he found himself behind the wheel of a cream-colored Hyundai Accent that reminded him of an old-fashioned Minute Maid juice can. Armed with a poor map and a few slapdash directions, he bravely ventured forth and immediately got lost. Boston was not a city that was at all kind to a visiting driver. Nor were the Boston drivers. It was like a rally as Jack struggled to find the suburban town where Alexis lived. On his rare previous visits, he'd always met his sister in town.

Shaken but not down-and-out, Jack pulled into the Bowman driveway at a quarter to nine. It was still not completely dark, thanks to the approaching summer solstice, but the interior incandescent lights were on, giving the home what Jack assumed to be the falsely cozy appearance of the happy family. The house was impressive, like others in the immediate Newton neighborhood. It was a large two-and-a-half-story structure made of brick and painted white with a series of dormers poking out of the roof. Also, like the other homes, there was an expansive lawn, lots of shrubs, towering trees, and extensive flower beds. Below each window on the ground floor was a window box brimming with blossoms. Next to Jack's Hyundai was a Lexus. Inside the garage, Jack knew from one of Alexis's earlier conversations there was the de rigueur station wagon.

No one came flying out of the house waving a banner of welcome. Jack turned off the engine and for a moment entertained the idea of just turning around and leaving. Yet he couldn't do that, so he reached into the backseat for his carry-on bag and got out of the car. Outside, there were the familiar noises of the crickets and other creatures. Save for those sounds, the neighborhood seemed devoid of life.

At the front door, Jack peered in through the side-lights. There was a small foyer with an umbrella stand. Beyond that was a hallway. He could see a flight of stairs that rose up to the second floor. Still, there were no people, not a sound. Jack rang the bell, which was actually chimes that he could hear distinctly through the door. Almost immediately a small, androgynous figure appeared bounding down the stairs. She was dressed in a simple T-shirt and shorts and no shoes. She was a lithe towhead with milky white blemish-free skin and delicate-appearing arms and legs. She threw open the door. It was obvious she was strong-willed.

"You must be Uncle Jack."

"I am, and you?" Jack felt his heart quicken. He could already see his late daughter Tamara.

"Christina," she declared. Then, without taking her greenish eyes from Jack, she yelled over her shoulder, "Mom! Uncle Jack is here."

Alexis appeared at the end of the hallway. As she approached, she exuded major domesticity. She was wearing an apron and wiping her hands on a checkered dishtowel. "Well, ask him in, Christina."

Although looking appropriately older, Alexis appeared pretty much the same as Jack remembered her back in their childhood home in South Bend, Indiana. There was no doubt they were siblings. They had the same sand-colored hair, the same matching maple-syrup eyes, the same defined features, and the same complexion, which suggested they'd been in the sun even when they hadn't. Neither was completely pale, even in the dead of winter.

With a warm smile, Alexis walked directly up to Jack and gave him a sustained hug. "Thanks for coming," she whispered in his ear. While still embracing Alexis, Jack saw the other two girls appear at the top of the stairs. It was easy to tell them apart, since Tracy at age fifteen was more than a foot taller than Meghan at eleven. As if not sure what to do, they came down the stairs slowly, hesitating at each step. As they neared it was easy for Jack to see their personalities differed as much as their height. Tracy's sky-blue eyes burned with a brazen intensity, whereas Meghan's hazel eyes flitted about, not willing to make eye contact. Jack swallowed. Meghan's eye movement suggested she was shy and introverted just like Jack's Lydia.

"Come down here and say hello to your uncle," Alexis ordered good-naturedly.

As the girls reached the floor level, Jack was surprised at Tracy's height. He was regarding her at nearly eye level. She was a good three to four inches taller than her mother. The other thing he saw was that she had two obvious piercings. One was on her nostril, topped with a small diamond. The other was a silver ring tucked into her exposed navel. Her attire included a cropped sleeve-less cotton top that stretched across precociously impressive breasts. On her lower half, she wore low-rise billowy harem pants. The outfit and accessories gave her a saucy sensuality as brazen as her stare.

"This is your uncle, girls," Alexis said as a way of introduction.

"How come you've never visited us?" Tracy demanded right off. She had both hands defiantly thrust into pants pockets.

"Did your daughters really die in a plane crash?" Christina asked almost simultaneously.

"Girls!" Alexis blurted, drawing the word out as if it were five or six syllables long. Then, she apologized to Jack. "I'm sorry. You know children. You never know what they are going to say."

"It's all right. Unfortunately, they are both reasonable questions." Then, looking into Tracy's eyes, he said, "Maybe over the next day or so we could talk. I'll try to explain why I've been a stranger." Then, looking down to Christina, he added, "In answer to your question, I did lose two lovely daughters in a plane tragedy."

"Now Christina," Alexis said, butting in. "Since you're the only one who's finished her homework, why don't you take Uncle Jack down to the basement guest room. Tracy and Meghan, you two head back upstairs and finish your work. And Jack, I assume you've not eaten."

Jack nodded. He'd wolfed down a sandwich at LaGuardia Airport, but that had long since disappeared into the lower reaches of his digestive tract. Although he hadn't expected to be, he was hungry.

"How about some pasta. I've kept the marinara sauce hot, and I can throw together a salad."

"That would be fine."

The basement guest room was as expected. It had two high windows that looked into brick-lined window wells. The air had a damp, cool feeling like a root cellar. On the plus side, it was tastefully decorated in varying shades of green. The furniture included a king-size bed, a desk, a club chair with a reading lamp, and a flat-screen TV. There was also a bathroom en suite.

While Jack pulled his clothes out of his carry-on bag and hung what he could in the closet, Christina threw herself into the easy chair. With her arms flat on the chair's arms and her feet sticking straight out into space, she regarded Jack critically. "You're skinnier than my dad."

"Is that good or bad?" Jack questioned. He put his basketball sneakers on the floor of the closet and carried his shaving kit into the bathroom. He liked the fact that there was a generous shower stall rather than a generic bathtub.

"How old were your daughters when they crashed in the plane?"

Although Jack should have expected Christina to return to the sensitive issue after his inadequate response, such a direct, personal question snapped him back to that disturbing sequence when he'd said good-bye to his wife and daughters at the Chicago airport. It had been fifteen years ago almost to the day that he'd driven his family to the airport to take a commuter flight back to Champaign while a band of rogue thunderstorms and tornadoes were approaching through the vast midwestern plains. He'd been in Chicago, retraining in forensic pathology after a health-care giant had gobbled up his ophthalmology practice back in the heyday of managed care's expansion. Jack had been trying to get Marilyn to agree to move to Chicago, but she had rightfully refused for the children's sake.

The passage of time had not numbed Jack's memory of the last good-bye. As if it had been yesterday, he could see in his mind's eye, watching through the glass partition, Marilyn, Tamara, and Lydia descend the ramp behind the departure gate. As they reached the maw of the Jetway, only Marilyn turned to wave. Tamara and Lydia, with their youthful enthusiasm, had just disappeared.

As Jack was to learn later that night, only fifteen or twenty minutes after takeoff the small prop plane had plowed full-speed into the fertile black earth of the prairie. It had been struck by lightning and caught in a profound wind shear. All aboard had been killed in the blink of an eye.

"Are you okay, Uncle Jack?" Christina asked. For several beats, Jack had been motionless as if caught in a freeze-frame.

"I'm fine," Jack said with palpable relief. He'd just relived the moment in his life that he strenuously avoided thinking about, and yet the episode concluded without the usual visceral sequelae. He didn't feel as if his stomach had flip-flopped, his heart had skipped a beat, or as if a heavy, smothering blanket had descended over him. It was a sad story, but he felt enough distance that it could have involved someone else. Perhaps Alexis was right. As she'd said on the phone: Perhaps he'd processed his grief and moved on.

"How old were they?"

"The same as you and Meghan."

"That's awful."

"It was," Jack agreed.

Back up in the kitchen/great room, Alexis had Jack sit at the family table while she finished boiling the pasta. The girls had all retreated upstairs to get ready for bed. It was a school night. Jack's eyes ranged around the room. It was an expansive yet cozy room befitting the house's external appearance. The walls were a light, sunburst yellow. A deep, comfortable sofa upholstered in a bright green floral fabric and covered with cushions faced a fireplace surmounted by the largest flat-screen television Craig had ever seen. The curtains were the same print as the sofa and framed a bow window looking out on a terrace. Beyond the terrace was a swimming pool. Beyond that was lawn with what looked like a gazebo in the gloom.

"It's a beautiful house," Jack commented. In his mind it was more than beautiful. Compared to how he had been living over the last ten years, it was the epitome of luxury.

"Craig has been a wonderful provider, as I said on the phone," Alexis said as she poured the pasta into a colander.

"Where is he?" Jack questioned. No one had mentioned his name. Jack assumed he was out, perhaps on an emergency medical call or possibly conferring with his attorney.

"He's asleep in the upstairs guest room," Alexis said. "As I implied, we're not sleeping together and haven't been since he left to live in town."

"I thought maybe he was out on a medical call."

"No, he's free of that for the week. He's hired someone to cover his practice during the trial. His attorney recommended it. I think it's a good thing. As dedicated a doctor as he is, I wouldn't want him for my doctor right now. He's too preoccupied."

"I'm impressed he's asleep. If it were me, I'd be up, pacing the house."

"He's had a little help," Alexis admitted. She brought the pasta and salad over to the table and put it in front of Jack. "It was a hard day with the opening of the trial, and he's understandably depressed. I'm afraid he's been self-prescribing sleeping pills to deal with insomnia. There's also been some alcohol: scotch, to be exact, but not enough to worry about, I don't think. At least not yet."

Jack nodded but didn't say anything.

"What would you like to drink? I'm going to have a glass of wine."

"A little wine would be nice," Jack said. He knew more than he wanted to about depression. After the plane crash, he'd fought it for years.

Alexis brought over an opened bottle of white wine and two glasses.

"Did Craig know I was coming?" Jack asked. It was a question he should have asked before he'd agreed to come.

"Of course he knew," Alexis said while pouring the wine. "In fact, I discussed the idea with him before I called you."

"And he was okay with it?"

"He questioned the rationale but said he'd leave the decision up to me. To be truthful, he wasn't excited about it when we discussed it, and he said something that surprised me. He said he thought you disliked him. You never said anything like that, did you?"

"Absolutely not," Jack said. As he began to eat, he wondered how far to take the conversation. The truth of the matter was that back when Alexis and Craig had gotten engaged, he didn't think Craig was appropriate for Alexis. But Jack had never said anything, mainly because he thought, without knowing exactly why, that doctors in general were a poor risk, marriagewise. It was only relatively recently that Jack's tortured road to recovery had given him the insight to explain his earlier gut reaction—namely, that the whole medical training process either selected narcissistic people or created them, or some combination of the two. In Jack's estimation, Craig was the poster boy in this regard. His single-minded dedication to medicine almost guaranteed that his own personal relationships would be correspondingly shallow, a kind of psychological zero-sum game.

"I told him you didn't feel that way," Alexis continued. "In fact, I said you admired him because you told me that once. Am I remembering correctly?"

"I told you I admired him as a consummate physician," Jack said, aware that he was being mildly evasive.

"I did qualify it by saying you were envious of his accomplishments. You did say something to that effect, didn't you?"

"Undoubtedly. I have always been awed by his ability to do real, publishable basic science research while handling a large, successful clinical practice. That is the romantic goal of a number of physicians who never even come close. I made a stab at it back when I was an ophthalmologist, but in retrospect, my supposed research was a joke."

"I can't imagine that's true, knowing what I do about you."

"Getting back to the critical issue, how does Craig feel about me actually being here? You really didn't answer that."

Alexis took a sip of her wine. It was apparent she was considering the answer, and the longer she paused while doing so, the more uneasy Jack became. After all, he was a guest in the man's house.

"I suppose my not answering it was deliberate," she admitted. "He's embarrassed to be asking for help, as you suggested he might be on the phone. There's no doubt he sees dependency as a weakness, and this whole affair has made him feel totally dependent."

"But I have a feeling he's not the one asking for help," Jack said. He finished his pasta and started in on his salad.

Alexis put her wineglass down. "You are right," she said reluctantly. "I'm the one who's asking for help on his behalf. He's not all that happy about you being here because he's embarrassed. But I'm ecstatic you are here." Alexis reached across the table and took Jack's hand. She squeezed it with unexpected ferocity. "Thank you for caring, Jack. I've missed you. I know it's not the best time for you to be away, and that makes it even more special. Thank you, thank you, thank you."

A sudden flash of emotion washed over Jack, and he felt his face flush. At the same time, the avoidant nature of his personality kicked in and asserted itself. He detached his hand from Alexis's, took a gulp of wine, than changed the subject. "So, tell me about the opening day of the trial."

Alexis's slight smile turned up the corners of her mouth. "You are smooth, just like the old days! That was an impressively quick U-turn from an emotionally charged arena. Did you think I might not notice?"

"I keep forgetting you're a psychologist," Jack said with a laugh. "It was an instinctual reaction for self-preservation."

"At least you admit to your emotional side. Anyway, about this trial, all that's happened so far are the two opening statements by the opposing attorneys and the testimony of the first witness."

"Who was the first witness?" Jack finished the salad and picked up the wineglass.

"Craig's accountant. As Randolph Bingham explained later, the whole reason he was included was merely to establish that Craig owed a duty to the deceased, which was easy, since the deceased had paid the retainer fee, and Craig had been seeing her on a regular basis."

"What do you mean 'retainer fee'?" Jack asked with surprise.

"Craig switched from a traditional fee-for-service practice to a concierge practice almost two years ago."

"Really?" Jack questioned. He'd had no idea. "Why? I thought Craig's practice was booming, and he loved it."

"I'll tell you the main reason even if he won't," Alexis said, moving herself in closer to the table as if she was about to reveal a secret. "Over the last number of years, Craig has felt he has been progressively losing control of patient decisions. I'm sure you know all this, but with more and more involvement of insurance companies and various health plans with cost containment, there's been more and more intrusion into the doctor-patient relationship, essentially telling doctors what they can and cannot do. For someone like Craig, it has been a progressive, ongoing nightmare."

"If I were to ask him why he made the change, what reason would he give?" Jack questioned. He was fascinated. He'd heard of concierge medicine, but he thought it was a small fringe group or a mere trendy quirk in the system. He'd never talked with a doctor who practiced in such a setting.

"He wouldn't admit he'd ever compromised a patient decision because of outside influence, but he'd be fooling himself. Just to keep his practice solvent, he has had to see progressively more patients in any given day. The reason he gives for switching to concierge medicine is that it affords him the opportunity to practice medicine the way he was taught in medical school, where he could spend as much time as needed with each patient."

"Well, it's the same thing."

"No, there's a subtle difference, although there's an aspect of rationalization on his part. The difference is between a negative push and a positive pull. His explanation emphasizes the patient."

"Is the style of his practice playing a role in the malpractice case?"

"Yes, at least according to the plaintiff's attorney, who I have to say is performing better than anticipated."

"How do you mean?"

"To look at him, and you'll see for yourself if you come to the courtroom, you'd not imagine on first glance he'd be effective. How should I say this: He's a composite stereotype of the tawdry, ambulance-chasing personal-injury lawyer and the mafioso defense attorney, about half Craig's defense attorney's age. But he's relating to the jury in a surprisingly effective manner."

"How is Craig's practice style supposed to play into the case? Did the plaintiff's attorney address it in his opening statement?"

"Absolutely, and very effectively. The whole concept of concierge medicine is predicated on being able to satisfy patient needs, like a concierge at a hotel."

"I get the association."

"To that end, each patient has access to the doctor through cell phone and/or e-mail so that they can contact the doctor at all hours and be seen if necessary."

"Sounds like an invitation to abuse on the part of the patient."

"I suppose with some patients. But it didn't bother Craig. In fact, he seemed to like it because he started making house calls at off-hours. I think to him there was something retro and nostalgic about it."

"House calls?" Jack questioned. "Making house calls is usually a waste of time. As a modern-age doctor you're so limited in what you can do."

"Nonetheless, some of the patients love it, including the deceased. Craig had seen her often after hours. In fact, he had seen her at her home the morning of the very day the malpractice was supposed to have occurred. That evening she took a turn for the worse, and Craig made a house call."

"It seems to me it would be hard to find fault with that."

"One would assume so, but according to the plaintiff's attorney, it was Craig's making the house call rather than sending the patient to the hospital that caused the malpractice, since it delayed the diagnosis and emergency treatment of a heart attack."

"That seems absurd," Jack said indignantly.

"Not when you hear it coming from the plaintiff's attorney during his opening statement. You see, there are other circumstances surrounding the episode that are important. It happened when Craig and I were officially separated. At the time, he was living in an apartment in Boston with one of his nubile secretary-cum-file clerks named Leona."

"Good God!" Jack exclaimed. "I don't know how many stories I've heard of married physicians having affairs with their office help. I don't know what it is about male medical doctors. In this day and age, most men in other endeavors know not to date their employees. It's asking for legal troubles."

"My sense is you are being too generous to the middle-aged married males who find themselves locked in a reality that didn't live up to their romantic expectations. I think Craig falls into such a group, but it wasn't Leona's twenty-three-year-old body that was the initial lure. It was, ironically enough, the change to the concierge practice, which provided something he'd never had: free time. Free time can be a dangerous thing for someone who'd spent half of his life as single-minded as Craig. It was like he woke up and looked at himself in the mirror and didn't like what he saw. All of a sudden he had this manic interest in culture. He wanted to make up for lost time and become overnight his image of a well-rounded person. But it wasn't enough for him to do it alone like a hobby. Just as he did with medicine, he wanted to indulge it with one hundred percent effort, and he insisted I go along with it. But obviously I couldn't, not with my job and the responsibility of the girls. That's what drove him out, at least as far as I know. Leona came later, as he realized he was lonely."

"If you're trying to make me feel sorry for him, it's not going to work."

"I just want you to know what we're up against. The plaintiff's attorney knows that Craig and Leona had tickets for the symphony on the night the plaintiff's wife died. He says witnesses will prove that Craig made the house call even though he suspected the patient had a heart attack on the outside chance it wasn't. If he had found that to be the case, he would have been able to make the concert. Symphony Hall is closer to the plaintiff's house than Newton Memorial Hospital."

"Let me guess—this Leona is scheduled to be a witness."

"Of course! She's now the spurned lover. To make matters worse, she is still working in Craig's office and he can't fire her for fear of another lawsuit."

"So the plaintiff's attorney is contending that Craig put the patient at risk by playing the odds against the possible diagnosis."

"That's essentially it. They're saying that it's not up to the standard of care in terms of making a timely diagnosis, which for a heart attack is critical, as events have shown. They don't even have to prove that the woman would have survived had she been taken to the hospital immediately, just that she might have. Of course, the cruel irony is that the allegation is diametric to Craig's practice style. As we've said, he's always put patients first, even before his own family."

Jack ran a hand through his hair in frustration. "This is more complicated than I thought it would be. I assumed the question revolved around some specific medical issue. This kind of case means there is even less chance of my being any help than I thought."

"Who knows?" Alexis said fatalistically. She pushed back from the table, went over to the service desk, and hefted a sizable manila envelope stuffed with papers. She brought it back to the table and plopped it down. It made a resounding thump. "Here's a copy of the case I put together. It's pretty much everything, from interrogatories to depositions to medical records. The only thing that's not included is a transcript of today's proceeding, but I've given you a good idea of what was said. There's even a couple of Craig's recent research papers he suggested I include. I don't know why: maybe to save face, imagining you'll be impressed."

"I probably will be if I can understand them. Anyway, it looks like I have my work cut out for me."

"I don't know where you want to work. You have a lot of choices. Can I show you a few alternatives besides your room downstairs?"

Alexis led Jack on a tour of the first floor of the house. The living room was huge but appeared uncomfortably pristine, as if no one had ever stridden across its deep pile carpet. Jack nixed that. Off the living room was a mahogany-paneled library with a wet bar, but it was dark and funereal with poor lighting. *No thanks!* Down the hall was a media room with a ceiling-mounted projector and several rows of lazy-boy chairs. Inappropriate, and worse lighting than the library. At the end of the hall was a sizable study with matching his-and-hers desks on opposing walls. His desk was neat with each pencil in a pencil cup sharpened to a needle-like point. Her desk was the opposite, with haphazard stacks of books, journals, and reprints. There were several reading chairs and hassocks. A bow window similar to the one in the great room looked out onto a flower bed with a small fountain. Directly opposite the window was floor-to-ceiling shelving on either side of the entrance door. Among a mixture of medical and psychology texts was Craig's old-fashioned leather doctor's bag and a portable ECG machine. As far as being a work area, the best thing about the room was the lighting setup, with recessed ceiling fixtures, individual desk lamps, and floor lamps by each club chair.

"This is a terrific space," Jack said. "But are you sure you don't mind me in your personal study?" He switched on one of the floor lamps. It cast a wide, warm glow.

"Not in the slightest."

"What about Craig, since it's his space, too?"

"He wouldn't mind. One thing I can assure you about Craig. He's not territorial."

"Okay, then, here's where I'll be. I have a feeling it will take me quite a few hours." He put the bulging manila envelope down on the table between the two reading chairs.

"As the saying goes, knock yourself out. I'm off to bed. With the need to get the kids off to school, tomorrow comes early around here. There are plenty of drinks in the kitchen refrigerator and more in the wet bar, so help yourself."

"Terrific! I'm all set."

Alexis let her eyes wander down Jack's frame, then back to his face. "I have to tell you, brother, you look good. When I visited you out in Illinois, and you had your ophthalmology practice, you looked like a different person."

"I was a different person."

"I was afraid you were going to become overweight."

"I was overweight."

"Now you look hale, hungry, and hollow-cheeked, like an actor in a spaghetti western."

Jack laughed. "That's a creative description. Where did that come from?"

"The girls and I recently watched some old Sergio Leone movies. It was an assignment for a film class Tracy's taking at her school. Seriously, you look like you're in good shape. What's your secret?"

"Street basketball and bike riding. I treat them like second careers."

"Maybe I should give them a try," Alexis said with a wry smile. Then she added: "Good night, brother. See you in the morning. As you might expect, it's always a bit chaotic with three girls."

Craig watched Alexis walk down the hall and then with a final wave disappear up the stairs. He turned around and scanned the room again. A sudden silence descended like a blanket. The place looked and smelled so different from his own surroundings, it could have been on a different planet.

Somewhat self-conscious about being in someone else's space, Jack sat down in the easy chair illuminated by the floor lamp. The first thing he did was take out his cell phone and turn it on. There was a message, and it was from Warren, with the promised name and phone number of his friend in Boston. The name was David Thomas, and Jack called immediately, thinking he might be in need of exercise if the morrow turned out to be as stressful as he feared. Alexis's evasiveness about Craig's response to Jack's visit was enough to make anyone feel less than welcome.

Warren must have been full of praise about Jack when he talked to David, because David was overly enthusiastic about Jack coming for a run.

"This time of year we play every night starting about five o'clock, man!" David had said. "Get your honky ass over there and we'll see what you got." He gave Jack directions to the court on Memorial Drive near Harvard. Jack said he'd try to get there in the late afternoon.

Next, Jack called Laurie to report that he was settled as best as could be expected so far.

"What do you mean?" she asked warily.

"I have yet to see Craig Bowman. The story is, he's not all that happy I'm here."

"That's not very nice, all things considered, particularly the timing."

Jack then described what he thought was the positive news about his response to Alexis's daughters. He told Laurie that one of the girls had even brought up the crash right off the bat, but that he had taken it in stride, to his pleasant surprise.

"I'm amazed and pleased," Laurie said. "I think it's terrific, and I'm relieved."

Jack went on to say that the only bad news was that the malpractice didn't involve a technical medical issue, but rather something far more convoluted such that there was even less chance that he could help them than he'd thought.

"I hope that means you'll be on your way back here straight away," Laurie said.

"I'm about to read the file," Jack said. "I imagine I'll know more at that point."

"Good luck."

"Thanks. I'll need it."

Jack ended the call and put his phone away. For a moment, he strained to hear any noise in the vast house. It was as silent as a tomb. Picking up the manila envelope, he dumped the contents onto the side table. The first thing he picked up was a research paper Craig had coauthored with a renowned Harvard cell biologist and had published in the prestigious *New England Journal of Medicine*. It was about the function of sodium channels in cell membranes responsible for nerve and muscular action potentials. There were even some diagrams and electron micrographs of subcellular molecular structure. He glanced at the materials-and-methods section. It was amazing to him that someone could conceive of such arcane concepts, much less study them. Seeing as it was all beyond his current comprehension, he tossed the paper aside and picked up a deposition instead. It was the deposition of Leona Rattner.

CHAPTER SEVEN

The first thing Jack was aware of was a distant verbal disagreement followed by the concussive force of a door slamming. For a brief moment, he tried to incorporate the sounds into his dream, but it didn't make any sense. Instead, he opened his eyes only to have not a clue where he was. After checking out the fountain bathed in bright sunlight outside the bow window as well as the interior of the study, it all came back to him in a flash. In his hand was a deposition of a nurse named Georgina O'Keefe from the Newton Memorial Hospital, which he had been in the process of rereading when he'd fallen fast asleep.

Gathering up all the papers from the *Stanhope vs. Bowman* malpractice case, Jack slipped them into the manila envelope. It took some doing to get them all in. Then he got to his feet. A wave of momentary dizziness made him pause briefly.

He had no idea what time he'd fallen asleep. He'd read through the entire collection of papers and had been in the process of going back over those parts he thought most interesting when his eyes closed involuntarily. To his surprise, he'd been captivated by the material from the start. If the story didn't indirectly involve his sister, he would have thought it an entertaining script for a soap opera, since the colorful characters' personalities leapt off the pages. There was the gifted and dedicated but arrogant and adulterous doctor; the nubile, spurned, and angry lover; the precise and rather laconic bereaved spouse; the knowledgeable but contentious experts; the parade of other witnesses; and finally the apparently hypochondriacal victim. It was a comedy of human foibles, except for the unfortunate fatal outcome and the fact that it had ended up as a malpractice suit. As far as the probable outcome of the suit was concerned, at least from reading the material, Jack thought Alexis's concern and pessimism were well founded. With his grandiosity and arrogance, which came out in the latter stages of his deposition, Craig did not help his cause. The plaintiff's attorney had succeeded in making Craig sound as if he believed it was an outrage that his clinical judgment was being questioned. That wouldn't play well with any jury. And on top of that, Craig had implied that it was his wife's fault he'd had an affair with his secretary.

Whenever Jack was pressed to describe the goal of his job as a medical examiner, his usual response, depending to a degree on the inquirer and the occasion, was to say he "spoke for the dead." As he read over *Stanhope vs. Bowman,* he found himself ultimately thinking mostly about the victim and the unfortunate but obvious circumstance that she could not be deposed or serve as a witness. Playing a game in his mind, he considered how it would influence the case if she were able to participate, and thinking along those lines made him believe that she was the key to a successful resolution of the case. It seemed to him that if the jury believed she was the hypochondriac Craig said she was, they'd have to find for the defense, despite her final symptoms being all too real and despite Craig's narcissistic personality. Thinking in this vein emphasized the unfortunate reality that there had been no autopsy and, accordingly, there was no medical examiner on the defense's witness list to speak for the deceased.

With the manila envelope under his arm, Jack snuck down the hallway toward the basement stairs beneath the main staircase. As scruffy as he was, he preferred not to run into anybody. As he started down the stairs, he heard more yelling above by one of the girls and another door slam.

Down in his quarters, Jack shaved, showered, and dressed as quickly as he could. When he got back upstairs, the entire Bowman clan was in the great room. The atmosphere was strained. The three girls were at the table behind cereal boxes. Craig was on the sofa hidden behind *The New York Times* with a mug of coffee on the coffee table in front of him. Alexis was at the counter, busily making sandwiches for the girls' lunches. The TV above the fireplace was tuned to the local news, but the sound was barely on. Sun streamed in through the bow windows. It was almost blinding.

"Good morning, Jack," Alexis said lightly when she noticed him standing in the doorway. "I hope you slept okay downstairs."

"It was very comfortable," Jack said.

"Say good morning to your uncle," Alexis advised the girls, but only Christina did so.

"I don't know why I can't wear the red top," Meghan whined.

"Because it belongs to Christina, and she says she prefers you don't," Alexis said.

"Did the plane burn with your daughters in it?" Christina asked.

"Christina, that's enough!" Alexis said. She rolled her eyes for Jack's benefit. "There's fresh juice in the fridge and fresh coffee in the maker. What do you usually have for breakfast?"

"Just fruit and cereal."

"We have both. Help yourself."

Jack went over to the coffeemaker. As his eyes began to search for a cup, a mug came sliding down the granite countertop, thanks to Alexis. He filled it with coffee and plopped in a spoonful of sugar and a dollop of cream. As he stirred, he again took in the room. Christina and Alexis were now embroiled in a conversation about afterschool plans. The two other girls seemed silent and sulky. Craig had not emerged from behind his newspaper, which to Jack seemed an obvious slight.

Refusing to be cowed and believing a good offense was the best defense, Jack walked over to the mantel. He was now looking directly at Craig's newspaper, which Craig was holding up to its full extent like a barrier wall.

"Anything interesting in the news?" Jack asked while taking a sip of his steaming coffee.

The top edge of the paper came down slowly, progressively revealing Craig's puffy, slack face. His eyes were like bull's-eyes with dark surrounding rings, while his sclerae were webbed with minute red capillaries, giving him the visage of a man who'd been out on an all-night binge. In contrast to his weary face, he was dressed in a freshly pressed white shirt and conservative tie, while his sandy-colored hair was neatly brushed with a slight sheen suggesting a dab of gel.

"I'm hardly in the mood for small talk," Craig said morosely.

"Nor am I," Jack responded. "At least we agree right out of the starting gate. Craig, let's clear the air! I'm here on my sister's behest. I'm not here to help you. I'm here to help her. If I help you, it's fallout. But let me tell you something; I think it stinks that you've been sued for malpractice. In my estimation from what I know of you professionally, you're the last one who should be sued for malpractice. Now, there are some other social areas in which you don't shine from my perspective, but that's another story entirely. As far as the case is concerned, I've read the material and I have some thoughts. You can hear them or not, that's your call. As far as my staying in your house, that's also your call, since I demand unanimity on the part of couples when I'm a guest. I can easily move to a hotel."

Except for the muted sounds of the local news and some twittering of birds outside, the room went silent and still. No one moved until Craig noisily collapsed his papers, folded them haphazardly, and tossed them aside. A moment later came the renewed clink of flatware against cereal bowls from the table. From the sink came the sound of the faucet being turned on. Sound and action had returned.

"I have no problem being up-front," Craig said. His voice now sounded more tired and sad than morose. "When I heard you were coming, I was irritated. With everything that's going on, I didn't think it was an appropriate time for company, especially since you'd never bothered previously to come for a visit. Frankly, it irked me that you might harbor the mistaken illusion you were the cavalry riding in at the nick of time to save the party in peril. Having you tell me right off that that's not the case makes me feel differently. You're welcome to stay, but I'm sorry I'm not up to being much of a host. As far as your thoughts about the case are concerned, I'd like to hear them."

"I don't expect you to be a host at all, considering what you are going through," Jack said. He sat on the corner of the coffee table diagonally across from Craig. The conversation was going better than he'd anticipated. He had in mind to further the cause by paying Craig a compliment. "Along with all the court-related material, there were a couple of your most recent research papers. I was impressed. Of course, I'd be more impressed if I understood them."

"My attorney has in mind to introduce them as evidence of the extent of my commitment to medicine. The plaintiff's attorney according to his opening statement is going to try to prove the opposite."

"Certainly can't hurt. I can't imagine how he's going to present them, but I'm no lawyer. If he does, I have to give you credit, Craig. You are amazing. Most every doctor I know thinks they would like to do a combination of clinical work and research. It's the ultimate ideal absorbed in medical school, but you're one of the few that actually does it. What's so surprising, it's real research and not those 'reports of an interesting case' type papers that try to masquerade as research."

"There's no doubt it is real research," Craig said, perking up a tad as he warmed to the subject. "We are learning more and more about voltage-gated sodium channels in nerve and muscle cells, and it has immediate clinical application."

"In your last paper in *NEJM*, you talked about two

different sodium channels, one for heart muscle and one for nerves. How are they different?"

"They are structurally different, which we are now determining at a molecular level. How we knew they were different was because of their marked difference in their response to tetrodotoxin. There's a thousandfold difference, which is extraordinary."

"Tetrodotoxin?" Jack questioned. "That's the toxin that kills people in Japan who eat the wrong sushi."

Craig laughed in spite of himself. "You're right. It's sushi made by an inexperienced sushi chef from puffer fish at a particular time of their reproductive cycle."

"Remarkable," Jack commented. Having accomplished getting Craig to perk up, he was eager to move on. Craig's research, although interesting, was far too esoteric for his liking. Jumping directly from one subject to another, Jack brought up his feelings about how the victim, Patience Stanhope, was the key element to win his malpractice case. "If your attorney can indisputably establish the fact in the jurors' minds that this woman was the kind of hypochondriac she was, the jury will have to find against the plaintiff."

For a few seconds, Craig merely stared back at Jack. It was as if the conversational transition had been so abrupt that his brain had to reboot itself. "Well," he said at length. "It's interesting you say that, because I already said as much to Randolph Bingham."

"Well, there you go. We're thinking on the same plane, which lends more credibility to the idea. What did your attorney say?"

"Not much, as I recall."

"I think you should bring it up again," Jack said. "And while we're on the subject of the deceased, I didn't see an autopsy report. I'm assuming there was none. Am I correct?"

"Unfortunately, there wasn't an autopsy," Craig said. "The diagnosis was confirmed by the biomarker assay." He shrugged. "No one expected a malpractice suit. I'm sure if they had, the medical examiners would have opted for a postmortem and I would have requested one."

"There was one other small point in the record I thought was curious," Jack said. "An ER nurse by the name of Georgina O'Keefe, who was the admitting nurse at Newton Memorial Hospital. She wrote in her notes that the patient had marked central cyanosis. The reason it jumped out was because she didn't mention it in her deposition. I went back and checked. Of course, the reason I was sensitive to the issue was because in your deposition, you said you were shocked at the degree of cyanosis when you saw the patient. In fact, this issue was a point of disagreement between you and Mr. Stanhope."

"It certainly was a disagreement," Craig said defensively. Some of the original sullenness returned to his voice. "Mr. Stanhope had said on the phone, and I quote, 'She looked rather blue,' whereas when I got to the house, she was floridly cyanotic."

"Would you have labeled it central cyanosis like Ms. O'Keefe?"

"Central or peripheral, what's the difference in this kind of case? Her heart wasn't pumping her blood fast enough through her lungs. There was a lot of deoxygenated blood in her system. That's what generally causes cyanosis."

"The issue is the amount of cyanosis. I agree the deep cyanosis certainly suggests not enough blood was going through her lungs or that not enough air was getting into her lungs. If it were peripheral cyanosis, meaning blood just pooling in her extremities, it wouldn't have been so conspicuous or even."

"What are you implying?" Craig asked aggressively.

"To be honest, I don't know. As a medical examiner, I try to keep an open mind. Let me ask you this: What kind of relationship did the deceased have with her surviving husband?"

"Somewhat strange, I suppose. They certainly weren't affectionate in public. I doubt they were close, since he did commiserate with me about her hypochondriasis."

"You see, we medical examiners from experience are naturally suspicious. If I were doing this autopsy and considering the cyanosis, I would look for any signs of smothering or strangulation just to rule out homicide."

"That's absurd," Craig snapped. "This wasn't a homicide. Good grief, man!"

"I'm not suggesting it was. I'm just thinking about it as a possibility. Another possibility could be the woman had an undiagnosed right-to-left cardiac shunt."

Craig impatiently ran his fingers through his hair, which changed his appearance from looking tired but neat to tired and mildly disheveled. "She didn't have a right-to-left shunt!"

"How do you know? She didn't let you do any non-invasive cardiac imagery like you wanted after her questionable stress test, which, by the way, I couldn't find."

"We haven't been able to locate the tracing yet at the office, but we have the results. But you're right. She refused any cardiac studies."

"So she could have had a congenital right-to-left shunt that was undiagnosed."

"What difference would it make if she had?"

"She could have had a serious structural problem with her heart or major vessels, which raises the issue of contributing negligence, since she refused follow-up studies to your stress test. More importantly, if she had a serious structural defect, then one might argue the outcome would have been the same even if she had been taken to the hospital immediately. If that had been the case, then the jury would have to find for you and you'd prevail."

"Those are interesting arguments, but unfortunately for me, it is all academic. An autopsy was not done, so it will never be known if she had a structural abnormality."

"Not necessarily," Jack said. "An autopsy wasn't done, but that doesn't mean one couldn't still be done."

"You mean exhume the body?" Alexis asked from the kitchen area. She'd obviously been listening.

"Provided it wasn't cremated," Jack added.

"It wasn't cremated," Craig said. "It was buried in Park Meadow Cemetery. I know because I was invited to the funeral by Jordan Stanhope."

"I guess that was before he sued you for malpractice."

"Obviously. It was another reason I was so taken aback when I was served with the summons and the complaint. Why would the man invite me to the service and then sue me? Like everything else, it doesn't make sense."

"Did you go?"

"I did. I felt obligated. I mean, I was upset I'd not been able to resuscitate the woman."

"Is it difficult doing an autopsy after she's been buried

for almost a year?" Alexis asked. She'd come over and taken a seat on the couch. "It sounds so ghoulish."

"You never know," Jack said. "Two factors are the most important. First: how well the body was embalmed. Second: whether the grave stayed dry or if the seal on the casket remained intact. The reality is you never know until you open up the grave. But regardless of the situation, a lot of information can be gleaned."

"What are you guys talking about?" Christina yelled from the table. The two other girls had disappeared upstairs.

"Nothing, sweetie," Alexis said. "Run up and get your things. The school bus is going to be here any minute."

"This could be my contribution to the case," Jack said. "I could find out the procedure for exhumation here in Massachusetts and do an autopsy. Short of my providing mere moral support, it's probably the only way I could offer to help in this affair. But it's up to you guys. You tell me."

Alexis looked at Craig. "What do you think?" she asked.

Craig shook his head. "To be honest, I don't know what to think. I mean, if an autopsy were to prove she had some major congenital cardiovascular problem such that any delay getting her to a hospital had no significance, I'd be all for it. But what are the chances? I'd have to guess rather small. On the flip side, if an autopsy were to show her myocardial infarction was even more extensive than one might expect, maybe the autopsy would make things worse. It seems to me to be a wash."

"I'll tell you what," Jack said. "I'll look into it. I'll find out all the details, and I'll let you know. Meanwhile, both of you can give it some thought. What do you say?"

"I say it's a plan," Alexis responded. She looked at Craig.

"Why not?" Craig said with a shrug. "I've always said more information is better than less."

CHAPTER EIGHT

"All rise!" the court officer called as Judge Marvin Davidson emerged from his chambers and mounted the stairs to the bench. The black robes shielded his feet, so he seemed to glide like an apparition. "Be seated," the court officer called out after the judge had done so.

Jack looked behind himself so he could lower his posterior onto the seat without knocking over his Starbucks coffee. After the fact, he'd noted that no one else had brought any refreshments into the courtroom, so he'd guiltily stashed his coffee beside him on the bench.

He was sitting next to Alexis in the crowded spectators' section. He'd asked her why there were so many observers, but she'd told him she had no idea whatsoever. Almost all the spectator seats were taken.

The morning at the Bowman residence had gone better than Jack had imagined. Although Craig had flip-flopped to a degree from being conversational to brooding, they'd at least had a mutually honest talk, and Jack felt infinitely better being a guest in their home. After the girls had left for school, there'd been more conversation, but then it was mostly between Alexis and Jack. Craig had reverted to his sullen, preoccupied state.

There'd been a long discussion about transportation

to and from town, but ultimately Jack had firmly insisted he'd drive. He wanted to come to the courtroom to get a feel for the principals, particularly the lawyers, but then around midmorning, he wanted to drive to the Boston medical examiner's office, where he'd start his investigation about Massachusetts's rules regarding exhumation. After that, he didn't know what he'd do. He'd told them he might come back to the courtroom, but if he didn't, he'd meet them at the Newton house in the late afternoon.

As the court took its time getting ready to begin by handling the usual housekeeping motions, Jack studied the principal actors. The African-American judge looked like a former college football player gone to seed, yet the sense of authority he radiated through the confident deliberativeness with which he handled the paperwork on his desk and conversed sotto voce with his clerk gave Jack the reassuring feeling he knew what he was doing. The two lawyers were exactly as Alexis had described. Randolph Bingham was the picture of the elegant, polished, big-firm attorney in the way he dressed, moved, and spoke. In sharp contrast, Tony Fasano was the brazen, flashy young lawyer who flaunted his trendy clothes and clunky gold accessories. Yet the characteristic of Tony that Jack noticed right off and which Alexis had not mentioned was that Tony appeared to be enjoying himself. Although the bereaved plaintiff sat rigidly, Tony and his assistant were carrying on an animated conversation with smiles and suppressed laughter, which was a far cry from the defense table, which sat in either frozen propriety or defiant despair.

Jack's eyes moved staccato down the line of jurors as they filed into the jury box. It was obviously a diverse group, which he thought appropriate. It struck him that if he ducked out of the court and strolled down the street, the first twelve people he'd confront would be an equivalent group.

While Jack was studying the jurors, Tony Fasano called the first witness of the day. It was Marlene Richardt, Craig's matronly secretary-cum-receptionist, and she was duly sworn and seated in the witness box.

Jack turned his attention to the woman. To him, she looked like the strong-willed Frau that her German name suggested. She was of sizable proportions and built square, not too dissimilar from Tony. Her hair was up in a tight bun. Her mouth was set bulldog-style, and her eyes sparkled with defiance. It wasn't hard to sense she was a reluctant witness, whom Tony had the judge declare a hostile witness.

From the podium, Tony started out slowly, trying to joke with the woman, but he was unsuccessful, at least that's what Jack thought until he switched his attention to the jurors. In contrast to the witness, most of them smiled at Tony's attempts at humor. All at once, Jack could see what Alexis had implied, namely that Tony Fasano had a flair for connecting with the jury.

Jack had read Marlene's deposition, which had very little connection to the case, since the day of Patience Stanhope's demise she'd not been in contact with the patient, because the patient had not come into the office. The two times Craig had seen the patient had been at her home. So Jack was surprised that Tony was taking as long as he was with Marlene, painstakingly charting her association with Craig and her own troubled personal life. Since she and Craig had worked together for fifteen years, there was a lot to talk about.

Tony maintained his humorous style. Marlene ignored it at first, but after about an hour of what was starting to smack of a filibuster on Tony's part, she began to get angry, and as she did so she started to respond emotionally. It was at that point that Jack correctly sensed that the joky style was a deliberate ploy on Tony's part. Tony wanted her off-balance and angry. As if sensing something unexpected was coming, Randolph tried to object that the testimony was endless and immaterial. The judge seemed to agree, but after a short sidebar conversation, which Jack could not hear, the questioning resumed and quickly hit pay dirt for the plaintiff's cause.

"Your Honor, may I approach the witness?" Tony asked. He was holding a folder in the air.

"You may," Judge Davidson said.

Tony stepped up to the witness box and handed the folder to Marlene. "Could you tell the jury what you are holding?"

"A patient file from the office."

"And whose file is it?"

"Patience Stanhope."

"Now there is a file number on the file."

"Of course there's a file number!" Marlene snapped. "How would we find it otherwise?"

"Could you read it aloud for the jury," Tony said, ignoring Marlene's mini-outburst.

"PP eight."

"Thank you," Tony said. He retrieved the file and returned to the podium.

Expectantly, several of the jurors leaned forward.

"Mrs. Richardt, would you explain to the jury what the initials PP stand for."

Like a cornered cat, Marlene's eyes darted around the room before settling for a moment on Craig.

"Mrs. Richardt," Tony prodded. "Hello! Anybody home?"

"They are letters," Marlene snapped.

"Well, thank you," Tony said sarcastically. "I believe most of the jurors recognized them as letters. What I'm asking is what they stand for. And permit me to remind you that you are sworn, and giving false testimony is perjury, which carries a severe penalty."

Marlene's face, which had become progressively red during her testimony, got redder still. Even her cheeks swelled as if she were straining.

"If it will help you remember, later testimony will suggest that you and Dr. Craig Bowman came up with this filing designation, which is not typical in your office. In fact, I have two other patient file numbers from your office." Tony held up the two additional folders. "The first one is Peter Sager's, and the number is PS one twenty-one. We chose this particular file since the individual's first initials are the same as the deceased, yet the letters on her file are PP, not PS.

"And my third file is Katherine Baxter, and this number is KB two thirty-three. There were others as well, and in each instance, the two first letters corresponded with the patient's initials. Now, we are aware that there are a few other PPs, but very few. So I ask again. What does the PP stand for, since it is not the patient's initials?"

"PP stands for 'problem patient,' " Marlene snapped defiantly.

Tony's face twisted into a wry smile for the jury's benefit. "Problem patient!" he repeated slowly but loudly.

"What in heaven's name does that mean? Do they act up in the office?"

"Yes, they act up in the office," Marlene spat. "They're hypochondriacs. They have a bunch of stupid complaints that they make up and take the doctor's time away from the people who are really sick."

"And Dr. Bowman agreed with your giving the patients this designation."

"Of course. He's the one who told us which ones."

"And just so there is no misunderstanding, Patience Stanhope's file was a PP file, meaning she was a problem patient. Is that true?"

"Yes!"

"No further questions."

Jack leaned over toward Alexis and whispered, "This is a public-relations nightmare. What was Craig thinking?"

"I haven't the slightest idea. But something like this is not helping. In fact, things are looking even bleaker."

Jack nodded but didn't say anything more. He couldn't believe Craig could be so foolish. Every doctor had patients he or she labeled "problem patients," but it was never indicated in the record. Every practice had patients that were hated or despised, and that the doctors would try to get rid of as patients but often couldn't. Jack could remember in his own ophthalmology practice he'd had two or three who were so unpleasant that when he saw their names on the schedule, it would influence his mood for the whole day. He knew such a response was human nature, and being a doctor does not absolve the physician from such feelings. It was an issue that was swept under the rug during training, except in psychiatry.

Randolph smoothly tried on cross-examination to repair the damage as best he could, although it was clear the issue had blindsided him. With the ritualized process of discovery, such surprises were rare. Tony sported a smug smile.

"Labeling a patient as a 'problem patient' is not necessarily disparaging, is it, Mrs. Richardt?"

"I guess not."

"In fact, the reason to flag such a patient is to plan on giving them more attention rather than less."

"We did schedule them more time."

"That's exactly my point. Is it correct to say that as soon as you spotted PP, you scheduled the doctor to be with the patient longer?"

"Yes."

"So it was for the patient's benefit to have the PP designation."

"Yes."

"No more questions."

Jack leaned over to Alexis again. "I'm going to head over to the medical examiner's office. This has given me a bit more motivation."

"Thank you," Alexis whispered back.

Jack felt definite relief as he emerged from the courthouse. Being ensnared in the legal system had always been one of his phobias, and having it happen to his brother-in-law hit too close to home. The notion that justice would miraculously prevail was unreasonably idealistic, as Craig's case was threatening to show. Jack didn't trust the system, although he couldn't think of a better one.

He retrieved his rented Hyundai from beneath the Boston Common. He'd parked it there that morning,

having stumbled on the public garage after vainly looking for street parking in Boston's Government Center
district. He had no idea where Craig and Alexis had
parked. The original idea had been for him to follow
them into the city, but whenever he let so much as a car
length develop between himself and the Bowmans'
Lexus, another car always immediately slid in. It was
especially true once they got on the turnpike, and, not
willing to be as aggressive at highway speeds as would
have been necessary to stay directly behind Craig and
Alexis, he lost them in the sea of commuters. From his
perspective, the Boston driving, which had been difficult
the night before, was a hundred times more challenging
in true rush-hour traffic.

Using the Hertz map, he'd been able to get into
Boston proper easily enough. From the garage, it had
been a relatively short and quite pleasant walk to the
courthouse.

Once he was out of the dimly lit garage, Jack pulled
to the side of the road and consulted the Hertz map. It
took him a while to find Albany Street, but once he had,
he was able to orient himself with the help of the Boston
Common, which was to his right, and the Boston Public
Garden, which was to his left. The garden was ablaze
with late-spring flowers. Jack had forgotten what a
charming, attractive city Boston was once you got into
it.

While he drove, which took most of his concentration, he tried to think of any other way to help Craig's
cause. It seemed an ironic absurdity that Craig was going
to be found liable for malpractice because he'd been gracious enough to make a house call.

Albany Street was relatively easy to find, as was the

medical examiner's office. Making it even easier was a multistory public parking facility immediately adjacent. Fifteen minutes later, Jack was talking through a protective glass screen to an attractive young female receptionist. In contrast to the outdated medical examiner's facility in New York, the Boston headquarters was spanking new. Jack couldn't help being both envious and impressed.

"Can I help you?" the woman asked cheerfully.

"I imagine you can," Jack said. He went on to explain who he was and that he wanted to talk to one of the medical examiners. He said he wasn't choosy, just whoever was available.

"I think they are all in the autopsy room, doctor," the woman said. "But let me check."

While the woman made several calls, Jack glanced around. It was a utilitarian décor with the characteristic odor of fresh paint. There was an office for the liaison with the police department, and through the open door Jack saw a uniformed officer. There were several other rooms, but Jack could only guess at their function.

"Dr. Latasha Wylie is available after all, and she'll be right down," the receptionist said. She had to practically yell for Jack to hear through the glass partition.

Jack thanked her and began to wonder exactly where the Park Meadow Cemetery was. If Craig and Alexis wanted him to do the autopsy, he was going to have to move very quickly, since they were already at day two of a predicted five-day trial. Actually doing the autopsy wouldn't be the challenge. The challenge would be the bureaucratic red tape, and in a city as old as Boston, Massachusetts, Jack feared the red tape might be formidable.

"Dr. Stapleton?" a voice questioned.

Jack started. He'd been nosily and surreptitiously glancing into one of the other rooms off the lobby, trying to figure out its role. Guiltily, Jack turned to face a surprisingly youthful African-American woman with flowing, coal-black tresses and beauty-pageant good looks. Jack went from feeling guilty to being momentarily nonplussed. There had been too many times lately when he'd faced professional female medical colleagues who looked to him like college coeds. It made him feel ancient.

After introductions, which included Jack's showing his ME badge just to emphasize that he wasn't some deranged creep off the street, he gave a thumbnail sketch of what he wanted—namely, information about the exhumation procedure in Massachusetts. Latasha immediately invited Jack upstairs to her office, which made Jack even more envious when he compared it to his own. The room wasn't huge or sumptuous, but it had both a desk and work area, so the inevitable paperwork and microscopic work could be kept separated such that one didn't have to be put away to switch to the other. It also had windows. It was only a view of the nearby parking garage, but it let in a significant amount of daylight, something he didn't see in his office.

Once in the office, Jack gave a detailed account of Craig's malpractice case. He stretched reality by saying Craig was one of the city's premier internists even though he practiced in the suburbs, and by suggesting he was going to be found liable for the deceased's death unless the deceased was exhumed and autopsied. His rationale for this embellishment was that he thought that if the Boston ME's office was motivated enough, they could slice through any bureaucratic problems. In New

York, that would have been the case. Unfortunately, Latasha disabused him of this idea immediately.

"We medical examiners in Massachusetts cannot get involved in ordering an exhumation unless it's a criminal case," she observed. "And even then, it has to go through the district attorney, who in turn has to go to a judge to get a court order."

Jack groaned inwardly. Bureaucracy was rearing its ugly head.

"It's a lengthy process," Latasha continued. "Essentially, it involves this office convincing the district attorney there is a high suspicion of criminality. On the other hand, if there is no crime involved, then it's a pro forma procedure here in Massachusetts."

Jack's ears pricked up. "Really? How is that?"

"All you need is a permit."

Jack felt his pulse quicken. "And how do you get a permit?"

"From the town clerk where the cemetery is located or from the Board of Health if it's here in Boston. The easiest way would be to contact the funeral director who did the burial in the first place. If the funeral home is in the same town as the cemetery, and it usually is, he knows the town clerk or Board of Health personnel personally. It could probably be obtained in an hour with the right contacts."

"That's good news," Jack said.

"If you go ahead with an autopsy, we could help, not doing it here, of course, since this is a public facility, and I can't imagine our chief authorizing something like that. But we could help by providing specimen jars and fixatives, and help processing the specimens. We could also help with toxicology if it's appropriate."

"Will the death certificate have the funeral home on it?"

"Absolutely. Disposition of the body has to be recorded. What's the name again?"

"Patience Stanhope. She died about nine months ago."

Latasha used her computer to bring up the death certificate. "Here it is. September eighth, 2005, to be exact."

"Really?" Jack questioned. He got up and peered over Latasha's shoulder at the date. It seemed a coincidence. September 8, 2005, had been significant in his life as well. It had been the date of the dinner at Elio's when he and Laurie had gotten engaged.

"It's the Langley-Peerson Funeral Home in Brighton who took the body. Want me to write the address and phone number down?"

"Thank you," Jack said. He was still marveling about the date. He retook his seat. He wasn't superstitious, but the coincidence intrigued him.

"What's the time frame? When do you see yourself doing this autopsy?" Latasha asked.

"To be perfectly honest, it hasn't been decided to actually do it," Jack admitted. "It's up to the doctor and his wife. It's my feeling it would help, which is the reason I suggested it, and why I'm looking into how to go about it."

"There is something about the exhumation permit I forgot to mention," Latasha said as an afterthought.

"Oh," Jack said, reining in his enthusiasm.

"You'll need the approval and signature of the next of kin."

Jack's shoulders visibly sagged. He chided himself for

not remembering what was now so obvious. Of course the next of kin would have to agree. He'd allowed his zeal of helping his sister overwhelm his rationality. He couldn't imagine the plaintiff agreeing to allow his dead wife to be dug up in hopes of helping the defense. But then he remembered that stranger things have happened, and since doing an autopsy might be the only thing he could offer Alexis, he wasn't going to accept an unchallenged defeat. But then again, there was Laurie back in New York. If he were to do an autopsy, it would mean staying in Boston, which would get her upset. Like so many things in life, the situation was far more complicated than he'd like.

Fifteen minutes later, Jack was back in his Hyundai Accent, drumming his fingers on the driver's-side air-bag cover. What to do was the question. He looked at his watch. It was twelve twenty-five. Any thoughts of returning to the courtroom were nixed, since the court would be in recess for lunch. He could have called Alexis's cell phone, but instead he decided on paying a visit to the funeral home. With that decided, he unfolded his Hertz city map and plotted his course.

Driving out of Boston was no easier than driving in, but once he stumbled onto the Charles River, he was oriented. Twenty minutes later, he was on the appropriate street in the suburban area of Brighton, and five minutes after that, he found the funeral home. It was housed in a large, white, wood-frame, previously single-family home built in the Victorian style, complete with a turret and Italianate details. Extending from the rear was a modern addition of an indeterminate style built of concrete block. Most important from Jack's perspective was that it had ample parking.

After locking the car, Jack walked around to the front of the building and mounted the stairs to a spacious wraparound porch. There was no porch furniture. The front door was unlocked, so he walked into the building's foyer.

Jack's immediate impression was that the interior was as serene as a deserted medieval library, with muted Gregorian chants providing the appropriate background noise. He would have liked to have said it was as severe as a deserted funeral home, but since it was a funeral home, he felt obligated to come up with something else. To his left was a casket gallery with all the caskets propped open to reveal their velvet or satin interiors. Comforting names like Eternal Bliss were displayed, but prices were not. To the right was a viewing room, which was currently vacant. Rows of collapsible chairs faced a raised dais with an empty catafalque. Floating in the air was a whiff of incense, as though it were a Tibetan souvenir shop.

At first Jack was confused as to where to go to find a live human, but before he could wander too far, one appeared as if by magic. Jack hadn't heard a door open or even approaching footsteps.

"Can I help you?" a man inquired in a barely audible voice. He was slender and austere in his black suit, white shirt, and black tie. With his pasty and cadaverous face, he looked like a candidate for the establishment's services. His thin, short, and deeply colored dyed hair was plastered to the scabrous dome of his head. Jack had to suppress a smile. The man embodied a familiar but false stereotype of a funeral home employee. It was as if he'd been called by central casting for a part in a ghoulish movie. Jack knew that reality didn't support the Hollywood image. In his role as a medical examiner, Jack had a lot of interaction with funeral home employees, and none of them resembled the man standing in front of him.

"Can I help you?" the man repeated slightly louder but almost in a whisper despite there being no one, not even the dead, whom he could have disturbed. He held himself rigidly in check, with his hands clasped piously over his abdomen and his elbows tucked in against his body. The only thing moving were his narrow lips. He didn't even seem to blink.

"I'm looking for the funeral director."

"At your service. My name is Harold Langley. We are a family-owned and -operated establishment."

"I'm a medical examiner," Jack said. He flashed his official badge quickly enough to be reasonably certain Harold didn't have time to notice it was not from Massachusetts. Harold visibly stiffened as if Jack were an emissary from the Massachusetts Division of Professional Licensure. Suspicious by nature, Jack thought the reaction curious, but he pressed on. "You people handled the arrangements for Patience Stanhope, who passed away this past September."

"Indeed, we did. I remember it well. We also handled the services for Mr. Stanhope, a very prominent gentleman in the community. Also for the only Stanhope child, I'm afraid."

"Oh!" Jack grunted in response to information he'd not been seeking. He quickly stored it away and returned to the issue at hand. "Some questions have arisen surrounding Mrs. Stanhope's death, and an exhumation and autopsy are being considered. Has the Langley-Peerson Home had experience doing such a thing?"

"We have, but on an infrequent basis," Harold said,

relaxing back to his originally restrained, ceremonious self. Jack was apparently no longer viewed as a possible threat. "Are you in possession of the required paper-work?"

"No. What I'm hoping is that you could help in that regard."

"Certainly. What's needed is an exhumation permit, a transportation permit, and a reinterment permit, and, most importantly, the permit must have the signature of the current Mr. Stanhope as the next of kin. It is the next of kin who must give authorization."

"So I understand. Would you have the necessary forms here?"

"Yes, I believe so. If you'll follow me, I can give them to you."

Harold led Jack through an archway in the direction of the main stairs but immediately turned left into a dark-ened, deep-pile carpeted hallway. It was now apparent to Jack how Harold had managed to silently appear.

"You mentioned that the first Mr. Stanhope was prominent in the community. How so?"

"He was founder of the Stanhope Insurance Agency of Boston, which was very successful in its heyday. Mr. Stanhope was a wealthy man and quite a philanthropist, which is rare in Brighton. Brighton is a working-class community."

"Meaning the current Mr. Stanhope must be a wealthy man."

"Undoubtedly," Harold said as he led Jack into an office as austere as he was. "The current Mr. Stanhope's history is a marvelous Horatio Alger story. He was born Stanislaw Jordan Jaruzelski, a local boy from a working-class immigrant family who started working at the agency right out of Brighton High School. He was a whiz kid, even though he didn't go to college, who worked himself up by his bootstraps to management. When the old man passed on, he married the widow, sparking some lurid speculation. He even took the family name."

Although it was a bright, sunshine-filled June day outside, inside Harold's office it was dark enough to necessitate the desk lamp and a floor lamp to be on. The windows were covered by heavy, dark green velvet drapes. After finishing the current Mr. Stanhope saga, Harold went to an upright, four-drawer file cabinet covered with mahogany veneer. From the top drawer, he pulled out a folder. From within the folder, he took three papers, one of which he handed to Jack. The other two he placed on his desk. He motioned toward one of the velvet-upholstered chairs facing the desk for Jack before sitting himself down in his high-backed desk chair.

"That's the exhumation permit I gave you," Harold said. "There's a place for Mr. Stanhope to sign, giving authorization."

Jack glanced at the paper as he sat down. Getting the signature was obviously going to be the deal-breaker, but for the moment, he wasn't going to worry about it. "Who will fill in the rest after Mr. Stanhope signs?"

"I will do that. What is the time frame you are looking at?"

"If it's to be done, it has to be done immediately."

"Then you'd better let me know quickly. I'd have to arrange for the vault company's truck and a backhoe."

"Could the autopsy be done here at the home?"

"Yes, in the embalming room, working around our schedule. The only problem is we might not have all the

tools you would like. For instance, we don't have a cra-
nial saw."

"I can get the tools." Jack was impressed. Harold
looked rather weird, but he was informed and efficient.

"I should mention this will be an expensive under-
taking."

"What are we talking about?"

"There'll be the vault company and backhoe charge,
as well as cemetery fees. On top of that will be our
charges for obtaining the permits, supervision, and use
of the embalming room."

"Can you give me a ballpark idea?"

"At least several thousand dollars."

Jack whistled softly as if he thought the figure high,
whereas in actuality he thought it was cheap with all that
was involved. He stood up. "Do you have an off-hours
phone number?"

"I'll give you my cell phone number."

"Terrific," Jack said. "One other thing. Do you know
the address of the Stanhope home?"

"Of course. Everybody knows the Stanhope house.
It's a landmark in Brighton."

A few minutes later, Jack was back in the rent-a-car
again, drumming the steering wheel while he thought of
what he should do next. It was now after two p.m.
Returning to the courtroom didn't thrill him. He'd
always been more of a performer than a spectator.
Instead of going back into Boston, he reached for the
Hertz map. It took him a few minutes, but he located
the Newton Memorial Hospital and oriented himself,
and eventually arrived at his destination.

Newton Memorial Hospital resembled almost every
suburban hospital Jack had been in. It was built in a

confusing hodgepodge of various wings added over the years. The oldest section had period details like decoration on a cake, mostly Greek Revival, but the new structures were progressively plainer. The most recent addition was just brick and bronze-tinted glass with no embellishments whatsoever.

Jack parked in the visitors' area, in a lot that backed onto a wetland with a small pond. A flock of Canada geese were floating motionless on the surface like a bunch of wooden decoys. Consulting the fat case file, Jack memorized the names of the people he wanted to speak with: the emergency-room doctor, Matt Gilbert; the emergency-room nurse, Georgina O'Keefe; and the staff cardiologist, Noelle Everette. All three were on the plaintiff's witness list, and all three had been deposed by the defense. What was troubling Jack was the cyanosis issue.

Instead of going to the front entrance of the hospital, Jack went to the emergency area. The ambulance bay was empty. To the side was an automatic sliding glass door. Jack walked in and headed directly to the admitting desk.

It seemed like a good time to visit. There were only three people in the waiting area; none of them appeared sick or injured. The nurse at the desk looked up as Jack approached. She was dressed in scrubs and had the usual stethoscope slung around her neck. She was reading *The Boston Globe*.

"Calm before the storm," Jack joked.

"Something like that. What can we do for you?"

Jack went through his usual spiel, including the ME badge flash. He asked for Matt and Georgina, purposefully using their first names to suggest familiarity.

"They're not here yet," the duty nurse said. "They work the evening shift."

"When does that start?"

"At three."

Jack looked at his watch. It was going on three. "So they will be here shortly."

"They better be!" the duty nurse said sternly but with a smile to show she was being humorous.

"What about Dr. Noelle Everette?"

"I'm sure she's here someplace. Want me to page her?"

"That would be helpful."

Jack retreated to the waiting area with the other three people. He tried to make eye contact, but no one was willing. He eyed an old *National Geographic* magazine but didn't pick it up. Instead, he marveled about Stanislaw Jordan Jaruzelski transforming himself into Jordan Stanhope, and then he brooded about how he was going to get Jordan Stanhope to sign an exhumation permit. It seemed impossible, like climbing Mount Everest not only without oxygen but also without clothes. He smiled briefly at the thought of a couple of bare-assed climbers standing triumphantly on the rocky summit. *Nothing is impossible,* he reminded himself. He heard Dr. Noelle Everette's name over an old-fashioned page system. Such a page system seemed like an anachronism in the information age, with grammar-school kids text-messaging.

Five minutes later the ER duty nurse called him back to the admitting desk. She told him that Dr. Everette was up in radiology and would be happy to talk with him. The nurse then gave him directions.

The cardiologist was busy reading and dictating cardioangiograms. She was sitting in a small viewing room with an entire wall filled with X-ray films on a movable conveyor belt. The only light came from behind the films and washed her with its fluorescent blue-whiteness, similar to moonlight but brighter. It made the cardiologist appear ghostlike, particularly in her white coat. Jack assumed he looked equally washed-out. Jack was completely forthright. He explained who he was and why he was associated with the case.

"I am to be an expert witness for the plaintiff," Noelle said, wishing to be equally forthright. "I'm going to testify that by the time the patient arrived here at the emergency room, we really had no chance to resuscitate her, and I was indignant to learn there had been an avoidable delay. Some of us old-fashioned physicians who treat all comers and not just those who pay us up front are angry about these concierge doctors. We're convinced they are self-serving rather than acting in the patients' best interests as they claim and which true professionalism dictates."

"So you are testifying because Dr. Bowman is practicing concierge medicine?" Jack asked. He was taken aback by Noelle's emotional response.

"Absolutely not," Noelle said. "I'm testifying because there had been a delay getting the patient to the hospital. Everyone knows that after a myocardial infarction, it is critical to start fibrinolytic and reperfusion treatment absolutely as soon as possible. If that opinion secondarily says something about my feelings vis-à-vis concierge medicine, so be it!"

"Listen, I respect your position, Dr. Everette, and I'm not here to try to convince you otherwise. Believe me! I'm here to ask you about the degree of cyanosis the patient apparently had. Is that something you remember particularly?"

Noelle relaxed to a degree. "I can't say particularly, since cyanosis is a frequent sign seen with severe cardiac illness."

"The ER nurse wrote in the notes the patient had central cyanosis. I mean, she specifically said 'central' cyanosis."

"Listen, when the patient got here, she was close to death, with dilated pupils, completely flaccid body, and a pronounced brachycardia with total AV black. Her heart could not be externally paced. She was on death's door. Cyanosis was just part of the whole picture."

"Well, thanks for talking with me," Jack said. He stood.

"You're welcome," Noelle responded.

As Jack made his way back down to the emergency room, he was even more pessimistic about the outcome of the case than he'd been earlier. Dr. Noelle Everette was going to be a powerful expert witness for the plaintiff, not only because of her expert status as a cardiologist but also because she was articulate and a dedicated physician, and because she had been directly involved in the case. "Times have changed," Jack murmured out loud, thinking that it used to be hard to find a doctor to testify against another doctor. It seemed to him that Noelle was looking forward to testifying, and despite what she'd said, part of her motivation was antipathy toward concierge medicine.

By the time Jack got back to the ER, the shift had changed. Although the ER was still peaceful, Jack had to wait to talk with the nurse and the doctor while they got themselves updated on the patients present who were

waiting for test results or for the arrival of their personal
physicians. It was close to three thirty when Jack finally
was able to sit down with them in a small staff lounge
area directly behind the admitting desk. Both were
young. Jack guessed early thirties.

Jack said essentially the same thing he'd said to Noelle
at the outset, but the emergency-room staff's response
was much less emotional or censorious. In fact,
Georgina, in her bubbly style, professed to have been
greatly impressed by Craig.

"I mean, how many doctors arrive at the ER riding
with the patient in the ambulance? I can tell you: not
many. The fact that he's being sued is a travesty. It shows
how far out of whack the system is when doctors like Dr.
Bowman are ambushed by the likes of the ambulance-
chaser lawyer on the case. I can't remember his name."

"Tony Fasano," Jack offered. He was enjoying hearing someone who shared his thoughts, although he
wondered if Georgina had heard the social side of Craig's
tale, especially since Leona had come to the ER that fatal
night.

"That was it: Tony Fasano. When he first came snooping around here, I thought he was an extra in one of
those gangster movies. I really did. I mean, I couldn't
imagine he was for real. Did he really go to law school?"

Jack shrugged his shoulders.

"Well, it wasn't Harvard, I can tell you that. Anyway,
I can't imagine him calling me as a witness. I told him
exactly what I thought of Dr. Bowman. I think he did a
great job. He even had a portable ECG machine and had
already tested for biomarkers before they arrived here at
the ER."

Jack nodded as Georgina spoke. He'd read all this in her deposition in which she'd fulsomely praised Craig.

When she fell silent, Jack said, "What I wanted to talk to you people about was the cyanosis."

"What about the cyanosis?" Dr. Matt Gilbert asked. It was the first time he'd spoken. His laid-back personality was overwhelmed by Georgina's vivacity.

"You remember the cyanosis, silly," Georgina said, giving Matt a playful slap on the shoulder before Jack could speak. "She was as blue as a blue moon when they brought her in here."

"I don't think that expression has anything to do with color," Matt said.

"It doesn't?" Georgina questioned. "Well, it should."

"Do you not remember the cyanosis?" Jack asked Matt.

"Vaguely, I suppose, but her general condition trumped everything else."

"You described it as 'central cyanosis' in your notes," Jack said to Georgina. "Was there some specific reason for that?"

"Well, of course! She was blue all over, not just her fingers or legs. Her whole body was blue until they got her on oxygen with the respirator and started doing cardiac massage."

"What do you think might have been the cause?" Jack asked. "Do you think it could have been a right-to-left shunt or maybe severe pulmonary edema?"

"I don't know about a shunt," Matt said. "But she didn't have any pulmonary edema at all. Her lungs were clear."

"One thing I remember," Georgina said suddenly.

"She was completely flaccid. When I started another IV line, her arm was like a rag doll's."

"Is that unique, in your experience?" Jack asked.

"Yeah," Georgina said. She looked at Matt for confirmation. "There's usually some resistance. I guess it varies with the degree of consciousness."

"Did either of you see any petechial hemorrhages in her eyes, any strange marks on her face or neck?"

Georgina shook her head. "I didn't." She looked at Matt.

"I was worrying too much about the big picture to see any such details," Matt said.

"Why do you ask?" Georgina questioned.

"I'm a medical examiner," Jack explained. "I'm trained to be cynical. Smothering or strangulation has to be at least considered in any sudden death with cyanosis."

"Now that's a new angle," Georgina said.

"A biomarker assay confirmed a heart attack," Matt said.

"I'm not questioning there was a myocardial infarction," Jack said. "But I'd be interested if something other than a natural process brought it on. Let me give you an example. I once had a case of a woman, arguably a few years older than Mrs. Stanhope, who had a heart attack immediately after being robbed at gunpoint. It was easy to prove a temporal connection, and the perpetrator is sitting on death row to this day."

"My word!" Georgina said.

After giving both individuals a business card that included his cell phone number, Jack headed back to his car. By the time he unlocked the door and climbed in, it was after four o'clock. He sat for a moment, looking out at the small pond. He thought about his conversation with the hospital staff, thinking it was a wash in regard to Craig's cause between Noelle and Georgina, with one avidly for and one avidly against. The trouble was that Noelle was surely going to testify, whereas Georgina, as she expected, probably would not since she wasn't on the defense list. Other than that, he hadn't learned much, or if he had, he was too dumb to recognize it. One thing was for certain: He'd liked and was impressed by all these people, and if he got into an accident and was brought in there, he'd feel he was in good hands.

Jack thought about his next move. What he would have liked to do was drive back to the Bowman house, suit up in his basketball gear, and have a run with David Thomas, Warren's friend, over on Memorial Drive. But realistically speaking, Jack knew that if there were any chance of his contributing to the case by doing an autopsy on Patience Stanhope's earthly remains, he had to force himself to face Jordan Stanhope with the idea of getting him to sign the exhumation permit. The problem was how to get him to do it short of procuring a pistol and holding it to his temple. Jack could not think of a single reasonable stratagem and ultimately resigned himself to ad-libbing while trying to appeal to the man's sense of justice and fairness.

Jack took out the three-by-five index card that Harold Langley had given him with Harold's cell phone number and Jordan Stanhope's address. Balancing it on the steering wheel, he picked up the trusty Hertz map and tried to find the street. It took a bit of patience, but he located it near both Chandler Pond and Chestnut Hill Country Club. Assuming that the court would have recessed somewhere in the three thirty to four o'clock range, he thought now would be as appropriate a time as any to drop in for a visit. Whether he'd get into the man's house or not he had no idea, but it wasn't going to be for lack of trying.

It took him a half-hour of navigating a maddening maze of twisty streets to find the Stanhope house. The fact that Jordan Stanhope was a wealthy man was immediately apparent. The house was huge, with spacious, immaculate grounds, carefully pruned trees and shrubs, and flowering gardens. A shiny, new, dark blue Bentley two-door coupe was parked in the circular drive that fronted the house. A separate three-car garage with a carriage house above was just visible through the trees to the right of the main building.

Jack pulled his Hyundai Accent up alongside its obscenely expensive counterpart. The juxtaposition was a study in contrasts. He got out of his car and approached the other. He had to look inside the extravagant machine, humorously attributing his unexpected interest to a heretofore unexpressed gene on his Y chromosome. The windows were down, so the aroma of the luxurious leather bathed the whole area. The car was obviously brand-spanking-new. After making sure he wasn't being observed, Jack stuck his head through the driver's-side window. The control panel had a simple, rich elegance. Then he noticed something else: The keys were in the ignition. Jack stepped back. Although he thought it was the height of ridiculousness to spend the kind of money he imagined the car cost, the fact that the keys were available unleashed a pleasant fleeting fantasy of breezing down a scenic road in the Bentley with Laurie at his side. It was a reverie that reminded him of a recurrent dream of flying he'd had in his youth. But the daydream quickly dissolved to be replaced by a mild embarrassment of coveting another man's car, even if just for an imagined joyride.

Jack skirted the Bentley and approached the front door. His reaction to the car had surprised him on several levels, most important of which concerned the idea of unabashedly enjoying himself. For many years after the fateful plane crash, he'd been unable to do so, since it aroused his guilt of being the only one in the family still alive. The fact that he could entertain the idea now was the best suggestion yet that he'd made significant progress toward recovery.

After ringing the doorbell, Jack turned back to the gleaming Bentley. He'd thought about what the car meant to him, but now he pondered what it said about Jordan Stanhope, aka Stanislaw Jordan Jaruzelski. It suggested that the man was seriously indulging himself with his new wealth.

Hearing the door open brought Jack's attention around and to the issue at hand. In his inside jacket pocket was the signatureless exhumation permit, and it crinkled as he brought his hand up to shield his eyes. The late afternoon sun was reflecting off the polished brass door knocker and momentarily blinded him.

"Yes?" Jordan questioned. Despite the glare, Jack could tell he was being eyed suspiciously. Jack was wearing his usual jeans, blue chambray shirt, knitted tie, and summer-weight blazer that hadn't been cleaned or pressed for longer than he cared to admit. In contrast, Jordan had on a plaid smoking jacket with a cravat. From around his silhouette wafted cool, dry air, suggesting the home's air-conditioning was on despite the mild outdoor temperature.

"I'm Dr. Stapleton," Jack began. With a sudden decision to suggest a quasi-official explanation for his visit, Jack fumbled to extract his wallet with his medical examiner badge. He held it up for moment. "I'm a medical examiner, and I'd like a moment of your time."

"Let me see!" Jordan said as Jack tried to quickly return the wallet and badge to its normal location.

Jack was surprised. Rarely did people actually examine his official credentials.

"New York?" Jordan questioned, glancing back up into Jack's face. "Aren't you rather far afield?" To Jack's ear, Jordan spoke with a mock-melodiousness and a hint of an English accent that Jack associated with elite New England boarding schools. To Jack's double surprise, Jordan had reached out to grasp Jack's hand to steady it while he'd studied the badge. His precisely manicured fingers were cool to the touch.

"I take my job seriously," Jack said, defensively reverting to sarcasm.

"And what is your job that brings you from New York all the way to our humble home?"

Jack couldn't suppress a smile. The man's comment suggested he had an ironic sense of humor similar to Jack's. The home was anything but humble.

"Who is it, Jordie?" a crystalline voice called from the cool depths of the home's interior.

"I don't precisely know yet, dearest," Jordan affectionately called back over his shoulder. "It's a doctor from New York."

"I've been asked to help with the legal case you are currently involved in," Jack said.

"Really!" Jordan said with a hint of amazement. "And exactly how are you intending to help?"

Before Jack could answer, an attractive, doe-eyed young woman half Jordan's age appeared from around Jordan and stared at Jack. She had slipped an arm around Jordan's neck and the other around his middle. She smiled pleasantly, revealing startlingly white, perfect teeth. "Why are you standing here? Invite the doctor in! He can join us for tea."

Following the woman's suggestion, Jordan stepped to the side, motioned for Jack to come into the house, and then led him on a lengthy journey through a central hall, an expansive living room, and out into a conservatory built off the building's rear. Surrounded on three sides and roofed with glass, the room gave Jack the feeling he was back outdoors in the garden. Although Jack initially had thought "tea" was to be a euphemism for cocktails, he was wrong.

Ensconced in an oversized white wicker chair with pastel chintz cushions, Jack was served tea, whipped cream, and biscuits by a reserved woman in a French maid's uniform who quickly disappeared. Jordan and his girlfriend, Charlene McKenna, were seated opposite on a matching wicker sofa. Between Jack and his hosts was a low glass table supporting a silver service with additional sweets. Charlene could not keep her hands off Jordan, who acted as if he were unaware of her overt affection. The conversation initially ranged freely before centering on their plans for the summer, which were to include a cruise along the Dalmatian coast.

It was amazing to Jack that the couple were willing to do all the talking. He sensed that they were starved for entertainment, since he didn't have to say much beyond where he was from and that he was currently a house-guest at his sister's in Newton. After that, all he had to do was give an occasional "un-huh" to indicate he was paying attention. This gave Jack lots of opportunity to merely observe, and he was fascinated. Jack had heard that Jordan was enjoying himself, and apparently had been enjoying himself practically from the day Patience Stanhope had died. There had been little time for mourning since Charlene had moved in with him several weeks after the funeral. The Bentley in the driveway was only a month old, and the couple had spent a portion of the winter in St. Bart's.

Thanks to a melding of this new information with his cynical nature, the possibility in Jack's mind of foul play being involved in Patience's death became more than a passing thought and made the idea of doing an autopsy even more appropriate and necessary. He thought about going back to the Boston medical examiner's office with his suspicions, even if entirely circumstantial, to see if they would be willing to approach the district attorney about going to a judge to order the exhumation, because surely Jordan would never agree to one if he'd been in any way responsible for Patience's death. But the longer Jordan talked and the more apparent it was that he was playing the role of an ersatz, cultured, aristocratic gentleman, the less sure Jack was of Jordan's response to an autopsy. There had been criminal cases where the perpetrators thought themselves so intelligent that they actively helped law enforcement just to prove how smart they were. The pretender Jordan seemed to be might fall into that category and agree to an autopsy to make the game that much more exciting.

Jack shook his head. His rationality suddenly kicked in, and he knew without a shadow of a doubt that he was letting his imagination run wild.

"You don't agree?" Jordan asked. He'd seen Jack's head motion.

"No, I mean yes," Jack said as he verbally stumbled, trying to cover his blunder. The truth was he'd not been following the conversation at that point.

"I'm saying the best time to go to the Dalmatian coast is during the fall and not the summer. You don't agree?"

"I agree," Jack insisted. "There's no doubt whatsoever."

Mollified, Jordan returned to what he'd been saying. Charlene nodded appreciatively.

Jack went back to his musing and admitted to himself that the chance of foul play being involved with Patience's death was infinitesimally small. The main reason was that Patience had had a heart attack and that there'd been too many accomplished physicians involved, including Craig. Craig wasn't Jack's favorite person, particularly to be married to his sister, but he was one of the sharpest, most knowledgeable physicians that Jack had ever known. There was no way Jordan could have fooled such a collection of professionals by somehow causing his wife to have a heart attack.

Such a realization yanked Jack back to square one. The medical examiner's office could not get him an exhumation and autopsy. If it were to happen, he had to do it himself. In that regard, Jordan's masquerading as the Boston Brahmin might help. Jack could appeal to him as a gentleman, since true gentlemen have a duty to set the example in ethical behavior by making sure justice prevails. It was a long shot, but it was all he could come up with.

While Jordan and Charlene debated the best time of year to go to Venice, Jack put down his cup and saucer and reached into his side pocket to pull out one of his business cards. When a break occurred in the conversation, he leaned forward and with his thumb snapped the card down onto the glass tabletop.

"I say! What do we have here?" Jordan questioned, immediately taking the bait. Bending forward, he glanced at the card before picking it up to examine it more closely. Charlene took it from him and looked at it as well.

"What's a medical examiner?" Charlene asked.

"It's the same thing as a coroner," Jordan explained.

"Not quite," Jack said. "A coroner historically is an appointed or elected official tasked to look into causes of death, who may or may not have any specific training. A medical examiner is a medical doctor who's had graduate training in forensic pathology."

"I stand corrected," Jordan said. "You were about to tell me how you intend to help with my suit, which I have to say I'm finding rather a bore."

"And why is that?"

"I thought it would be exciting, like watching a boxing match. Instead, it is tedious, like watching two people arguing."

"I'm certain I could make it more interesting," Jack said, snatching the opportunity Jordan's unexpected opinion about the trial afforded him.

"Please be more specific."

"I like your simile comparing the trial to boxing, but the reason the match is uninteresting is because the two boxers are blindfolded."

"That's a droll image. Two fighters unable to see each other and just flailing away."

"Precisely! And they are blinded because they don't have all the information they need."

"What do they need?"

"They are arguing about the care of Patience Stanhope without Patience being able to tell her side of the story."

"And what story would she tell if she could tell it?"

"We won't know unless I can ask her."

"I don't understand what you two are talking about," Charlene complained. "Patience Stanhope is dead and buried."

"I believe he's talking about doing an autopsy."

"That's exactly what I'm talking about."

"You mean dig her up?" Charlene questioned with consternation. "Yuck!"

"It's not all that uncommon," Jack said. "It's been less than a year. I guarantee something will be learned by doing it, and the boxing match, as you call it, will be in broad daylight and far more engaging."

"Like what?" Jordan questioned. He'd gone quiet, pensive.

"Like what portion of her heart was involved with the heart attack, how it progressed, whether there was any preexisting condition. Only when these issues are known can the question of her care be addressed."

Jordan chewed his lower lip while he considered what Jack had said.

Jack was encouraged. He knew what he was trying to do was still an uphill struggle, but Jordan had not dismissed the idea outright. Of course, he might not realize that permission to do the exhumation rested with him.

"Why are you offering to do this?" Jordan asked. "Who's paying you?"

"No one is paying me. I can honestly say that I'm motivated to see that justice prevails. At the same time, I have a conflict of interest. My sister is married to the defendant, Dr. Craig Bowman."

Jack carefully watched Jordan's face for signs of anger or irritation and saw neither. To the man's credit, he seemed to be rationally mulling over Jack's comments without emotion.

"I'm all for justice," Jordan said at length. For the moment, his mild English accent had abandoned him. "But it seems to me it would be hard for you to be completely objective."

"Fair enough," Jack said. "It's a good point, but if I were to do an autopsy, I would preserve all specimens for expert review. I could even get a medical examiner to assist me who had no conflict."

"Why wasn't an autopsy done originally?"

"Not all deaths result in autopsies. If there had been any question of the manner of death, an autopsy could have been ordered by the medical examiner's office. At the time, there were no questions. Patience had had a documented heart attack and was attended by her physician. If the lawsuit had been anticipated, an autopsy could have been done."

"I hadn't planned on filing suit, although I wouldn't be honest if I didn't admit your brother-in-law angered me that night. He was arrogant and accused me of not communicating adequately about Patience's condition when I was pleading with him to take Patience directly to the hospital."

Jack nodded. He'd read about this particular point in both Jordan's and Craig's depositions, and had no intention of getting involved in the issue. He knew that the

origins of many malpractice suits involved poor communication from the physician or his staff.

"In fact, I hadn't intended to file suit until Mr.
Anthony Fasano contacted me."

Jack's ears pricked up. "The attorney sought you out
and not vice versa?"

"Absolutely. Just like you did. He came to the door
and rang the bell."

"And he talked you into filing."

"He did, and for essentially the same justification you
are using: justice. He said it was my responsibility to see
that the public was protected from doctors like Dr.
Bowman and what he called the 'inequities and inequal-
ities' of concierge medicine. He was quite persistent and
persuasive."

Good Lord, Jack thought to himself. Jordan's gulli-
bility for the come-on of an ambulance-chasing
personal-injury lawyer undermined the regard Jack had
begun to feel for the man. Jack reminded himself that the
man was a phony: a wealthy phony, but a phony nonetheless who had married up. Having laid the groundwork,
Jack decided it was time to go for the jugular and get the
hell out. He reached into his pocket and pulled out
the exhumation permit. He placed it on the table in front
of Jordan. "In order for me to do the autopsy, you would
have to merely sign this authorization. I'll take care of the
rest."

"What kind of paper is it?" Jordan questioned, his
put-on accent returning. He leaned over and glanced at
it. "I'm not a lawyer."

"It's just a routine form," Jack said. He could think
of several sarcastic quips, but he restrained himself.

Jordan's response caught Jack off guard. Instead of

any more questions, he reached into the pocket of his jacket, but unfortunately not for a pen. Instead, he pulled out a cell phone. He speed-dialed a number and sat back. He eyed Jack as the call went through.

"Mr. Fasano," Jordan said while looking out at his lush lawn. "I've just been handed a form by a medical examiner from New York that might impact the trial. It's to give my permission to dig up Patience for an autopsy. I want you to view it before I sign."

Even from where he was sitting more than ten feet away, Jack could hear Tony Fasano's response. Jack couldn't understand the actual words, but the tone was quite clear.

"All right, all right!" Jordan repeated. "I shan't sign it until you review it. You have my word." He flipped his phone shut, then looked at Jack. "He's on his way over."

The last thing Jack wanted was to involve the lawyers. As he'd told Alexis the day before, he didn't like lawyers, particularly personal-injury lawyers with their self-serving claims of fighting for the little guy. After the plane crash, he'd been hounded by lawyers trying to get him to sue the commuter airline.

"Maybe I'll head out," Jack said, getting to his feet. He couldn't help but feel that with Tony Fasano involved the chances of getting an authorization signature were close to zero. "You have my cell phone number on my card in case you want to get ahold of me after your lawyer checks out the form."

"No, I want to deal with this now," Jordan said. "If I don't do it now, I don't do it at all, so sit down! Mr. Fasano will be here before you know it. How about a cocktail. It's after five, so it's legal." He smiled at his

hackneyed quip and rubbed his hands together in anticipation.

Jack eased himself back down into the wicker chair.
He resigned himself to the visit's conclusion, whatever it
was to be.

Jordan must have had a hidden call button, because
the woman in the French maid outfit suddenly materialized. Jordan asked for a pitcher of vodka martinis and a
dish of olives.

As if nothing had transpired in the interim, Jordan
comfortably lapsed back into the discussion of his and
Charlene's imminent travel plans. Jack declined the offer
of a martini. He couldn't think of anything he would
have wanted less. He was entertaining the idea of getting
some exercise as soon as he could break away.

Just when Jack was reaching the limits of his patience,
a carillon of bells announced visitors at the front door.
Jordan didn't move. In the distance, the front door was
heard opening, followed by muted voices. A few minutes
later, Tony Fasano swept into the room. A few steps
behind was another man dressed identically to Tony but
intimidatingly larger.

In a reflex show of respect, Jack stood up. He noticed
that Jordan didn't.

"Where is this supposed form?" Tony demanded. He
had no time for niceties. Jordan pointed with his free
hand. The other was holding his martini. Charlene was
sitting snugly at his side, toying with the hair on his nape.

Tony snatched up the exhumation permit from the
glass-topped table and gave it a rapid once-over with his
dark eyes. While he did so, Jack looked him over. In contrast to his earlier blithe demeanor in the courtroom, he
was now ostensibly irate. Jack estimated he was in his

mid- to late thirties. He had a broad face with rounded features and square teeth. His hands were clublike, with short fingers. Jack's attention switched to the significantly larger associate who was dressed in the same gray suit, black shirt, and black tie. He had come to the room's threshold and stopped. He was obviously Tony's strong-arm crony. The fact that Tony apparently thought he needed such an associate on a visit to a client gave Jack pause.

"What's this nonsense?" Tony demanded, waving the form in Jack's direction.

"I'd hardly call an official city form nonsense," Jack said. "It's an exhumation permit."

"What are you, some kind of hired gun for the defense?"

"Absolutely not."

"He's Dr. Bowman's wife's brother," Jordan explained. "He's in town, staying at his sister's home to make sure justice prevails. That's in his own words."

"Justice, my ass!" Tony growled at Jack. "You have some nerve busting in here, talking to my client."

"Wrong!" Jack said lightly. "I was invited in for a tea party."

"A wiseass on top of it," Tony snapped.

"It's true! He was invited in," Jordan said. "And we did have tea prior to the martinis."

"I'm just trying to pave the way to do an autopsy," Jack explained. "The more information available, the better the chance justice will be served. Someone needs to talk for Patience Stanhope."

"I can't believe this bullshit," Tony said, throwing up his hands in exasperation. Then he waved to his associate. "Franco, get over here and get this dog turd out of Mr. Stanhope's home!"

Franco obediently stepped into the room. He grasped Jack's arm around the elbow, hiking up Jack's shoulder in the process. Jack debated the rationale for as well as the consequences of resisting as Franco started out of the room with Jack in tow. Jack glanced at his host, who'd not budged from the wicker sofa. Jordan appeared surprised at the proceedings but didn't intervene as Tony apologized for the interruption and promised to take care of the intruder.

Maintaining his firm grip on Jack's arm, Franco marched through the formal living room and out into the marbled central hall with the grand staircase, pulling Jack along.

"Can't we discuss this like gentlemen?" Jack said. He began to mildly resist their forward progress as his internal debate continued about how to handle the situation. Jack wasn't keen on getting physical, even though he had been provoked. Franco was the kind of blocky individual Jack associated with linebackers when he played football in college. Running into a mass of similar size and proportion had been the end of Jack's brief football career.

"Shut up!" Franco snapped without even so much as a glance back at Jack.

Franco stopped when he reached the front door. After opening it, he propelled Jack outside, letting go of his arm in the process.

Jack adjusted his jacket and walked down the two steps to the gravel driveway. Parked at an angle behind the Bentley and the Hyundai was a large, black Cadillac of indeterminate vintage. It looked like a houseboat compared with the other two vehicles.

Although Jack had started for his car and had the keys in his hand, he stopped and turned around. His rationality told him to get into the car and drive away, but that same area on his Y chromosome that had admired the Bentley was outraged at this summary dismissal. Franco had stepped out of the house and was standing on the stoop with his legs planted apart and arms akimbo. A taunting smirk lingered on his acne-scarred face. Before anything could be said, Tony barreled out of the house, pushing past Franco. Shaped like a considerably smaller version of the bricklike Franco, he had to swing his hips in a peculiar way to walk with his thick, short legs. He came directly up to Jack, poking into Jack's face with his index finger.

"Let me tell you the reality here, cowboy," Tony snarled. "I got at least a hundred grand tied up in this case, and I'm expecting one hell of a payoff. Are you hearing me? I don't want you screwing things up. Everything is going just fine, so no autopsy. *Capisce?*"

"I don't know why you are so upset," Jack said. "You could arrange to have your own medical examiner work with me." He knew the autopsy issue was dead in the water, but he felt a certain satisfaction in aggravating Tony. The man, who was slightly bug-eyed to begin with, was even more so now. The veins on the sides of his forehead stuck out like dark worms.

"What do I have to say to you?" Tony snarled rhetorically. "I don't want an autopsy! The case is just fine as is. No surprises are needed or wanted. We're going to nail that arrogant, concierge M.D.'s ass, and he deserves it."

"Sounds like you've lost your objectivity," Jack remarked. He couldn't help but notice how Tony's full lips curled back in unmitigated derision as he pronounced "concierge." Jack wondered if the man had latched onto the issue as a personal crusade. There was a touch of zealotry in his expression.

Tony glanced up at Franco for support. "Can you believe this guy? It's like he's from another planet."

"Sounds to me like you are afraid of facts," Jack said.

"I ain't afraid of facts," Tony yelled. "I got plenty of facts. That woman died of a heart attack. She should have been at that hospital an hour earlier, and if she had, we wouldn't be standing here talking."

"What's a 'hah'd attack'?" Jack asked, poking fun at Tony's accent. There hadn't been a hint of an "r" sound, and the "t" was like a soft "d."

"That's it!" Tony blurted. He snapped his fingers for Franco's attention. "Get this idiot in his car and out of my sight."

Franco came down the steps quickly enough to jangle the coins in his pocket. He stepped around Tony and tried to give Jack a shove with the flats of his hands. Jack stood his ground.

"You know, I've been meaning to ask you guys how you coordinate your outfits," Jack said. "Do you decide the night before, or is it something you do first thing in the morning? I mean, it's kind of sweet."

Franco reacted with a speed that caught Jack by surprise. With an open palm, he slapped Jack on the side of his face hard enough to cause Jack's ears to ring. Jack recoiled instantly and returned the favor with a similar and equally effective blow.

Unaccustomed to people unintimidated by his size,

Franco was more astonished than Jack at having been struck. As his hand reflexively rose to touch his burning face, Jack grabbed him by the shoulders and kneed him in the groin. Franco doubled over into a crouch for a brief instant, struggling to get his breath. When he came back up, he was holding a gun.

"No!" Tony shouted. He grabbed Franco's arm from behind and pulled it down.

"Get the hell out of here!" Tony growled to Jack, holding back the enraged Franco like a handler with a mad dog. "If you screw up my case in any way, you'll be history. There's not going to be an autopsy."

Jack backed up until he bumped into the Hyundai. He didn't want to take his eyes off Franco, who was still not standing completely upright and still had the gun in his hand. Jack's legs felt rubbery from the adrenaline coursing around in his bloodstream.

Once in the car, he quickly started it. As he looked back at Tony and his sidekick, he caught sight of Jordan and Charlene standing in the doorway.

"You ain't seen the last of me," Franco yelled through Jack's open passenger-side window as Jack drove away.

For more than a quarter of an hour, Jack drove in a circuitous route through residential areas, taking turns haphazardly but not wanting to stop. He did not want anyone following him or finding him, particularly a large, black Cadillac. He knew he'd been stupid at the end of his visit to the Stanhope mansion. It had been a brief resurgence of the risk-taking, defiant personality that had emerged after the depression the plane crash and the loss of his family had caused. As he came down from the adrenaline rush, he felt weak. Totally lost but within sight of several street signs, he pulled over to the side of the road in the shade of a gigantic oak tree to get his bearings.

As he'd been driving, Jack had toyed with the idea of driving out to the airport, washing his hands of the whole affair, and flying back to New York. The burning skin on the left side of his face was an argument in favor, as was the fact that the possibility of doing an autopsy to help his sister and brother-in-law was now defunct. The other compelling argument was that his wedding was approaching at warp speed.

Yet Jack couldn't do it. Sneaking out of town was a cowardly thing to do. He picked up the Hertz map and tried to guess which main thoroughfare he should try to find and in which direction it would be. It wasn't easy, because the street he was on wasn't on the map. It was either too small or beyond the map's range. The problem was he didn't know which was the case.

Just as he was about to start driving again blindly to find a main street, his cell phone came to life. Reaching into his pocket, he pulled it out. He didn't recognize the number. He answered the call and said hello.

"Dr. Stapleton, this is Jordan Stanhope. Are you okay?"

"There have been happier times in my life, but basically I'm okay." Jack was taken aback by the call.

"I wanted to apologize for the way Mr. Fasano and his associate treated you at my home."

"Thank you," Jack said. He thought of other, more clever retorts, but he held his tongue.

"I saw you being slapped. I was impressed by your response."

"You shouldn't have been. It was an embarrassingly

dim-witted thing to do, especially considering the man was armed."

"I felt he had it coming."

"I doubt he shares your opinion. That was my least favorite part of my visit."

"I've come to realize just how boorish Mr. Fasano is. It's embarrassing."

It's not too late to call off the hounds, Jack thought but did not say.

"I'm also questioning his tactics and his blithe disregard for finding the truth."

"Welcome to the legal profession," Jack said. "Unfortunately, in civil procedures, the goal is dispute resolution, not finding the truth."

"Well, I'm not going to be a party to it. I'll sign the exhumation permit."

CHAPTER NINE

By the time Jack got back to the Bowman residence, it was too late to consider going for exercise. He'd also missed dinner with the girls, who had retired to their respective rooms and were studying for their imminent final exams. Apparently, his presence was already commonplace because none of them came down to say hello. To make up for the girls, Alexis had been effusively welcoming but had immediately noticed the redness, bruising, and swelling on the left side of his face.

"What in heaven's name happened?" she had questioned with concern.

Jack had brushed her off, saying it was nothing, but offered to explain it later after he'd cleaned up. He'd changed the subject by asking for Craig. Alexis had told him merely that he was in the great room without elaborating.

Jack had jumped into the shower to wash away the day, and now, as he got out, he wiped the mist from the bathroom mirror to look at his face. After the hot water, the redness was even more intense than it had been before. What he had not noticed was a small, bright crimson flame-shaped hemorrhage on the white, scleral part of his eye. Leaning closer to the mirror, he saw a few tiny subcutaneous hemorrhages over the lateral aspect of his cheekbone. There was no doubt that Franco had packed a wallop. Jack couldn't help but wonder how Franco looked, because Jack's palm was still tender from the impact, suggesting he'd hit him equally hard.

After a change of clothes, Jack tossed his laundry into the basket in the laundry room, per Alexis's instructions.

"How about some supper?" Alexis offered. She was standing in the kitchen area.

"That would be terrific," Jack said. "I'm starved. I never had time for lunch."

"We all had steaks from the grill, roasted potatoes, steamed asparagus, and salad. How does that sound?"

"Like a dream," Jack said.

During this exchange, Craig hadn't said a word. He was sitting forty feet away on the sofa in the great room, in exactly the same place he'd been that morning, but without the newspaper. He was dressed in the same clothes he'd had on during the day although the shirt was now wrinkled and its top collar button open and his tie loosened. Like a statue, he was staring at the flat-screen television, completely motionless. Jack wouldn't have thought anything abnormal except that the TV wasn't on. On the coffee table in front of him stood a half-empty bottle of scotch and an old-fashioned glass brimming with the amber fluid.

"What's he doing?" Jack asked, lowering his voice.

"What does it look like he's doing?" Alexis responded. "He's vegetating. He's depressed."

"How did the rest of the day go in court?"

"I'd have to say pretty much the same as the part you watched. That's why he's depressed. The plaintiff's first expert witness out of three testified. It was Dr. William

Tardoff, who is chief of cardiology at the Newton Memorial Hospital."

"What kind of witness was he?"

"Unfortunately, very credible, and he didn't talk down to the jurors. He was able to make it crystal clear why the first hour, even the first minutes, are so important for a heart-attack victim. After a number of attempted objections from Randolph, he was able to get it into the record that it was his opinion that Patience Stanhope's chances of survival had significantly decreased because of Craig's delay in confirming his diagnosis and getting her to the treatment facility—namely, the hospital."

"Sounds rather damning, especially coming from a department head in Craig's own hospital."

"Craig has reason to be depressed. Criticism from anyone is hard for a doctor to take, since they put themselves on the pedestal, but coming from a respected colleague is a quantum leap worse."

"Was Randolph able to reduce Dr. Tardoff's impact on cross-examination?"

"I'm sure, at least to an extent, but it's like he's always playing catch-up."

"It's the rule for the plaintiff to present his case first. Defense will have its time."

"The system doesn't seem fair, but it's not like we have an alternative."

"Were there only two witnesses today?" Jack asked.

"No, there were three total. Before Dr. Tardoff, Darlene, Craig's nurse, testified, and she was grilled on the 'problem patient' designation the same way Marlene had been, with the same result. During the lunch break,

Randolph was furious at Craig for not having told him about it, and it's easy to understand why."

"It still boggles my mind that Craig would permit something like that in his practice."

"I'm afraid it speaks to a kind of arrogance."

"I'd be less generous. To me, it's pure stupidity, and it's certainly not going to help his cause."

"I'm amazed it's been allowed to be introduced. It's clearly prejudicial in my mind, and has nothing to do with alleged negligence. But you know what bothers me the most?"

"What?" Jack asked. He noticed that Alexis's face had flushed.

"Craig's case is going to suffer, but the secretaries' designation for those patients was actually appropriate."

"How so?" Jack asked. He couldn't help but notice that Alexis's color had deepened. This was an issue she felt strongly about.

"Because they were problem patients, each and every one of them. In fact, calling them problem patients wasn't strong enough. They were hypochondriacs of the worst sort. I know, because Craig would tell me about them. They were wasting his time. They should have gone to a psychiatrist or a psychologist, someone who could possibly have helped them process their issues. Patience Stanhope was the worst of the lot. There had been an interval of time about a year ago when she was dragging Craig out of bed once a week to make an unnecessary house call. It was affecting the whole family."

"So you were upset about Patience Stanhope?"

"Of course I was upset. It wasn't long after that particular period when she was so demanding that Craig moved out."

Jack studied his sister's face. He knew her personality tended toward the histrionic back when they were kids, and this reaction about Patience Stanhope suggested the trait hadn't completely disappeared. She had gotten herself completely worked up.

"So you weren't sorry when she passed on?" Jack said, more as a statement than a question.

"Sorry? I was happy. I had told him he should drop her from his practice many times: find her another doctor, preferably a psychiatrist. But you know Craig. He always refused. He had no trouble referring patients to specialists for specialty care, but the idea of giving up on a patient was tantamount to failure. He couldn't do it."

"How much has he been drinking?" Jack asked to change the subject. He nodded toward Craig's motionless form.

"Too much, just like every night."

Jack nodded. He knew that abuse of drugs and alcohol by doctors was not an uncommon sequel to being sued for malpractice.

"While we're on the subject, what would you like to drink?" Alexis asked. "Beer or wine? We've got both in the fridge."

"A beer would hit the spot," Jack said.

Jack got his own beer, and while Alexis busied herself with Jack's dinner, he wandered out of the kitchen area and over to the sofa. Although Craig did not move his body, his bloodshot eyes rose up and engaged Jack's.

"I'm sorry it was a discouraging day in court," Jack said, in hopes of engaging Craig in conversation.

"How much of it did you see?" Craig asked in a monotone.

"Only the testimony of your receptionist, Marlene, which was upsetting to hear."

Craig waved a hand as if he were shooing away invisible insects but didn't comment. His eyes switched back to the dead TV screen.

Jack would have liked to ask about the "PP" designation to try to fully understand the mind-set that would have allowed Craig to so something so politically incorrect and foolish, but he didn't. It wouldn't have helped anything and was just for his morbid curiosity. Alexis had been right. It had been arrogance. Craig was one of those doctors who unquestioningly thought everything he did was noble because the core of his life in terms of dedication and sacrifice was indeed noble. It was an unfortunate sense of entitlement.

With Craig incommunicative, Jack wandered back into the kitchen and then out onto the patio with Alexis while she grilled his steak. Alexis was eager to talk about something more upbeat than the malpractice suit. She wanted to hear about Laurie and the wedding plans. Jack related the basics but wasn't thrilled about the conversation, since he was feeling guilty about being in Boston and leaving all the last-minute details to Laurie. In many respects, it was an untenable position. He was fated to feel guilty no matter what he did; if he left for New York, he'd feel he was abandoning Alexis. Either way, he was slighting someone. But rather than wallow in the dilemma, he went for another beer.

Fifteen minutes later, Jack sat down at the large, round family table while Alexis put a plate of heavenly food in front of him. For herself, Alexis had made a cup of tea, and she joined him, sitting directly opposite. Craig had rallied enough to turn on the TV and was watching a local news broadcast.

"I'd like to tell you about my day," Jack said in between mouthfuls. "There's a decision to be made about my role here and what you people want me to do. I have to say, I had a rather productive afternoon."

"Craig!" Alexis called over to her husband. "I think you should turn off the life support and come over here to hear what Jack has to say. Ultimately, this is your decision."

"I don't appreciate being made fun of," Craig snapped, but he did turn off the TV with the remote. As if exhausted, he got up, picked up the scotch bottle and the glass, and walked to the table. He put the glass down first, filled it with scotch before putting the bottle down, and took a seat.

"I'm going to have to cut you off," Alexis said. She reached out for the scotch bottle and slid it out of Craig's reach.

Jack expected Craig to throw a temper tantrum about his bottle, but he didn't. Instead, he gave Alexis an overly fake smile to sarcastically thank her.

While he ate, Jack told them about his activities chronologically, and he tried to be complete. He told about going to the medical examiner's office and meeting Dr. Latasha Wylie and what she was able to tell him about exhuming a body in Massachusetts—particularly, about needing the approval of the next of kin.

"Wouldn't that be Jordan Stanhope?" Alexis questioned.

"He'll never agree," Craig said.

"Let me finish the whole story," Jack said.

Jack told about visiting the Langley-Peerson Funeral Home and his discussion with Harold Langley and getting the permit forms. He then told the Bowmans what he had learned about Jordan Stanhope.

Both Alexis's and Craig's mouths sagged open simultaneously as Jack gave them Jordan's short biography.

Craig was the first to speak. "Do you think it is true?" he sputtered.

"Harold Langley has no reason to lie. It must be common knowledge in Brighton; otherwise, Harold Langley certainly wouldn't have told me. Funeral directors are generally and rather notoriously tight-lipped."

"Stanislaw Jordan Jaruzelski," Alexis repeated with disbelief. "No wonder he changed his name."

"I knew Jordan was younger than Patience," Craig said, but I never suspected anything like that. They acted as if they had been married for twenty-five-plus years. I'm amazed."

"I think the interesting part is that Patience was the one with the money."

"She's not the one with the money anymore," Craig commented. He shook his head with disgust. "Randolph should have discovered this. This is another example of his ineptitude. I should have demanded another lawyer."

"Normally, this is not the kind of information necessary to litigate a malpractice claim," Jack said, although he was surprised himself it didn't come out in Jordan's deposition. "It's not relevant."

"I'm not so sure," Craig said.

"Let me finish," Jack interrupted. "Then we can talk about the whole situation."

"Fine," Craig said. He put his drink down and eagerly

leaned forward. He was no longer a pathetically brooding individual.

Jack then took the Bowmans to the Newton Memorial
Hospital with his dialogue and related his conversations
with Dr. Noelle Everette, Dr. Matt Gilbert, and Ms.
Georgina O'Keefe. He talked about his sense that the
cyanosis issue was unresolved. He said that Georgina's
main point was that the cyanosis was even, not just in the
extremities. Jack asked Craig if he had had the same
impression.

"I suppose," Craig said. "But I was so overwhelmed
by her grave general state that I really didn't look at her
with that question in mind."

"That's exactly what Dr. Gilbert said as well," Jack
added.

"Wait a second!" Craig said, holding up his hand.
"Did learning what you did about Jordan make you
think this cyanosis issue is more significant? I mean, this
money situation with a younger man marrying a wealthy
widow . . ." Craig let his sentence trail off as his mind
toyed with the idea and its implications.

"I have to say it did," Jack agreed, "but relatively
briefly. In many respects, it's too soap-operaish, if that's
a word. Besides, it's been documented by the biomarkers that Patience had suffered a heart attack, as Dr.
Gilbert rightfully reminded me today. At the same time,
Jordan's curious biography should not be dismissed
entirely." Jack then went on to tell the story he'd related
to Matt and Georgina about his case involving the elderly woman who'd died of a heart attack after being
robbed at gunpoint.

"I think this is all very significant," Craig said, "and

it continues to make me question Randolph's competence."

"What about the bruising on the side of your face?" Alexis asked, as if suddenly remembering that Jack had agreed to explain it.

"What bruising?" Craig asked. Jack was to his left, meaning the left side of Jack's face was angled away.

"You didn't notice?" Alexis questioned with amazement. "Take a look."

Craig stood up and leaned over the table. Reluctantly, Jack turned his head so the left side of his face was in Craig's view.

"My gosh," Craig said. "That does look raw." He reached out and touched Jack's cheekbone with the tip of his index finger to assess the amount of edema. "Does it hurt?"

Jack pulled his face away. "Of course it hurts," he said irritably. He'd always hated how doctors did that. They always poked the place you said hurt. Orthopedic guys were the worst, in Jack's experience, which he had a lot of, thanks to all the bumps and bruises he got playing street basketball.

"Sorry," Craig said. "It looks raw. Maybe a cold pack would be a good idea. Want me to get one?"

Jack declined Craig's ministrations.

"How did it happen?" Alexis asked.

"I'm coming to it," Jack said. He then related the visit to the Stanhopes'.

"You went to the Stanhope mansion?" Craig questioned with obvious disbelief.

"I did," Jack admitted

"Is that legal?"

"What do you mean legal? Of course it's legal. I mean,

it's not like seeking out the jurors or anything. If there was any chance of getting a signature, I had to go." Jack then told them about the Bentley and then the unexpected Charlene.

Craig and Alexis exchanged glances of surprise. Craig gave a short, derisive laugh.

"So much for a long mourning period," Alexis said indignantly. "The man is shameless, likewise for the elaborate gentleman façade."

"This is starting to remind me of another notorious case that took place in Rhode Island but involved diabetes," Craig said.

"I know the case you are referring to," Jack said. "But even in that case, the suddenly wealthy heir was acquitted."

"What about your face?" Alexis said impatiently. "The suspense is killing me."

Jack told them about how he brought up the issue about exhuming Patience's body, fully expecting to be rebuffed. He then described Tony Fasano's arrival, along with an associate dressed in an almost identical outfit.

"His name is Franco," Alexis said.

"You know him?" Jack questioned. He was surprised.

"I don't know him. I've just seen him. He's hard to miss. He comes to the courtroom with Tony Fasano. I only know his name because I heard Tony Fasano call to him yesterday when they were leaving the courtroom."

Jack related Tony's vehement objection to the idea of exhuming Patience and doing an autopsy. He told them he'd been threatened that he'd be "history" if he did the autopsy.

For a few moments, both Alexis and Craig merely

stared at Jack. They were both dumbfounded by what he had just told them.

"That's weird!" Craig said finally. "Why would he be so against an autopsy?"

Jack shrugged. "Presumably, because he feels confident in the case he has and doesn't want to rock the boat. He's invested some serious money on contingency, and he's expecting a mammoth payoff. But I have to tell you, it makes me more motivated."

"What about your face?" Alexis asked. "You keep avoiding telling us about it."

"That happened at the end, after Franco gave me the bum's rush. I was being cute and stupid. I told both of them I thought their matching outfits were sweet."

"So he struck you?" Alexis questioned with consternation.

"Well, it wasn't a love pat," Jack said.

"I think you should press charges," Alexis said indignantly.

"I don't agree," Jack said. "Stupidly, I hit him back, so trying to press charges would just get into an argument of who hit whom first."

"You hit that hulky hoodlum?" Alexis questioned with disbelief. "What have you become in your adulthood, self-destructive?"

"People have accused me of that in the not-too-distant past. I like to think of myself as occasionally impulsive with a touch of self-righteous recklessness."

"I don't find this at all funny," Alexis said.

"Nor do I," Jack agreed. "But the episode, especially me getting whacked, helped my argument with Jordan that I originally thought was hopeless." Jack reached into his inner jacket pocket and pulled out the exhumation permit. He placed it on the table and smoothed it out with the palm of his hand. "Jordan signed the exhumation permit."

Alexis drew the form closer to herself. She looked at Jordan's signature and blinked several times as if she expected it might disappear.

"That kind of eliminates any suspicion of his involvement," Craig said, looking over Alexis's shoulder.

"Who knows," Jack said. "What it does for certain is that it puts the idea of an autopsy on the table as a legitimate option. It's no longer a mere theoretical possibility, although now we're up against a time constraint. Assuming that can be overcome, the question is whether you people want me to do it or not. It has to be decided tonight."

"My feelings have not changed from this morning," Craig said. "There's no way to be sure whether it would help or hurt, and I can make an argument in either direction."

"I think there's slightly more chance it might help than hinder because of the cyanosis issue," Jack said. "There must be some anatomical explanation, some contributory pathology. But you are right: There are no guarantees." Jack shrugged. "But I don't want to push the idea. I'm not here to make things worse. It's your decision."

Craig shook his head. "As confused as I am, it's hard to make a decision. I think I'm against it because of the unknown, but what do I know. I'm hardly in a position to be objective."

"How about asking Randolph?" Alexis suggested. "If something positive were found by the autopsy, he'd have to figure out how to get it admitted as evidence. With rules of discovery, it is not the given it could be."

"You're right," Jack said. "Randolph should be consulted. It would be an exercise in futility if the findings couldn't be introduced."

"There's something not right in this picture," Craig said. "I'm questioning the man's competence and considering replacing him, and you both think we should let him decide whether or not to do an autopsy."

"We can tell him Jordan Stanhope's story at the same time," Alexis said, ignoring Craig.

"Can we get him on the phone and discuss it with him tonight?" Jack asked. "The decision about whether or not to do the autopsy really cannot wait. Even if it's given a green light, I can't be certain it will happen. There are too many variables and not a lot of time."

"We can do better than call him," Alexis said. "He lives just around the corner."

"Fine," Craig said, throwing up his hands. He didn't feel strongly enough about it to overrule both Alexis and Jack. "But I'm not going to be the one to call."

"I don't mind calling," Alexis said. She got up and went over to the desk.

"You seem to be feeling better," Jack said to Craig while Alexis was using the phone.

"It's up and down," Craig said. "One minute I'm depressed and the next minute hopeful that truth will win out. It's been that way since this mess started back in October. Yet today had to be one of the worst days, hearing Bill Tardoff testify against me. I've always been friendly with the man. I really don't understand it."

"Is he a good doctor?"

Craig glared at Jack before saying, "Ask me that in a

couple of days. At the moment, I'd be giving you an emotional response. Right now, I'd like to kill the guy."

"I understand," Jack said, and he did. "What about Dr. Noelle Everette? Does she have a good reputation?"

"With me or the hospital community?"

"Both."

"Like with Bill, my feelings changed after this malpractice suit. Before I thought she was okay, not great but okay, and I referred to her on occasion. After the suit, I'm as mad at her as I am at Bill. As far as her general reputation is concerned, it's fine. She's well liked although not so dedicated as most."

"Why do you say that?"

"She only works half-time officially, although it's more like three-quarters time. Her excuse is her family, which is nonsense. I mean, we all have families."

Jack nodded as if he agreed, but he didn't. He thought Craig should have given Noelle's work ethic a try. He probably would have been happier and a far better husband and father.

"The reason I asked about Noelle Everette," Jack said after a pause, "is because she said something interesting today. She said some of the old-fashioned physicians, a group in which she included herself, were angry about you concierge doctors. Does that surprise you?"

"Not really. I think they might be jealous. Not everybody can switch to a retainer practice. It depends a lot on their patient base."

"You mean whether the patient base is wealthy or not."

"That's a big part of it," Craig admitted. "Concierge practice is an enviable lifestyle compared with the mess standard practice is being put in. I'm making more money in a lot less time."

"What happened to your patients from your old practice who couldn't come up with the retainer fee?"

"They were referred to other people's standard practice."

"So they were in a sense abandoned."

"No, not at all. We spent a lot of time giving them names and numbers of other doctors."

To Jack it sounded very much like abandonment, but he didn't argue. Instead, he said, "So you see the kind of anger Noelle was talking about as stemming from envy."

"I can't think of any other reason."

Jack could think of a number, including the concept of professionalism Noelle had mentioned, but Jack wasn't interested in a debate. It was the malpractice case he was most interested in, so he asked, "Was Patience Stanhope an old patient of yours from your old practice?"

"No. She was a patient of the physician who started the concierge practice that I'm now essentially running. He's in Florida and not in the best of health."

"So in a sense you inherited her?"

"In a sense."

Alexis came back to the table. "Randolph is coming right over. He's interested in the autopsy idea but has reservations, including its admissibility, like I feared."

Jack nodded, but he was more interested in his conversation with Craig, and he had been debating how to word his next question. "Craig, remember this morning when I mentioned the idea of smothering or strangula-

tion in relation to Patience Stanhope, which I later realized was ridiculous, since she died of a heart attack?"

"How could I forget?"

"It's an example of how medical examiners like me
think. I mean, I wasn't making any allegations of any
sort. I was kind of thinking out loud, trying to relate central cyanosis to the rest of the facts. In retrospect, you
understand, don't you? At the time, you were bothered
by the suggestion."

"I understand, but I'm not myself these days for obvious reasons. I'm sorry."

"No need to apologize. I'm bringing it up only
because I want to ask you a question which occurred to
me when Noelle Everette made her comment about a
group of old-fashioned doctors being angry about
concierge doctors. It's a question you might think outlandish the same way you responded to the mentioning
of strangulation and smothering this morning."

"You've piqued my curiosity. Ask your question."

"Can you think of any remotely possible way you
could have been set up by Patience Stanhope's death?
What I'm suggesting is that someone might have seen
her passing as a way to put concierge medicine in a bad
light. Does this idea resonate at all, or am I once again
somewhere beyond the orbit of Pluto?"

A small smile appeared at the corners of Craig's
mouth and slowly spread inward until he laughed and
shook his head in wonderment. "What you lack in
rationality, you certainly make up for in creativity."

"Remember, it is a rhetorical question. I don't expect
an answer; just tuck it away in the archives of your brain
and see if it resonates with any other facts you've not told
anyone."

"Are you suggesting some kind of conspiracy?" Alexis asked. She was as taken aback as Craig.

"Conspiracy implies more than one," Jack said. "Like you asked me to do on the phone, I'm thinking out of the box."

"That's way out of the box," Craig said.

The doorbell precluded any more talk of malevolent medical machinations, which was how Craig referred to Jack's idea as Alexis went to the door. When Alexis returned with Randolph Bingham in tow, Jack and Craig were chuckling at other clever names Craig was able to conjure up. Alexis was pleasantly surprised. Craig was showing more normal behavior than he had in months, which was even more unusual, considering the stressful day in court.

Jack was reintroduced to Randolph. The first time had been outside the courtroom that morning before the trial had recommenced. There hadn't been much time, and Alexis, who'd done the introducing, merely said that Jack was her brother, whereas now she included details of Jack's professional qualifications.

Randolph didn't say anything during Alexis's monologue, although he nodded a few times at key points. "I'm pleased to make your acquaintance again," he said when Alexis concluded.

"Likewise," Jack said. He felt there was an unease about the situation. Randolph was irrepressibly staid. Although he'd changed from his meticulously tailored courtroom suit, his idea of relaxed wear was a heavily starched, freshly pressed, long-sleeved white oxford shirt, pleated summer-weight wool pants with a knifelike crease, and a summer-weight cashmere sweater. As further evidence of his primness, he appeared to have shaved, in contrast to Jack and Craig, who both had the expected evening stubble, and his silver hair was as perfectly styled as it had been in court.

"Should we sit here at the table or go into the living room?" Alexis asked as the host.

"Wherever you'd like," Randolph said. "But we must be expeditious; I have a lot of preparation yet to do tonight."

They ended up sitting around the table where they'd been before Randolph's arrival.

"Alexis has told me about your suggestion of doing an autopsy on the deceased," Randolph said. "Perhaps you can tell me why this might be important at this eleventh hour."

To Jack's ear, he spoke with the true melodiousness that Jack associated with elite New England schools, and it suddenly occurred to him that Randolph was the archetype to which Jordan aspired. The question of why Jordan wanted to do so was another matter, since Jack found Randolph a passionless man, a prisoner of his restrained formality.

Jack ran down his short list in favor of an autopsy sans any reference to conspiracy or individually motivated foul-play theories. Then he gave his patented spiel about the role of a medical examiner's talking for the dead. "In short," Jack said as a kind of summation, "I believe an autopsy would afford Patience Stanhope her last day in court. My hope is to find enough pathology to clear Craig or, worst case, provide an argument for contributory negligence, since there is documentation the deceased refused a recommended cardiac workup."

Jack looked across at Randolph's arctic-blue eyes for some response. There was none, nor was there from his mouth, which was a small, almost lipless horizontal slash halfway between his nose and the point of his chin. "Any questions?" Jack asked, hoping to generate a response.

"I don't believe so," Randolph said at length. "You've stated your case succinctly and well. It is an intriguing possibility, which I had not thought of since the clinical aspects of the case are so clear. My biggest concern involves the admissibility of whatever you might find. If something were to be found truly relevant and exculpatory, I would have to petition the court for a continuance to allow for proper discovery. In other words, it could be up to the judge."

"Couldn't I be called as a surprise rebuttal witness?"

"Only to refute previous testimony, not to offer new testimony."

"I would be refuting the testimony of the plaintiff's experts claiming malpractice."

"It's stretching the rule, but I see your point. It would be up to the judge at any case, and he'd be ruling over strenuous objections from the plaintiff's attorney. It would be an uphill struggle and would afford the plaintiff foundation for appeal if it were granted.

"A final thought that adds to the difficulties of presenting such new evidence is my experience with Judge Davidson. He is known to like to move things along and is already irritated at the slow pace of this trial. There's no doubt he wants to bring it to a close. He would not look kindly on new evidence brought in at the very last minute."

Jack shrugged and raised his eyebrows questioningly. "So you are against it?"

"Not necessarily. This is a unique case with unique challenges, and we would be foolish not to do everything we possibly can for a positive outcome. New exculpatory evidence could be used as the basis to argue for a new trial through appeal. On the other hand, I believe the chances of finding something exculpatory are slim indeed. With that said, I'd come out sixty-forty in favor of doing it. So there you have it."

Randolph stood, as did the others. "Thank you for inviting me over and briefing me," he said, shaking hands all around. "See you all in court."

As Alexis accompanied Randolph to the door, Jack and Craig sat back down. "He fooled me," Jack said. "Just when I thought he was telling us he was against my doing the autopsy, he tells me he's for it."

"I had the same reaction," Craig said.

"One thing this little meeting made me realize is that I don't think you should change attorneys," Jack said. "Randolph might be priggish, but he strikes me as keenly intelligent, and under that gentleman veneer, he's a competitor. He definitely wants to win."

"Thanks for your opinion," Craig said. "I wish I unquestioningly shared it."

Alexis returned. She acted mildly irritated. "Why didn't you tell him about your run-in with Tony Fasano and the threat he gave you?"

"I didn't want to confuse the issue," Jack said. "Same reason I didn't bring up my wild theories of foul play or the surprising biography of Jordan Stanhope, aka Stanislaw Jaruzelski."

"I think that threat issue is more important," Alexis said. "Doesn't that bother you, being threatened like that?"

"Not really. Tony Fasano's worried about his investment, since he's surely taken the case on contingency.

With that said, he strikes me as someone who blows a lot of hot air."

"I don't know," Alexis said. "It concerns me."

"Well, folks!" Jack said. "It's time to fish or cut bait. Am I going to try to do this autopsy or not? One thing I haven't mentioned. From my experience, juries use a commonsense gut reaction in their decision-making, but they like facts. Autopsy results are facts that they can grasp in contrast to testimony that is ephemeral and open to interpretation. Try to keep that in mind."

"If you can honestly tell me you are not concerned about Tony Fasano's threat, then I'll vote for the autopsy."

"And you, Craig?" Jack asked. "You're the principal here. Your vote can trump the rest of us."

"My feelings haven't changed," Craig said. "I think there's more chance finding stuff we don't want to know than things we do. But I'm not going to vote against the two of you and Randolph." He stood up. "Now I'm going to go up and put myself in the warm and fuzzy hand of a strong hypnotic. With the rest of the plaintiff experts, Jordan Stanhope, and possibly Leona Rattner slated to testify, it's going to be a taxing day tomorrow."

For a few minutes after Craig had disappeared upstairs, Jack and Alexis sat at the table, lost in their own thoughts. Jack was the first to speak after reaching out and picking up the scotch bottle. "Mixing this hard stuff and a strong hypnotic is not a good idea."

"I can't argue with that."

"Have you been at all worried about Craig injuring himself?"

"You mean overdosing?"

"Yes, either intentionally or otherwise." Jack could

remember his own struggles with self-destructive thoughts during his years of fighting depression.

"Of course I've thought about it, but that's one aspect of narcissism in his favor. The devotees generally don't hurt themselves. Also, his depression has been far from incapacitating, and he has been cycling regularly through periods of normalcy—like tonight, for instance. He probably wouldn't admit it, but I think you have raised his spirits by being here. It means you care, and he respects you."

"That's nice. But what's he been taking for sleep? Do you know?"

"Just the usual. I've kept close tabs. I'm embarrassed to say, I've even been counting the pills behind his back."

"You shouldn't be embarrassed. That's being prudent."

"Whatever," Alexis said. She stood up. "I think I'll head upstairs, check on the girls, and turn in myself. I hate to abandon you, but if Leona Rattner testifies tomorrow, it's going to be particularly taxing for me, too."

"No problem," Jack said. He got to his feet as well. "I'm tired myself, although I want to read over some of the depositions again. I keep thinking I might be missing something that would be key to keep in mind if and when I do the autopsy."

"I certainly don't envy you working on someone who's been buried for almost a year. How do you do this kind of work day in, day out? Isn't it repulsive?"

"I know it sounds unpleasant, maybe even ghoulish, but it's actually fascinating. I learn something every day, and I don't have any problem patients."

"Don't remind me about problem patients," Alexis

said. "Talk about self-inflicted wounds; that's a prime example!"

The silence of the big house settled over Jack after Alexis said good night and climbed the stairs. For a few minutes, he reflected on Alexis's curiously emotional response to Patience Stanhope being a problem patient and how Alexis was willing to say she was glad Patience was gone. She'd even alluded to thinking that Patience Stanhope had had something to do with Craig's moving out. Jack shook his head. He didn't know what to think. Instead, he finished the beer he'd been nursing, then went down to his room to retrieve the case file and his cell phone. With those in hand, he made his way back to the study where he'd inadvertently spent the night. The room had a comfortable, familiar feel.

After getting himself situated in the same reading chair he'd been in the night before, Jack flipped open his cell phone. He felt ambivalence about calling Laurie. He wanted to hear her voice, but he was not excited about dealing with her inevitable resentment when he told her about the possible exhumation and autopsy. It was already Tuesday night, which meant there were only two more full days before Friday. The other problem was that Jack had phoned Calvin during the day to say he wasn't going to be at the OCME on Wednesday and that he'd keep him informed. There was a chance Calvin had said something to Laurie, so she'd be miffed hearing things secondhand.

As the call went through, Jack wiggled to get as comfortable as possible, and his eyes swept over the shelving that filed the opposite wall. His line of sight stopped on a large, black, old-fashioned doctor's bag next to a portable ECG machine.

"The busy traveler at last," Laurie said brightly. "I was hoping it would be you."

Jack launched into an immediate apology for calling late but explained that he wanted to wait until a decision had been made.

"What kind of decision?"

Jack took a breath. "A decision to do an autopsy on the patient whose death is the basis of Craig's lawsuit."

"An autopsy?" Laurie questioned with consternation. "Jack, this is Tuesday night. The wedding is one thirty on Friday. I don't have to tell you that's right around the corner."

"I know there's a time crunch here. I'm keeping it in mind. Don't worry!"

"Are you doing the autopsy in the morning?"

"I don't think so, but there's a chance, I suppose. The problem is that the body is still in the ground."

"Jack!" Laurie whined, pulling out his name like taffy. "Why are you doing this to me?"

Jack gave Laurie the details of the case, everything he'd learned from the file, and then everything that had happened that day sans the episode with Franco. Laurie listened without interrupting until Jack was finished. Then she completely surprised Jack. She said, "Would you like me to fly up and assist you with the case?"

Wishing he could reach across the miles and give her a hug of appreciation, Jack said, "Thank you for your offer, but there's no need. It will not be a difficult case unless there's been a lot of water intrusion."

"Let me know. I'm certain as a team we could do it quickly."

After a bit of loving small talk and a promise to call as soon as he knew more, Jack flipped his phone closed. He was about to pull the case file into his lap when his eyes again spotted the doctor's bag. Jack got up and went over to the shelf. As he had implied to Alexis, he didn't think house calls were an appropriate use of a doctor's time, since they were limited to what could be done without the diagnostic tools available in a well-equipped doctor's office. But remembering the reference in the case file about a bedside assay kit for biomarkers to confirm heart attack, the thought passed through his mind that he might be outdated. In truth, Jack had not even heard about such a kit and was curious to see one. He pulled the bag from the shelf and placed it on Craig's desk. He turned on the gooseneck lamp and opened the bag. It opened like a fishing tackle box, with a number of small, chock-full compartments in trays on the top that opened to the sides. Below was the main space, with a collection of instruments including blood-pressure cuff, ophthalmoscope, and otoscope. Jack pulled out the ophthalmoscope. Just holding the instrument brought back a flood of memories.

Replacing the ophthalmoscope, Jack looked through the plethora of other material, including IV fluid, IV lines, thermometer, emergency medication, hemostats, culture media, and bandages. In the bottom, far corner of the bag he found the biomarker kit. He pulled it out and read the exterior. Hoping for an insert that might be more informative, he opened the box. The insert was directly on top.

After reading the insert, Jack realized he'd have to reassess his evaluation of house calls. With such products, including new and accurate ways of determining diabetic status, a physician could be quite effective in a home environment, especially with the portable ECG machine Jack had seen next to the doctor's bag.

Jack replaced the insert and then the biomarker assay kit. When he did so, he noticed some debris, including an empty atropine vial and an empty epinephrine vial. He wondered if they could have been from the time Craig had been treating Patience Stanhope. From the record, both medications had been used. Then Jack found something that made him sure they were. He found a small sample bottle of the antidepressant Zoloft with Patience Stanhope's name and the notation #6: one pill at hour of sleep. Jack opened the bottle and glanced in at the five pale blue tablets. Replacing the lid, Jack put the bottle back. Next, he lifted out the atropine and epinephrine vials. Both were empty.

Hearing what he thought were footsteps coming down the front steps caused Jack a pang of guilt about snooping into private property, even if just in a doctor's bag. It was a clear violation of the trust extended to him as a guest. With a bit of panic, he quickly replaced the vials, closed the bag, and jammed it back onto the shelf. He dashed across the room, leaped back into the club chair, and pulled the case-file material onto his lap.

It was none too soon. Craig shuffled into the study a few moments later. He was dressed in a bathrobe with open-backed slippers on his feet. He went over and sat in the other reading chair.

"I hope I'm not disturbing you," he said.

"Don't be silly," Jack answered. He couldn't help notice that Craig's voice had a monotone that hadn't been there when he'd gone upstairs and that when he'd walked in, his arms had hung limply at his sides as though they were paralyzed. It was abundantly clear the man had already taken his sleep medication and hadn't skimped on the dose.

"I just wanted to say thank you for coming up here to Boston. I know I wasn't much of a host last night and this morning."

"No problem. I have a good sense of what you're going through."

"I also wanted to say that I'm behind the autopsy idea after giving it additional thought."

"That makes it unanimous. Now, after convincing everybody, I can only hope I can pull it off."

"Well, I appreciate your efforts." He struggled back to a standing position and wobbled before gaining his balance.

"I glanced in your doctor's bag," Jack said to clear his conscience. "I hope you don't mind."

"Of course not. Do you need something? Back when I was making a lot of house calls, I amassed a small pharmacy."

"No! I was curious about the biomarker kit for heart attacks. I never knew they existed."

"It's hard to keep up with technology. Good night."

"Good night," Jack said. From where he was sitting, he could see down the lengthy hall as Craig plodded toward the stairs. He was moving like a zombie. For the first time, Jack started to feel sorry for the man.

CHAPTER TEN

NEWTON, MASSACHUSETTS
Wednesday, June 7, 2006
6:15 a.m.

The morning routine was as chaotic as it had been the previous morning, including another disagreement between Meghan and Christina over an article of apparel. Jack never knew what it was, but the tables had been turned. Now it was Meghan denying Christina, resulting in Christina rushing back upstairs in tears.

Alexis was the only one acting normally. It was as if she were the glue holding the family together. Craig was somnolent and spoke little, apparently still feeling the effects of his sleeping medication on top of his scotch.

After the kids had left for school, Alexis turned to Jack. "What do you want to do about transportation? Do you want to come with us or drive yourself?"

"I've got to drive myself. My first stop is the Langley-Peerson Funeral Home. I've got to get the signed papers over there to start the exhumation process." What he didn't say was that he hoped to get in a little basketball in the late afternoon.

"Then we'll see you in the courtroom?"

"That's my intention," Jack said, although he harbored a hope that Harold Langley could work miracles and get Patience Stanhope out of her eternal resting place that very morning. If that could happen, then Jack

could do the autopsy, have the gross results by that afternoon, present them to Craig and Alexis, and be on the
shuttle back to New York. That would give him Thursday to wrap things up in his office prior to the
honeymoon that was to begin on Saturday morning. It
would also give him the opportunity to pick up the tickets and hotel vouchers.

Jack left before Alexis and Craig. He got into his rent-
a-car and headed for the Massachusetts Turnpike. He
had assumed that having already visited the Langley-
Peerson Funeral Home, it would be easy to find it again.
Unfortunately, he was wrong. It took him almost forty
minutes of highly aggravating driving to cover approximately five miles as the crow flew.

Muttering obscenities to himself over the stressful
experience, Jack finally pulled into the funeral home's
parking lot. It was more crowded than the previous day,
forcing Jack to park at the very back. When he got
around to the front of the building, there were people
milling about on the porch. It was at that point that he
guessed a service was about to get under way. His suspicions were confirmed when he entered the foyer. In the
viewing room to the right, people were scurrying about,
arranging flowers and unfolding additional chairs. On
the catafalque was an open coffin with its occupant comfortably resting. The same pious soundtrack as the day
before inundated the scene.

"Would you care to sign the book?" a man asked in a
quiet, sympathetic voice. In many respects, he was a
significantly heavier version of Harold Langley.

"I'm looking for the funeral director."

"I am the funeral director. Mr. Locke Peerson at your
service."

Jack mentioned he was looking for Mr. Langley and was directed back to Harold's office. He found the man at his desk.

"The current Mr. Stanhope has signed the authorization," Jack said, wasting no time with small talk. He handed over the form. "Now it's a matter of utmost urgency to get the body back here to your embalming room."

"We have a service this morning," Harold said. "After that, I'll get on it."

"Do you see any chance of it happening today? We're really up against a strict deadline."

"Dr. Stapleton, do you not remember that the city, the vault company, a backhoe operator, and the cemetery are all involved in this endeavor? Under normal conditions, we're talking about a week at least."

"It cannot be a week," Jack said emphatically. "It's got to be today or tomorrow at the very latest." Jack shuddered at the implication of having to wait until Thursday and wondered what he could tell Laurie.

"That's an impossibility."

"Perhaps an extra five hundred dollars on top of your usual fee is in order to make up for the inconvenience." Jack watched Harold's expression. He had an almost parkinsonian lack of mobility and a pair of narrow lips that recalled Randolph's.

"All I can say is that I will give the affair my utmost effort. There can be no promises."

"I can't ask for anything more," Jack said while giving Harold one of his business cards. "By the way, do you have any idea of what condition we can expect the body to be in?"

"Absolutely," Harold said emphatically. "The body

should be in pristine condition. It was embalmed with our usual care, and the coffin is a top-of-the-line Perpetual Repose mated with a premier cement vault."

"What about the grave site: much water?"

"None. It's on the crest of the hill. The original Mr. Stanhope had picked it out himself for the family."

"Call me as soon as you know something."

"I most certainly will."

As Jack left the funeral home, the people on the porch had begun somberly filing in. Jack got into his car and consulted his map, which had been significantly upgraded by Alexis, who had laughed when she'd heard he'd been trying to navigate around the city with the rent-a-car map. Jack's next destination was back to the medical examiner's office. Thanks to significantly less traffic, Jack was able to make the journey in comparatively short time.

The receptionist remembered him. She told him that Dr. Wylie was definitely in the autopsy room on this occasion, and she took it upon herself without being asked to call down and talk with her. The result was that a mortuary tech came up to reception and escorted Jack down to the autopsy anteroom. Two men in mufti were milling about; one was African-American, the other Caucasian. The Caucasian was a big, red-faced Irishman. Everyone else was in Tyvek protective gear. Jack was to learn a few minutes later that the men were detectives interested in the case Latasha Wylie was doing.

Jack was given gear, and after suiting up he pushed into the room. Like the rest of the facility, the autopsy room was state-of-the-art and made the New York room look like an anachronism in comparison. There were five

tables, three of which were in operation. Latasha's was
the farthest away, and she waved for him to come over.

"I'm almost finished," Latasha said behind her plastic
face mask. "I thought you might like to take a look."

"What do you have?" Jack asked. He was always interested.

"It's a fifty-nine-year-old female found dead in her
bedroom after having been visited by a man she met on
the Internet. The bedroom was in disarray, suggesting a
struggle, with the bedside table upended and the bedside lamp broken. The two detectives waiting out in the
dressing area are thinking homicide. The woman had a
gash on her forehead at her hairline."

Latasha pulled the woman's scalp down from where it
had been reflected over the face to gain access to the
brain.

Jack bent down to look at the laceration. It was round
and punched in, as if delivered by a hammer.

Latasha went on to describe how she had been able to
reconstruct what turned out to be an accident and not a
homicide. The woman had slipped on a small throw rug
on the polished wood flooring and had collided with the
bedside table, hitting her forehead on the lamp's finial
with the full force of her body weight. The case turned
out to be an example of how important knowledge
of the scene was. It seemed that the lamp's finial was
a rather tall spire ending in a flat disc that resembled a
hammerhead.

Jack was impressed and told Latasha so.

"All in a day's work," she said. "What can I do for
you?"

"I want to take you up on your offer of autopsy supplies. It appears that it is a go, provided they can be

expeditious getting the body out of the ground. I'm going to do it at the Langley-Peerson Funeral Home."

"If you end up doing it after hours, I'd be willing to help, and I could bring a bone saw."

"Really?" Jack questioned. He'd not expected such generosity. "I'd be happy to have your help."

"Sounds like a challenging case. Let me introduce you to our chief, Dr. Kevin Carson."

The chief, who was doing a case on table number one, turned out to be a tall, lanky, pleasant individual with a southern accent who mentioned he was on a first-name basis with Jack's chief, Dr. Harold Bingham. He said Latasha had told him about what Jack was trying to do, and he supported her offer to process specimens and help with toxicology if needed. He said they did not yet do their own toxicology but had access to a superb twenty-four-seven facility at the university.

"You tell Harold hello from Boston," Kevin said before going back to his case.

"I certainly will," Jack responded, although the man was already bent over the body in front of him. "And thanks for your assistance."

"He seems like a pleasant chief," Jack said as he and Latasha went out into the anteroom.

"He's very personable," Latasha agreed.

Fifteen minutes later, Jack stashed a box of autopsy supplies in the trunk of his Accent, moving his basketball gear out of the way in the process. He also slipped Latasha's card with cell phone number into his wallet before climbing in behind the steering wheel.

Although Alexis had suggested another parking facility near Faneuil Hall, Jack was content to return to the one beneath the Boston Common, since it was easier for him to find. He also enjoyed the walk skirting the Massachusetts State House.

Pushing into the courtroom, Jack tried to let the door close as silently as possible behind him. At that moment, the court clerk was swearing in a witness. Jack had heard the name; it was Dr. Herman Brown.

As he stood by the door, Jack's eyes scanned the room. He saw the backs of Craig's and Jordan's heads along with those of their attorneys and the attorneys' associates. The jury seemed as bored as they had the day before, while the judge appeared preoccupied. He was shuffling papers, glancing at them, and reorganizing them as if he were alone in the room.

Jack's eyes scanned the spectators and immediately locked onto Franco's. From the distance, Franco's eye sockets appeared like featureless black holes beneath his Neanderthal-like brow.

Against his better judgment, Jack smiled and waved. He knew it was foolish, since he was taunting the man, but Jack was unable to stop himself. It was a reemergence of the risk-taking mentality that he had glommed on to for a number of years as a juvenile coping mechanism for his guilt about surviving his family. Jack thought he saw the man tense, but he could not be certain. Franco continued to scowl at him for several beats longer but then shifted his gaze when his boss scraped his chair back from the plaintiff's table and headed toward the podium.

Berating himself for deliberately provoking the man, Jack thought about finding a hardware store and buying some pepper spray. If there was to be a second confrontation, Jack had no intention of trading blows again. Their difference in size made that an unfair exchange.

Jack returned to scanning the spectators. Once again,

he was taken by the number. He wondered how many were the proverbial courtroom junkies, vicariously thrilled by people receiving their comeuppance, particularly the wealthy and powerful. As a successful doctor, Craig was fair game.

Finally, Jack found Alexis. She was sitting in the first row over against the wall, close to the jury box. Next to her seemed to be one of the few empty seats. Jack walked down to the bar, and then by excusing himself, he stepped into the aisle. Alexis saw him coming and moved her belongings to make room. Jack gave her shoulder a squeeze before sitting down.

"Any luck?" Alexis whispered.

"Progress, I hope, but it's now out of my hands. What's been happening here?"

"More of the same, I'm afraid. It was a slow start, since the judge had to deal with some arcane legal stuff. The first witness was Dr. Noelle Everette."

"That couldn't have been good."

"It wasn't. She came across as a superbly trained, thoughtful, and sensitive professional with the added benefit that she's from the community and was involved in the resuscitation attempt. Tony handled it well, I'm sorry to say. The way he questioned her and the way she answered kept the jurors' attention. I even saw the homemakers nodding at one point—not a good sign. Her testimony was essentially the same as Dr. William Tardoff's, but to me more effective. She comes off like the doctor everyone wishes they had."

"How was Randolph on cross?"

"Not as effective as he was with Dr. Tardoff but, personally, I couldn't see how he could be, considering how well Dr. Everette came across. I had the feeling he just wanted to get her off the stand."

"That might have been the best stratagem," Jack said. "Did the issue of concierge medicine come up?"

"Oh, yeah. Randolph tried to object, but Judge Davidson is letting it all in."

"Did the issue of cyanosis come up?"

"No. Why do you ask?"

"It continues to be a nettle in my brain. It will be one of the prime things on my mind when and if I do the autopsy."

A sixth sense made Jack turn around and look across the room at Franco. The man was again glaring at Jack with an expression that hovered between a grimace and a cruel smile. On a positive note, from the angle in which Jack was looking, he could see that the left hand side of Franco's face was as red as Jack's. So far, things were apparently equal.

Settling back on the rock-hard oak pew, Jack directed his attention to the proceedings. Tony was at the podium, while Dr. Herman Brown was in the witness box. In front of the bench, the court reporter's fingers were playing incessantly on her small machine to create a verbatim record. Tony was having the witness testify to his impressive academic and clinical credentials, and it had been going on for a quarter of an hour. As chief of cardiology at the Boston Memorial Hospital, he also occupied the chair of the Department of Cardiology at Harvard Medical School.

Randolph had stood on several occasions and offered to stipulate as to the witness's qualifications as an expert to save the court's time, but Tony had persisted. He was trying to impress the jury, and it was working. It became

increasingly apparent to everyone that it would be hard
to find a witness more qualified in cardiology, or even
equivalently qualified. The man's appearance and bearing added to his image. There was a Boston Brahmin
aura that was similar to Randolph's but without the hint
of disdain and condescension. Instead of cold and distant, he appeared kind and gentle: the sort of person who
would go out of his way to put a baby bird back into its
nest. His hair was grandfatherly white and well groomed,
his posture straight. His clothes were neat but not overly
elegant, and they had a comfortable, lived-in look. He
wore a paisley bow tie. There was even a hint of self-
deprecation, as Tony had to work to get the man to
admit reluctantly to his awards and accomplishments.

"Why is this medical Olympian testifying for the plaintiff in a malpractice trial?" Jack whispered to Alexis, but
it was more of a rhetorical question, and he didn't expect
an answer. He began to wonder if the reason had something to do with Noelle Everette's unexpected comment
about concierge medicine when she had said, "Some of
us old-fashioned physicians are angry about concierge
doctors." Maybe Dr. Brown was one of that group
because the concept of concierge medicine flew in the
face of the new professionalism that academia was trying
to espouse, and more than anyone else at the trial, Dr.
Herman Brown was representing academia.

"Dr. Brown," Tony Fasano said, gripping the sides of
the lectern with his short, thick fingers. "Before we get
to Patience Stanhope's unfortunate and avoidable
death—"

"Objection," Randolph said emphatically. "There has
been no establishment that Mrs. Stanhope's death was
avoidable."

"Sustained!" Judge Davidson declared. "Rephrase!"

"Before we get to Patience Stanhope's unfortunate death, I'd like to ask you if you've had previous contact with the defendant, Dr. Craig Bowman."

"I have."

"Can you explain the nature of your contact to the jury?"

"Objection, Your Honor," Randolph said with exasperation. "Immaterial. Or if it is material in some unfathomable way, then I object to Dr. Brown as an expert witness for bias."

"Counsels approach the bench, please," Judge Davidson said.

Tony and Randolph dutifully grouped at the side of the judge's bench.

"I'm going to be very upset if we have a repeat of Monday," Judge Davidson said. "You're both experienced lawyers. Behave as such! You both know the rules. As to the current line of questioning: Mr. Fasano! Am I to assume you have a relevant rationale for your current line of questioning?"

"Absolutely, Your Honor! The core of the plaintiff's case revolves about Dr. Bowman's attitude toward his patients in general and Patience Stanhope in particular. I call to the court's attention the deprecatory 'PP' classification. Dr. Brown has the ability to provide some insight into the development of these traits during Dr. Bowman's critical third year in medical school and during his residency training. Subsequent testimony will relate them directly to the case of Patience Stanhope."

"Okay, I will allow this line of questioning," Judge Davidson said. "But I want it related quickly to establish its relevance. Am I clear about that?"

"Perfectly clear, Your Honor," Tony said, unable to suppress a slight smile of satisfaction.

"Don't look so goddamned pained," Judge Davidson said to Randolph. "Your objection has been recorded. My judgment, provided Mr. Fasano is being totally honest about relevancy, is that the probative value will outweigh the prejudicial. I admit it is a judgment call, but that's why I'm here. In return I will grant the defense wide leniency on cross-examination. As for the question of bias, there's been ample opportunity to determine that during discovery, and it wasn't. But the issue can be examined on cross.

"And I want the pace to pick up," Judge Davidson said. "I've allocated this week for this trial, and here it is Wednesday already. For the sake of the jurors and my schedule, I want it to conclude on Friday unless there are some particularly extenuating circumstances."

Both lawyers nodded. Randolph repaired to his seat at the defense table while Tony returned to the podium.

"Objection overruled," Judge Davidson called out. "Proceed."

"Dr. Brown," Tony said after clearing his throat. "Would you tell the jury the nature of your contact with Dr. Craig Bowman?"

"My first contact was as his preceptor at Boston Memorial Hospital on his internal-medicine rotation during his third year of medical school."

"Could you explain what this means, since no one in this wonderful jury went to medical school?" Tony made a sweeping gesture down the line of jurors, some of whom nodded in agreement. Everyone was paying rapt attention, except for the plumber's assistant, who was focusing on his nails.

"Internal medicine is the most important rotation and the most demanding during the third year, and perhaps for the entire four years. It is the first time the students have prolonged contact with the patients from the patient's admission to their discharge, and they participate in the diagnosis and therapy under strict observation and supervision by the resident house staff and by the preceptor."

"Was this preceptor group that included Dr. Bowman a large group or a small group?"

"A small group: six students, to be exact. The teaching is intense."

"So you as the preceptor see the students on a regular basis."

"Every day."

"So you can observe the overall performance of each student."

"Very much so. It is a critical time in the student's life, and it marks the beginning of the individual's transformation from a student to a physician."

"So that attitudes that are observed or develop are important."

"Exceedingly so."

"And how do you rate your responsibility as a preceptor vis-à-vis attitudes?"

"Again, exceedingly important. As a preceptor, we have to balance the explicit attitudes toward patients as promulgated by the medical school versus the implicit attitudes often exhibited by the overworked and stressed house staff."

"There's a difference?" Tony questioned with exaggerated disbelief. "Can you explain the difference?"

"The amount of knowledge medical trainees must

assimilate and have immediate recall of is staggering and increasing every year. As pressed as residents are, they can sometimes lose sight of the ultimate humanistic aspects of what they are doing and which form the basis of professionalism. There are also defensive coping mechanisms in the face of suffering, dying, and death that are not healthy."

Tony shook his head in bewilderment. "Let me ask you if I have this correct. In simplified terms, there can be a tendency on the part of medical trainees to devalue individual people, like losing sight of the trees by paying too much attention to the forest."

"I suppose," Dr. Brown said. "But it is important not to trivialize this issue."

"We'll all try," Tony said with a short chuckle, which brought a few tentative smiles from the jurors. "Now, let's get back to the defendant, Dr. Craig Bowman. How did he do during his rotation in third-year internal medicine?"

"Generally excellent. In the group of six students, he was far and away the most knowledgeable and the most prepared. I was often astonished at his recall. I remember one episode of asking what a patient's BUN was."

"The BUN is a laboratory test?" Tony asked.

"Yes. I asked it more as a rhetorical question, to emphasize that knowledge of kidney function was key in the treatment of the patient's condition. Dr. Bowman rattled if off without hesitation, making me wonder if he had made it up, a frequent medical student ploy to cover unpreparedness. Later, I looked it up. It was exactly right."

"So Dr. Bowman got a good grade for the course."

"He got an A."

"Yet you qualified excellent by saying 'generally excellent.' "

"I did."

"Can you tell us why?"

"I had a nagging feeling, which I again got while
supervising Dr. Bowman when he was a resident at the
Boston Memorial Hospital."

"And what was this feeling?"

"I had the impression that his personality—"

"Objection!" Randolph called out. "Foundation: The
witness is neither a psychiatrist or psychologist."

"Overruled," Judge Davidson said. "As a physician,
the witness has had exposure to those fields, the amount
of which can be challenged on cross. The witness may
proceed."

"It was my impression that Dr. Bowman's desire to
succeed and his lionization of our then chief resident
made him view patients as a means to compete. He
actively sought out the most difficult patients so his presentations were intellectually the most interesting and
achieved the widest acclaim."

"In other words, it was your impression Dr. Bowman
saw patients as a way to further his career?"

"Essentially, yes."

"And that kind of attitude is not consistent with the
current concept of professionalism?"

"That's correct."

"Thank you, doctor," Tony said. He paused and
looked from one juror to another, making eye contact
with each, allowing the testimony to sink in.

Jack leaned over toward Alexis and whispered, "Now
I understand what you said about Tony Fasano; this guy
is good. Now he's putting academic medicine and its

inherent competitiveness on trial along with concierge medicine."

"What's bothering me is that he's changing Craig's successes into a liability in anticipation of Randolph trying to do the opposite."

When Tony recommenced his questioning, he zeroed in on the Patience Stanhope episode with a vengeance. In short order, he got Dr. Brown to testify how important it was to begin treatment for victims of a heart attack absolutely as soon as possible and that from reviewing the records Patience's chances of survival had substantially diminished due to Craig's delay in confirming the diagnosis.

"Just a few more questions, Dr. Brown," Tony said. "Are you acquainted with Dr. William Tardoff?"

"Yes, I am."

"Are you aware he trained at Boston University?"

"I am."

"And likewise are you acquainted with Dr. Noelle Everette, and are you aware that she trained at Tufts?"

"I am, on both accounts."

"Does it surprise you that three cardiology experts from our area's three prestigious medical schools all concur that Dr. Craig Bowman did not meet the standard of care in relation to Patience Stanhope?"

"It does not. It merely shows unanimity on the issue of the need for rapid treatment of heart attack victims."

"Thank you, doctor. No more questions." Tony picked up his papers from the lectern and walked back to the plaintiff's table. Both his assistant and Jordan acknowledged his performance with pats on the arm.

Randolph slowly stood to his commanding height and approached the podium. He adjusted his jacket and put one of his heavy, thick-soled, wingtip lawyer shoes on the rail.

"Dr. Brown," Randolph began, "I agree that there is unanimity on the need of treating heart attack victims as soon as possible in an appropriately equipped facility. However, that is not the issue before the court. The issue involves whether or not Dr. Bowman met the standard of care."

"Insisting on going to the Stanhope residence rather than meeting the victim at the hospital caused a delay."

"But prior to Dr. Bowman's arrival at the Stanhope residence, there was not a definitive diagnosis."

"According to the plaintiff's testimony at deposition, Dr. Bowman told him his wife was having a heart attack."

"That was the plaintiff's testimony," Randolph said, "but it was the defendant's testimony that he specifically said a heart attack must be ruled out. He did not categorically say Patience Stanhope was having what you doctors call a myocardial infarction, or MI. If there had not been a heart attack, there would not have been a delay. Is that not true?"

"That is true, but she had a heart attack. That's been documented. It was also in the record she had a questionable stress test."

"But my point is that Dr. Bowman did not know for certain Patience had had an MI," Randolph said. "And he will testify to that in this court. But let us turn our attention to your earlier testimony about medical school. Let me ask you if you got an A in your third-year rotation on internal medicine?"

"I did."

"Did all your fellow students in your preceptor group get A's?"

"No, they did not."

"Did they all want to get A's?"

"I suppose."

"How do you get into medical school? Must you routinely get A's in your premedical curriculum?"

"Of course."

"And how do you get the most coveted residencies, like at the Boston Memorial Hospital?"

"By getting A's."

"Is it not hypocritical for academicians to decry competition as antihumanistic and yet base the whole system upon it?"

"They do not have to be mutually exclusive."

"Perhaps in the best of worlds, but reality is something different. Competition does not breed compassion in any field. As you eloquently testified, medical students must absorb a staggering amount of information, which is what they are graded on. And one further question in this regard. In your experience both as a student and as a preceptor, is there competition for the, quote, 'most interesting patients' rather than the routine degenerative afflictions?"

"I guess there is."

"And that's because their presentations gather the most acclaim."

"I suppose."

"Which suggests that all of the students, but particularly the top students, to a degree use the patients both to learn from and advance their careers."

"Perhaps."

"Thank you, doctor," Randolph said. "Now, let's turn to the issue of medical house calls. What is your professional impression of house calls?"

"They are of limited value. One doesn't have access to the tools that are necessary to practice twenty-first-century medicine."

"So doctors generally are not in favor of house calls. Would you agree?"

"I would. Besides the lack of equipment, it represents an inappropriate utilization of resources, since there is too much downtime traveling to and from the home. In the same time frame, many more patients could be seen."

"So it is inefficient."

"Yes, you could say that."

"What is the opinion of patients about house calls?"

"Objection!" Tony called out, semi-rising from his chair. "Hearsay."

Judge Davidson snapped off his reading glasses and glared down at Tony with irritable disbelief.

"Overruled!" he snapped. "As a patient, which we all are at some point, Dr. Brown would be talking from experience. Proceed."

"Would you like me to repeat my question?" Randolph asked.

"No," Dr. Brown said. He hesitated. "Patients generally like house calls."

"How do you think Patience Stanhope felt about house calls?"

"Objection!" Tony said, rising again. "Supposition. There's no way the witness would know how the deceased felt about house calls."

"Sustained," Judge Davidson said with a sigh.

"I assume you read the medical records supplied to the plaintiff."

"Yes, I read them."

"So you are aware that Dr. Bowman made many

house calls to tend to Patience Stanhope prior to the evening in question, often in the middle of the night. From reading these records, what was the usual diagnosis on these visits?"

"Anxiety reaction manifesting itself mostly in gastrointestinal complaints."

"And the treatment?"

"Symptomatic and placebo."

"Was pain ever involved?"

"Yes."

"Where was the pain?"

"Mostly low abdominal but occasionally midepigastric."

"Pain in the latter location is occasionally reported as chest pain. Is that correct?"

"Yes, that's correct."

"From your reading of the record, would you say that Patience Stanhope exhibited at least some evidence of hypochondriasis?"

"Objection!" Tony called out but stayed in his chair. "Hypochondriasis is never mentioned in the record."

"Overruled," Judge Davidson said. "The court would like to remind the plaintiff's attorney that the witness is his medical expert."

"From reading the record, I believe it would be a safe assumption that some element of hypochondriasis was involved."

"Does the fact that Dr. Bowman made repeated house calls, which you have said most doctors do not favor, often in the middle of the night to a woman with avowed hypochondriasis, say something to you as a physician about Dr. Bowman's attitude and compassion for his patients?"

"No, it does not."

Randolph stiffened with surprise, and his eyebrows rose. "Your response defies rationality. Can you explain?"

"It is my understanding that house calls are one of the perquisites that patients expect when they pay high retainer fees, sometimes as high as twenty thousand dollars a year, to be part of a concierge medical practice. Under such a circumstance, one cannot say Dr. Bowman's making house calls necessarily reflects beneficence or altruism."

"But it might."

"Yes, it might."

"Tell me, Dr. Brown, are you biased against concierge medicine?"

"Of course I'm biased against concierge medicine," Dr. Brown sputtered. Up until that moment, he had maintained a detached coolness, not too dissimilar to Randolph's. It was clear that Randolph's questions had challenged him.

"Can you tell the court why you feel so strongly?"

Dr. Brown took a breath to calm himself. "Concierge medicine flies in the face of one of the three basic principles of medical professionalism."

"Perhaps you could elaborate."

"Of course," Dr. Brown said, lapsing into his familiar professional role. "Besides patient welfare and patient autonomy, the principle of social justice is a key underpinning of twenty-first-century medical professionalism. The practice of concierge medicine is the absolute opposite of trying to eliminate discrimination in health care, which is the key issue of social justice."

"Do you believe that your strong feelings in this

regard might compromise your ability to be impartial concerning Dr. Bowman?"

"I do not."

"Perhaps you could tell us why, since, to use your words, it 'flies in the face' of rationality."

"As a well-informed internist, Dr. Bowman knows that the symptoms women experience with myocardial infarction do not follow the classic symptoms experienced by men. As soon as an internist thinks about a heart attack in a female, particularly a postmenopausal female, he should act as if it were a heart attack until proven otherwise. There's a parallel in pediatrics: If the thought of meningitis occurs to a physician with a pediatric patient, the physician is obligated to proceed as if it is and do a spinal tap. Same with a female and a possible heart attack. Dr. Bowman suspected a heart attack, and he should have acted accordingly."

"Dr. Brown," Randolph said. "It is often said that medicine is more of an art than a science. Can you tell us what that means?"

"It means that factual information is not enough. A doctor must use his judgment as well, and since this is not an objective arena that can be studied, it is labeled an art."

"So scientific medical knowledge has its limits."

"Exactly. No two humans are exactly the same, even identical twins."

"Would you say that the situation Dr. Bowman faced on the evening of September eighth, 2005, when he was called to see for the second time in the same day a woman whom he knew was hypochondriacal called for a large measure of judgment?"

"All medical situations call for judgment."

"I'm asking specifically about the evening in question."

"Yes. It would have called for a large measure of judgment."

"Thank you, doctor," Randolph said, gathering up his notes. "No more questions."

"The witness may be excused," Judge Davidson said. Then, turning to the jurors, he added, "It is nearing the noon hour, and it looks to me as if you could all use some sustenance. I know I could. Remember not to discuss the case with anyone or among yourselves." He cracked the gavel. "Court's adjourned until one thirty."

"All rise," the court officer called out as the judge stepped down from the bench and disappeared into his chambers.

CHAPTER ELEVEN

Alexis, Craig, and Jack had found a small, noisy sandwich shop that looked out onto the broad Government Center esplanade. Randolph had been invited, but he'd begged off, claiming he had preparation to do. It was a beautiful late-spring day, and the esplanade was full of people escaping from their confining offices for a bit of sunshine and fresh air. Boston struck Jack as an out-door city much more so than New York.

Craig had been his usual brooding self at first, but had begun to relax and join the conversation.

"You haven't mentioned the autopsy," Craig said suddenly. "What's the status?"

"It's in the hands of a funeral director at the moment," Jack said. "He's got to take the paperwork to the health department and arrange for opening the grave and transporting the coffin."

"So it's still a go?"

"We are trying," Jack said. "Earlier I was hoping it might happen this afternoon, but since there's been no word, I guess we'll have to aim for tomorrow."

"The judge wants the case to go to the jury on Friday," Craig said discouragingly. "Tomorrow might be

too late. I hate to put you through all this effort for nothing."

"Maybe it is futile," Alexis agreed dejectedly. "Maybe
it is all for nothing."

Jack looked from one to the other. "Hey, come on,
you guys. I don't see it for nothing. It gives me the
sense I'm doing something. And besides, I'm interested
the more I think about the cyanosis issue."

"Why exactly?" Alexis questioned. "Explain it to me
again."

"Don't get him started!" Craig said. "I don't want
to raise any false hopes. Let's analyze this morning's
proceedings."

"I didn't think you wanted to talk about it," Alexis
said with some surprise.

"Actually, I'd rather forget about it, but unfortunately, I don't have that luxury if we're going to make
any changes."

Both Craig and Alexis eyed Jack expectantly.

"What is this?" Jack questioned with a wry smile,
looking from one to the other. "An interrogation? Why
me?"

"You can be the most objective of all of us," Alexis
said. "That's obvious."

"How do you feel Randolph is doing, now that you've
seen more of him in action?" Craig asked. "I'm worried.
I don't want to lose this case, and not just because there
was no negligence involved. My reputation will be in the
gutter. That last witness had been my preceptor in medical school, as he said, and my attending as a resident. I
worshipped that guy, and still do professionally."

"I can understand how devastating and humiliating
this has to be," Jack replied. "With that said, I think

Randolph is doing a good job. He neutralized most of what Tony established with Dr. Brown. So I suppose I have to say from what I saw this morning it was a wash. The problem is that Tony is more entertaining, but that's not enough to switch attorneys in midstream."

"What Randolph didn't neutralize was Dr. Brown's powerful analogy about a pediatric patient and meningitis. He's right, because that is the way you have to respond to a postmenopausal female when you even think she might be having a heart attack. Women don't have the same symptoms as men in a surprising number of cases. Maybe I screwed up, because a heart attack did pass through my mind."

"Second-guessing oneself is a rampant tendency in physicians in every case of adverse outcome," Jack reminded Craig. "It's especially so when there's alleged malpractice. The reality is you bent over backward with this woman, who was actually taking advantage of you. I know it's not politically correct to say that, but it is true. With all her false alarms, calling you out in the middle of the night, there's no wonder your index of suspicion of real illness would have been down in the lower basement."

"Thank you," Craig said with his shoulders sagging. "It means a lot to me to hear you say that."

"The trouble is, Randolph must make the jury understand that. That's it in a nutshell. And keep in mind Randolph hasn't presented his case. You have your own experts who are willing to testify to exactly what I outlined."

Craig took a deep breath and let it out noisily. He nodded a few times. "You're right. I can't give up, but tomorrow I'll have to testify."

"I would think you would be looking forward to it," Jack said. "You are the one more than anyone else who knows exactly what happened and when."

"I understand that perfectly well," Craig said. "The problem is I despise Tony Fasano so much, I have trouble keeping my cool. You've read the deposition. He got to me. Randolph advised me not to appear arrogant; I appeared arrogant. Randolph advised me not to get into an argument; I got into an argument. Randolph advised me not to get angry; I got angry. Randolph advised me only to answer each question; I flew off on a tangent, trying to justify honest mistakes. I was terrible, and I'm afraid it might happen all over again. I'm not good at this."

"Consider your deposition a learning experience," Jack said. "And remember: The deposition lasted two days. The judge will not allow that. He's the one who wants this trial brought to an end by Friday."

"I suppose it boils down to the fact that I don't trust myself," Craig said. "The one good aspect of this whole damn affair is that it has forced me to look at myself in the proverbial mirror. The reason Tony Fasano got me to appear arrogant is because I am arrogant. I know it's not politically correct to say so, but I am the best doctor I know. I've had confirmation in so many different ways. I've always been one of the best students, if not the best, throughout my training, and I've become addicted to acclaim. I want to hear it, which is why the reverse, like what I'm hearing throughout this malpractice ordeal, is so goddamn distressing and humiliating."

Craig fell silent after his outburst. Both Alexis and Jack were dumbfounded and momentarily speechless. The waiter came over and bused away the dirty dishes.

Alexis and Jack glanced briefly at each other and went back to staring wide-eyed at Craig.

"Somebody say something!" Craig demanded.

Alexis spread her hands palms up and shook her head. "I don't quite know what to say. I don't know whether to respond emotionally or professionally."

"Try professionally. I think I need the reality check. I'm in free fall here. And you know why? I'll tell you why. When I went to college and worked my balls off, I thought it sucked but that once I got into medical school, I'd be home free. Well, medical school sucked, too, so I looked forward to residency. You're probably getting the picture. Well, residency was no picnic, yet around the corner was opening my practice. That's when reality really set in, thanks to insurance companies and managed care and all the bullshit that has to be endured."

Jack looked at Alexis. He could tell she was struggling with what to say to these sudden revelations, but he was hoping she'd come up with something, since he was incapable. He was shocked by Craig's monologue. Psychology was not his forte by any stretch of the imagination. There'd been a time when it was all he could do to hold himself together.

"Your insight is dramatic," Alexis began.

"Don't give me any patronizing bullshit," Craig snapped.

"Believe me, I'm not," Alexis said. "I'm impressed. Truly! What you are trying to communicate is that your romantic nature has been constantly suffering disillusionment as reality has failed to meet your idealized expectations. Every time you get to a goal, it was not what you thought it would be. That's tragic."

Craig rolled his eyes. "That sounds like bullshit to me."

"It's not," Alexis insisted. "Think about it."

Craig pressed his lips together and knitted his brows for a long moment. "Okay," he said finally. "It does make sense. Yet it seems like a damn convoluted way of saying, 'Things just haven't quite worked out.' But then again, I've never been up on psychologyspeak."

"You have been struggling with some conflicts," Alexis continued. "It's not been easy for you."

"Oh, really," Craig said with a touch of superciliousness.

"Now, don't get defensive," Alexis urged. "You specifically asked for my professional response."

"You're right! Sorry! Let me hear the conflicts."

"The easiest one is your conflict between clinical medicine and research medicine. That has caused you some anxiety in the past because of your need to apply yourself one hundred percent in any pursuit, but in this case, you've been able to strike a balance. A more problematic conflict is between devoting yourself to your practice or devoting yourself to your family. This has caused a lot of anxiety."

Craig stared back at Alexis but remained silent.

"For obvious reasons, I cannot be objective," Alexis continued. "What I'd like to do is encourage you to explore these insights of yours with a professional individual."

"I don't like to ask for help," Craig said.

"I know, but even that attitude says something that might be valuable for you to explore." Alexis turned to Jack. "Do you want to add anything?"

Jack raised his hands. "Nope. This is an arena I'm not

good at." Actually, what he was thinking was that he'd been struggling with his own conflicts—namely, whether to start a new family with Laurie, as he was scheduled to do come Friday. For many years he'd said no, he didn't deserve to be happy, and that another family would demean his first. But then as the years had gone by, it had changed to a fear of putting Laurie at risk. Jack had struggled with the admittedly irrational fear that his loving someone put them in jeopardy.

The conversation took a lighter turn, and Jack seized the moment to excuse himself to use his phone. Walking out onto the bricked esplanade, he dialed the OCME. He had meant to leave a message with Calvin's secretary. His hope was that Calvin would be out of the office at lunch. Unfortunately, that wasn't the case. It was the secretary who was out to lunch. Calvin answered the phone.

"When the hell are you getting yourself back here?" Calvin demanded when he heard Jack's voice.

"It's looking bad," Jack said. He then had to hold the phone away from his ear while Calvin cursed and carried on about Jack's irresponsibility. After Jack heard, "What the hell are you doing, anyway?" he put the phone back to his ear and explained the proposed autopsy. He told Calvin about being introduced to the Boston chief medical examiner, Dr. Kevin Carson.

"Really! How is that old southern boy?" Calvin questioned.

"Seemed fine to me. He was in the middle of a case when I met him, so we chatted only briefly."

"Did he ask for me?"

"Oh, yeah!" Jack lied. "He said to say hello."

"Well, tell him hello from me if you see him again. And then get back here. I don't have to tell you that you've got Laurie all up in arms with the big day just around the corner. You're not going to try to rush down here at the last minute, are you?"

"Of course not," Jack said. He knew that Calvin was one of the people from the office she'd insisted on inviting. If it had been up to him, he wouldn't have invited anyone other than Chet, his office mate. The office already knew too much about their private life.

After finding Craig and Alexis, whom Jack joined for a short stroll in the sunshine, they returned to the courthouse. When they arrived outside the courtroom, other people were just filing in. It was quarter after one. They followed suit.

Craig went through the bar with Randolph and his assistant. Jordan Stanhope was already at the plaintiff's table with Tony Fasano and Renee Relf. Jack guessed that Tony was giving Jordan last-minute advice before his testimony. Although the sound of his voice was lost in the general babble of the room, his lips were moving rapidly, and he was gesticulating with both hands.

"I have a nagging suspicion this is going to be pure theater this afternoon," Jack said as they worked their way into the same row they'd occupied that morning. Alexis had said she liked to be near the jurors to watch their expressions and gestures. At that moment, the jurors had yet to be brought in.

"I'm afraid you are right," Alexis said, taking her seat and putting her bag down on the floor in front of her.

Jack sat down and adjusted himself as best he could on the unforgiving oak. His eyes wandered aimlessly around the courtroom, taking in the bookcase filled with law books behind the judge's bench. Within the well was a blackboard on wheels in addition to the plaintiff's and defendant's tables, all of which stood on a speckled carpet. When Jack's eyes moved all the way to the right to take in the court officer's box, they overshot their mark. Once again he found himself confronting Franco's beady-eyed stare. In contrast with the morning, and thanks to the sun's current position, Jack could now see the man's eyes within their deep sockets. They were like two gleaming black marbles. Jack felt the urge to wave again, but rationality prevailed. He'd had his fun that morning. Being overly provocative made no sense whatsoever.

"Did you find Craig's comments at lunch as surprising as I did?" Alexis questioned.

Happy to break off with Franco, Jack swung around to face his sister. "I think astounding would be a better word. I don't mean to be cynical, but it seems out of character. Do narcissists recognize themselves as such?"

"Not usually, unless they are in therapy and motivated. Of course, I'm talking now about someone with a real, dysfunctional personality disorder, not just a personality trait, where most doctors fall."

Jack held his tongue on that issue. He wasn't about to get into an argument with Alexis about which group Craig belonged in. Instead, he asked, "Is this the kind of insight that's a temporary response to stress or a real change in self-knowledge?"

"Time will tell," Alexis said. "But I'll be hopeful. It would be something very positive. In a real way, Craig is a victim of a system that pushed him to compete and excel, and the only way he knew when he was excelling was when he got praise from his teachers, like Dr. Brown. As he admitted, he became addicted to that kind of approbation. Then, when he finished his training, he was cut off like an addict being denied his drug of choice while simultaneously feeling disillusioned about the reality of the kind of medicine he was forced to practice."

"I think that happens to a lot of doctors. They need praise."

"It didn't happen to you. How come?"

"It did to a degree, back when I was an ophthalmologist. Randolph got Dr. Brown to admit that it's due to the competitive way medical training is structured. But when I was a student, I wasn't as monomaniacal as Craig. I had other interests than just medicine. I only got an A-minus in my third-year internal-medicine rotation."

Jack started when his phone began to vibrate in his pocket. He'd taken it off the ring mode. Frantically, he tried to get it out of his pocket. For reasons he couldn't fathom, the phone always startled him.

"Is something bothering you?" Alexis asked, eyeing his contortions. He'd slid his pelvis forward to straighten himself out.

"The damn phone," Jack explained. At last he was able to pull it free. He glanced at the LCD. It was a 617 area code, meaning Boston. Then he remembered the number. It was the funeral home.

"I'll be right back," Jack said. He got up and quickly moved out of the row. Once again, he was conscious of Franco's stare, but Jack did not return it. Instead, he headed out of the courtroom. Only then did he answer the call.

Unfortunately, the reception was bad, so he disconnected. He quickly took the elevator down to the first floor and then out the door. He used his received-calls function to retrieve the number. A moment later, he had

Harold on the phone, and Jack apologized for the poor connection earlier.

"No problem," Harold said. "I have good news. The paperwork is done, the permits have been granted, and everything is arranged."

"Terrific," Jack said. "When? This afternoon?"

"No! That would have been a miracle. It will be tomorrow, mid-morning. It's the very best I could do. Both the vault truck and the backhoe are fully committed today."

Disappointed a miracle had not been forthcoming, Jack thanked the director and hung up. He stood for a few minutes, debating whether to call Laurie to let her know about the autopsy timing. Although he knew calling was appropriate, he was less than enthusiastic about doing it, since he had little doubt what her response would be. Then he had a cowardly idea. Instead of calling her landline at the office, where he'd probably get her, he had the idea of calling her cell phone and just leaving a message on her voicemail, since she rarely turned on her cell phone during the day. In that way, he'd avoid her immediate response and give her a chance to adjust before he phoned her that night. As the call went through, he was relieved to hear the recorded message.

With that mildly unpleasant task out of the way, Jack returned to his seat next to Alexis. Jordan Stanhope was in the witness box, and Tony was at the podium, but no one was talking. Tony was busy with his papers.

"What did I miss?" Jack whispered to Alexis.

"Nothing. Jordan was just sworn, and he's about to begin testifying."

"The autopsy is on for sometime tomorrow. The body is to be exhumed in the morning."

"That's good," Alexis said, but her reaction was not what Jack had expected.

"You're not sounding very enthusiastic."

"How can I be? As Craig said at lunch: Tomorrow might be too late."

Jack shrugged. He was doing the best he could.

"I know this is difficult for you," Tony called out in an empathetic voice so everyone in the courtroom could hear. "I will try to make this as short and painless as possible, but the jury needs to hear your testimony."

Jordan nodded appreciatively. Instead of the erect posture he had been maintaining at the plaintiff's table, he now had his shoulders hunched over, and instead of his previously neutral facial expression, he now had the corners of his mouth turned down in a look of despondency and despair. He was dressed in a black silk suit, white shirt, and black tie. Peeking from his breast pocket was a barely visible black pocket square.

"I suppose you miss your wife," Tony said. "She was a wonderful, passionate, cultured woman who loved life, wasn't she?"

"Good grief!" Jack moaned in a whisper to Alexis. "Having visited the man, this is going to make me sick. And I'm surprised at Randolph. I'm not a lawyer, but that's certainly a leading question. Why doesn't he object?"

"He told me that the testimony of the widow or widower is always the most problematic for the defense. He says that the best strategy is to get them off the stand as soon as possible, which means giving the plaintiff attorney rather free rein."

Jack nodded. The pain of losing a family member was an emotion that resonated with everyone as a fundamental human experience.

Jordan proceeded to wax cloyingly sentimental about Patience: how wonderful she was, how storybook their life together was, and how much he loved her. Tony asked additional leading questions whenever Jordan faltered.

As this stage of Jordan's testimony tediously proceeded, Jack turned his head and searched the spectator gallery. He saw Franco, but the man was watching the witness, which was a minor relief. Jack hoped bygones would remain bygones. He was looking for someone else, and he found her in the back row. It was Charlene. The woman looked quite fetching in her black mourning outfit. Jack shook his head. There were times when he truly couldn't believe the degeneracy of which humans were capable. Even if just for appearances, she shouldn't have been there.

As the eulogy dragged on, Jack began to get progressively antsy. There was no need for him to listen to the drivel the phony Jordan was offering. He glanced at the back of Craig's head. Craig was motionless, as if in a trance. Jack tried to imagine what it would be like if he were ensnared in such a nightmare. Jack hazarded a quick glance in Alexis's direction. She was concentrating intensely with her eyes slightly narrowed. He wished the best for her and was sorry there wasn't more he could do.

Just when Jack had decided he could not listen to another word of Jordan's testimony, Tony switched gears.

"Now let's talk about September eighth, 2005," Tony

said. "I guess your wife wasn't feeling so well that day. Could you tell us in your own words what happened?"

Jordan cleared his throat. He pulled his shoulders back and sat up straight. "It was mid-morning when I was first aware she was not feeling well. She called to me to come into her bedroom. I found her in great distress."

"What was she complaining about?"

"Pain in her abdomen, gas, and congestion. She said she was coughing more than usual. She said she'd not slept all night, and she couldn't take it any longer. She told me to call Dr. Bowman. She said she wanted him to come right over. She said she would not be able to go to the office."

"Were there any other symptoms?"

"She said she had a headache, and she felt hot."

"So that was it, as far as the symptoms were concerned: abdominal pain, gas, coughing, headache, and feeling hot."

"Essentially, yes. I mean, she always had a lot of complaints, but those were the main ones."

"Poor woman," Tony said. "And it was hard on you, too, I presume."

"We did our best to cope," Jordan said stiffly.

"Now, you called the doctor, and he did come over."

"Yes, he did."

"And what happened?"

"Dr. Bowman examined her and recommended that she take the medication he'd already prescribed for her digestive system. He also recommended she get out of bed and cut down on her smoking. He also told her he thought she was more anxious than usual and suggested she try a small dose of an antidepressant medication, which she was to take at bedtime. He said he thought it was worth trying."

"Was Patience satisfied with these recommendations?"

"No. She wanted an antibiotic, but Dr. Bowman refused. He said she didn't need one."

"Did she follow the doctor's recommendations?"

"I don't know what medications she took, but she did eventually get out of bed. I thought she was doing quite a bit better. Then around five, she said she was going back to bed."

"Did she complain of anything at that point?"

"Not really. I mean, she always had a few complaints, which is why she was going back to bed."

"What happened next?"

"She suddenly called me sometime around seven to come to her bedroom. She wanted me to call the doctor again because she felt terribly."

"Did she have the same complaints as that morning?"

"No, they were completely different."

"What were they now?" Tony asked.

"She had chest pain that she'd had for an hour."

"Which was different from the abdominal pain she had in the morning?"

"Completely different."

"What else?"

"She was weak, and she said she had vomited a little. She could barely sit up, and she said she was numb and had a feeling as if she were floating. And she said she was having difficulty breathing. She was very ill."

"It sounds like a very serious circumstance. It must have been frightening."

"I felt very upset and worried."

"So," Tony intoned for dramatic effect, "you called the doctor, and what did you say?"

"I told him Patience was very sick, and she should go to the hospital."

"And how did Dr. Bowman respond to your urgent request to go to the hospital immediately?"

"He wanted me to describe her symptoms."

"And you did? You told him what you told us today?"

"Almost word for word."

"And what was Dr. Bowman's response? Did he tell you to call an ambulance and say he'd meet you at the hospital?"

"No. He kept asking me more questions, such that I had to go back to Patience and ask her."

"Let me make sure I understand. You told him your wife was in this terrible condition, and he had you going back to her multiple times to ask specific details. Is that what you are saying?"

"That's precisely what I am saying."

"During this question-and-answer period, while valuable time was passing, did you again mention your belief she should go directly to the hospital without delay?"

"Yes, I did. I was terrified."

"And you should have been terrified, since your wife was dying before your eyes."

"Objection," Randolph said. "Argumentative and prejudicial, and move to strike."

"Sustained," Judge Davidson said. He looked at the jury. "You will disregard that last statement by Mr. Fasano, and it should play no part in your consideration of this case." He then switched his attention to Tony. "I warn you, counsel, I will not tolerate any more comments like that."

"I apologize to the court," Tony said. "My emotions overcame my better judgment. It won't happen again."

Alexis leaned toward Jack. "Tony Fasano scares me. He is slick. He knew what he was doing."

Jack nodded in agreement. It was like watching a street fighter in a no-holds-barred brawl.

Tony Fasano went to the plaintiff's table for a drink. Out of the view of the judge, Jack caught him give a wink to his associate, Renee Relf.

Back at the podium, Tony returned to the narrative. "During your telephone conversation with Dr. Bowman while your wife was gravely ill, did he mention the word *heart attack*?"

"Yes, he did."

"Did he say she was having a heart attack?"

"Yes. He said that was what he was thinking."

Jack noticed Craig lean over and whisper something to Randolph. Randolph nodded.

"Now," Tony continued. "When Dr. Bowman arrived at your house and saw Patience, he acted differently than he had on the phone. Is that correct?"

"Objection," Randolph said. "Leading."

"Sustained," Judge Davidson said.

"Mr. Stanhope, would you tell us what happened when Dr. Bowman arrived at your home the night of September eighth of this past year."

"He was shocked at Patience's condition and told me to call an ambulance immediately."

"Had Patience's condition changed dramatically between your telephone conversation with Dr. Bowman and his arrival?"

"No, it had not."

"Did Dr. Bowman say anything to you at that point that you found inappropriate?"

"Yes. He blamed me for not having described Patience's condition adequately."

"Did that surprise you?"

"Of course it surprised me. I had told him how bad she was, and I had urged more than once that she should be taken directly to the hospital."

"Thank you, Mr. Stanhope. I appreciate your testimony about this tragic event. I have one more question: When Dr. Bowman arrived that fateful night, what was he wearing? Can you remember?"

"Objection," Randolph said. "Immaterial."

Judge Davidson twirled his pen and looked at Tony. "Is this relevant or mere embellishment?"

"Very relevant, Your Honor," Tony said, "as will be clear with testimony from the very next plaintiff witness."

"Objection overruled," Judge Davidson said. "Witness may answer the question."

"Dr. Bowman arrived in a tuxedo with a young woman in a low-cut dress."

Some of the jurors exchanged glances with their immediate neighbors, as if wondering what he or she was thinking.

"Did you recognize the young woman?"

"Yes, I had seen her at Dr. Bowman's office, and he said she was his secretary."

"Did their formal attire strike you as odd or significant?"

"Both," Jordan said. "It was odd because it suggested they were en route to a social function, and I knew Dr. Bowman was married, and significant because I wondered if their attire had anything to do with Dr. Bowman's decision to come to the house rather than meet us at the hospital."

"Thank you, Mr. Stanhope," Tony said, gathering his papers. "No more questions."

"Mr. Bingham," Judge Davidson said, nodding in Randolph's direction.

Randolph hesitated for a moment. It was clear he was in deep thought. Even when he stood up and approached the podium, he seemed to be moving by reflex rather than by conscious intention. The courtroom was hushed in attentive expectancy.

"Mr. Stanhope," Randolph began. "I will ask you only a few questions. All of us at the defense table, including Dr. Bowman, are saddened by your loss and can appreciate how difficult it is for you to revisit that fateful evening, so I will be brief. Let us go back to the telephone conversation you had with Dr. Bowman. Do you recall telling Dr. Bowman that it was your recollection that Patience had never complained of chest pain before?"

"I'm not certain. I was very upset."

"And yet with Mr. Fasano, your memory of the same telephone conversation seemed impressively complete."

"I might have said she'd never had chest pain. I'm just not sure."

"I should remind you that in your deposition, you did so state. Should I read it to you?"

"No. If it is there, then it is true. And now that you remind me, I believe I did say she'd never had chest pain. It was eight months ago, and I was under duress. The deposition was much closer to the event."

"I can appreciate that, Mr. Stanhope. But I'd like you

to search your memory for Dr. Bowman's response. Do you recall what he said?"

"I don't believe I do."

"He corrected you and reminded you she had had chest pain on several previous occasions, for which he came to the house."

"Maybe he did."

"So it seems that your memory of what was said during this phone conversation is not as clear as we were led to believe just a few minutes ago."

"The phone conversation was eight months ago, and I was frantic at the time. I don't think it's unreasonable."

"It is certainly not unreasonable, yet you are certain Dr. Bowman specifically said Patience was having a heart attack."

"He said that it had to be ruled out."

"Your choice of words suggests that Dr. Bowman was not the one who brought up the subject."

"I brought up the subject. I asked him if that was what he was thinking. I guessed, from the questions he was asking me to ask Patience."

"Saying it has to be ruled out is a lot different than stating Patience was having a heart attack. Would it surprise you if I told you Dr. Bowman never used the words *heart attack* in your conversation?"

"We talked about it. That I remember."

"You brought it up. He merely said, 'It has to be ruled out.' He never even said the term."

"Maybe that is the way it happened, but what difference does it make?"

"I believe it makes a lot of difference. Do you believe that whenever someone has chest pain—like yourself, for instance—and a doctor is on call, he or she thinks a heart attack has to be ruled out?"

"I assume so."

"So when you told Dr. Bowman Patience had chest pain, it is not surprising that Dr. Bowman would think it had to be ruled out, even if the chances were very, very small."

"I suppose not."

"And on those previous house calls Dr. Bowman made to see Patience in response to a complaint of chest pain, what was the ultimate diagnosis on each occasion?"

"It was assumed to be intestinal gas."

"Correct! Intestinal gas in the splenic flexure of the colon, to be exact. It was not heart attacks or heart pain, since ECGs and enzymes were normal and stayed normal on subsequent examinations."

"They were not heart attacks."

"Dr. Bowman made a lot of house calls to attend to Patience. In fact, the records show a rate of visitation approximately once per week over an eight-month interval. Is that consistent with your recollection?"

Jordan nodded, which brought an admonition from the judge: "The witness will speak up for the benefit of the court reporter and the record."

"Yes," Jordan called out.

"Was it Patience's preference to be seen at home?"

"Yes. She did not like to go to the doctor's office."

"Was she fond of hospitals?"

"She was terrified of hospitals."

"So by making house calls, Dr. Bowman was catering to your wife's needs and wishes."

"Yes, he was."

"Since you are semiretired and spent a good deal of

your time at home, you had a lot of opportunity to interact with Dr. Bowman, with his making so many house
calls."

"Indeed," Jordan agreed. "We spoke on each visit and
were quite congenial."

"I assume you were always in attendance when Dr.
Bowman attended Patience."

"Either I or our maid."

"During any of these conversations with Dr. Bowman,
which I assume dealt primarily with Patience, did the
term *hypochondriasis* come up?"

Jordan's eyes darted to Tony's and then back to Randolph. "Yes, it did."

"And I assume you know the definition of the term."

Jordan shrugged. "I suppose."

"It's applied to an individual who has a preoccupation
with normal sensations and functions and believes them
to be indicative of severe problems needing medical
attention. Is that generally your understanding of the
term?"

"I would not have been able to define it quite like
that, but yes, that's my understanding."

"Did Dr. Bowman ever apply that term to Patience?"

"He did."

"Did he use the term in a derogatory context?"

"No, he did not. He said that it was always important
to remember that hypochondriacs could have real illnesses as well as their psychological ones, and even if
their imaginary illness were not real, they still suffered."

"A few moments ago, when Mr. Fasano was questioning you, you testified that Patience's condition did not
change dramatically between your telephone conversation and Dr. Bowman's arrival."

"That's correct."

"During your conversation, you told Dr. Bowman that you believed Patience was having some difficulty breathing. Do you remember that?"

"Yes, I do."

"You also said you believed she appeared rather blue. Do you remember that as well?"

"I don't know if those were my exact words, but it is the gist of what I was saying."

"I contend that it was exactly what you said or extremely close. In your deposition, you agreed it was extremely close. Would you like to read the relevant portions?"

"If I said it was extremely close, then it was. At this point, I don't remember."

"When Dr. Bowman arrived, he found Patience totally blue and hardly breathing at all. Would you say that was a big difference from your description over the phone?"

"I was trying to do my best in a difficult situation. I made it very clear to him she was very ill and that she should be seen at the hospital."

"One further question," Randolph said, straightening his tall, lean frame to its six-foot-plus limit. "Taking into account Patience's long history of hypochondriasis, along with a number of previous episodes of chest pain caused by intestinal gas, do you believe on the evening of September eighth, 2005, that Dr. Bowman thought Patience Stanhope was having a heart attack?"

"Objection," Tony cried, getting to his feet. "Hearsay."

"Sustained," Judge Davidson said. "The question can be posed to the defendant himself during his testimony."

"No more questions," Randolph said. He strode back toward the defense table.

"Do you wish to redirect?" Judge Davidson asked Tony.

"No, Your Honor," Tony said.

As Jordan stepped down from the witness box, Jack turned to Alexis. He flashed her a thumbs-up on Randolph's cross-examination, but then his eyes went to the jurors. They didn't strike him as being nearly as riveted as he had been. Instead of many of them leaning forward as they'd been earlier, they were all leaning back in their chairs, arms folded across their chests, except for the plumber's assistant. He was back to fussing with his nails.

"Plaintiff, call your next witness!" Judge Davidson ordered.

Tony stood up and bellowed, "Ms. Leona Rattner to the stand, please."

CHAPTER TWELVE

Jack twisted around. He had a mildly prurient interest in seeing the nubile hussy turned spurned-lover vixen. Having read her racy deposition, he was sure her testimony was going to be a show.

Leona came through the courtroom door and strode unhesitantly down the courtroom's central aisle. In contrast to Craig's description of her typically sexy apparel, she was now dressed demurely in a dark blue pants suit with a white blouse buttoned to the neck. Jack assumed it was at Tony Fasano's suggestion. The only hint of her normal style was extra-high-heeled sandals that made her walk slightly wobbly.

Although the woman's clothing was modest, Jack could immediately appreciate what had attracted Craig. Her individual features were not special, nor was her straw-blonde, obviously dyed hair with its dark roots. But her skin was flawless and radiant. She was the picture of youthful sensuality brazenly projected.

Leona went through the bar with a saucy shake of her head. She knew she was onstage and she loved it.

Jack hazarded a glance in Alexis's direction. Her face was set in stone, reflecting a determined expression with her lips pressed firmly together. Jack had the sense that she was steeling herself for what was coming. He thought that was a good self-preservation ploy, having read Leona's deposition.

The court clerk administered the oath while Leona held her right hand heavenward. "Do you swear or affirm to tell the truth, the whole truth, and nothing but the truth so help you God?"

"I do," Leona said in a slightly nasal voice. She glanced modestly at the judge through eyelashes heavy with mascara as she stepped up into the witness box.

Tony took his time getting to the podium and arranging his notes. Then he hiked one of his tasseled loafers onto the brass rail, as was his habit, and began the direct. First off, he established a short biography: where she was born (Revere, Massachusetts); where she'd gone to high school (Revere, Massachusetts); where she was currently living (Revere, Massachusetts). He asked how long she had worked in Dr. Craig Bowman's office (more than a year) and where she was going to night school three nights a week (Bunker Hill Community College).

As Leona answered these neutral initial questions, Jack had more of an opportunity to observe her. He noticed she and Tony shared the same accent, which to him seemed as much like a Brooklyn accent as a Boston accent. Jack could also see more evidence of the personality traits Craig had described: opinionated, high-spirited, and willful. What he had yet to observe was the mercurial petulance.

"Now, let's talk about your relationship with your boss, Dr. Craig Bowman," Tony said.

"Objection," Randolph said. "Immaterial."

"Counsels, approach the bench!" Judge Davidson ordered irritably.

Randolph complied immediately. Tony motioned to Leona to sit tight and followed.

Using his reading glasses similar to the way a person uses a newspaper roll to threaten a dog, Judge Davidson directed his attention to Tony. "This better not be an elaborate sham, and I want to be assured again that this social crap is germane to the plaintiff's case. Otherwise, we are going to be dealing with a mistrial and potentially a directed verdict for the doctor."

"It's absolutely germane. The witness will testify that Dr. Bowman did not consider meeting Patience Stanhope at the hospital because of their relationship and their evening plans."

"All right. I'm going to give you a lot of rope, and I hope you don't hang yourself with it. I'm going to allow the social testimony for the reasons I've already given in the past, specifically, the assurance that its probative value outweighs its prejudicial value." Judge Davidson waved the glasses in Randolph's direction. "As far as the defense is concerned, I will allow you wide latitude on your cross-examination, which Mr. Fasano will respect. Now, within this framework, I want to move things along. Between the two of you, these interruptions are annoying me to death. Understood?"

"Yes, Your Honor," both counsels echoed in unison. They turned on their heels and returned to their respective spots.

"Objection overruled," Judge Davidson called out for the court reporter's benefit. "Continue the direct of Ms. Rattner."

"Miss Rattner," Tony said. "Could you tell the court about your relationship with Dr. Bowman?"

"Sure. At first I was, like, just one of the employees.

But about a year ago, I could tell Dr. Bowman was giving me the eye. You know what I'm saying?"

"I think I do," Tony responded. "Go on!"

"At first I was embarrassed and everything because I knew he was married with kids and the whole works. But then one evening when I was working late, he came into the file room where I was working and started talking. One thing led to another, and we began hanging out with each other. I mean, it was okay since I found out he had moved out of his house and gotten an apartment in Boston."

"Was this a platonic affair?"

"Hell, no! He was a tiger. It was a very physical relationship. We even did it on the examination table one afternoon at the office. He said his wife didn't like sex and, besides, she'd gained all this weight after she'd had her kids and never lost it. It was like he was starving and needed a lot of attention, so I went out of my way. A lot of good it did me!"

"Your Honor, this is beyond—" Randolph began, rising to his feet.

"Sit down, Mr. Bingham," Judge Davidson snapped. Then he looked at Tony over his reading glasses. "Mr. Fasano, it is time to establish foundation, and it better be convincing."

"Of course, Your Honor," Tony said. He made a quick detour to take a sip of water at the plaintiff's table. Then, running his tongue around his lips as if they were dry, he returned to the podium and shuffled his papers.

There was a murmur of expectancy from the spectator area, and the jurors appeared more attentive than usual, with many leaning forward. Salacious material never failed to titillate.

Once again, Jack furtively glanced at Alexis out of the corner of his eye. She'd not moved. Her grim expression had not changed. He couldn't help but feel a tender, brotherly compassion for her. He hoped her professional psychology training could provide some element of ego protection, as humiliating as the situation was.

"Miss Rattner," Tony began. "On the evening of September eighth, 2005, you were in Dr. Bowman's Boston apartment, where you were at that time residing."

"That's correct. I'd moved from the dump where I'd been in Somerville, because the landlord was an ass."

Judge Davidson leaned over toward Leona. "The witness will restrict herself to answering questions and refrain from spontaneous monologues."

"Yes, Your Honor," Leona said meekly through batting eyelashes.

"Could you tell the jury in your own words what you and Dr. Bowman were doing that evening?"

"What we had planned to do and what we did were two different things. We had planned to go to Symphony Hall for some kind of performance. Craig, I mean, Dr. Bowman, was on this Renaissance-man kick to make up for lost time, and he had bought me this terrific pink dress that came down low." She traced a deeply concave arc across her chest with her finger. "We were both excited. The most fun was arriving at the Symphony Hall with all the bustle and excitement. I mean, the music was pretty good, too, but walking in was the best part for both of us. Dr. Bowman had season tickets and the seats were way down in the front. It was like being on stage walking down the aisle, which is why he liked me to look real sexy."

"It sounds as if Dr. Bowman liked to show you off."

"Something like that, " Leona agreed. "It was okay with me. I thought it was fun."

"But to do this, you had to get there on time or maybe a little early."

"That's right! If you got there late, sometimes you had to wait until intermission to sit down, and it wasn't the same."

"What happened on September eighth, 2005?"

"We were rushing around getting ready to go when Dr. Bowman's cell phone rang."

"I presume it was Jordan Stanhope," Tony said.

"It was, and it meant the evening was up in the air because Dr. Bowman decided he had to make a house call."

"Did you stay at the apartment while Dr. Bowman made the house call?"

"No. Dr. Bowman told me to come. He said if it turned out to be a false alarm, we could go directly to the concert from the Stanhopes'. He said the Stanhope house was not that far away from Symphony Hall."

"Meaning it was closer than Newton Memorial Hospital."

"Objection," Randolph said. "Lack of foundation. The witness said nothing about Newton Memorial Hospital."

"Sustained," Judge Davidson said with a tired voice. "Jury will disregard! Proceed."

"Miss Rattner," Tony intoned, licking his lips as he was wont to do. "On the way to the Stanhope residence, did Dr. Bowman say anything to you about his sense of Patience Stanhope's condition? Did he feel the house call he was about to make would be a false alarm?"

"Objection," Randolph said. "Hearsay."

"Sustained," Judge Davidson said with a sigh. "The witness will confine herself to Dr. Bowman's actual comments and not offer an opinion as to his mind-set."

"I repeat," Tony said, "did Dr. Bowman say anything to you about what he thought Patience Stanhope's condition was?"

Leona looked up at the judge. "I'm confused. He's asking, and you're telling me not to answer."

"I'm not telling you not to answer, dear," Judge Davidson said. "I'm telling you not to try to imagine what Dr. Bowman was thinking. He will be able to tell us that himself. Mr. Fasano is asking you what Dr. Bowman specifically said about Patience's condition."

"Okay," Leona said, finally understanding. "He said he was scared that the visit was legit."

"Meaning that Patience Stanhope was legitimately sick."

"Yes."

"Did he say anything about how he felt about patients like Patience Stanhope, the PPs, or problem patients?"

"That night while we were in the car?"

"Yes, that night."

"He said she was a hypochondriac, which he could not stand. He said hypochondriacs were the same to him as malingerers. I remember because I had to look the word up later. It means someone who fakes illness to get something they want. It's pretty bad."

"Looking up *malingerer* is very commendable. What motivated you?"

"I'm studying to be a medical lab technician or nursing assistant. I've got to know the lingo."

"Did Dr. Bowman ever say anything else to you about his feelings toward Patience Stanhope?"

"Oh, yeah!" Leona said with a fake laugh for emphasis.

"Could you explain to the jury when this occurred?"

"It was on the evening he was served with the lawsuit. We were at Sports Club/LA."

"And what exactly did he say?"

"It's what he didn't say. I mean, he ran off at the mouth like you wouldn't believe."

"Give the jury some sense of what you are talking about."

"Well, it's hard to remember the whole tirade. He said he hated her because she drove everybody crazy, including herself. He said she drove him crazy because all she ever talked about was her BMs and that sometimes she'd save it to show it to him. He also said she drove him crazy because she never did anything he said. He called her a hypochondriacal, clinging excuse for a wife, and an entitled bitch that demanded he hold her hand and listen to her complaints. He said her passing was a blessing to everybody, including herself."

"Wow!" Tony said, pretending he'd heard the testimony for the first time and was shocked. "So I guess it was your impression that from what Dr. Bowman had said, he was glad Patience Stanhope had died."

"Objection," Randolph said. "Leading."

"Sustained," Judge Davidson said. "Jurors will disregard."

"Tell us what you thought after Dr. Bowman's tirade."

"I thought he was glad she died."

"Hearing such a tirade, as you put it, you must have

thought Dr. Bowman was really upset. Did he say any-thing specific about his being sued, meaning that his performance and decision-making would be reasonably questioned in a court of law?"

"Yes. He said it was an outrage that the oddball bastard Jordan Stanhope was suing him for loss of consortium when he couldn't imagine Mr. Stanhope having sex or wanting to have sex with such a miserable hag."

"Thank you, Miss Rattner," Tony said, collecting his widely spread papers from the lectern's surface. "No more questions."

Once again, Jack glanced over at Alexis. This time, she met his eyes. "Well," she whispered philosophically, "what can Craig expect? He certainly dug his own hole. Leona's testimony was about as bad as I imagined it would be. Let's hope you can come up with something on the autopsy."

"Maybe Randolph can do something on cross. And don't forget Randolph has yet to start the case for the defense."

"I'm not forgetting. I'm just being realistic and put-ting myself in the place of one of the jurors. It doesn't look good. The testimony is convincingly making Craig sound like a completely different person than he is. He has his faults, but the way he cares about his patients is not one of them."

"I'm afraid you're right," Jack said.

CHAPTER THIRTEEN

NEWTON, MASSACHUSETTS
Wednesday, June 7, 2006
3:30 p.m.

Let me see the floor plan again," Renaldo said to Manuel. They were sitting in a black Chevrolet Camaro parked on a tree-lined side street around the corner from the Bowmans' residence. They were dressed in nondescript brown work clothes. On the backseat was a canvas carpetbag similar to those carried by plumbers for tools.

Manuel handed Renaldo the plans. They crinkled as Renaldo unrolled them. Renaldo was sitting behind the steering wheel. He had to fight to get the paper to flatten out enough to look at it.

"Here's the door we're going in," Renaldo said, pointing. "You oriented?"

Manuel leaned over, almost touching Renaldo's shoulder so the top of the page was pointing away from him. He was sitting in the front passenger seat.

"For shit sake," Renaldo complained. "It's not that complicated."

"I'm oriented!" Manuel said.

"What we have to do is locate all three of the girls fast so none of them has a chance to alert the others. You know what I'm saying?"

"Sure."

"So they'll either be here in the family room/kitchen,

probably watching TV," Renaldo said, pointing to the area on the plans, "or they will be in their separate bedrooms." He struggled to get to the second page. The plans wanted to roll back up into their original tight cylinder. He ended up tossing the first page into the backseat. "Here are the bedrooms along the back of the house," he said when he got the second page flattened. "And here are the stairs. You got it? We don't want to be searching, and it has to happen fast."

"I understand. But there's three of them and only two of us."

"It's not going to be hard to scare the shit out of them. The only one that might be trouble is the oldest, but if we can't handle this, we're in the wrong business. The plan is to tape them up fast. I mean, really fast. I don't want any screaming. Once we get them taped up with gags, then the fun begins. Okay?"

"Okay," Manuel said. He straightened.

"You have your gun?"

"Of course I have my gun." He pulled a snub-nosed thirty-eight out of his pocket.

"Put it away, for Christ's sake," Renaldo snapped. His eyes darted around to make sure there were no strollers. The area was quiet. Everyone was at work. The widely spaced houses seemed deserted.

"What about your mask and gloves?"

Manuel pulled those out of his other pocket.

"Good," Renaldo said. He checked his watch. "Okay, this is it. Let's move it!"

While Manuel got out of the car, Renaldo reached into the backseat and got the canvas bag. He joined Manuel, and they walked back to the intersection, turning right. They didn't hurry, nor did they talk. Due to the canopy of leaves, the street was shaded yet each house blazed in bright sunlight. An elderly woman was walking a dog in the distance, but she was heading away from them. A car approached and passed by without stopping. The driver ignored them.

Coming abreast of the Bowman property, they briefly stopped, looking up and down the street.

"Looks good," Renaldo said. "It's a go!"

Maintaining a normal gait, they crossed the edge of the Bowmans' front lawn. They appeared like two workmen on a legitimate errand. They entered the treeline separating the two neighboring homes and were soon even with the backs of the houses. Eyeing the back of the Bowman house, they could see the door they intended to enter. It was about forty feet away, across a patch of sun-drenched lawn.

"Okay," Renaldo said. "Time for the masks and gloves."

Each quickly donned the items: masks first, gloves second. They eyed each other and nodded.

Renaldo snapped open the canvas bag. He wanted to be certain he had everything. He handed Manuel a roll of duct tape, which Manuel pocketed. "Let's do it!"

Reflecting their professionalism, they were across the lawn and through the door in a blink of the eye and with almost no sound. Once inside, they hesitated and listened. They could hear a TV with canned laughter from the family room. Renaldo flipped a thumbs-up and motioned for Manuel to move forward. Treading lightly and moving quietly, they passed through the study and down the central corridor. Renaldo was in the lead. He stopped just shy of the arched entrance to the family room. Slowly, he looked around the edge of the arch, seeing an ever-expanding view first of the kitchen and then of progressively more of the family room. When he saw the girls, he pulled himself back. He raised two fingers, indicating two girls. Manuel nodded.

Renaldo then used his hand to indicate a wide, counterclockwise circle in the air to suggest they move through the kitchen, then approach the couch in front of the TV from the rear. Manuel nodded. Renaldo brandished his roll of duct tape. Manuel pulled out his.

After silently placing the canvas bag on the floor, Renaldo readied himself. He looked at Manuel, and Manuel indicated that he was ready.

Moving quickly but quietly, Renaldo followed the route he'd mapped out. The girls' heads could just be seen over the back of the brightly colored couch. The TV volume, which had seemed low when they'd first heard it, was not low, especially the laughing sequences. Renaldo and Manuel were able to move up directly behind the unsuspecting girls.

With a nod from Renaldo, each man sprang around either end of the couch and glommed on to the respective girl. The men were rough and decisive, grabbing the children by the necks and pressing their faces into the soft pillows of the couch. Both girls had made feeble reflex squawks, but the sounds were immediately muffled. Using their teeth, the men pulled off lengths of duct tape from each of their rolls, and, keeping their weight on the girls, they managed to bind each of their hands behind their backs. Almost simultaneously, they rolled the girls over. The girls gasped for breath, wide-eyed with terror. Renaldo put his finger over his closed lips to indicate that the girls must remain silent, but there was no need. Both girls did all they could do to satisfy their air hunger, and they were frightened to near paralysis.

"Where's your sister?" Renaldo hissed through clenched teeth. Neither girl spoke, watching their captors with unblinking intensity. Renaldo snapped his fingers at Manuel and pointed to Meghan, who was trembling in his grasp.

Manuel let go of Meghan long enough to pull out a square rag, which he roughly pressed into her mouth. She tried to resist by twisting her head from side to side, but it was to no avail. Manuel slapped a short piece of duct tape over the lower part of the girl's face, securing the gag. Rapidly, a second piece of tape was added, forcing Meghan to breathe loudly through her nose.

Seeing what had happened to Meghan, Christina quickly tried to be cooperative. "She's upstairs taking a shower," she cried breathlessly.

Renaldo rewarded her by quickly gagging her in the same fashion as Manuel had gagged Meghan. Then both men bound the girls' feet before yanking them upright and then together to tape them back to back. At that point, Renaldo gave them a push and they toppled over in an awkward heap, both still struggling for breath.

"Stay here!" Renaldo growled as he picked up his roll of duct tape.

Moving silently but quickly, Renaldo ascended the stairs. Once in the upstairs hallway he could hear the shower. It was a distant, soft, sibilant sound, which he followed, passing several bedrooms with open doors. The third door on the right opened into a bedroom unique in its disarray. Clothes, books, shoes, and magazines were haphazardly tossed about on the floor and on all horizontal surfaces.

Black thong panties and a bra were draped over the bathroom's marble threshold. From within the bathroom, clouds of steam billowed out into the room.

With rising anticipation, Renaldo quickly traversed the room, being careful to avoid the debris. He poked his head into the bathroom but could barely see through the dense mist. The mirror was completely fogged over.

It was a small bathroom with a pedestal sink, a toilet, and a low tub that also served as a shower. An opaque white shower curtain with black sea horses hung from a silver-colored rod, and it was moving both from the forces of the water and rising steam and also from occasional contact by the shower's occupant.

Renaldo briefly debated how best to handle the situation. With the other girls already secured, it really wasn't a problem. In fact, knowing the girl was naked was a turn-on, and that had to be factored in as well. He reached out with the roll of duct tape and placed it on the edge of the sink. He couldn't help but smile, thinking he was being paid to do something he might pay to do. He knew the girl in the shower was fifteen going on twenty-one, with a couple of knockers worth a second look.

After thinking about a few different alternatives, including waiting for the girl to finish and get out of the shower herself, Renaldo merely grabbed the shower curtain and whipped it back. It was a tension rod, and the force of Renaldo's jerk pulled the whole apparatus off the wall, and it tumbled onto the floor in a heap.

At the moment of the shower rod and curtain's disappearance, Tracy had her back to the shower with her head under the torrent, forcibly rinsing her thick tresses. She hadn't heard the clatter, but she must have felt the

surge of significantly cooler air because she leaned forward out of the gush of water and opened her eyes. As
soon as she caught sight of the black-ski-masked
intruder, she screamed.

Renaldo reached in and grabbed a handful of wet hair
and yanked Tracy from the bathtub. Her feet tripped on
the rim, and she fell headlong to the floor. Renaldo let
go of her hair and put a knee into the small of her back
while he lunged for her flailing wrists. Using decisive
strength, he forced her hands behind her back, snatched
the duct tape off the sink, and as he'd done downstairs,
used his teeth to pull a strip of tape from the roll. With
rapid movements, he wound the tape in and out and
around Tracy's wrists. Within only a few seconds, her
hands were securely bound.

Through this procedure, Tracy had maintained a
scream, but it was dampened by the sound of the shower.
Renaldo rolled her over. He pulled a square rag from his
pocket, balled it up, and began stuffing it into her
mouth. Tracy was a quantum stronger than Christina,
and she was able to resist until Renaldo straddled her and
used his knees to secure her head. Then she succeeded
in biting his finger, which infuriated him.

"Bitch!" he yelled. He slapped her hard, splitting her
lip. She still resisted, but he was able to get the gag into
her mouth and place several pieces of duct tape to hold
it in place. Then he got up and stared down at the
terrified teenager.

"Not bad." Renaldo commented as he took in Tracy's
nubile figure and the belly button piercing. His eyes
stopped at a small tattoo of a snake just north of her
mons pubis. "Already shaving your snatch, and you got

a tattoo. I wonder if Mommy and Daddy know that. Aren't you a little ahead of yourself, girl?"

Renaldo reached down and hooked a hand under one of Tracy's armpits and hoisted her roughly to her feet. She responded by bolting out of the bathroom, catching Renaldo off guard. He had to race to catch her before she got out of her bedroom.

"Not so fast, sister," Renaldo snarled, yanking her around to face him. "If you're smart and cooperative, you won't be hurt. If you're not, I guarantee you'll be a very sorry girl. Read me?"

Tracy stared defiantly back at her attacker with fiery eyes.

"Feisty thing, huh?" Renaldo questioned derisively. He glanced down at her breasts, which he found considerably more impressive with her upright posture. "And sexy, too. How many snakes have you had in that snake den of yours? I bet a lot more than your parents think, huh?" He nodded his head knowingly.

Tracy continued to glare at Renaldo, with her chest heaving from her adrenaline rush.

"Let me tell you what's going to happen here. You and me are going to march downstairs to the family room for a family reunion with your sisters. We'll tape you girls together so you'll be one big happy family unit. Then I'm going to tell you a few things I want you to tell your parents. Then we're out of here. Does that sound like a plan?"

With a push, Renaldo directed Tracy out into the hall. He still had ahold of her arm just above the elbow. When they came to the stairs, he urged her to descend.

In the family room, Manuel was dutifully standing over Meghan and Christina. Meghan was silently crying, as evidenced by her tears and the intermittent trembling of her torso. Christina was still wide-eyed with terror.

"Nice work," Manuel said as the naked Tracy was led over to the couch. He couldn't help eyeing Tracy as Renaldo had done.

"Sit the two up facing either end of the sofa," Renaldo commanded.

Manuel yanked the two preteens up and rotated them as Renaldo had directed.

Renaldo directed Tracy to sit on the sofa's edge with her back to her sisters. When she was in place, he wound tape around all three. When he was finished, he straightened up and checked his handiwork. Satisfied, he handed the tape to Manuel and told him to gather up their stuff.

"Listen, sweeties," Renaldo said to the girls, but mostly to Tracy, with whom he made direct eye contact. "We want you to deliver a message to your parents. But first let me ask you something. Do you know what an autopsy is? Just nod your head if you do!"

Tracy didn't move. She didn't even blink.

Renaldo slapped her again, further opening her split lip. A trickle of blood ran down her chin.

"I'm not going to ask you again. Nod or shake your head! Whatever is appropriate."

Tracy nodded quickly.

"Good!" Renaldo said. "Here's the message for Mommy and Daddy. No autopsy! You got that? No autopsy! Nod your head if you got it."

Tracy dutifully nodded.

"Okay. That's the main message: no autopsy. I could write it for you, but I don't think that's wise under the circumstances. Tell them if they ignore this warning that we will be back to visit you kids, and it won't be pretty.

You know what I'm saying? It will be bad, not like this time, because this is just a warning. It might not be tomorrow and maybe not next week, but sometime. Now, I want to know you understand the message so far. Nod your head if you do."

Tracy nodded. Some of the brashness had disappeared from her eyes.

"And the last part of the message is just as simple. Tell your parents to keep the police out of this affair. It's just between us and your parents. If they go to the police, I'm going to have to visit you again sometime, someplace. It's pretty clear. Are we on the same page about all this?"

Tracy nodded again. It was now obvious she was terrified just like her younger sisters.

"Great," Renaldo said. Then he reached out with his gloved finger and tweaked one of Tracy's nipples. "Nice boobs. Tell your parents not to make me come back."

After a quick visual sweep around the room, Renaldo motioned for Manuel. As quickly as they had come in, they left, picking up the canvas bag on the way and taking off their masks and gloves. They closed the door behind them and followed the same route back to the street. En route to the car, they passed a couple of kids on bikes, but it didn't bother them. They were just two handymen returning from having done some work. Back in the car, Renaldo looked at his watch. The whole exercise had taken less than twenty minutes, which wasn't bad for a thousand bucks.

CHAPTER FOURTEEN

Randolph took longer than usual to get up from the defense table, organize his notes, and situate himself behind the podium. Even when ostensibly prepared, he eyed Leona Rattner long enough for her to briefly look away. Randolph could be intimidating with his powerful, paternal aura.

"Miss Rattner," Randolph said in his refined voice. "How would you describe your choice of apparel at the office?"

Leona laughed uncertainly. "Normal, I guess. Why?"

"Would you label your usual attire conservative or modest?"

"I never thought about it."

"Did Marlene Richardt, who is the de facto office manager, ever suggest your attire was inappropriate?"

For a moment, Leona looked like the fox caught in the henhouse. Her eyes darted from Tony to the judge and then back to Randolph.

"She said something to that effect."

"How many times?"

"How should I know? A number of times."

"Did she use terms like 'sexy' or 'provocative'?"

"I suppose."

"Miss Rattner, you testified that Dr. Bowman was giving you 'the eye' about a year ago."

"That's correct."

"Do you think it might have had anything to do with your choice of apparel?"

"How am I supposed to know?"

"You testified that at first it made you embarrassed, because he was married."

"That's true."

"But a year ago, Dr. Bowman was officially separated from his wife. There were strains in his marriage that were being addressed. Wasn't that common knowledge in the office?"

"Maybe it was."

"Could it be that you were giving Dr. Bowman the eye rather than vice versa?"

"Maybe subconsciously. He's a good-looking guy."

"Did it ever go through your mind that Dr. Bowman might be susceptible to provocative clothing, considering he was living alone?"

"I never thought about it."

"Miss Rattner, you testified that on September eighth, 2005, you were living in Dr. Bowman's Boston apartment."

"I was."

"How did that happen? Did Dr. Bowman invite you to move in?"

"Not exactly."

"Did your moving in ever come up in a conversation so that the benefits and the disadvantages could be discussed?"

"Not really."

"The reality was that you decided to move in on your own accord. Is that correct?"

"Well, I was staying there every night. Why pay rent on two apartments?"

"You did not answer the question. You moved into Dr. Bowman's apartment without discussing it with him. Is that correct?"

"It's not like he complained," Leona snapped. "He was getting it every night."

"The question is whether you moved in on your own accord."

"Yeah, I moved in on my own accord," Leona spat. "And he loved it."

"We shall see when Dr. Bowman testifies," Randolph said, consulting his notes. "Miss Rattner, on the evening of September eighth, 2005, when the call came in from Mr. Jordan Stanhope about his wife, Patience, did Dr. Bowman ever say anything about the Newton Memorial Hospital?"

"No, he did not."

"He didn't say it would be better to go to the Stanhope residence than the hospital, because the Stanhope residence was closer to Symphony Hall."

"Nope. He didn't say anything about the hospital."

"When you and Dr. Bowman arrived at the Stanhope residence, did you remain in the car?"

"No. Dr. Bowman wanted me to come inside and help him."

"I understand you were carrying the portable cardiogram."

"That's right."

"And when you got to Mrs. Stanhope's bedroom, what happened?"

"Dr. Bowman started to work on Mrs. Stanhope."

"Did he act concerned at that point?"

"He sure did. He had Mr. Stanhope call an ambulance right away."

"I understand he had you breathe for the patient while he did what he had to do."

"That's right. He showed me how to do it."

"Was Dr. Bowman concerned about the patient's condition?"

"Very concerned. The patient was very blue, and her pupils were big and unreactive."

"I understand the ambulance came quickly to take Mrs. Stanhope to the hospital. How did you and Dr. Bowman get to the hospital?"

"I drove his car. Dr. Bowman went with the ambulance."

"Why did he go in the ambulance?"

"He said if she has trouble, he wants to be there."

"You did not see him again until much later, after Mrs. Stanhope had died. Is that correct?"

"It is. It was in the emergency room. He was all blood-spattered."

"Was he discouraged because his patient had died?"

"He was pretty down."

"So Dr. Bowman made a strenuous effort to save his patient."

"Yes."

"And he was despondent when all his efforts were unsuccessful."

"I guess I'd say he was depressed, but he didn't dwell on it. In fact, we ended up having a pretty damned good Friday night back at the apartment."

"Miss Rattner, allow me to ask you a personal question. You strike me as a high-spirited young woman. Have you ever said things you didn't really mean when you've been angry, maybe exaggerate your feelings?"

"Everybody does," Leona said with a shallow laugh.

"On the night Dr. Bowman was served with the lawsuit, did he become upset?"

"Very upset. I'd never seen him so upset."

"And angry?"

"Very angry."

"Under such circumstances, do you believe there was a chance when he, quote, 'ran off at the mouth' and voiced inappropriate comments about Patience Stanhope that he was merely blustering, especially considering the strenuous effort he'd made to resuscitate her on the fateful evening, and the weekly house calls he'd made during the year leading up to her death?"

Randolph paused, waiting for Leona to answer.

"The witness will answer the question," Judge Davidson said after a period of silence.

"Was that a question?" Leona said with apparent befuddlement. "I didn't get it."

"Repeat the question," Judge Davidson said.

"What I'm suggesting is that Dr. Bowman's comments about Patience Stanhope on the evening he was served were a reflection of his agitation, whereas his true feelings about the patient were accurately demonstrated by his dedicated commitment to attend to her at her home on a weekly basis for almost a year and his strenuous efforts to resuscitate her the night she passed away. I'm asking, Miss Rattner, if this sounds plausible to you."

"Maybe. I don't know. Maybe you should ask him."

"I believe I will do that," Randolph said. "But I first

want to ask you if you are still living in Dr. Bowman's rented apartment in Boston."

Jack leaned over toward Alexis and whispered, "Randolph is getting away with some questions and statements that should have raised objections from Tony Fasano. Fasano has always been quick on the trigger before. I wonder what's going on."

"Maybe it has something to do with that hushed conversation the judge had with the lawyers earlier in Leona's testimony. There's always a bit of give-and-take for fairness."

"That's a good point," Jack agreed. "Whatever the reason, Randolph's making the best of it." Jack listened while Randolph cleverly began questioning Leona about her feelings since the malpractice suit began and Craig moved back with his family. Jack knew exactly what Randolph was doing; he was setting the stage for a "spurned love" defense, where the previous testimony would be rendered suspect as having been motivated by spite.

Jack leaned back toward Alexis and whispered, "Let me ask you a question, and be truthful. Would you mind if I slipped out? I'd like to get in some basketball for exercise. But if you want me to stay, I will. I have a sense the worst is over. From here on, she'll just be making herself look bad."

"Please!" Alexis said sincerely. "Go get some exercise! I appreciate your having been here, but I'm fine now. Go and enjoy yourself. The judge is going to wind things up here momentarily. He always does around four."

"You are certain you're okay," Jack asked.

"Absolutely," Alexis insisted. "I'll eat early with the girls, but there'll be something for you to eat later. Take your time, but be careful, Craig always gets hurt when he plays. You have your key?"

"I've got the key," Jack said. He reached around his sister for a quick hug.

Jack got to his feet, and by excusing himself to those people sitting in his row, he worked his way to the aisle. When he arrived, he glanced over at Franco's typical location. Jack was surprised. The man wasn't in his accustomed seat. Although Jack did not stop, he searched among the spectators for the hoodlum's familiar silhouette. When Jack got to the door, he turned around and quickly scanned the spectators again. No Franco.

Using his back to press down the door's lever, Jack backed out of the courtroom. Not seeing Franco in his usual place gave him pause. The thought of running into the man in some difficult location with limited egress, such as the underground parking garage, passed through his mind. Although several years previously he wouldn't have given the issue a second thought, now that he was getting married in two days, he wasn't quite so nonchalant. With someone else to think about besides himself, he needed to be careful, and being careful meant being prepared. The idea of getting some pepper spray had occurred to him the previous day, but he'd failed to act on it. He decided to change that.

The third-floor elevator lobby was full of people. The doors to one of the four courtrooms were propped open, and people were being disgorged. A trial was in recess. There were clumps of people chatting; others hurried to the elevators, trying to determine which of the eight elevators would come next.

Jack joined the group and found himself looking

around warily and wondering if he'd run into Franco. Jack doubted there would be any problem in the courthouse building. It was outside that he was concerned about.

At the security checkpoint at the entrance, Jack stopped to ask one of the uniformed guards if he knew of a nearby hardware store. He was told there was one down on Charles Street, which Jack was told was the main drag of neighboring Beacon Hill.

Jack was assured he'd have no trouble finding the street, especially since it also bisected the park, meaning it was the street Jack had used to get into the car park where his rent-a-car was waiting. Armed with that information and the advice that he should wander westward, down through the maze of Beacon Hill, Jack left the courthouse.

Again, Jack scanned for signs of Franco, but he was nowhere to be seen, and Jack chuckled at his paranoia. Having been told the general direction was opposite the courthouse's entrance, Jack made his way around the courthouse building. The streets were narrow and twisty, hardly the grid he'd become accustomed to in New York. Following his nose, Jack found himself on Derne Street that mysteriously became Myrtle. The buildings for the most part were modest, narrow four-story brick town houses. To his surprise, he suddenly came upon a charming toddler playground awash with kids and moms. He passed aptly named Beacon Hill Plumbing with a friendly chocolate Labrador doing a poor job of guarding the entrance. As Jack crested the hill and began a slow descent, he asked a passerby if he was going in the right direction for Charles Street. He was told he was but advised to take a left at the next corner where there was a small convenience store, and then a quick right onto Pinkney Street.

As the street became progressively steeper, he realized that Beacon Hill was not just a name but a real hill. The houses became larger and more elegant, although still understated. On his left he passed a sun-filled square with a stout wrought-iron fence circling a line of hundred-year-old elms and a patch of green grass. A few blocks on, he came to Charles Street.

In comparison with the side streets he'd been following, Charles Street was a major boulevard. Even with parallel parking on either side, there was still room for three lanes of traffic. Lining the street on either side were a wide variety of small shops. After stopping one of the many pedestrians and asking for a hardware store, Jack was directed to Charles Street Supply.

When he walked into the store, he silently questioned if purchasing the pepper spray was necessary. Away from the courthouse and Craig's lawsuit, Franco's threat seemed a distant possibility. But he had come that far, so he bought the pepper spray from the square-jawed, friendly proprietor, whose name coincidentally was Jack. Jack had learned this fact by chance when another employee had called out the owner's name.

Turning down the offer of a small bag, Jack slipped the pepper spray into his right jacket pocket. As long as he made the effort to buy the narrow canister, he wanted to keep it handy. Thus armed, Jack strolled the rest of the way along Charles Street to the Boston Common and retrieved his Hyundai.

While in the dim, dank, deserted underground garage, Jack was glad he had the pepper spray. It was in just such a circumstance that he would not like to confront Franco.

But once in his car and on his way to the tollbooth he
again laughed at his paranoia and wondered if it was mis-
placed guilt. In retrospect, Jack knew he should not have
kneed the man in Stanhope's driveway, although there
was a lingering thought that had he not done so, the situation could have quickly gotten out of hand, especially
with Franco's apparent lack of impulse control and penchant for violence.

As Jack pulled out of the murky depths of the garage
and into the bright sunshine, he made a conscious decision to stop thinking about Franco. Instead, he pulled to
the side of the road and consulted Alexis's city map. As
he did so, he felt his pulse quicken with the thought of
a good pickup basketball game.

What he was searching for was Memorial Drive, and
he quickly found it running alongside the Charles River
Basin. Unfortunately, it was in Cambridge on the opposite side of the river. Judging from his Boston driving
experience, he guessed that getting there might be somewhat of a struggle, since there were few bridges. His
concerns were well founded as he was hampered by a
confusing interplay of no left turns, one-way streets, the
spottiness of street signs, and the overly aggressive
Boston drivers.

Despite the handicaps, Jack eventually managed to get
on Memorial Drive and then quickly found the outdoor
basketball courts Warren's friend David Thomas had
described. Jack parked on a small side street, got out, and
raised the trunk of his car. Pushing aside the autopsy supplies he'd gotten from Latasha, he got out his basketball
gear and looked around for a place to change. Not finding
any, he climbed back into the car, and like a contortion-
ist managed to get out of his clothes and into his shorts

without offending any of the multitudes of bicyclists, in-line skaters, and joggers along the banks of the Charles River.

After making sure the car was locked, Jack jogged back to the basketball courts. There were about fifteen men, ranging in age from about twenty up. At forty-six, Jack assumed he'd be the senior player. The game had yet to begin. Everybody was shooting or showboating, with a bit of playground trash talk being exchanged by the court's regulars.

Being wise to the complicated playground etiquette from his many years of experience in a similar environment in New York, Jack acted nonchalant. He began by merely rebounding and passing the balls out to those people who'd made their practice shots. Only later did Jack begin shooting, and as he expected, his accuracy caught the attention of a number of players, although nothing was said. After fifteen minutes, feeling loose, Jack casually asked for David Thomas. The person he'd asked didn't answer, he merely pointed.

Jack approached the man. He'd been one of the more vociferous of the trash-talkers. As Jack had surmised, he was African-American, mid- to late thirties, slightly taller than Jack, and heavier. He had a full beard. In fact, he had more hair on his face than on the crown of his head. But the most distinguishing characteristic was the twinkle of his eye; the man was quick to laugh. It was evident he enjoyed life.

When Jack approached and introduced himself, David unabashedly threw his arms around Jack, hugged him, and then pumped Jack's hand.

"Any friend of Warren Wilson is a friend of mine,"

David said enthusiastically. "And Warren says you're a playmaker. Hey, you're running with me, okay?"

"Sure!" Jack said.

"Hey, Aesop!" David called out to another player. "It's not your night, man. You ain't running with us. Jack is!" David gave Jack a thump on the back and then added as an aside, "That boy always has a story. That's why we call him Aesop!"

The play turned out to be terrific: as good as Jack had experienced in New York. Very quickly, Jack realized he'd been lucky to be included on David's pickup team. Although the games were all close, David's team continually triumphed, which meant that for Jack the play was continuous. For more than two hours, he, David, and the three others David had selected for the evening's run did not lose. By the time it was over, Jack was exhausted. At the sidelines, he looked at his watch. It was well after seven.

"You going to come by tomorrow night?" David asked as Jack gathered up his things.

"Can't say," Jack said.

"We'll be here."

"Thanks for letting me run with you."

"Hey, man. You earned it."

Jack walked out of the chain-link fenced court on slightly rubbery legs. Although he'd been drenched with sweat at the end of the play, it was already gone from the dry, warm breeze wafting in off the river. Jack walked slowly. The exercise had done him a world of good. For several hours, he'd not thought of anything besides the immediate requirements of the game, but now reality was setting in. He was not looking forward to his conversation with Laurie. Tomorrow was Thursday, and he didn't even know what time he'd be able to start the autopsy, much less when it would be over and when he'd be able to fly back to New York. He knew she was going to be understandably upset, and he wasn't sure what he should say.

Jack got to his little cream-colored car, unlocked the door, and started to open it. To his surprise, a hand came over his shoulder and slammed it shut. Jack twisted around and found himself looking into Franco's deep-set eyes and not-too-pretty face. The first thing that flashed through his mind was that the damn ten-dollar-forty-nine-cent pepper spray was inside his jacket pocket inside the car.

"We've got some unfinished business," Franco growled.

Jack was close enough to Franco to almost be bowled over by the smell of garlic on his breath.

"Correction," Jack said, trying to lean back. Franco was crowding him against the car. "I don't believe we have ever had business together, so it can't be unfinished." Jack noticed that behind Franco and a little to the side was another man who was also involved in the confrontation.

"Wiseass," Franco muttered. "What's between us concerns you sucker-punching me in the nuts."

"It's not a sucker punch when you hit me first."

"Grab him, Antonio!" Franco ordered while moving back a step.

Jack responded by trying to dart between Franco and the car. With his sneakers on, he thought he could easily outrun the two thugs despite his fatigue from the basketball game. But Franco lunged forward and managed to get a handful of Jack's shirt with his right hand, pulling Jack up short while at the same time hitting him in the mouth with his left fist. Antonio grabbed one of Jack's arms and tried to get ahold of the other to pin them behind Jack's back. Meanwhile, Franco cocked his right hand back for a knockout blow.

But the blow never landed. Instead, a short piece of pipe came down on Franco's shoulder, causing him to cry out in surprise and pain. His right arm dropped limply to his side while his left hand shot to his injured shoulder, and he hunched over.

The pipe was pointed at Antonio. "Let him go, man!" David said. More than a dozen other basketball players had materialized in a threatening U around Jack, Franco, and Antonio. Several had tire irons; one had a baseball bat.

Antonio let Jack go and glared at the newcomers.

"I don't believe you guys are from the neighbor-hood," David commented, his voice no longer truculent. "Aesop, pat them down!"

Aesop stepped forward and quickly removed Franco's gun. Franco did not resist. The second thug was not armed.

"Now I recommend you boys remove yourself from the neighborhood," David said, taking the gun from Aesop.

"This ain't over," Franco muttered to Jack as he and Antonio walked away. The basketball players parted to allow them through.

"Warren warned me about you," David said to Jack. "He said you were prone to get into trouble and that he'd had to save your ass on more than one occasion. You're lucky we saw these honkies hanging around while we were playing. What's the deal?"

"It's just a misunderstanding," Jack said evasively. He touched his finger to his lip. There was a spot of blood.

"If you need some help, you let me know. Right now you better get some ice for that fat lip, and why don't you take this gun? You might need it if that asshole shows up on your doorstep."

Jack declined the gun and thanked David and the others before climbing into the car. The first thing he did was get the canister of pepper spray out. Next, he looked at himself in the rearview mirror. The right side of his upper lip was swollen, with a bluish cast. A trickle of congealed blood ran down his chin. "Good God," he murmured. Warren was right, he did have a penchant for getting himself in compromising circumstances. He cleaned off the blood as best he could with the bottom of his T-shirt.

On the way back to the Bowmans', Jack considered fibbing and saying his injury was from basketball. Bruises were not uncommon with as much as he played and the fact that basketball was a contact sport in his experience. The problem was that Craig and Alexis were going to be downcast after the day's testimony, and he didn't want to add to their burden. He was afraid they might feel inappropriately responsible if he told the truth.

Being as quiet as possible, Jack used the key Alexis had given him to come in the front entrance. He was carrying his clothes and shoes in his arms. His goal was to slip downstairs and quickly shower before running into anyone. He was eager to ice his lip, but it had already been long enough since the injury that another fifteen minutes was hardly critical. As he silently closed the front door, he stopped with his hand on the doorknob. His sixth sense was nagging him; the house was too quiet.

Every other time he'd entered, there'd been background noise: a radio, a ringing cell phone, children's chatter, or the TV. Now there was nothing, and the silence was foreboding. From having seen the Lexus in the driveway, he was reasonably sure at least the parents were home. His immediate concern was that something had gone wrong at the trial.

Continuing to clutch his clothes against his chest, Jack moved quickly and silently down the hall to the archway leading into the great room. He leaned through the opening, expecting the room beyond to be deserted. To his surprise, the whole family was there on the couch, with the parents at either end. They appeared as if they were watching television, but the TV was off.

From his vantage point, Jack could not see any faces. For a moment he stood still, watching and listening. No one moved or spoke. Mystified, Jack stepped into the room and approached. When he got about ten feet away, he tentatively called out Alexis's name. He didn't want to disturb them if it was some family thing, but he couldn't seem to walk away, either.

Both Craig's and Alexis's heads shot around. Craig glared back at Jack. Alexis got to her feet. Her face was drawn and her eyes were red. Something was wrong. Something was very wrong.

CHAPTER FIFTEEN

"So there you have it," Alexis said. She'd told Jack the story about how she and Craig had come home after the trial had been recessed to find their terrified daughters bound and gagged with duct tape. She'd spoken slowly and deliberately. Craig had spat out a few gory details, like the fact Tracy had been dragged from the shower stark naked and rudely struck.

Jack was speechless. He was sitting on the coffee table, facing his sister and her family. As the story unfolded, his eyes jumped from Alexis, who was anxious, fearful, and concerned, to Craig, who was beside himself with outrage, to three children who were shocked and clearly traumatized. All three children were sitting silent and immobile. Tracy had her legs tucked under herself and her arms folded across her chest. She was dressed in oversized sweat clothes. Her hair was frizzed. There was no bare midriff. Christina and Meghan both had their arms clutched around their legs with their knees jutting up into the air. All three had raw, red bands across their lower faces from the duct tape. Tracy had a split lip.

"Are you guys all right?" Jack asked the children. It appeared to him that only Tracy had been physically abused, and thankfully, it looked minor.

"They are as well as can be expected," Alexis said.

"How did the intruders get in?"

"They forced the back door," Craig snapped. "They were obviously professionals."

"Has anything been stolen?" Jack asked. His eyes rapidly scanned the room for any damage, but everything seemed to be in order.

"Not that we can determine," Alexis said.

"What did they want then?" Jack asked.

"It was to convey a message," Alexis said. "They gave Tracy a verbal message to give to us."

"What?" Jack asked impatiently when Alexis didn't elaborate.

"No autopsy," Craig snapped. "The message was no autopsy or they'd be back to hurt the kids."

Jack's eyes rocketed back and forth between Craig and Alexis. He could not believe his offer to help could have caused such a situation. "This is crazy," he blurted. "This can't be happening."

"Tell that to the kids!" Craig challenged.

"I'm sorry," Jack said. He looked away from the Bowmans' faces. He was crushed he'd been the cause of such a disaster. He shook his head and looked back, particularly at Craig and Alexis. "Well, fine then, no autopsy!"

"We're not sure we're ready to give in to this kind of extortion," Alexis said. "Despite what's happened, we're not ruling an autopsy out. It seems to us that if someone is willing to go to the extent of threatening children to block the autopsy, that's all the more reason to do it."

Jack nodded. The thought had occurred to him as well, but it wasn't for him to put Tracy, Meghan, and Christina any more at risk. Besides, the only culprit that came to his mind was Tony Fasano, and his motivation could only involve fear of losing his contingency fee. Jack looked at Craig, whose anger had seemingly lessened a degree as the conversation progressed.

"If there's any risk at all, I'm not for it," Craig said. "But we're thinking we can eliminate the risk."

"Have you called the police?" Jack asked.

"No, we haven't," Alexis said. "That was the second part of the message: no autopsy, no police."

"You have to call the police," Jack said, but his words rang hollow since he'd not reported either his confrontation with Fasano et al. the previous day or his confrontation with Franco a half-hour earlier.

"We're considering our options," Craig explained. "We've been talking it over with the girls. They are going to stay with their grandparents for a few days, until this trial is over. My mom and dad live up in Lawrence, Massachusetts, and they are on their way down here to pick them up."

"I'll probably be going along with them," Alexis said.

"You don't have to, Mom," Tracy said, speaking for the first time. "We'll be fine with Gramps and Grandma."

"No one knows where the girls will be," Craig explained. "They'll stay out of school at least for the rest of this week and maybe for the year since there's only a few days left. They've promised not to use their cell phones or tell anyone where they are."

Jack nodded, but he didn't know what he was agreeing to. It seemed to him he was getting mixed messages. There was no way the risk for the children could be completely eliminated. He was concerned that Alexis and Craig might not be thinking clearly under the stress of the trial. The only thing Jack was certain of was that the police had to be notified.

"Listen," Jack said. "The only person that comes to mind who might be behind this outrage is Tony Fasano and his cronies."

"We thought the same," Craig said. "But it seems almost too venal, so we're trying to keep an open mind. The one thing that has particularly surprised me during my trial is the animosity colleagues feel about my concierge practice. It gives some credence to the rhetorical questions you posed last night about a conspiracy."

Jack allotted the idea a quick thought, but other than being grist for an avowed conspiracy-theory aficionado, he gave the chances of such a scenario an extremely low probability, even though he'd suggested it the previous evening. Tony Fasano and his tag team were a much more likely possibility, especially since Tony had already threatened him. "I don't know if you've noticed my fat lip," he said, gingerly touching the swelling.

"It would be hard to miss," Alexis said. "Was it from basketball?"

"I was going to pass it off as such," Jack admitted. "But it was from another run-in with Tony Fasano's Franco. It's becoming a regrettable, daily ritual."

"Those bastards," Craig snarled.

"Are you okay?" Alexis questioned with concern.

"I'm better than I would have been had my newly made Boston basketball buddies not intervened on my behalf in the nick of time. Franco had an accomplice."

"Oh my God," Alexis said. "We're sorry to involve you in this."

"I take full responsibility," Jack said. "And I'm not looking for sympathy. What I'm trying to suggest is that Fasano et al. were probably behind what happened here as well. The point is: The police have to be notified on both accounts."

"You can call the police about your problem," Craig said. "But I don't want to gamble on my children's safety. I don't think there's a damn thing the police can do. These people that came here were professionals with ski masks, nondescript workers' uniforms, and gloves. And the Newton police force is not accustomed to this kind of thing. It's just a suburban town."

"I disagree," Jack said. "I bet your local police have seen a lot more than you imagine, and forensics is a powerful tool. You have no idea what they could find. They could associate this event with others. They can surely increase surveillance. One of the problems if you don't report it is that you are playing into the hands of whoever did this. You are allowing yourselves to be extorted."

"Of course we're being extorted," Craig yelled loud enough for the kids to jump. "Good God, man. You think we're stupid?"

"Easy, Craig!" Alexis advised. She put her arms around Tracy, who was sitting next to her.

"I have a suggestion," Jack said. "I have a very good friend in New York who is a senior detective with the New York City Police Department. I can call him and just get the benefit of his expertise and experience. We can ask him what you should do."

"I don't want to be coerced," Craig said.

"No one is going to coerce you," Jack said. "I guarantee it."

"I think Jack should call his friend," Alexis said. "We hadn't decided for sure about the police."

"Fine!" Craig said, throwing up his hands. "What do I know?"

Jack went through the pockets of his jacket and located his phone. He flipped it open and speed-dialed Lou Soldano at home. It was a little after eight p.m., which was probably the best time to catch the detective, but he wasn't home. Jack left a message on his voicemail. Next he tried Lou's cell phone and got the detective in his car on his way out to a homicide in Queens.

While the Bowmans listened, Jack gave Lou a thumbnail sketch of what he'd been doing and what had happened in Boston. He concluded by saying he was sitting with his sister, her husband, and the children at that very minute and the question was: Should they notify the police or not?

"There's no question," Lou said without hesitating. "They have to notify the police."

"They are concerned the Newton police might not be experienced enough to justify the risk."

"You say they are right there with you?"

"Yes. Right across from me."

"Put me on speakerphone!"

Jack did as Lou requested and held the phone out in front of himself. Lou formally introduced himself, expressed his sympathies for their ordeal, and then said, "I have a very, very good friend who is my counterpart with the Boston Police Department. We were in the service together aeons ago. He is very experienced in every kind of crime, including what you people are victims of. I'll be happy to call him and ask him to personally become involved. He lives either in your town or West Newton. It's Newton something. I'm sure he knows the guys on the Newton force. It's up to you. I can call him right away. His name is Liam Flanagan. He's a terrific guy. And let me tell you something. Your kids are at more risk if you don't report the incident than if you do. I know that for a fact."

Alexis looked at Craig. "I think we should take him up on his offer."

"All right," Craig said with some reluctance.

"Did you hear that?" Jack asked.

"I did," Lou said. "I'll get right on it."

"Hang on, Lou," Jack said. He took him off speaker-phone, excused himself from the Bowmans, and walked into the hall, out of earshot. "Lou, when you talk to Flanagan, see if he could get me a gun."

"A gun?" Lou questioned. "That's a tall order."

"See if it's possible. I'm feeling more vulnerable than usual."

"Is your permit current?"

"Yes, for New York. I went through the formal train-ing and everything. You're the one who pushed me to do it. I just never got the gun."

"I'll see what I can do."

As Jack flipped his phone closed, the front doorbell chimed. Alexis came hurrying past. "It must be Grandma and Gramps," she said. But she was wrong. It was Ran-dolph Bingham, dressed casually but as elegantly as usual.

"Is Craig ready for his rehearsal?" Randolph inquired, noticing Alexis's surprise. "He's expecting me."

Alexis acted confused for a beat after having been so certain it was Craig's parents at the door. "Rehearsal?" she questioned.

"Yes. Craig will be testifying in the morning, and we agreed some rehearsal was in order."

"Come in," Alexis said, embarrassed at her hesitation.

Randolph took note of Jack's shorts and soiled, bloodstained T-shirt but said nothing as Alexis led him down the hall and into the family room. Randolph was next to be apprised of what had happened that afternoon at the Bowman home. As the story unfolded, his expression changed from his normal, mildly condescending aloofness to one of concern.

"Have the girls been seen by a doctor?" he asked.

"Not other than Craig," Alexis responded. "We didn't call their pediatrician."

Randolph looked at Craig. "I could make a motion for a continuance of your case if you'd like."

"What are the chances of the judge granting it?" Craig asked.

"There's no way to know. It would be entirely at Judge Davidson's discretion."

"To be honest with you, I think I'd rather get this nightmare trial over with," Craig said. "And it's probably the safest for the kids."

"As you wish," Randolph said. "I assume you have contacted the police?"

Alexis and Craig exchanged a glance. Then Alexis looked over at Jack, who'd come back into the room.

"That's in the process," Jack said. He then quickly outlined the plan. When he finished, he went on to explain their belief that Tony Fasano had something to do with the episode, using Tony's very specific threat to Jack that he would be "history" if Jack carried out the autopsy.

"That is clearly assault," Randolph said. "You could bring charges."

"The episode is a little more complicated," Jack said.

"The only witness was Fasano's thug, who I ended up striking after he struck me. The bottom line is that I personally have no intention of pressing charges."

"Is there any proof whatsoever Tony Fasano was behind today's criminal acts?" Randolph asked. "If there is, I'm certain I could get a mistrial."

"No proof," Craig said. "My daughters said they might be able to recognize a voice, but they are not at all certain."

"Perhaps the police will have more luck?" Randolph said. "What about the autopsy? Is that going to be done or not?"

"We're trying to decide," Alexis said.

"Obviously it is the girls' safety that is the issue," Craig said.

"If it were to be done, when would it be?"

"The body is scheduled to be exhumed in the morning," Jack said. "I'll do the autopsy immediately, but the initial results will only involve gross pathology."

"That's very late in the course of events," Randolph said. "Perhaps it's not worth the effort or the risk. Tomorrow, after Dr. Bowman testifies, I'm certain the judge will rule that the plaintiff has met his burden. I will then present the defense, which will be the testimony of our experts. That means Friday morning will be closing arguments."

Jack's phone rang. He still had it in his hand, and it startled him. He quickly left the room before answering. It was Lou.

"I got ahold of Liam, and I told him the story and gave him the address. He's going to be right over with some of the Newton police. He's a good guy."

"Did you ask about the gun?"

"I did. He was not excited about the idea, but I gave him glowing reports about your integrity and all that bullshit."

"Well, what's the bottom line? Is he going to come through or what? If all goes well, they'll be digging up the body in the morning, and thanks to all these threats, I'll feel like a sitting duck."

"He said he'd fix you up, but he's going to hold me responsible."

"What does that mean?"

"I assume he's going to give you a gun, so be careful with the damn thing!"

"Thanks for the advice, Dad," Jack said. "I'll try my damnedest to shoot as few people as possible."

Jack returned to the family room. Craig, Alexis, and Randolph were still discussing the autopsy issues. The consensus had tripped in favor of still doing it despite the time constraint. The main argument from Randolph was the possibility of using any potentially significant findings to help with the appeal process, if an appeal became necessary, either to vacate the verdict, to obtain a new trial, or to allocate the award according to contributory negligence. Randolph called to everyone's attention that the records clearly documented that Patience Stanhope refused on several occasions against medical advice to have any more cardiac evaluation after her questionable ECG stress test.

When a break came in the conversation, Jack informed the group that Detective Lieutenant Liam Flanagan was on his way.

"We want you to do the autopsy if you are still willing," Alexis said to Jack, seemingly ignoring his statement.

"I gathered as much," he said. "I'm happy to do it if that's what you people want." He looked at Craig. Craig shrugged.

"I'm not going to go against the grain," Craig said. "With all the stress I'm under, I don't trust my judgment."

"Fair enough," Jack said. Once again, Jack felt Craig was demonstrating unexpected insight.

The doorbell rang again, and again Alexis ran to get it, saying it must be the grandparents. But for the second time she was wrong. Standing at the door were five policemen, two of which were in Newton Police Department uniforms. Alexis invited them into the house and led them to the great room.

"I am Detective Lieutenant Liam Flanagan," the big, red-faced Irishman said in a booming voice. He had bright, baby-blue eyes, and a smattering of freckles across his flat, prizefighter's nose. He proceeded to introduce the others, who included Detective Greg Skolar, officers Sean O'Rourke and David Shapiro, and crime-scene investigator Derek Williams.

As Liam made the introductions, Jack studied him. There was something familiar, as if Jack had met the man sometime in the past, yet he thought that unlikely. Suddenly, it came to him. When he had a chance to introduce himself to Liam, he asked, "Did I see you at the medical examiner's office this morning?"

"Yes, you did," Liam said effusively. He laughed. "Now I remember you. You went into the autopsy room."

After getting a brief overview of the incident at the Bowman residence, the crime-scene investigator and the two uniformed officers went off to check out the yard while there was still a little daylight. The sun had set, but it was not yet completely dark. The two detectives were mostly interested in the children, and the children responded to being the center of attention.

While that was going on, Randolph asked Craig if he was up to the rehearsal they'd planned for the following day's testimony.

"How necessary do you think it is?" Craig protested. He was understandably preoccupied.

"I'd say exceedingly crucial," Randolph commented. "Perhaps you should recall your performance during your deposition. It would be calamitous to repeat it in front of the jurors. It has become apparent that the opposing side's stratagem is to present you as an arrogant, uncaring M.D. who was more interested in getting to Symphony Hall on time with your trophy girlfriend than your seriously ill patient's welfare. We must prevent you from presenting yourself in any way that substantiates such allegations. The only way is to rehearse. You are a good doctor, but you are a poor witness."

Chastened by Randolph's less-than-flattering assessment, Craig docilely agreed to a practice session. He interrupted the detectives long enough to tell the children he'd just be in the library.

Suddenly, Jack and Alexis found themselves regarding each other. At first they had been listening intently to the children's description of their ordeal, but when it became repetitious as the detectives diligently searched for any possible missed but significant information, their interest waned. In order to talk, they stepped back into the kitchen area.

"I want to say again how sorry I am about everything

that has happened," Jack offered. "My intentions were good, but I've been more of a hindrance than a help."

"None of this could have been anticipated," Alexis said. "You needn't apologize. You have been an enormous help to me moralewise, and also to Craig. He's been a different man since you've been here. In fact, I'm still shocked at the insight he expressed at lunch."

"I hope it's lasting insight. What about the girls? How do you see them reacting to this experience?"

"I'm not sure," Alexis admitted. "They're pretty together kids, despite their father generally not having been available as they've been growing up. On the other hand, I've been very close to each one. There's good communication. We'll just have to take it day by day and let them voice their feelings and concerns."

"Do you have any specific plans for them?"

"Mainly to get them to their grandparents. They adore their grandmother. They all have to sleep in the same room, which they usually complain about, but under the circumstances, I think it will be good for them."

"Are you going?"

"That had been what we were discussing when you came in. My inclination is to go. It's a way of acknowledging that their fears are legitimate, which is important. The last thing that should be done is to offer them platitudes that they'll be fine and they shouldn't have to be afraid. They should be afraid. It was obviously a very traumatizing ordeal. I thank God they weren't physically injured more than they were."

"How are you going to make your decision whether to go or not?"

"I'm probably going. The reason there was a question was because Craig voiced some interest in my staying and because Tracy said she didn't want me to go. You heard her. But I think it's teenage bluster. And as much as I'm concerned about Craig and his needs, if it comes down to an either-or decision, the kids win hands down."

"Do you think they'll need professional help, like some sort of therapy?"

"I don't think so. Only if their fearfulness is prolonged or blows out of proportion. I suppose ultimately it will be a judgment call. Luckily, I have some colleagues at work who I can exploit for an opinion if need be."

"I've been thinking," Jack said. "Since my presence has caused so much trouble, maybe it would be best for everyone if I move into a hotel in town."

"Absolutely not," Alexis said. "I won't hear of it. You're here, and you are saying here."

"Are you sure? I won't take it personally."

"I'm positively sure. Let's not even discuss it."

The front doorbell chimed yet again. "This has to be the grandparents," Alexis said categorically, pushing off from the kitchen counter where she'd been leaning.

Jack glanced back toward the sitting area where the detectives and children were. It appeared that their interview was coming to an end. The two uniformed policemen and the crime-scene technician had returned to the great room and were dealing with the duct-tape strips that had bound the children.

A few minutes later, Alexis brought in the elder Bowmans. Leonard was a thick, pasty man with a two-day growth of beard, an old-fashioned crew cut, and an expansive gut suggesting he spent far too much time drinking beer in his favorite recliner in front of the TV. When Jack was introduced to him, Jack learned something even more idiosyncratically distinctive; Leonard was a man of few words who would have put the laconic Spartans to shame. When Jack shook hands with the man, he merely grunted.

Rose Bowman was the antipode. When she appeared and the children rushed her, she bubbled with delight and concern. She was a short, stocky woman with frizzed white hair, bright eyes, and yellow teeth.

As the children dragged their grandmother to the couch, Jack found himself momentarily isolated with Leonard. In an effort to make conversation, Jack commented on how much the kids liked their grandmother. All Jack got in return was another muffled grunt.

With the police doing their thing, the kids involved with the grandmother, Alexis busy packing for the kids and herself, and Craig sequestered with Randolph in the library, Jack was stuck with Leonard. After a few more vain attempts to wring words out of the retiree's mouth, Jack gave up. He checked with Liam Flanagan to be sure he would be there for at least another thirty minutes; picked up his pile of clothes and shoes from where he'd stacked them on the hearth; found Alexis, who was up in one of the kids' rooms, and told her he was going to shower; and went downstairs to his room.

As he was showering, he guiltily remembered he'd not yet called Laurie. As he got out of the shower, he glanced at himself in the mirror and winced. He'd completely forgotten about the ice, and his lip was still swollen and blue. Combining that with the left side of his face, which was still red, he looked as if he'd been in a barroom brawl. He considered getting some ice from the refrigerator he'd seen in the basement proper but decided it would have minimal effect since too much time had elapsed, so he passed on the idea. Instead, he dressed and got out his cell phone.

With the signal strength almost nonexistent, Jack gave up on the phone idea as well. He climbed the stairs and met Alexis, the girls, and the grandparents in the main hall. Alexis had finished packing and had already put the luggage in the station wagon. The girls were pleading with Rose to ride with them, but Rose said she had to go with Gramps. It was then that Jack heard Leonard's only words: "Come on, Rose," he said, grimly drawing the words out. It was an order, not a request. Dutifully, Rose detached herself from the children and hurried after her husband, who'd stepped out the front door.

"Will I see you in court tomorrow?" Alexis asked Jack as she herded the children toward the door to the garage. The girls had already said their good-byes to Craig, who was still working in the library with Randolph. "At some point," Jack said. "I honestly don't know what to expect the schedule to be. It's out of my hands."

All at once Alexis spun around, her expression reflecting a sudden realization. "Oh, my gosh," she exclaimed. "I just remembered you are getting married on Friday. Tomorrow is already Thursday. I've been so preoccupied, I've completely forgotten. I'm sorry. Your wife-to-be must hate me for dragging you up here and keeping you hostage."

"She knows me well enough to know where to assign blame if she's inclined."

"So you'll do the autopsy and then head back to New York?"

"That's the plan."

At the door to the garage, Alexis told the girls to say

good-bye to their uncle. Each gave Jack an obedient hug. Only Christina spoke. She whispered in Jack's ear that she was sorry his daughters had burnt up in the plane. The totally unexpected comment took Jack by such surprise that it undermined his emotional equilibrium, and he had to choke back a tear. When Alexis gave him a hug, she sensed his new emotion and pulled back to look him in the eyes, mistaking its origin. "Hey," she said. "We're fine. The kids are going to be fine. Trust me!"

Jack nodded and found his voice. "I'll see you sometime tomorrow, and I hope to hell to have something to offer that will make this all worthwhile."

"Me, too," Alexis said. She climbed into the station wagon and activated the garage door, which rolled up with a fearful clanking.

It was at that point that Jack realized he had to move his car. It was parked next to Craig's Lexus and blocking the driveway. Jack sprinted past Alexis, motioning her to wait. He backed his Hyundai into the street and waited while Alexis did the same. With a beep and a wave, she drove off into the night.

As Jack pulled back into the driveway, he glanced at the two Newton police patrol cars and the two other nondescript, dark sedans belonging to the two detectives parked along the street. He wondered how close to finishing they were, since he was eager to talk to them in private, particularly Liam Flanagan. In answer to his question, all five police officers emerged from the Bowmans' front door as Jack climbed from his car.

"Excuse me!" Jack called. He jogged in their direction, catching up to them midway on the Bowmans' serpentine front walk.

"Dr. Stapleton," Liam said. "We were looking for you."

"Have you finished checking out the scene?" Jack asked.

"For the moment."

"Any luck?"

"The duct tape will be analyzed at the crime lab, as will some fibers from the kid's bathroom. There wasn't a lot. We did find something on the grounds that I'm not at liberty to divulge, which could be promising, but all in all, it was obviously a professional job."

"What about the autopsy that's at the center of this extortion attempt?" Detective Greg Skolar asked. "Is it going to happen or what?"

"If the exhumation happens, then the autopsy will happen," Jack said. "I'll be doing it as soon as the body is available."

"Strange to have such an incident over an autopsy," Detective Skolar said. "Are you expecting some shocking revelations?"

"We don't know what to expect. All we know for certain is the patient had a heart attack. Obviously, this has heightened our curiosity."

"Weird!" Detective Skolar said. "For your peace of mind, as well as the Bowmans', we'll have the house under twenty-four-hour surveillance for a few days."

"I'm sure the Bowmans will be appreciative. I know it will make me sleep better."

"Keep us informed of any new developments," Detective Skolar said. He handed Jack a business card before shaking his hand. The other three uniformed officers shook his hand as well.

"Can I speak to you for a few minutes?" Jack asked Liam.

"By all means," Liam replied. "I was about to ask you the same question."

Jack and Liam said good-bye to the Newton police, and the police drove off in their respective vehicles, which were rapidly swallowed by the inky darkness. Night had fallen reluctantly, but now the transition was complete. The only light in the neighborhood was from the Bowmans' front windows and from a lonely street-lamp in the opposite direction the police had gone. Above in the dark sky a narrow scimitar-shaped sliver of a moon peeked through the leafy canopy of the trees lining the street.

"Want to sit in my limo?" Liam asked as they reached his bottom-of-the-line Ford.

"Actually, it's beautiful outside," Jack said. It had cooled from the day, and the temperature was invigorating.

With both men leaning against the vehicle, Jack told the story of his confrontation with Tony Fasano, the threat he'd received, and his two fisticuffs with his crony, Franco. Liam listened intently.

"I'm acquainted with Tony Fasano," Liam responded. "He's an individual who's going in a lot of different directions, including personal injury litigation and now medical malpractice. He's even done some criminal work defending a handful of low-level nasties, which is how I am aware of him. I have to say he's more clever than you might initially give him credit for."

"I've had the same impression."

"Do you think he's behind this professional but crude

extortion attempt? With the people he's in bed with, he's got the contacts."

"It stands to reason, considering the way he threatened me, but then again, it seems almost too simple and too stupid, considering how clever he apparently is."

"Do you have anyone else you suspect?"

"Not really," Jack said. He briefly considered bringing up the conspiracy idea, but he thought the chances the notion had any validity were so infinitesimally small he was embarrassed to mention it.

"I'll check into the Fasano angle," Liam said. "His office is in the North End, so he falls under our jurisdiction, but with no evidence, at least so far, there is little we can do, especially in the short run."

"I know," Jack said. "Listen, I appreciate your taking the time to come out here tonight and get involved. I was afraid the Bowmans might not have reported the episode."

"I'm always willing to do a favor for my old buddy Lou Soldano. I got the impression you guys are really tight."

Jack nodded and smiled inwardly. He'd originally met Lou when both of them were pursuing Laurie. He felt it was a tribute to Lou's personality that when Lou's chances with Laurie dimmed by his own doing, he was gracious enough to become Jack's advocate, which turned out to be key. Jack's pursuit of Laurie had not been without its bumps, thanks to Jack's psychological baggage.

"Which brings me to the final issue," Liam said. He unlocked his car and rummaged in a duffel bag on the front seat. He turned to Jack and handed him a snub-nose .38 Smith and Wessen. "You'd better be tight with him, because this is something I don't usually do."

Jack turned over the revolver in his hand. It glistened in the darkness, reflecting the light coming from the Bowmans' windows.

"You'd better have one hundred ten percent good reason to use this thing," Liam said. "And I hope to hell you don't."

"Rest assured it would have to be life or death," Jack said. "But with the girls not here, maybe I don't need it." He extended the revolver back toward Liam.

Liam held up his hand, palm out. "Keep it. You've been smacked a couple of times. This Franco sounds like he's got a couple of screws loose. Just be sure I get it back. When are you leaving?"

"Sometime tomorrow, which is all the more reason I shouldn't take it."

"Take it!" Liam insisted. He handed Jack his business card before walking around the car and opening the driver's-side door. "We can hook up when you leave or you can drop it by headquarters in a bag with my name on it. Don't go advertising what it is!"

"I'll be sure to be subtle," Jack said. Then he added humorously, "It's my middle name."

"Not according to Lou," Liam laughed. "But he said you were an enormously responsible guy, and that's what I am counting on."

With a final good-bye, Liam climbed into his car and quickly disappeared in the same direction as the Newton police.

Jack handled the gun in the darkness. It felt deceptively innocent, like the toy guns he had as a child, yet as a medical examiner, he knew its destructive potential.

He'd traced more bullet tracks in cadavers than he'd care to admit, always marveling at the degree of trauma. Putting the gun in one pocket, Jack took out his cell from another. He had understandable ambivalence about calling Laurie because he knew she would be justly upset and angry over his remaining in Boston. From her perspective, his returning home Thursday, maybe even Thursday night, with the wedding at 1:30 p.m. on Friday was ludicrous, unreasonable, and even hurtful, yet he felt powerless. He'd become ensnared in a quicksand of circumstance. After all that had happened, some of it his doing, there was no way he could just abandon Alexis and Craig. Moreover, he was genuinely intrigued because someone for some reason seriously did not want an autopsy. And as this reality tumbled around inside his brain, something new occurred to him: *What about the hospital? Could something have happened at the hospital the night Patience Stanhope had been brought in that needed to be covered up?* He hadn't thought about that angle, and even though it was unlikely, it seemed a hell of a lot more likely than the outlandish concierge-medicine conspiracy idea.

With trepidation and just about every neuron in his brain associated with feeling guilty firing, Jack speed-dialed Laurie's cell phone.

CHAPTER SIXTEEN

"It's about time!" Laurie said curtly

Jack winced. Her greeting was 180 degrees from the night before, heralding the kind of conversation he feared.

"It's almost ten o'clock!" Laurie complained. "Why haven't you called? It's been eight hours since your cowardly message on my voicemail."

"I'm sorry," Jack said as contritely as he could. "It's been a rather strange evening."

Although such a comment was a deliberate understatement, it was hardly the kind of sarcastic humor that Jack was capable of. He was making a conscious effort to resist the tendency that had become reflex with his devil-may-care approach to life after his family tragedy. Being careful with his vocabulary and as succinctly as possible, Jack told Laurie about the break-in, the terrorizing of the children, and the visit by the police made possible by Lou's timely intercession. Jack then told her about Tony Fasano and his threat, as well as about Franco, including the previous day's episode, which he had not mentioned to her the evening before.

"This is incredible!" Laurie said after a pause. Most of the anger had gone out of her voice. "Are you all right?"

"I've got a swollen lip and a few busted capillaries over a cheekbone, but I've had worse from basketball. I'm okay."

"I'm nervous about this Franco. He sounds like a lunatic."

"He's been on my mind as well," Jack said. He thought about mentioning the gun but decided it might make her more nervous.

"I'm gathering you believe Tony Fasano is behind the episode with the children."

Jack repeated some of the conversation he'd had with Liam Flanagan.

"How are the children?"

"They seem remarkably poised, considering what they've been through. Maybe it has something to do with their mother being a psychologist. Alexis is terrific with them. She took them to their grandparents', Craig's parents', for a few days. To give you an idea, the littlest one was together enough to empathize with me about my kids when they were saying good-bye. It took me completely by surprise."

"She sounds precociously self-possessed," Laurie said. "That's a blessing for the Bowmans. Now, let's talk about us. What's the bottom line about you coming back here?"

"Worst case is tomorrow evening," Jack said. "I'll do the autopsy, write up the results, whatever they turn out to be, and give them to Craig's lawyer. Even if I wanted to, he doesn't think he could get me on the stand as a witness, so that's not an issue."

"You are cutting this mighty close," Laurie said. "If I end up being the bride left at the altar, I'll never forgive you. I just want you to know that."

"I said worst case. Maybe I'll be there in the middle of the afternoon."

"Promise me you're not going to do anything foolish."

Jack could think of a lot of great retorts for that setup, but he resisted. Instead, he said, "I'll be careful." Then he added, to make her even more comfortable, "The Newton police have promised extra surveillance."

Confident Laurie was reasonably assuaged, Jack extended some appropriate endearments and then said good-bye. He then made two other quick calls. He spoke briefly to Lou to explain what had happened with Liam Flanagan and to thank him for his help. He told him he'd see him at the church on Friday. Next, he called Warren and told him that not only was David a good b-ball player, but he'd also saved Jack's ass. Jack had to hold the phone away from his ear when Warren responded. Jack told him he'd see him at the church also.

With all his calls out of the way, Jack once again took in the peaceful scene. The concave snippet of moon had moved a little higher in the sky and had cleared the black silhouettes of the trees. A few stars even twinkled in the sky despite the general nighttime glow sent heavenward from the entire Boston metropolitan area. Jack took in a big lungful of the cool, fresh air. It was bracing. In the distance, a dog barked. The serenity made him wonder what the morrow would bring. Would there be violence at the exhumation? He didn't know, but the thought made him glad Liam had insisted he keep the gun. He patted it in his pocket. Its weighty solidness made him feel more secure, even though he knew statistics suggested the opposite. With a sense of fatalism that whatever was going to happen would happen no matter what he did, Jack shrugged, turned, and headed into the house.

Without Alexis and the children at home, Jack felt somewhat like an intruder. After he closed the front door, the silence of the house was almost palpable, even though he could hear Craig's and Randolph's muffled voices from the library. He walked into the great room and went to the refrigerator. There were plenty of fixings, and he quickly made a sandwich. He popped open a beer and took both over to the couch. Careful to keep the sound low, he turned on the TV, and after rapidly scanning the channels, he found a news broadcast. Still feeling like a stranger in a strange land, he sat back and ate.

By the time he had finished the food and most of the beer, he heard raised voices coming from the library. It was obviously a disagreement. Jack quickly turned up the TV to keep from hearing. It made him feel similar to when he'd almost been caught snooping into Craig's doctor's bag. A few minutes later, the front door to the house slammed hard enough for Jack to feel the vibration. A few minutes after that, Craig came into the great room. It was apparent he was fuming from the way he acted, particularly the way he threw ice cubes into an old-fashioned glass and slammed shut the glass-front cabinet door. He helped himself to a healthy dollop of scotch, then brought the drink and bottle over to the couch.

"Do you mind?" Craig asked, motioning to the couch where Jack was sitting.

"Not at all," Jack said, wondering why he bothered to ask. Jack moved closer to the opposite end. He turned off the TV and twisted around to face his host, who'd plopped down, still holding both bottle and glass.

Craig took a large slug of his scotch and swished it around in his mouth before swallowing. He was staring into the empty fireplace.

"How did the rehearsal go?" Jack asked. He felt obligated to try to have a conversation.

Craig merely laughed scornfully.

"Do you feel prepared?" Jack persisted.

"I suppose I'm as ready as I'll ever be. But that's not saying a whole bunch."

"What was Randolph's advice?"

Craig forced another laugh. "You know, the usual. I'm not supposed to pick my nose, fart too loudly, or laugh at the judge."

"I'm serious," Jack said. "I'd like to know."

Craig regarded Jack. A bit of the tenseness that had been so apparent drained from his face. "The usual admonitions like I mentioned at lunch and maybe a few more. I'm supposed to avoid stuttering and inappropriate laughter. Can you believe that? Tony Fasano is going to verbally attack me, and I'm supposed to calmly let it happen. If anything, I'm supposed to look hurt and not angry so the jury will sympathize with me. Can you imagine?"

"I think it sounds reasonable."

Craig's eyes narrowed as he looked at Jack. "Maybe to you, but not to me."

"I couldn't help but hear raised voices. I mean, I couldn't hear what it was about. Did you and Randolph disagree on something?"

"Not really," Craig said. "He just pissed me off. Of course, that was what he was trying to do. He was play-acting as if he were Fasano. You see the problem is that when I'm on the stand, I'm sworn, whereas Tony Fasano won't be. That means he can make up and say whatever allegation he wants, and I'm supposed to have thick skin, but I don't. I even got mad at Randolph. I'm hopeless."

Jack watched as Craig drained his glass and then poured another drink. He knew that often the personality traits of really good clinicians like Craig made them susceptible to malpractice suits, and the same traits made them poor witnesses in their own defense. He also knew that the opposite was true: Really bad doctors made an effort at bedside manner to make up for their professional deficiencies and avoid suits, and the same doctors, if they were sued, could often offer Oscar-worthy performances on their behalf.

"It's just not looking good," Craig continued, more sullen than angry. "And I'm still worried Randolph is not the right guy, despite his experience. He's so damn pretentious. As slimy as Tony Fasano is, he has the jurors eating out of his hands."

"Juries have a surprising way of eventually seeing through the fog," Jack said.

"The other thing that really pisses me off about Randolph is he keeps talking about the appeal," Craig said as if he'd not heard Jack. "That was what put me over the top right at the end of our session. I couldn't believe he'd bring it up at that point. Of course, I know I have to think about it. Just like I have to think about what I'll be doing with the rest of my life. If I lose, I'm sure as hell not going to stay in practice."

"That's a double tragedy," Jack said. "The profession cannot afford to lose its best clinicians, nor can your patients."

"If I lose this case, I'm never going to be able to look at a patient without worrying about being sued and having to go through this kind of experience again. This has been the worst eight months of my life."

"But what would you do if you don't practice? You've got a young family."

Craig shrugged. "Probably work for big pharma in some capacity. There are lots of opportunities. I know several people who have gone that route. The other possibility is managing somehow to do my research full-time."

"Could you really do that sodium-channel work full-time and be content?" Jack questioned.

"Absolutely. It's exciting stuff. It's basic science yet has immediate clinical application."

"I suppose big pharma is interested in that arena."

"Without doubt."

"Switching subjects," Jack said. "While I was outside saying good-bye to everyone, I had a thought that I wanted to run by you."

"About what?"

"About Patience Stanhope. I've got the whole case file, which I've read over several times. It includes all your records, but the only thing from the hospital is the emergency-room sheet."

"That's all there was. She was never admitted."

"I know that, but there's no labwork other than what is mentioned in the notes, and no order sheet. What I'm wondering is whether a major mistake could have occurred at the hospital, like the wrong drug given or a large overdose. If so, whoever was responsible could be desperate about covering up their tracks and be more than happy you are set up to take the fall. I know it's a theory somewhere out there in left field, but it's not as far out as the conspiracy idea. What's your take? I mean, it's clear from what happened here this afternoon to your children that someone is very, very against my doing an autopsy, and if Fasano is not to blame, the reason has to involve something other than money."

Craig stared off for a minute, mulling over the idea. "It's another wild but interesting thought."

"I assume that during discovery all the pertinent records from the hospital were obtained."

"I believe so," Craig said. "And an argument against such a theory is that I was there with the patient the whole time. I would have sensed something like that. If there's a major overdose or the wrong drug, there's usually a marked change in the patient's status. There wasn't. From the time I first saw her at the Stanhope residence until she was pronounced, she just faded away, unresponsive to anything we did."

"Right," Jack said. "But maybe the idea is something to be kept in mind when I get to do the autopsy. I was planning on a toxicology screen regardless, but if there's a chance of an overdose or the wrong drug, it's more critical."

"What does a toxicology screen pick up?"

"The usual drugs, and even some unusual ones if they have high enough concentrations."

Craig polished off his second drink, eyed the scotch bottle, and thought better of pouring a third. He stood up. "Sorry not to be a better host, but I have a date with my favorite hypnotic agent."

"It's bad news mixing alcohol with sleeping pills."

"Really?" Craig questioned superciliously. "I never knew that!"

"See you in the morning," Jack said. He felt Craig's provocative comment did not deserve a response.

"Are you worried about the bad guys coming back?" Craig asked in a taunting tone.

"I'm not," Jack said.

"Me neither. At least not until after the autopsy is done."

"Are you having second thoughts?" Jack asked.

"Of course I'm having second thoughts, especially with you telling me the chances of finding something relevant are small and Randolph saying it's not going to influence the trial irrespective of what's found, because it won't be admissible."

"I said the chances of finding something were small before someone broke into your house warning you not to allow me to do it. But this isn't an argument. It's up to you and Alexis."

"She's set on it."

"Well, it's up to you guys. You have to tell me, Craig. Do you want me to do it?"

"I don't know what to think, especially after two double scotches."

"Why don't you just give me your final word in the morning," Jack said. He was losing patience. Craig was not the easiest guy to like, even without two double scotches.

"What kind of person would be willing to terrorize three young girls to make a point?" Craig asked.

Jack shrugged. It was the kind of question that didn't need an answer. He said good night, and Craig did the same before walking unsteadily out of the room.

While staying on the sofa but leaning his head way back and hyperextending himself, Jack could just catch a glimpse of Craig slowly mounting the stairs. It seemed to him Craig was already evidencing a touch of alcohol-induced dyskinesia, as though he didn't quite know where his feet were. Always the doctor, Jack wondered if he should check on Craig in the middle of the night. It was a question with no easy answer, since Craig would not take kindly to such solicitousness, with its implication of neediness, an anathema to him.

Jack got himself up and stretched. He could feel the weight of the revolver, and it was comforting even though he was not concerned about any intruders. He looked at his watch. It was too early to try to fall asleep. He looked at the blank TV: no interest there. For lack of a better plan, he went to get Craig's case file and carried it to the study. As a man of habit, he sat in the same chair he'd occupied on previous occasions. After turning on the floor lamp, he searched through the file for the hospital ER record.

Pulling out the sheet, Jack settled back. He'd skimmed through it before, particularly the part about the cyanosis. Now he wanted to read every word. But as he was doing so, he became distracted. His eyes had drifted to Craig's old-fashioned doctor's bag. All of a sudden a new thought occurred to him. He wondered what the incidence of false positives was with the bed-side biomarker kit.

First Jack went to the door to determine whether he could hear Craig moving about upstairs. Even though Craig had implied he didn't care if Jack looked in his bag, Jack still felt uncomfortable. But when he was convinced all was quiet, he pulled the leather doctor's bag from its shelf, opened it, and got out the biomarker kit. Opening up the product insert, he read that the technology was based on monoclonal antibodies, which are highly specific, meaning the chance of a false positive was probably close to zero.

"Oh, well," Jack said out loud. The insert went back in the box and the box went back to its location in the very bottom of the bag among the three discarded vials, and the bag went back on the shelf. *So much for another clever idea,* he thought.

Jack returned to the reading chair and to the ER sheet. Unfortunately, there was nothing even remotely suspicious, and as he'd noticed on the first reading, the cyanosis notation was the most interesting part.

All of a sudden the two phones on the two desks sprang to life simultaneously. The raucous ring shocked Jack in the otherwise silent house. The insistent ring continued, and Jack counted them. After the fifth ring, he began to believe Craig might not be hearing it, and Jack heaved himself out of the reading chair. Turning on the lamp on Alexis's desk, he looked at the caller I.D. The name was Leonard Bowman.

After the seventh ring, Jack was certain it was not going to be answered, so he lifted the handset. As he suspected, it was Alexis.

"Thanks for picking up," she said after Jack's hello.

"I was waiting on Craig, but I guess his combination nightcap has him in dreamland."

"Is everything okay there?" Alexis asked.

"Peaches and cream," Jack said. "How are things there?"

"Quite well. All things considered, the girls are doing terrific. Christina and Meghan are already asleep. Tracy is watching an old movie on TV. We all have to sleep in the same room, but I think that's a good idea."

"Craig is having second thoughts about my doing the autopsy."

"Why? I thought that was all decided."

"He's having the jitters for the girls' sake, but it was after he'd had two double scotches. He's going to let me know tomorrow."

"I'll call him in the morning. I think it should be done, all the more so because of today's threat. I mean, that's one of the reasons the girls and I came out here. Plan on doing it! I'll bring him around."

After some final small talk, including that they would see each other in the courtroom, they both hung up.

Back in the reading chair, Jack tried to concentrate on the case file, but he couldn't. He kept marveling about how much was going to happen in the next few days and wondering whether there would be any surprises. Little did he know.

CHAPTER SEVENTEEN

NEWTON, MASSACHUSETTS
Thursday, June 8, 2006
7:40 a.m.

The unease that Jack had experienced after Alexis and the kids left the evening before was magnified in the morning. Jack didn't know if Craig's mind-set was from the stress of his upcoming testimony or a hangover from his alcohol and sleeping pills, but he had reverted to his silent, brooding sullenness, similar to how he'd been on Jack's first morning at the Bowman residence. Back then Alexis and the children had made the situation sufferable, but without them it was decidedly unpleasant.

Jack had tried to be upbeat when he'd first emerged from his basement lair but had received a cold stare for his efforts. It was only after Jack had gotten himself some cereal and milk that Craig had said anything.

"I got a call from Alexis," Craig said in a husky, forlorn voice. "She said you two had spoken last night. Anyway, the message is: The autopsy is on."

"Fine," Jack responded simply. As bad a mood as Craig seemed to be in, Jack couldn't help but wonder what he would say if Jack owned up to having gone upstairs in the middle of the night to take a look at him and listen to his breathing. Everything had seemed normal enough, so Jack had not tried to wake him, which had been his original plan. It was a good thing he hadn't, considering Craig's current disposition without the intrusion and reminder of his neediness.

After Craig was ready to leave, he partially compensated for his behavior by coming over to Jack, who was at the dining table drinking coffee and glancing at the newspaper.

"I'm sorry for being a lousy host," Craig said in a more normal voice, devoid of either superciliousness or sarcasm. "This isn't my shining moment."

Out of respect, Jack pushed back his chair and stood up. "I understand what you are going through. I've never experienced a malpractice suit, but several of my friends did back in my ophthalmology days. I know it's awful and as bad as divorce."

"It sucks," Craig said.

Then Craig did something totally unexpected. He gave Jack an awkward hug, then immediately let go before Jack had had a chance to react. He avoided looking Jack in the eyes while he adjusted his suit jacket. "For what it's worth, I appreciate you coming up here. Thanks for your efforts, and I'm sorry you had to take a couple of whacks for me."

"I'm glad to have done it," Jack said, struggling to avoid sarcastically saying, "My pleasure." He hated being less than truthful, but he'd been caught off guard by the switch in Craig's behavior.

"Will I see you in the courtroom?"

"At some point."

"All right. See you then."

Jack watched Craig leave. Once again, he'd underestimated the man.

Jack went down to his basement guest room and put his belongings in his carry-on bag. He didn't know what to do about the bed linens. He ended up stripping them off the bed and leaving them and the towels in a heap. He folded the blankets. There was a notepad by the phone. He wrote a short thank-you note and put it on the blankets. He debated about the front door key but decided to keep it and give it back in person when he returned the case file to Alexis. He wanted to keep the case file until after the autopsy, in case the autopsy raised questions that the case file could shed light on or answer. He pulled on his jacket. He could feel the gun in one side and his cell phone on the other.

With the bulging manila envelope under one arm and his carry-on in the other hand, Jack climbed the stairs and opened the front door. Although the weather had been terrific since he'd been in Boston, it had taken a decided turn for the worse. It was darkly overcast and raining. Jack eyed his Hyundai. It was about fifty soggy feet away. Just to the side of the door was an umbrella stand. Jack pulled one out that said Ritz-Carlton. There was no reason he couldn't give it to Alexis when he returned the other things.

With the umbrella, it took several trips leaping over puddles to get his things in the car. When all was ready, he started the engine, turned on the wipers, and cleared away the windshield's mist with the side of his hand. He then backed out of the driveway, waved to the policeman sitting in his cruiser, apparently watching the house, and accelerated down the street.

He had to use his hand to clear the windshield mist again after only a short distance. With one eye on the road, he used the other to locate the defrost button. Once the defrost got up to speed, the mist problem abated. To help, Jack cracked the driver's-side window.

As Jack wound his way through the suburban streets, traffic gradually increased. Due to the dark, low cloud cover, many cars had their lights on. When he got to the entrance to the Massachusetts Turnpike, where he had to wait for a traffic light, he was reminded it was rush hour. Ahead, the toll road was swarming with racing autos, buses, and trucks creating a swirling, vaporous mist. Jack girded himself to enter the fray as he waited for the light to turn green. He was aware he was not a particularly good driver, especially since he rarely drove after moving to New York City a decade ago. Jack much preferred his beloved mountain bike, even though most people thought it dangerous to bike in city traffic.

The next thing Jack knew, something crashed into his car's rear, causing his head to bounce off his headrest. The moment he had recovered enough, he twisted in his seat to look out the water-streaked back window. He couldn't see much other than a large black vehicle pressed up against the rear of his. It was at this point that Jack realized his car was moving forward despite his foot continuing to compress the brake pedal.

Twisting back around to face forward, Jack's heart skipped a beat. He was being pushed through the red light! Outside, he could hear the horrid grating noise of his locked wheels against the pebble-strewn macadam as well as the growl of the powerful engine propelling him. The next thing Jack was aware of was a headlight bearing down on him from his left and a car horn blaring a dire warning. Then came a harrowing, screeching sound of rubber against pavement, followed by the glaring headlights being diverted ahead.

Reflexively Jack's eyes closed, expecting an impact into his car's left side. When it came, it was more of a brush than a crash, and Jack became aware of the water-blurred image of a car pressed sideways against his Hyundai alongside his driver's-side door. There was a scraping of metal against metal.

Jack lifted his foot from the brake, thinking the brake was not working and needed to be pumped. The second he did so, his car shot forward toward the press of racing cars on the turnpike. Jack jammed his foot back down on the brake pedal. He could feel his wheels lock and the grating sound of his tires against the road's surface reoccurred, but his forward speed did not lessen. Jack glanced behind him again. The large black car was ineluctably pushing him toward the dangerous toll road that was less than fifty feet away. Just before spinning his head around to face forward yet again, he caught sight of the pushing car's hood ornament. Although the fleeting image was indistinct in the fog and drizzle, Jack saw that it consisted of two crescent-shaped sprigs bordering a coat of arms. He instantly made the association. It was the hood ornament of a Cadillac, and in Jack's mind, a black Cadillac meant Franco until proven otherwise.

Since the brake was useless against the Cadillac's excessive horsepower, Jack released it and stomped on the accelerator instead. The Accent responded nimbly. There was another agonizing sound of metal against metal, and with a perceptible pop, the Hyundai managed to detach itself from its bullying fellow automobile.

Gripping the steering wheel in desperation, Jack merged into the four lanes of speeding highway traffic like he'd never merged before. At the last second, he actually closed his eyes, since there was no shoulder on that part of the road, so there was no choice but to join the stream of cars in the far right-hand lane. Although the Boston drivers had seemed overly aggressive to Jack during his previous driving experiences, he had to give them credit for being alert and for having rapid reflexes. Despite a cacophony of horn blowing and screeching tires, Jack's car managed to merge into the traffic. When he blinked his eyes open, he found himself compressed between two vehicles with no more than six feet in front and seemingly inches behind. Unfortunately, the car behind was an intimidating Hummer, and it stayed where it was, suggesting the driver was venomously angry.

Jack tried to adjust his speed exactly equal to the car in front, despite feeling it was much too fast for the weather. He felt he had little choice. He was reluctant to slow down for fear the Hummer would ram him in a similar fashion as the black Cadillac had. Meanwhile, he frantically tried to search for the Cadillac in his side- and rearview mirrors, but it wasn't easy. It required taking his eyes off the car in front, which was nothing but a hazy blur despite the windshield wipers working at top speed. Jack didn't see the Cadillac, but he did catch glimpses of the Hummer driver alternately shaking his fist and giving him the finger when he sensed Jack was looking in his direction.

The need to concentrate on driving was not the only handicap in the search for his vehicular assailant. Whirling eddies of fog and water vapor were whipped up into a frenzy by the rushing vehicles, particularly the trucks whose eighteen wheels, each almost the size of Jack's car, flailed against the wet pavement, sending billows of mist into the air around the edges of their mud flaps.

Suddenly, to Jack's right a short stretch of shoulder appeared as a turnout for disabled vehicles. He had to make a snap decision, since the length of the turnout was not long, and at the speed his car and the others were traveling, the opportunity would soon be lost. Impulsively, Jack veered to the right out of the line of traffic, jammed on the brake, then fought against the car's tendency to skid first one way, then the other.

With great relief, Jack was able to bring the car to a stop, but he didn't get a moment to rest. In the rearview mirror, he caught sight of the black Cadillac pulling out of the lines of traffic exactly as he had.

Jack sucked in a chestful of air, gripped the steering wheel with white knuckles, and stomped the accelerator to the floor. The acceleration wasn't neck-snapping, but it was still impressive. Ahead, the fenced end of the pullout rapidly loomed, forcing Jack again to merge abruptly into the traffic. This time it wasn't blind, but it caused the same fury in the driver behind. Yet with the Cadillac obviously still in pursuit, Jack didn't concern himself. In fact, there was a good side. The man continued to express his anger by riding Jack's tail. Under normal circumstances, Jack would have considered such a situation dangerous and irritating. But now it meant that there was no room for the Cadillac, which would have been far worse than a mere irate driver.

Jack knew that coming ahead some miles down the road was his turnoff that surprisingly forked from the far left lane. Not too far beyond that were tollbooths marking the end of the toll road. Jack tried to reason which was better. The tollbooths meant staff and maybe even State Troopers, which was good, but it also meant long lines, which was bad. Although David Thomas had

relieved Franco of his gun, Jack knew the man undoubtedly had access to others. If Franco was crazy enough
to ram him in an attempt to push him out into traffic,
Jack felt he'd have little qualms about shooting at him.
The exit road had less staff and no troopers, which was
bad, but no lines, particularly in two fast lanes, which
was good.

As Jack was weighing these possibilities, he'd been
vaguely aware that some distance beyond the buildings
spanning the toll road, a true shoulder appeared. He'd
not thought much about it since he had no intention of
pulling out of the traffic for a second time. What he'd
not considered was the Cadillac using the breakdown
lane to catch up.

It wasn't until the Cadillac pulled alongside that Jack
caught sight of it. And when he did, he saw that its
driver's-side window was down. More important, Franco
was driving with one hand. In his other hand was a gun,
which he proceeded to stick out the window. Jack
touched his brakes and simultaneously his passenger-side
window shattered into a million pieces and a bullet hole
appeared in the plastic cover over the windshield support
to Jack's immediate left.

The man behind Jack was back to blowing his horn
continuously in utter exasperation. Jack could fully
understand his agitation. He was also impressed the man
had been able to avoid a collision, making Jack vow never
to complain about Boston drivers ever again.

The next instant after Jack had touched his brake, he
pressed the accelerator to the floor and used his newly
developed merging technique to move laterally across
several lanes of traffic. Now everybody around him was
beeping to beat the band. Jack couldn't rest on his lau-

rels since Franco had pulled an even greater merging feat and was now in the same lane as Jack with only one vehicle between them. Ahead, Jack saw the sign for his turnoff, Allston-Cambridge Left Lane, rapidly approach and then whip by. Impulsively, he made a snap decision that depended on his agile, compact Accent being able to make a tighter, high-speed turn than Franco's boat-like vintage Cadillac. Franco cooperated by remaining in lane, presumably avoiding using the relatively empty far-left lane to overtake Jack for fear of being forced off the road by the swiftly approaching exit.

Jack's entire body tensed as he fixed his eyes on his goal. What he wanted to do was execute a left turn as sharp as he could into the exit without rolling the car and clear a triangle of barrel-sized yellow plastic containers placed to cushion any vehicles destined to hit the concrete exit abutment. What he hoped was that Franco would have to sail on past.

At what he hoped was the proper instant, Jack whipped the steering wheel counterclockwise. He heard the tires screech in protest and felt the powerful centrifugal force attempting to fishtail the car or cause it to flip. Tentatively, he touched the brake, not knowing if it helped or hindered. For a second it felt as if the car was on two wheels, but it straightened itself and agilely missed the protective canisters with several feet to spare.

Rapidly throwing the steering wheel in the opposite direction, Jack straightened the car on the exit, heading for the line of tollbooths directly ahead. He began to brake. At that point, he glanced into the mirror just in time to see Franco slam sideways into the apex of yellow barrels. What was most impressive was that the Cadillac was already upside down, ostensibly having immediately rolled when Franco tried to follow Jack.

Jack winced at the force of the impact, which threw tires and other debris into the air. He found himself marveling at the degree of Franco's anger, which had obviously trumped any rationality.

As Jack approached the line of tollbooths, the two attendants leapt out from their stations, abandoning the drivers waiting to pay their tolls. One of the attendants was carrying a fire extinguisher. Jack checked his rearview mirror. He now saw tendrils of fire licking up the side of the upended vehicle.

With the reassurance that there was little he could do, Jack drove off. As he put some distance between himself and the whole episode beginning with Franco slamming into the back of his car, he got progressively more anxious, to the point that he was noticeably shaking. In some respects, such a response surprised him more than the experience itself had. It hadn't been that many years ago that he would have relished such a happening. Now he felt more responsible. Laurie was depending on him to stay alive and be at Riverside Church at one thirty the very next day.

When Jack pulled into the Langley-Peerson Funeral Home twenty minutes later, he'd recovered enough to recognize he had a responsibility to report what he knew about Franco's accident, although he didn't want to take time to go to the Boston police. Remaining in the car, he got out his phone and Liam Flanagan's business card, which had his cell number. Jack placed the call. When Liam answered, Jack could hear a babble of voices in the background.

"Am I calling at a bad time?" Jack asked.

"Hell, no. I'm in line in Starbucks to get my mocha latte. What's up."

Jack told the story of his latest run-in with Franco from its beginning to its dramatic and decisive conclusion.

"I've got one question," Liam said. "Did you return fire with my gun?"

"Of course not," Jack said. It was hardly the question he expected. "To tell the truth, the idea never even occurred to me."

Liam told Jack he'd relay the information to the State Troopers who patrol the turnpike, and if there were any questions, he'd have them call Jack directly.

Pleased that the reporting job was as easy as it had been, Jack leaned forward and examined the bullet hole in the car's plastic interior trim, knowing Hertz was not going to be happy. It was relatively neatly punched out, as he'd frequently seen with entrance wounds in victims' skulls. Jack inwardly shuddered at the thought of how close it had been to being his skull, which made him wonder if Franco's attacking him with his vehicle had been plan B. Plan A could have been either waiting for Jack to come out of the Bowmans' house or, worse yet, breaking into the house during the night. Maybe the police surveillance had been the deterrent, making Jack shudder anew at how sure he'd felt the previous night that there would be no intruders. Ignorance was bliss.

Making a conscious decision not to dwell on "what ifs," Jack got the umbrella from the backseat and went into the funeral home. With no services apparently scheduled, the establishment was back to its silent, sepul-chral serenity, save for the barely audible Gregorian

chants. Jack had to find his own way back to Harold's
heavily curtained office.

"Dr. Stapleton," Harold said, seeing Jack in his doorway. "I'm afraid I have bad news."

"Please!" Jack urged. "Don't say that. I've already had
a bumpy, difficult morning."

"I got a call from Percy Gallaudet, the backhoe operator. The cemetery has him on another job, then he's
going off-site to dig out someone's sewer line. He said
he won't be able to get to your job until tomorrow."

Jack took a breath and looked away for a moment to
calm himself. Harold's unctuous manner made this new
hurdle that much more difficult to bear. "Okay," Jack
said slowly. "How about we get another backhoe. There
must be more than one in the area."

"There are a lot, but only one is currently acceptable
to Walter Strasser, the superintendent of the Park
Meadow Cemetery."

"Are there kickbacks involved?" Jack said, more as a
statement than a question. Only one backhoe operator
smelled suspiciously like small-town graft.

"Heaven knows, but the reality is that we are stuck
with Percy Gallaudet."

"Shit!" Jack exclaimed. There wasn't any way he
could do the autopsy in the morning and still be at the
Riverside Church at one thirty in the afternoon.

"There's another problem," Harold said. "The vault
company's truck is not available tomorrow, and I had to
call them and tell them we were not going to use them
today."

"Wonderful!" Jack commented sarcastically. He took
another breath. "Let's go over this carefully so we know

what our options are. Is there some way we can accomplish this without the vault company?"

"Absolutely not," Harold said indignantly. "It would mean leaving the vault in the ground."

"Hey, I don't mind if the vault stays put. Why do you have to take it out anyway?"

"That's the way it is done. It is a top-of-the-line vault stipulated by the late Mr. Stanhope. The one-piece lid has to be removed with care."

"Couldn't the lid be removed without lifting the whole vault?"

"It could, I suppose, but it might crack."

"So what difference would that make?" Jack questioned, losing patience. He felt that burial practices in general were bizarre and was a fan of cremation. All someone had to do was look at mummies of Egyptian pharaohs gruesomely on display to realize allowing one's earthly remains to hang around was not necessarily a good idea.

"A crack could compromise the seal," Harold said with renewed indignation.

"I'm getting the picture the vault can be left in the ground," Jack said. "I'll take responsibility. If the lid cracks, we can get a new one. I'm certain that would please the vault company."

"I suppose," Harold said, moderating his stance.

"I'm going to go and personally speak to Percy and Walter and see if I can resolve this impasse."

"As you wish. Just keep me informed. I must be present if and when the vault is opened."

"I'll be sure to do that," Jack said. "Can you give me directions to the Park Meadow?"

Jack walked out of the funeral home in a different

frame of mind than he was when he had gone in. He was
now irritated as well as overstimulated. Three things that
never failed to rile him were bureaucracy, incompetence,
and stupidity, especially when they occurred together,
which they often did. Getting Patience Stanhope out of
the ground was proving to be more arduous than he had
expected when he first insouciantly suggested doing a
postmortem.

When he got to the car he looked at it critically for
the first time since the turnpike ordeal. Besides the
broken window and the bullet in the windshield post,
the whole left side was scraped and dented, and the rear
was pushed in. The back was so damaged he feared he
might not be able to open the trunk. Luckily, his fears
were unfounded when he was able to pop the lid. He
wanted to be certain he'd have access to the autopsy
materials Latasha had given him. What Hertz's reaction
was going to be to all the damage he didn't want to think
about, although he was happy he'd opted for full insurance.

Once inside the car he got out the map and, combining it with Harold's directions, he was able to plot his
route. The cemetery wasn't far, and he found it without
much effort or incident. It dominated a hill within sight
of an impressive religious institution that looked similar
to a college with numerous separate buildings. The
cemetery was quite pleasant, even in the rain, and looked
like a park with headstones. The main gate was an elaborate stone structure that spanned the entrance road and
bristled with statuary of the prophets. The individual
gates were black, cast-iron grates and would have been
forbidding except that they were permanently propped

open. The entire cemetery was encircled with a fence
that matched the entranceway gates.

Just beyond the portal and tucked behind it was a
Gothic building comprising an office and multi-bay
garage. It stood on a cobblestoned area from which
roads led up into the cemetery proper. Jack parked his
car and walked through the open door of the office.
There were two people at two desks. The rest of the furniture included several old four-drawer metal filing
cabinets and a library table with captain's chairs. On the
wall was a large map of the cemetery depicting all the
separate plots.

"Can I help you?" a dowdy woman asked. She was
neither friendly nor unfriendly as she gave Jack an
appraising look. It was a deportment Jack was beginning
to associate with New England.

"I'm looking for Walter Strasser," Jack said.

The woman pointed toward the man without looking
at him or back at Jack. She had already returned her
attention to her monitor screen.

Jack stepped over to the man's desk. He was of indeterminate late middle age and corpulent enough to
suggest he indulged in his share of the seven deadly sins,
particularly gluttony and sloth. He was sitting stolidly at
the desk with his hands clasped over his impressive girth.
His full face was red like an apple.

"Are you Mr. Strasser?" Jack asked when the man
made no attempt to speak or move.

"I am."

Jack made a rapid introduction that included flashing
his official ME badge. He went on to explain his need to
examine the late Patience Stanhope to help with a civil
lawsuit and that the required permits had been obtained

for the exhumation. He said all he needed was the corpse.

"Mr. Harold Langley has spoken to me about this issue at length," Walter said.

Thanks for telling me straight off, Jack thought but did not say. Instead, he asked, "Did he also mention there's a scheduling problem? We had planned on the exhumation happening today."

"Mr. Gallaudet has a conflict. I told him to call Mr. Langley this morning and explain the situation."

"I got the message. Why I came over here in person is to see if some small extra consideration for your efforts and for Mr. Gallaudet's could get the exhumation back on today's schedule. I'm afraid I must leave town this evening. . . ." Jack trailed off with his vague offer of a bribe, hoping that covetousness was as much a part of Walter's foibles as gluttony seemed to be.

"What kind of extra consideration?" Walter asked, to Jack's gratification. The man's eyes flicked warily toward the woman, suggesting she was not to be party to his shenanigans.

"I was thinking of double the usual fee in cash."

"There's no problem from this end," Walter said. "But you'll have to talk with Percy."

"How about another backhoe?"

Walter chewed on the suggestion for a moment, then declined. "Sorry! Percy has a long association with Park Meadow. He knows and respects our rules and regulations."

"I understand," Jack said agreeably while guessing Percy's long association most likely had more to do with kickbacks than with rules and regulations. But Jack was not going to belabor the issue unless he struck out with

Percy. "Word is that Mr. Gallaudet is doing work on-site as we speak."

"He's up by the big maple tree with Enrique and Cesar, preparing for a noontime burial."

"Who are Enrique and Cesar?"

"They are our caretakers."

"Can I drive up there?"

"By all means."

As Jack drove up the hill, the rain lessened and then conveniently stopped. He was relieved, since he was driving without a passenger-side window, thanks to Franco.

Jack turned off the windshield wipers. As he rose, he got a progressively better view of the surrounding area. To the west near the horizon was a band of clear sky promising better weather in the near future.

Jack found Percy and the others near the crest of the hill. Percy was in the glass-enclosed cab of his backhoe, scooping out a grave, while the two caretakers looked on, leaning on long-handled shovels. Percy had the backhoe's scoop down in the deep trench, and the vehicle's diesel engine was straining to draw it near and then up and out. The fresh soil was piled in a cone on a large, waterproof tarpaulin. A white pickup truck with the cemetery's name stenciled on the door was pulled to the side.

Jack parked his car and walked over to the backhoe. He tried to get Percy's attention by shouting his name, but the roar of the diesel drowned him out. It wasn't until he rapped on the glass of the cab that Percy became aware he was being accosted. Percy immediately eased up on the controls, and the diesel's roar became a more bearable purr. Percy opened the cab's door.

"What's up?" he yelled as if the backhoe's engine was still making a considerable racket.

"I need to talk to you about a job," Jack yelled back.

Percy bounced out of the cab. He was a short, squir-relly man who moved in sudden, quick jerks and had a perpetually questioning expression on his face, with fixed raised eyebrows and a furrowed forehead. His hair was short but spiked, and both forearms were heavily tat-tooed.

"What kind of job?" Percy asked.

Jack went through an even more elaborate introduc-tion and explanation than he had used with Walter Strasser, in hope of evoking whatever pathos Percy might have possessed in order to reschedule Patience Stan-hope's resurrection for that day. Unfortunately, it didn't work.

"Sorry, man," Percy said. "After this job, I got a buddy with a backed-up sewer and newborn twins."

"I heard you were busy," Jack said. "But as I told Mr. Strasser, I'm willing to pay double the fee in cash to get it done today."

"And what did Mr. Strasser say?"

"He said there was no problem from his end."

Percy's eyebrows hiked up a smidgen as he mulled over Jack's offer. "So you are willing to pay twice the cemetery fee and twice my fee?"

"Only if it gets done today."

"I still have to dig out my buddy," Percy said. "It would have to be after that."

"So what time would you be able to do it?"

Percy pursed his lips and nodded his head as he pon-dered. He checked his watch. "For sure, it would be after two."

"But it will get done?" Jack questioned. He had to be certain.

"It'll get done," Percy promised. "I just don't know what I'm going to run into with my buddy's sewer. If that goes fast, I could be back here around two. If there's a problem, then it's anybody's guess."

"But you'll still do it even if it is late in the afternoon."

"Absolutely," Percy said. "For twice my usual fee."

Jack stuck out his hand. Percy gave it a quick shake. While Jack returned to his beat-up car, Percy climbed back into his backhoe's cab. Before Jack started the engine, he called Harold Langley.

"Here's the story," Jack said in a voice that implied there was no room for discussion. "We're back on for digging up Patience sometime after two this afternoon."

"You don't have a more precise time?"

"It's going to be after Mr. Gallaudet finishes what he has scheduled. That's all I can tell you at the moment."

"I only need a half-hour's notice," Harold said. "I'll meet you graveside."

"Fine," Jack said. He struggled to keep the sarcasm out of his voice. Considering the fee he would be paying the Langley-Peerson Funeral Home, he felt Harold should be the one out running around and strong-arming Walter Strasser and Percy Gallaudet.

With the sound of Percy's backhoe grinding away, Jack tried to think of what else he had to do. He checked his watch. It was close to ten thirty. The way things were going, Jack's intuition told him that he'd be lucky to get Patience Stanhope back to the Langley-Peerson Home in the mid- to late afternoon, which meant that Dr. Latasha Wylie might be available. He wasn't sure her offer to help was entirely sincere, but he thought he'd give her the benefit of the doubt. With help the case would go faster, and he'd have someone to bounce ideas off of and to offer opinions. He also wanted the bone saw she offered to bring. Although he didn't think that the brain would be important in this particular case, Jack hated to do anything half-assed. More important, he thought there might be a chance he would want to use a microscope or a dissecting scope, and Latasha's presence would make that a viable possibility. Most important was her boss's offer of help with toxicology, which Latasha would be able to make happen. Now that Jack had the idea of an overdose or a wrong medication given at the hospital, he definitely wanted a toxicology screen, and he'd need it done immediately for it to be included in the report.

Such thoughts made Jack concede a distinct possibility that he had been unconsciously avoiding, namely, that there was a good chance he might not make the last shuttle flight from Boston to New York, meaning he'd be forced to fly in the morning. Since he knew the first flights were at the crack of dawn, there was no worry about making the one thirty church service, even with a stop at the apartment for his tuxedo. The concern was telling Laurie.

Acknowledging that he was not up to such a conversation and rationalizing that he didn't know for sure he wouldn't make the flight that evening, Jack opted not to try to phone at that time. He rationalized further that it would be far better to speak to her when he had definitive information.

Leaning to the side to facilitate getting his wallet from his back pocket, Jack got out Latasha Wylie's card and dialed her cell number. Considering the time, he wasn't surprised he got her voicemail. Undoubtedly, she was in the autopsy room. The message he left was simple. The exhumation was delayed, so the autopsy would be late in the afternoon, and he'd love to have help if she was inclined. He left his cell phone number.

With his telephoning out of the way, Jack switched his attention to a practical problem. Thanks to his amateur-ish bribing of Walter and Percy in which he'd obviously offered too much considering how rapidly they had accepted, he was now obligated to come up with the promised cash. The twenty or thirty dollars he normally carried in his wallet wasn't going to get him far. But cash wasn't a problem, thanks to his credit card. All he needed was an ATM, and there had to be plenty in the city.

When Jack had done everything he could think of, he resigned himself to going back to the courtroom. He wasn't excited about the idea. He'd seen quite enough of his sister being humiliated, and the initial slight twinge of schadenfreude he'd felt but barely admitted to himself at Craig's comeuppance had long since disap-peared. Jack had come to have strong empathy for both individuals and found it distasteful to witness them being skewered and their relationship debased by the likes of Tony Fasano for his venal self-interest.

On the other hand, Jack had promised both individ-uals he'd show up, and both had in their own ways expressed appreciation for his being there. With these thoughts in mind, Jack started his rent-a-car, managed a three-point turn, and drove out of the cemetery. Just outside the elaborate statue-encrusted gate, he pulled to the side of the road to glance at the map. It was a good thing, because he immediately discerned there was a much better way to get into Boston proper than retracing the route back past the funeral home.

Once under way, Jack found himself smiling. He wasn't quite laughing, but he was suddenly amused. He'd been to Boston for two and a half days, had been racking his brain over a senseless medical malpractice lawsuit, had been slapped and punched, had been shot at, and had been terrorized by a thug in a black Cadillac, and yet had, in reality, accomplished nothing. There was a kind of comic irony to the whole affair that appealed to his admittedly warped sense of humor.

Then another thought occurred to him. He'd become progressively concerned about Laurie's response to his being delayed in Boston to the point that he had become progressively reluctant to talk with her for fear of her response. But he wasn't concerned about the delay itself. If doing the autopsy forced him to fly to New York in the morning, he had to acknowledge that he might not make the wedding. Even though the chances were small that that would be the case, since there was a flight scheduled every thirty minutes from six thirty a.m. on, the probability was not zero, yet it didn't bother him. And the fact that it didn't bother him made him question his unconscious motivations. He loved Laurie, of that he was certain, and he believed he wanted to remarry. So why wasn't he more concerned?

Jack had no answers other than a concession that life was more complicated than his usual devil-may-care attitude would suggest. He apparently functioned on multiple levels, some of which were guarded if not actively suppressed.

With no cars chasing him, no misty fog to negotiate, and no rush-hour traffic, Jack made excellent time driving into downtown Boston. Even though he was approaching from a new direction, he was able to stumble onto the Boston Public Garden and the Boston Common where the two were bisected by Charles Street. And once he found that, he'd also found the underground garage he'd previously used.

After parking the car, Jack walked back to the attendant and asked about an ATM. He was directed to the commercial section of Charles Street and found the machine across from the hardware store where he'd purchased the unused pepper spray. With the upper limit of cash he could withdraw in hand, Jack followed his previous day's route in reverse. He walked up Beacon Hill, enjoying the neighborly ambience of the handsome town houses, many with carefully cultivated window boxes overflowing with flowers. The recent rain had washed the streets and the bricked sidewalks. The overcast sky made him aware of something he'd not noticed in the sunlight the day before: The nineteenth-century gas lamps were all ablaze, apparently day in, day out.

Pushing into the courtroom, Jack hesitated by the exit. Superficially, the scene looked exactly as he'd left it the afternoon before, except that Craig was on the stand instead of Leona. There was the same cast of characters mirroring the same attitudes. The jurors were impassive, as if they were cutout figures, save for the plumber's assistant, who made examining his nails a continuous endeavor. The judge was preoccupied with the papers on his desk, similar to the day before, and the spectators were contrarily attentive.

As Jack's eyes scanned the spectators, he saw Alexis in her usual spot with a seat next to her apparently saved for him. On the opposite side of the spectator

gallery in the spot normally occupied by Franco sat
Antonio. He was a smaller version of Franco but
significantly more handsome. He was now wearing the
Fasano team apparel: gray suit, black shirt, and black
tie. Although Jack had been reasonably confident
Franco would be out of the picture for a few days, he
wondered if he'd have trouble with Antonio. He also
wondered if either Franco or Antonio or both had
anything to do with the assault on Craig's children.

Appropriately excusing himself, Jack moved into the
aisle where Alexis was sitting at the very end, the closest
seat to the jury box. She saw him coming and flashed a
quick, nervous smile. Jack didn't take it as auspicious.
She gathered up her belongings so he could sit. They
gripped hands briefly before he sat.

"How's it going?" Jack whispered, leaning toward
her.

"Better now that Randolph is doing the cross."

"What happened with Tony Fasano on the direct?"

Alexis cast a fleeting glance at Jack, betraying her anx-
iousness. Her facial muscles were tense, and her eyes
were more wide open than usual. She had her hands
tightly clasped in her lap.

"Not good?" Jack questioned.

"It was terrible," Alexis admitted. "The only positive
thing that could be said was that Craig's testimony was
consistent with his deposition. In no way did he contra-
dict himself."

"Don't tell me he got angry: not after all that
rehearsal."

"He got furious after only an hour or so, and it was
downhill from there. Tony knew his buttons, and he
pressed every one. The worst part was when Craig told

Tony he had no right to criticize nor question doctors who were sacrificing their lives to take care of their patients. Craig then went on to call Tony a despicable ambulance-chaser."

"Not good," Jack said. "Even if it is true."

"It got worse," Alexis said forcibly, raising her voice.

"Excuse me," a voice said from behind. Someone had tapped Jack on the shoulder.

"We can't hear the testimony," the spectator complained.

"Sorry," Jack said. He turned back to Alexis. "Want to step out into the hall for a moment?"

Alexis nodded. She obviously needed a break.

They stood up. Alexis left her things. They worked their way to the main aisle. Jack opened the heavy courtroom door as quietly as possible. In the elevator lobby, they sat on a leather-covered bench, hunched over, elbows on knees.

"For the life of me," Alexis muttered. "I don't see what all those voyeurs get out of watching this damn trial."

"Have you ever heard the term *schadenfreude*?" Jack asked, marveling he'd just been musing about it a half-hour previously in relation to his initial reaction to Craig's imbroglio.

"Remind me," Alexis suggested.

"It's German. It refers to when people exult over someone else's problems and difficulties."

"I'd forgotten the German term," Alexis said. "But the concept I'm well aware of. As prevalent as it is, we should have a word for it in English. Hell, it's what sells tabloids. Anyway, I actually know why people are in there watching Craig's ordeal. They see doctors as powerful, successful people. So don't listen to me when I carp."

"Do you feel all right?"

"Other than a headache, I'm okay."

"What about the children?"

"Apparently, they're doing fine. They think they're on vacation, skipping school and staying at Grandma's. There have been no calls on my cell. Each of them knows the number by heart, and I would have heard if there was a problem of any sort."

"I've had an eventful morning."

"Really? What's going on with the autopsy? We're in the market for a miracle."

Jack told the story of his morning's ordeal on the Massachusetts Turnpike, which Alexis listened to with a progressive drooping of her lower jaw. She was equally astounded and alarmed.

"I should be asking you if you are all right," she said when Jack described Franco's final, spectacular upside-down crash.

"I'm fine. The rent-a-car is worse for wear. I know Franco's hurting. He's probably in a hospital somewhere. I wouldn't be surprised if he's also under arrest. I reported the incident to the same Boston detective that came to the house last night. I would assume the authorities would take a dim view of discharging firearms on the Massachusetts Turnpike."

"My God," Alexis said sympathetically. "I'm sorry all this has happened to you. I can't help but feel responsible."

"No need! I'm afraid I have a penchant for trouble. It's all my own doing. But I'll tell you, everything that's happened has done nothing but fan my determination to do this damn autopsy."

"What is the status?"

Jack described his machinations with Harold Langley, Walter Strasser, and Percy Gallaudet.

"My gosh," Alexis said. "After all this effort, I hope it shows something significant."

"You and me both."

"Are you okay with possibly putting off flying to New York to tomorrow morning?"

"What has to be has to be," Jack said with a shrug. He wasn't about to get into that personally thorny issue.

"What about with your wife-to-be, Laurie?"

"I haven't told her yet," Jack admitted.

"Good lord!" Alexis commented. "This is not a good way for me to start out a relationship with a new sister-in-law."

"Let's get back to what's going on in the trial," Jack said to change the subject. "You were about to tell me how Craig's testimony got worse."

"After he castigated Tony for being a despicable ambulance-chaser, he took it upon himself to lecture the jury that they were not his peers. He said they were incapable of judging his actions, since they'd never had to try to save someone like he tried to save Patience Stanhope."

Jack slapped a hand to his forehead in stupefaction. "What was Randolph doing during this?"

"Everything he could. He was jumping up and down objecting, but to no avail. He tried to get the judge to recess, but the judge asked Craig if he needed a rest, and Craig said no, so on it went."

Jack shook his head. "Craig is his own worst enemy, although . . ."

"Although what?" Alexis questioned.

"Craig has a point. In some respects, he's speaking for all us doctors. I bet most every physician who's gone through the hell of a medical malpractice trial feels the same way. It's just that they would have the sense not to say it."

"Well, he sure as hell shouldn't have said it. If I were a juror fulfilling my civic responsibility and got that kind of rebuke, I'd be incensed and much more apt to buy into Tony's interpretation of events."

"Was that the worst part?"

"There were many parts that qualified for being the worst. Tony got Craig to admit he'd had some concern that the fateful house call was for a legitimate emergency, as Leona had testified, and also that a heart attack was on his list of possible diagnoses. He also got Craig to admit that driving from the Stanhope residence to Symphony Hall would take a shorter time than from the Newton Memorial Hospital, and that he was eager to get to the concert before it began to show off his trophy girlfriend. And perhaps particularly incriminating, he got Craig to admit he'd said all those unflattering things about Patience Stanhope to the tart, Leona, including that Patience's passing was a blessing for everyone."

"Whoa," Jack said with yet another shake of his head. "Not good!"

"Not good at all. Craig managed to present himself as an arrogant, uncaring M.D. who was more interested in getting to Symphony Hall on time with his sex object than doing what was right for his patient. It was exactly what Randolph told him not to do."

Jack sat up straight. "So what is Randolph doing on cross-examination?"

"Attempted damage control would be the best description. He's trying to rehabilitate Craig on each individual issue, from the PP, problem patient, designation all the way to the events that happened on the night Patience Stanhope died. When you came in, Craig was testifying to the difference between Patience's condition when he arrived at the home and the description he'd gotten from Jordan Stanhope on the phone. Randolph had already made sure that Craig told the jury that he did not say Patience Stanhope was having a heart attack when he was speaking with Jordan, but rather it was something that had to be ruled out. Of course, that was in contradiction to what Jordan had said during his testimony."

"Did you get any sense of how the jury was responding to Craig's testimony during the cross as compared with the direct?"

"They seem more impassive now than before, but that may be just my pessimistic perception. I'm not optimistic after Craig's performance on direct. Randolph has a real uphill struggle ahead of him. He told me this morning that he's going to ask Craig to tell his life's story to counter Tony's character assassination."

"Why not," Jack said. Even though he wasn't all that enthusiastic, he felt a rekindling of sympathy for Alexis and wanted to be supportive. As they returned to their seats in the courtroom, he wondered how a finding for the plaintiff would affect Alexis's relationship with Craig. Jack had never championed their union, from the first time he'd met Craig some sixteen years previously. Craig and Alexis had met while in training at the Boston Memorial Hospital and had come as houseguests to Jack's home while they were engaged. Jack had found

Craig insufferably self-centered and one-dimensionally oriented toward medicine. But now that Jack had had a chance to see them together in their own environment, despite the current, difficult circumstance, he could see that they complemented each other. Alexis's very mildly histrionic and dependent character, which had been much more apparent as a child, melded well with Craig's more serious narcissism. In a lot of ways, from Jack's perspective, they complemented each other.

Jack settled back and got himself as comfortable as he could under the circumstances. Randolph was standing stiffly erect at the podium, exuding his normal blue-blooded resplendence. Craig was in the witness box, leaning slightly forward, his shoulders rounded. Randolph's voice was crisply articulate, melodic, and slightly sibilant. Craig's was vapid, as if he'd been in an argument and was now exhausted.

Jack felt Alexis's hand insinuate itself between his elbow and his side and then move forward to grab his hand. He squeezed in return, and they exchanged a fleeting smile.

"Dr. Bowman," Randolph intoned. "You've wanted to be a doctor since you were given a toy doctor's kit at age four and proceeded to administer to your parents and older brother. But I understand there was a particular event in your childhood that especially firmed this altruistic career choice. Would you tell the court about this episode."

Craig cleared his throat. "I was fifteen years old and in tenth grade. I was a manager for the football team. I'd tried to make the team but didn't, which was a big disappointment for my father, since my older brother had been a star player. So I was the manager, which was nothing more than the water boy. During the time-outs, I ran onto the field with a bucket, ladle, and paper cups. During a home game, one of our players was hurt and a time-out was called. I dashed onto the field with the bucket, but as I drew near I could see the injured player was a friend of mine. Instead of carrying my bucket to the huddle of players, I ran to my friend. I was the first one from the sidelines to get to him, and what I confronted was disturbing. He had badly broken his leg such that his cleated foot stuck off in a markedly abnormal direction, and he was writhing in agony. I was so struck by his need and my inability to help him that I decided on the spot that not only did I want to become a doctor, I had to become a doctor."

"That is a heartrending story," Randolph said, "and stirring because of your immediate compassionate impulse and the fact that it motivated you to follow what was to be a difficult path. Becoming a doctor was not easy for you, Dr. Bowman, and that altruistic urge you so eloquently described had to be strong indeed to propel you over the obstacles you faced. Could you tell the court something of your inspiring Horatio Alger story?"

Craig perceptively straightened in the witness chair.

"Objection," Tony shouted, getting to his feet. "Immaterial."

Judge Davidson took off his reading glasses. "Counsels, approach the bench."

Dutifully, Randolph and Tony congregated to the judge's right.

"Listen!" Judge Davidson said, pointing his glasses at Tony. "You made character a centerpiece of the plaintiff's case. I allowed that, over Mr. Bingham's objection, with the proviso you established foundation, which I believe you did. What's good for the goose is good for the gander. The jury has every right to hear about Dr. Bowman's motivations and training. Do I make myself clear?"

"Yes, Your Honor," Tony said.

"And furthermore, I don't want to hear a flurry of objections in this regard."

"I understand, Your Honor," Tony said.

Tony and Randolph retreated to their original spots, with Tony at the plaintiff's table and Randolph at the podium.

"Objection overruled," Judge Davidson called out for the court recorder's benefit. "Witness may proceed to answer the question."

"Do you recall the question?" Randolph asked.

"I should hope so," Craig said. "Where should I begin?"

"At the beginning would be appropriate," Randolph said. "I understand you did not get parental support."

"At least not from my father, and he ruled the house with an iron fist. He was resentful of us kids, particularly me, since I wasn't the football or hockey prodigy like my older brother, Leonard Junior. My father thought I was a 'candy ass,' and told me so on multiple occasions. When my browbeaten mother let it slip that I wanted to be a doctor, he said it would be over his dead body."

"Did he use those exact terms?"

"Absolutely! My father was a plumber who was dismissive of all professionals, which he labeled as a collective bunch of thieves. There was no way he wanted a son of his to become part of such a world, especially since he never finished high school. In fact, to the best of my knowledge, no one in my family on either side went to college, including my own brother, who ended up taking over my father's plumbing business."

"So your father wasn't supportive of your academic interests."

Craig laughed mirthlessly. "I was a closet reader as a youngster. I had to be. There were occasions on which my father whacked me around when he caught me reading instead of doing things around the house. When I got report cards, I had to hide them from my father and have my mother sign them secretly because I got all A's. With most of my friends, it was the other way around."

"Was it easier when you got to college?"

"In some ways yes and some ways no. He was disgusted with me, and instead of calling me a 'candy ass,' I became a 'highfalutin' ass.' He was embarrassed to talk about me to his friends. The biggest problem was that he refused to fill out the financial forms necessary to apply for a scholarship and, of course, refused to contribute a cent."

"How were you able to pay for college?"

"I relied on a combination of loans, scholastic awards, and every type of job I could manage to get and still keep a four-point-oh grade point average. The first couple of years it was mostly restaurant work, washing dishes and waiting tables. During the last two I was able to work in a variety of science labs. During summers I worked in the hospital at any job they would give me. Also, my brother helped me a little, although he couldn't do much, since he'd already started a family."

"Did your goal of medicine and your desire to help people support you during these difficult years?"

"Absolutely, especially the summer work in the hospital. I worshipped the doctors and the nurses, particularly the residents. I could not wait to become one of them."

"What happened when you got to medical school? Were your financial difficulties worse or less severe?"

"Much worse. The expenses were greater and the curriculum required more hours, essentially all day every day in contrast to college."

"How did you manage?"

"I borrowed as much as I was allowed; the rest I had to earn with a myriad of jobs all around the medical center. Luckily, jobs abounded."

"How did you find the time? Medical school is considered a full-time occupation and then some."

"I went without sleep. Well, not totally, since that is physically impossible. I learned to sleep in short snatches even during the day. It was difficult, but at least in medical school the goal was in sight, which made it easier to endure."

"What kind of jobs did you do?"

"All the usual medical center jobs like drawing blood, type- and cross-matching blood, cleaning animal cages: anything and everything that could be done at night. I even worked in the medical center kitchen. Then, during the second year, I landed a terrific job with a researcher studying sodium ion channels in nerve and muscle cells. I've even kept up that work today."

"With such a busy schedule in medical school, how were your grades?"

"Excellent. I was in the top ten percent of my class and a member of the Alpha Omega Alpha honorary scholastic society."

"What do you consider your biggest sacrifice? Was it the chronic lack of sleep?"

"No! It was the lack of any time for social contact. My classmates had time to interact and discuss the experience. Medical school is quite intense. During my third year, I was conflicted about whether to go into academic/basic-science medicine or clinical medicine. I would have loved to debate the pros and cons and have the benefit of others' opinions. I had to make the decision myself."

"And how did you make the decision?"

"I realized I liked taking care of people. There was an immediate gratification that I savored."

"So it was the contact with individuals that you found enjoyable and rewarding."

"Yes, and the challenge of coming up with the differential diagnoses, as well as the paradigm for narrowing the field."

"But it was the contact with the people and helping them that you cherished."

"Objection," Tony said. He had been progressively fidgeting. "Repetitious."

"Sustained," Judge Davidson said with a tired voice. "No need to belabor the point, Mr. Bingham. I am confident the jury has gotten it."

"Tell us about your residency training," Randolph said.

"That was a joy," Craig said. He was now sitting up straight, with his shoulders back. "Because of my grade point average, I was accepted to train at the prestigious Boston Memorial Hospital. It was a wonderful learning environment, and suddenly I was being paid, not a lot of money, but some. Equally important, I was no longer paying tuition, so I could begin to pay off the shocking debt I'd assumed from college and medical school."

"Did you continue to enjoy the necessarily close bonds that had to form between you and your patients?"

"Absolutely. That was by far the most rewarding part."

"Now tell us about your practice. I understand there were some disappointments."

"Not at first! Initially, my practice was everything I had dreamed it would be. I was busy and stimulated. I enjoyed going in each and every day. My patients were challenging intellectually and appreciative. But then the insurance companies began to withhold payments, often needlessly challenging certain charges, making it progressively difficult to do what was best for my patients. Receipts began to fall while costs continued to rise. In order to keep the doors open, I had to increase productivity, which is a euphemism for seeing more patients per hour. I was able to do this, but as it continued, I became progressively concerned about quality."

"I understand that your style of practice changed at that point."

"It changed dramatically. I was approached by an older, revered physician who was practicing concierge medicine but who was having health issues. He offered me a partnership."

"Excuse me for interrupting," Randolph said. "Perhaps you could refresh for the jurors the meaning of the term 'concierge medicine.' "

"It's a practice style in which the physician agrees to limit the practice size to offer extraordinary accessibility for an annual retainer fee."

"Does extraordinary accessibility include house calls?"

"It can. It's up to the doctor and the patient."

"What you are saying is that with concierge medicine, the doctor can tailor the service to the needs of the patient. Is that correct?"

"It is. Two fundamental principles of good patient care are the principle of patient welfare and the principle of patient autonomy. Seeing too many patients per hour threatens to violate these principles, since everything is rushed. When the doctor is pressed for time, the interview has to be forced, and when that happens, the patient's narrative is lost, which is tragic, since it is often within the narrative that the critical facts of the case are hidden. In a concierge practice, like mine, I can vary the time I spend with the patient and the location of the service according to the patient's needs and wishes."

"Dr. Bowman, is the practice of medicine an art or a science?"

"It is definitely an art, but it is based on a bedrock of proven science."

"Can medicine be appropriately practiced from a book?"

"No, it cannot. There are no two people alike in the world. Medicine has to be tailored for each patient individually. Also, books are invariably outdated by the time they come on the market. Medical knowledge is expanding at an exponential rate."

"Does judgment play a role in the practice of medicine?"

"Absolutely. In every medical decision, judgment is paramount."

"Was it your medical judgment that Patience Stanhope was best served by your making a visit to her home on the evening of September eighth, 2005."

"Yes, it was."

"Can you explain to the jury why your judgment led you to believe this was the best course of action?"

"She detested the hospital. I was even reluctant to send her to the hospital for routine tests. Visits to the hospital inevitably exacerbated her symptoms and general anxiety. She much preferred for me to come to her home, which I had been doing almost once a week for eight months. Each time it had been a false alarm, even on those occasions when I was told by Jordan Stanhope that she believed she was dying. On the evening of September eighth, I was not told she thought she was dying. I was confident the visit would be a false alarm like all the others, yet as a doctor, I could not ignore the possibility she was truly ill. The best way to do that was to go directly to her home."

"Ms. Rattner testified that you told her en route that you thought her complaints might be legitimate. Is that true?"

"It is true, but I didn't say that I considered the chances to be extremely small. I said I was concerned because I noted slightly more concern than usual in Mr. Stanhope's voice."

"Did you tell Mr. Stanhope on the phone that you believed Mrs. Stanhope had had a heart attack?"

"No, I did not. I told him that it would have to be ruled out with any complaint of chest pain, but Mrs. Stanhope had had chest pain in the past that had proved to be insignificant."

"Did Mrs. Stanhope have a heart condition?"

"I had done a stress test several months previous to her demise that was equivocal. It wasn't enough to say she had a heart condition, but I felt strongly that she

should have more definitive cardiac studies by a cardiologist at the hospital."

"Did you recommend that to the patient?"

"I strongly recommended it, but she refused, particularly since it involved going to the hospital."

"One last question, doctor," Randolph said. "In relation to your office's PP, or problem patient, designation,
did that signify the patient got more attention or less
attention?"

"Considerably more attention! The problem with
patients so designated was that I could not relieve their
symptoms, whether real or imagined. As a doctor, I
found that a continual problem, hence the terminology."

"Thank you, doctor," Randolph said as he gathered
up his notes. "No more questions."

"Mr. Fasano," Judge Davidson called. "Do you wish
to redirect?"

"Absolutely, Your Honor," Tony barked. He jumped
to his feet and rushed to the podium like a hound after
a rabbit.

"Dr. Bowman, in relation to your PP patients, did you
not say to your then live-in girlfriend while riding in your
new red Porsche on the way to the Stanhope home on
September eighth, 2005, that you couldn't stand such
patients and that you thought hypochondriacs were as
bad as malingerers?"

There was a pause as Craig fixed Tony with his eyes as
if they were weapons.

"Doctor?" Tony asked. "Cat got your tongue, as we
used to say in elementary school?"

"I don't remember," Craig said finally.

"Don't remember?" Tony questioned with exaggerated disbelief. "Oh, please, doctor, that's a too convenient

excuse, especially from someone who has excelled throughout his training at remembering trivial details. Ms. Rattner certainly remembered as she testified. Perhaps you can remember telling Ms. Rattner on the evening you were served your summons for this lawsuit that you hated Patience Stanhope and that her passing was a blessing for everyone. Is that possibly something you can recall?" Tony leaned forward over the podium as much as his short stature would allow and raised his eyebrows questioningly.

"I said something to that effect," Craig reluctantly admitted. "I was angry."

"Of course you were angry," Tony exclaimed. "You were outraged that someone, like my bereaved client, could possibly have the gall to question whether your judgment was in keeping with the standard of care."

"Objection!" Randolph said. "Argumentative!"

"Sustained," Judge Davidson said. He glared at Tony.

"We are all impressed with your rags-to-riches story," Tony said, maintaining his disdain. "But I'm not sure what that means now, especially considering the lifestyle your patients have provided you over the years. What is the current market value of your home?"

"Objection," Randolph said. "Irrelevant and immaterial."

"Your Honor," Tony complained. "The defense presented economic testimony to attest to the defendant's commitment to become a physician. It is only reasonable for the jury to hear what economic rewards have accrued."

Judge Davidson pondered for a moment before saying, "Objection overruled. The witness may answer the question."

Tony redirected his attention at Craig. "Well?"

Craig shrugged. "Two or three million, but we didn't pay that."

"I would now like to ask you a few questions about your concierge practice," Tony said, gripping the sides of the podium tightly. "Do you believe that demanding an annual, up-front payment of thousands of dollars is beyond some patients' means?"

"Of course," Craig snapped.

"What happened to those beloved patients of yours who either could not or did not for whatever reason come up with the retainer fee that was financing your new Porsche and your sex den on Beacon Hill?"

"Objection!" Randolph said. He stood up. "Argumentative and prejudicial."

"Sustained," Judge Davidson barked. "Counsel will restrict his questions to elicit appropriate factual information and will not word his questions to float theories or arguments better left for summation. This is my last warning!"

"I'm sorry, Your Honor," Tony said before turning back to Craig. "What happened to those beloved patients whom you had been caring for over the years?"

"They had to find new doctors."

"Which I'm afraid is often easier said than done. Did you help with this chore?"

"We offered names and numbers."

"Did you just get them out of the Yellow Pages?"

"They were local physicians, with whom my staff and I were acquainted."

"Did you call these physicians?"

"In some cases."

"Which means in some cases you did not call. Dr. Bowman, did it not bother you to abandon your

supposedly cherished patients who were desperate, looking to you for their health needs?"

"I didn't abandon them!" Craig spat indignantly. "I
gave them choices."

"No more questions," Tony said. He rolled his eyes
on the way back to the plaintiff's table.

Judge Davidson looked over his glasses at Randolph.
"Does the defense wish to recross?"

"No, Your Honor," Randolph said, half rising out of
his chair.

"The witness may step down," Judge Davidson said.

Craig stood, and with a deliberate step, walked back
to the defense table.

The judge turned his attention to Tony. "Mr.
Fasano?"

Tony stood. "Plaintiff rests, Your Honor," he said
confidently before retaking his seat.

The judge's eyes swept back to Randolph.

On cue, Randolph stood up to his full patrician
height. "Based on the inadequacy of the plaintiff's case
and lack of evidence thereof, the defense moves to dis-
miss."

"Overruled," Judge Davidson said crisply. "The evidence presented is sufficient for us to go forward. When
court reconvenes after a lunch break, you may call your
first witness, Mr. Bingham." He then brought his gavel
down sharply, and the sound echoed like a gunshot.
"Recess for lunch. You are admonished again not to discuss the case among yourselves or with anyone and to
withhold any opinions until the conclusion of the testimony."

"All rise," the court officer called out.

Jack and Alexis got to their feet along with everyone

else in the courtroom as the judge stepped down from the bench and disappeared through the paneled side door.

"What did you think?" Jack asked while the jury was ushered out.

"I'm continually amazed at the level of Craig's apparent inner anger at these proceedings, that he has such little self-control over his behavior."

"With you being the in-house expert, I'm surprised you're surprised. Isn't it consistent with his narcissism?"

"It is, but I was hoping that with the insight he expressed yesterday at lunch, he'd be able to control himself better. When Tony merely stood up even before he started his questions, I could see Craig's expression change."

"Actually, I was asking your opinion of how Randolph orchestrated the part of the cross-examination we heard."

"Unfortunately, I don't think it was as effective as I would have hoped. It made Craig sound too preachy, like he was giving a lecture. I would have preferred the whole cross to have been punchy and direct, like it was at the end."

"I thought Randolph's cross was pretty effective," Jack said. "I never realized Craig was such a self-made man. Working as hard as he did at gainful employment while going to medical school and still getting the grades he did is very impressive."

"But you're a doctor, not a juror, and you didn't hear Tony's direct. Craig might have struggled as a student, but from the juror's perspective, it's hard to have sympathy now that Craig and I are living in what is probably closer to being a four-million-dollar home, and Tony was very clever on his redirect, the way he brought back Craig's negative feelings about the patient, the red Porsche, the girlfriend, and the fact that he had to forsake many of his old patients."

Jack reluctantly nodded. He had been struggling to look on the bright side for Alexis's benefit. He tried a different tack: "Well, now it's Randolph's turn in the sun. It's time for the defense to shine."

"I'm afraid there's not going to be much sunshine. All Randolph is going to do is present two or three expert witnesses, none of whom are from Boston. He said he'll be finished this afternoon. Tomorrow will be the summations." Alexis shook her head dejectedly. "Under the circumstances, I don't see how he could turn this thing around."

"He's an experienced malpractice attorney," Jack said, attempting to generate enthusiasm he didn't feel. "Experience generally prevails in the final analysis. Who knows. Maybe he has a surprise up his sleeve."

Jack didn't realize he was half-right. There was to be a surprise, but it wasn't going to come from Randolph's sleeve.

CHAPTER EIGHTEEN

"Magazines?" the waiflike young woman questioned. Jack thought she was no more than ninety pounds, yet she was walking a half dozen dogs ranging in size from a gray Great Dane down to a small bichon frise. A clutch of clear plastic poop bags stuck out of her jeans' back pocket. Jack had stopped her after following his established route back down through the Beacon Hill neighborhood. He had it in his mind to buy some reading material in case the wait for the backhoe operator turned out to be overly protracted.

"Let's see," the woman said, scrunching her face in thought. "There's a couple of places on Charles Street."

"One would be fine," Jack said.

"There's Gary Drug on the corner of Charles and Mount Vernon Street."

"Am I going in the right direction?" Jack questioned. At the moment he was on Charles Street, heading toward the park area and the parking garage.

"You are. The drugstore is a block down on this side of the street."

Jack thanked the woman, who was pulled away by her impatient canines.

The shop was a true, ma-and-pop-type store with an

old-fashioned cluttered but welcoming ambience. The whole shebang was about the size of the shampoo section in a generic chain drugstore, yet it was a true emporium. Products that ranged from vitamins to cold remedies to notebooks were tucked into shelving that went from floor to ceiling along the single aisle. At the far end near the pharmacy counter was a surprisingly wide selection of magazines and newspapers.

Jack had mistakenly agreed to lunch with Alexis and Craig. It turned out to be like being invited to a wake where you were expected to converse with the deceased. Craig was furious at the system, as he called it, at Tony Fasano, at Jordan Stanhope, and mostly at himself. He knew he'd done a terrible job despite the hours of practice he'd been through with Randolph the night before. When Alexis tried to get him to talk about why he had so little control of his emotions, knowing full well it was in his best interest to do so, he flew off the handle, and he and Alexis had a short but nasty exchange. But mostly Craig just sat for the hour in sullen withdrawal. Alexis and Jack had tried to talk, but the intensity of Craig's irritation gave off vibes that were difficult to ignore.

At the end of lunch, Alexis was hoping Jack would return to the courtroom, but Jack had begged off with the excuse that he wanted to get to the cemetery by two in hopes that Percy Gallaudet had made short work of his contribution in rectifying his buddy's sewer system. At that point, Craig had angrily told Jack just to give up, that the die had been cast, so Jack needn't bother. Jack had responded that he'd gone too far involving too many people to abandon the idea.

With several magazines and a *New York Times* under his arm, Jack proceeded on to the parking garage, got his sad-looking Accent out into the daylight, and headed west. He had a bit of trouble finding the route that had brought him into the city that morning, but he eventually recognized a few landmarks that indicated he was on the correct road.

Jack pulled into the Park Meadow Cemetery at two ten and parked next to a Dodge minivan in front of the office building. Going inside, he found the frumpy woman and Walter Strasser exactly as he'd left them in the morning. The woman was typing into a monitor, and Walter was sitting impassively at his desk with his hands still clasped over his paunch. Jack wondered if he ever did any work, since there was nothing on his desk surface to suggest it. Both people looked in Jack's direction, but the woman immediately went back to her work without a word. Jack proceeded over to Walter, who followed him with his eyes.

"Any sign of Percy?" Jack asked.

"Not since he left this morning."

"Any word?" Jack asked. He marveled that the only way he could tell Walter was conscious was the rare blink and the moving mouth when he spoke.

"Nope."

"Is there any way to contact him? I'm supposed to meet him here sometime after two. He's agreed to dig out Patience Stanhope this afternoon."

"If he said he'd do it, he'll be here."

"Does he have a cell phone? I failed to ask him."

"Nope. We contact him by e-mail. Then he comes by the office."

Jack put one of his business cards on Walter's desk. "If you could contact him to find out when he's going to get to Patience Stanhope, I'd be much obliged. You can call me on my cell phone. Meanwhile, I'll head up to the grave site if you can tell me where it is."

"Gertrude, show the doctor the Stanhope plot on the map."

The wheels on Gertrude's desk chair squeaked as she pushed away from her desk. As a woman of few words, she merely tapped an arthritic index finger at the appropriate spot. Jack glanced at the site. Thanks to the contour lines, he could see it was on the very crest of the hill.

"Best view in the Park Meadow," Walter commented.

"I'll wait there," Jack said. He started for the car.

"Doctor!" Walter called. "Since the grave is scheduled to be opened, there's the issue of the fee, which must be settled before digging commences."

After parting with a significant number of twenty-dollar bills from his bulky stash, Jack returned to the rent-a-car and drove up the hill. He found a small turnout with an arbor shading a park bench. He left his car there and walked over to where he guessed the Stanhope plot was located. It was on the very crown of the hill. There were three identical, rather plain granite headstones. He found Patience's and glanced briefly at the incised inscription.

Getting the magazines and newspaper out of the car, Jack went over to the bench and made himself comfortable. The weather had improved dramatically from the morning. Bright sun beat down with a ferocity that it hadn't had on previous days, as if to remind everyone that summer was just around the corner. Jack was glad to have the shade from the ivy-covered arbor because it was tropically hot.

Jack glanced at his watch. It seemed hard to believe

that in less than twenty-four hours he would be married. That is, he admitted, unless there was some unforeseen disaster, such as his not getting there on time. He thought about that for a minute while a blue jay angrily scolded him from a nearby dogwood tree. Jack shook off the idea of not getting to the church on time with a shake of his head. There was no way it could happen. But the thought was an unpleasant reminder of his need to call Laurie. Yet with the reality of not knowing when he would get Patience's corpse, he was once again able to put it off.

It had been longer than Jack could remember since he'd spent solitary idle time. He'd found that keeping himself frantically busy, whether at work or at play, was the best way to keep his demons at bay. It had been Laurie who'd patiently coaxed him out of the habit over the last few years, but that was when they were together. This was different, since he was alone. Yet he felt no urge to dwell on the past and what could have been. He was content to think about what was going to be, unless . . .

Jack shook off the idea for the second time. Instead, he picked up the newspaper and started reading. It was a good feeling being al fresco in the sunshine, enjoying the news with birds singing in the background. The fact that he was sitting in the middle of a cemetery didn't bother him one iota. In fact, thanks to his ironic sense of humor, it added to his pleasure.

Finishing the newspaper, Jack turned to the magazines. After he read several rather long but interesting articles in *The New Yorker*, Jack's contentment began to wane, especially when he found himself in direct sunlight. He checked his watch and cursed. It was a quarter

to four. He stood up, stretched, and gathered the newspaper and magazines. One way or the other, he was
going to find Percy and pin him down for a start time.
Knowing that the last shuttle flight to New York was
somewhere around nine, he admitted he would not make
it. Unless he drove the rent-a-car to New York, which
he was not excited about doing for multiple reasons, he
would have to stay in Boston for one more night. The
idea of staying at the hotel he'd seen at the airport
occurred to him, because he had no intention of going
back to the Bowmans' without Alexis and the kids being
there. As much as he sympathized with Craig, he'd had
quite enough of his funk at lunch.

The newspapers and magazines went into the
Hyundai through the missing passenger-side window.
Jack was halfway around the car when he heard the
sound of the backhoe. Shielding his eyes from the sun
and peering down through the trees, Jack saw Percy's
yellow vehicle start up the cemetery's sinuous roadway.
It had its scoop folded up against its rear like a grasshop-
per's leg. Jack quickly called Harold Langley.

"It's almost four," Harold complained when Jack told
him the exhumation was about to get under way.

"It's the best I could do," Jack said. "I even had to
bribe the man as it is." Jack didn't say he'd also bribed
Walter Strasser.

"All right," Harold said with resignation. "I'll be over
in a half-hour. I need to make certain things are ready
here. If I'm a little late, do not open the vault until I am
on-site! I repeat, do not try to take the lid off the vault
until I am there to see it happen! I have to identify the
coffin and certify it was in that particular vault."

"I understand," Jack said.

Before Percy arrived, the Park Meadow pickup truck drove up. Enrique and Cesar climbed out and unloaded equipment from the truck's bed. With commendable efficiency and minimal conversation, they staked out Patience's grave site, spread out a waterproof tarpaulin like the one Jack had seen that morning at the grave that was being dug, cut and removed the sod, and stacked the rolled lengths on the tarpaulin's periphery.

By the time Percy rolled onto the scene, the site was ready for the backhoe. Although Percy gave Jack a quick wave, he didn't get out of his cab until he'd positioned the excavating machine to his liking. Only then did he leap out to position his outriggers.

"Sorry I was delayed," Percy called to Jack.

Jack merely waved. He wasn't interested in conversation. All he wanted to do was get the damn coffin out of the ground.

When Percy thought all was in order, he went to work. The scoop dug deeply into the relatively loose soil. The backhoe's diesel roared when the scoop was drawn inward, then lifted. Percy swung the boom around and began piling the dirt on the tarp.

Percy proved skillful at what he was doing, and within a short time, a wide trench with sharply perpendicular walls began to form. By the time he was down approximately four feet, Harold Langley arrived with the Langley-Peerson hearse. He did a three-point turn and backed the vehicle up alongside the deepening trench. With his hands on his hips, he inspected the progress.

"You're getting close," Harold yelled to Percy. "So ease up."

Whether Percy couldn't hear Harold or chose to ignore him Jack couldn't tell. Whatever the reason, he continued digging as if Harold wasn't there. After a short time, there was a jarring hollow sound as the scoop's teeth clunked against the vault's concrete top a foot or so beneath the soil at the bottom of the pit.

Harold went berserk. "I told you to ease up," he yelled, frantically waving his hands in an attempt to get Percy to lift the scoop out of the hole. Jack had to smile. Harold looked completely out of place outside the funeral home, in the sunshine with his somber black suit and pasty-colored skin, like a parody of a punk rocker. Spikes of darkly dyed hair, which had been carefully combed and pomaded over his bald crown, angled off from the side of his head.

Percy continued to ignore Harold's increasingly frenzied gestures. Instead, he drew in the scoop, creating a scraping, screeching noise as the scoop's metal teeth dragged along the vault's concrete lid.

In desperation, Harold dashed to the backhoe's cab and pounded on the glass. Only then did the scoop stop and the roar of the diesel abate. Percy opened the door and looked at the livid funeral director with an innocent questioning expression.

"You're going to break the vault's lid or tear off the eyehooks, you . . ." Harold yelled, unable to come up with a sufficiently vulgar descriptive noun to express what he thought of Percy. His anger had him tongue-tied.

Content to let the professionals sort out their differences, Jack climbed into his car. He wanted to use his phone, and he thought the car would shield him from the noise of the backhoe's diesel when Percy recommenced digging. The missing passenger-side window faced away from the action.

Jack called Dr. Latasha Wylie. This time, he got her directly.

"I got your message earlier," Latasha admitted. "Sorry I didn't get back to you. Thursdays are our Grand Rounds conference."

"No problem," Jack said. "I'm calling now because they are finally digging up the body as we speak. If all goes smoothly, which I have no reason to suspect, considering the obstacles I've had to deal with to get this far, I'm looking at doing the case between six and seven at the Langley-Peerson Funeral Home. You offered to help. Is that still a possibility?"

"The timing couldn't be better," Latasha said. "Count me in! I've got the bone saw packed and ready to go."

"I hope I'm not taking you away from something more fun."

"The pope was coming in for dinner, but I'll tell him we have to reschedule."

Jack smiled. Latasha had a sense of humor akin to his.

"I'll plan to meet you at the home around six thirty," Latasha continued. "If that's not appropriate for whatever reason, give me a call!"

"Sounds like a plan. Can I offer you dinner after all the fun and games?"

"If it's not too late. A girl needs her beauty sleep."

Jack disconnected. As he'd been speaking, Enrique and Cesar had disappeared into the pit and shovelfuls of dirt had begun flying up into the air. Meanwhile, Percy had started rigging steel cables from the scoop's teeth. Harold had returned to the edge of the pit, staring down into its depths with his hands on his hips. Jack was pleased that he was taking such personal interest.

Switching his attention to his phone, Jack considered
calling Laurie. He now knew that he'd missed even what
he'd called the worst-case scenario on the phone the
night before: getting home that evening. Events had
inexorably pushed his departure until tomorrow morning, the day of the wedding. Although his cowardly side
tried to talk him into putting off the call until after the
autopsy, he knew he had to make the call now. But that
wasn't the only conundrum: What to tell her about the
morning's demolition derby on the Mass Pike was
another issue. After a moment's thought, he decided to
come clean. He felt the sympathy factor trumped the
worry factor, since he could say he was reasonably
confident Franco had to be convalescing, at least for a
few days, and wouldn't be apt to pop up again. Of
course, that didn't exclude Antonio, whoever he was.
Jack could recall an image of the man standing behind
and to the side of Franco at the Memorial Drive basketball court confrontation, as well as his sitting in court
that morning. Jack had no idea how he fit in with the
Fasano team, but the fact that he existed had passed
through Jack's mind when Percy had started digging
Patience's grave. Unconsciously, Jack had touched the
revolver in his pocket at the time just to reassure himself
it was there. Considering the seriousness of the threat
communicated to the girls, it wasn't a wild leap of imagination to think of someone showing up and contesting
the exhumation.

Taking a fortifying breath, Jack speed-dialed Laurie's
number. There was always the hope he'd get her voicemail. Unfortunately, that didn't happen. Laurie answered
quickly.

"Where are you?" she demanded with no preliminaries.

"The bad news is that I'm in a cemetery in Boston. The good news is that I'm not one of the residents."

"This is no time for jokes."

"Sorry! I couldn't help myself. I am in a cemetery. The grave is being opened at this moment."

There was an uncomfortable pause.

"I know you are disappointed," Jack said. "I've done everything I could to speed up the process. I'd hoped to be on my way home at this time. It's not been easy." Jack went on to describe the morning's run-in with Franco. He told her everything that had happened, including the bullet lodging in the rent-a-car's windshield support.

Laurie listened in stunned silence until Jack finished his monologue, which had included the need to bribe both the cemetery superintendent and the backhoe operator. He also had mentioned that Craig's testimony had been a disaster.

"It pisses me off that now I don't know whether to be angry or sympathetic."

"If you are asking my opinion, I'd lean in the direction of sympathy."

"Please, Jack. No jokes! This is serious."

"After I finish the autopsy, I'll surely have missed the last shuttle flight tonight. I'll stay in a hotel at the airport. Flights start sometime around six thirty."

Laurie sighed audibly. "I'm going over to my parents' early to get ready, so I'll miss you here at the apartment."

"No problem. I think I'll be able to get into my tuxedo without any help."

"Will you come to the church with Warren?"

"That's my intention. He's inventive the way he always finds parking for his ride."

"All right, Jack. See you at the church." She disconnected abruptly.

Jack sighed and flipped his phone shut. Laurie wasn't happy, but at least he'd gotten the unpleasant chore out of the way. For a moment, he marveled that there was nothing in life that was simple and straightforward.

Slipping his phone into his pocket, Jack climbed out of the car. As he'd been talking with Laurie, things seemed to be coming to a head at graveside. Percy was back inside the backhoe's cab and had the diesel engine cranking. The scoop was poised over the excavation with attached steel cables stretching downward into the depths. It was apparent the backhoe was putting significant tension on the cables.

Jack walked to the edge of the hole to join Harold. Looking down, he could see that the cables were attached to eyehooks embedded in the vault's lid.

"What's happening?" Jack yelled over the diesel roar.

"We're trying to break the seal," Harold yelled back. "It's not easy. It's an asphalt-like material that's used to make it waterproof."

The backhoe grunted and strained and then eased off only to begin anew.

"What will we do if the seal holds?" Jack questioned.

"We'd have to come back another day with the vault company people."

Jack cursed but not audibly.

Suddenly, there was a low-pitched popping noise and a brief sucking sound.

"Well, hallelujah!" Harold said as he motioned for Percy to slow down by flapping his hand.

The vault lid rose up. When it got up to the edge of the pit, Enrique and Cesar grabbed it to keep it steady while Percy swung it away from the grave. Carefully, he set it down on the grass. Percy then climbed out of the cab.

Harold peered into the vault. The lining was mirror-like stainless steel. Resting inside was the white-gold metallic coffin. There was a good two feet of clearance all around.

"Isn't she a beauty?" Harold said with near religious veneration. "That's a Huntington Industries Perpetual Repose. I don't sell many of those. It's really a sight to behold."

Jack was more interested in the fact that the interior of the vault was as dry as a bone. "How do we get the coffin out?" he asked.

No sooner had Jack posed the question than Enrique and Cesar climbed down into the vault and passed wide cloth straps under the coffin and then through the four side handles. With the diesel back up to power, Percy swung the scoop back over the pit and lowered it so the straps could be attached. Harold opened the back of the hearse.

Twenty minutes later, the coffin was safely inside the hearse, and Harold closed the door.

"Will I be seeing you back at the home straight away?" Harold asked Jack.

"Absolutely. I want to do the autopsy immediately. Also, there's going to be another medical examiner involved. Her name is Dr. Latasha Wylie."

"Very well," Harold said. He got into the hearse's driver's seat, backed out into the roadway, and accelerated down the hill.

Jack settled up with Percy, giving him the bulk of his wad of twenty-dollar bills. He also gave a couple to Enrique and Cesar before getting into his car and beginning to head down the hill. As he drove, he couldn't help but feel pleased. After all the lead-up problems, he was surprised that the exhumation itself had gone so easily. In particular, no Fasano and no Antonio, and certainly no Franco, had shown up to spoil the party. Now all he had to do was the autopsy.

CHAPTER NINETEEN

To Jack's gratification, things continued to go smoothly. He drove from the Park Meadow to the Langley-Peerson Home without incident, as did Harold with the coffin. When Jack had arrived, Latasha was already there waiting. She had arrived only five minutes earlier, so the timing was nearly perfect.

Immediately on his arrival, Harold had had two of his beefy employees slide the Perpetual Repose coffin out of the hearse and onto a dolly. The dolly had been rolled into the embalming room, where it now stood.

"Here's the plan," Harold said. He was standing next to the coffin with a bony hand resting on its gleaming metallic surface. Thanks to the bright blue-white fluorescent light in the embalming room, any lifelike color he had was washed out, and he looked as if he should have been inside one of the Perpetual Reposes himself.

Jack and Latasha were standing a few feet away near the embalming table, which was going to substitute as the autopsy table. Both had pulled on Tyvek protective jumpsuits that Latasha had thoughtfully brought from the medical examiner's office along with gloves, plastic face screens, and a collection of autopsy tools. Also in the room were Bill Barton, a kindly senior gentleman whom

Harold had described as his most trusted employee, and Tyrone Vich, a robust African-American man twice Bill Barton's size. Both had kindly volunteered to stay late and would assist Jack and Latasha in any way needed.

"We'll now open the casket," Harold continued. "I will certify that it indeed contains the remains of the late Patience Stanhope. Bill and Tyrone will remove the clothing and put the body on the embalming table for the autopsy. Once you have finished, Bill and Tyrone will take over to redress the body and return it to the coffin so that it can be reinterred in the morning."

"Will you remain on the premises?" Jack asked.

"I don't think that is necessary," Harold said. "But I live nearby, and Bill or Tyrone can call me if there are any questions."

"Sounds like a plan to me," Jack said, enthusiastically rubbing his gloved hands together. "Let's get the show on the road!"

Taking a crank from Bill, Harold inserted its business end into a flush housing at one end of the metal coffin, seated it, and tried to turn it. The effort brought a fleeting bit of color to his face but failed to turn the locking mechanism. Harold gestured toward Tyrone, who changed places with the director. Tyrone's muscles bulged beneath his cotton scrub shirt, and with an abrupt, torturous screech, the lid began to open. A moment later, there was a short hiss.

Jack looked at Harold. "Is that hissing sound good or bad?" Jack asked. He hoped it was not indicative of gaseous decomposition.

"Neither good nor bad," Harold said. "It speaks to the Perpetual Repose's superb seal, which is not surprising, since it's a top-of-the-line, high-engineered product." Harold directed Tyrone to the opposite end of the casket, where he repeated the process with the crank.

"That should be it," Harold said when Tyrone was finished. He put his fingers under the edge of the coffin and had Tyrone do the same at the other end. Then, in a coordinated fashion, they lifted the lid and allowed light to wash in over Patience Stanhope.

The interior of the casket was lined in white satin, and Patience was clothed in a simple white taffeta dress. In keeping with the décor, her exposed face, forearms, and hands were covered with a white, cottony fluff of fungus. Beneath the mold, her skin was marmoreal gray.

"Without a shred of doubt, this is Patience Stanhope," Harold said piously.

"She looks terrific," Jack said, "all decked out and ready for the prom."

Harold cast a disapproving glance in Jack's direction but kept his thin lips pressed together.

"Okay! Bill and Tyrone," Jack said enthusiastically, "slip her out of her party duds, and we'll get to work."

"I will leave you now," Harold said with a hint of reprimand as if talking to a naughty child. "I hope you find this exercise worthwhile."

"What about your fee?" Jack questioned. He suddenly realized he'd not made any arrangement.

"I have your business card, doctor. We will bill you."

"Perfect," Jack said. "Thanks for your help."

"Our pleasure," Harold said, tongue in cheek. His funeral-director sensibilities had been offended by Jack's disrespectful language.

Jack pulled over a stainless-steel table on casters and put out paper and a pen. He had no recording device, and he wanted to write down his findings as he went along. Then he helped Latasha arrange specimen bottles and the instruments. Although Harold had laid out some of the embalming tools, Latasha had brought the more typical pathology knife, scalpels, scissors, and bone clippers along with the bone saw.

"Your thoughtfulness in bringing all this equipment is going to make this a thousand times easier," Jack said as he attached a new scalpel blade to a scalpel handle. "I was planning on making do with whatever they had here, which in hindsight was not a good idea."

"It was no trouble," Latasha said, glancing around the room. "I didn't know what to expect. I've never seen an embalming room. Frankly, I'm impressed."

The facility was about the same size as her autopsy room at the medical examiner's office but had only a single, central, stainless-steel table, giving the impression of wide-open space. The floor and walls were light green ceramic. There were no windows. Instead, there were areas of glass block that let in outside light.

Jack's eyes followed Latasha's around the room. "This is palatial," he said. "When I first conceived of doing this autopsy, I imagined myself using someone's kitchen table."

"Yuck!" Latasha responded. She glanced over at Bill and Tyrone, who were busily disrobing the corpse. "You told me the story about Patience Stanhope and your internist friend on Tuesday when you stopped by. Unfortunately, I've forgotten the details. Could you give me a quick synopsis?"

Jack did better than that. He told the whole story, which included his relationship to Craig as well as the threats he'd received and Craig's children had received

about the autopsy issue. He even told her about the incident that morning on the Massachusetts Turnpike.

Latasha was shocked, and her expression reflected it.

"I suppose I should have told you this sooner," Jack
said. "Maybe you wouldn't have agreed so readily to get
involved. But my feeling is that if there was to be trouble at this point, it would have happened before Patience
Stanhope came out of the ground."

"I agree with that," Latasha said, recovering to a
degree. "Now trouble, if it's going to happen, might
depend on what we find."

"You have a point," Jack agreed. "Maybe it would be
best if you don't help. If anybody is going to be a target
in any form or fashion, I want it to be me."

"What?" Latasha questioned with an exaggerated
expression. "And let you boys have all the fun? No
thanks! That's never been my style. Let's see what we
find and then decide how best to proceed."

Jack smiled. He admired and liked this woman. She
had smarts, pluck, and drive.

Bill and Tyrone lifted the corpse out of the casket, carried it over to the embalming table, and heaved it up
onto the surface. With a bucket of water and a sponge,
Bill gently rinsed away the mold. Like an autopsy table,
the embalming table had lips around its periphery and a
drain at the end to catch any wayward fluid.

Jack moved over to be on Patience's right while
Latasha was on her left. Both had donned their protective face and head gear. Tyrone excused himself to do his
nightly security check. Bill retreated to the sidelines to
be available if needed.

"The body's in fantastic shape," Latasha commented.

"Harold might be a tad stuffy, but he apparently knows his trade."

Both Jack and Latasha did their own silent external exam. When Latasha was finished, she straightened up.

"I don't see anything I wouldn't have expected," she said. "I mean, she went through a resuscitation attempt and an embalming, and there's plenty of evidence of that."

"I agree," Jack said. He'd been looking at some minor lacerations inside her mouth, which were consistent with having been intubated during the resuscitation. "So far, there's no suggestion of strangulation or burking, but smothering without chest compression still has to be kept in mind."

"It would be way low on my list," Latasha said. "The history pretty much rules it out, you know what I'm saying?"

"I'm with you," Jack said. He handed Latasha a scalpel. "How about you do the honors."

Latasha made the typical Y incision from the points of the shoulders to the midline and then down to the pubis. The tissue was dry like an overcooked turkey with a grayish-tan color. There was no putrefaction, so the smell was fusty but not offensive.

Working quickly and in tandem, Jack and Latasha had the internal organs exposed. The intestines had been completely evacuated with the embalming cannula. Jack lifted the firm edge of the liver. Beneath and affixed to its underside was the gallbladder. He palpated it with his fingers.

"We have bile," he said happily. "That will help with the toxicology."

"We've got vitreous as well," Latasha said, palpating

the eyes through the closed lids. I think we should also take a sample of that."

"Absolutely," Jack said. "And urine, too, if we can get it from either the bladder or kidneys."

Each took syringes and took the samples. Jack labeled his while Latasha did the same with hers.

"Let's see if there's an obvious right-to-left shunt," Jack said. "I keep thinking the cyanosis issue is going to prove important."

Carefully, Jack eased away the friable lungs to get a look at the great vessels. After a careful palpation, he shook his head. "Everything looks normal."

"The pathology is going to be in the heart," Latasha said with conviction.

"I think you are right," Jack agreed. He called Bill over and asked if there were any stainless pans or bowls they could use for the organs. Bill produced several from a cabinet below the embalming-room sink.

Proceeding as if they were accustomed to working together, Jack and Latasha removed the heart and lungs en bloc. While she held the pan, Jack lifted the specimen out of the chest and placed it inside. She put the pan down on the table beyond Patience's feet.

"Lungs look normal," Jack said. He rubbed his fingers over the lungs' surface.

"They feel normal, too," Latasha said as she gently prodded them in a few locations. "Too bad we don't have a scale."

Jack called Bill over and asked if a scale was available, but it wasn't.

"The weight feels normal to me," Jack said, hefting the block of tissue.

Latasha tried it but shook her head. "I'm not good at judging weights."

"I'm eager to get to the heart, but maybe we should first do the rest. What do you say?"

"Work first, play later: Is that your motto?"

"Something like that," Jack said. "Let's divide the job to speed things up. One of us could do the abdominal organs while the other does the neck dissection. For completeness' sake, I want to make sure the hyoid bone is intact, even though neither of us thinks strangulation was involved."

"If you are giving me a choice, I'll do the neck."

"You're on."

For the next half-hour they worked silently in their respective areas. Jack used the sink to wash out the intestines. It was in the large intestine that he found the first significant pathology. He called Latasha over and pointed. It was a cancer in the ascending colon.

"It's small, but it looks like it penetrated the wall," Latasha said.

"I think it has," Jack agreed. "And some of the abdominal nodes are enlarged. This is dramatic proof that hypochondriacs do get sick."

"Would that have been picked up by a bowel study?"

"Undoubtedly. If she'd had one. It's in Craig's records that she continually refused his recommendation to do it."

"So it would have killed her if she didn't have the heart attack."

"Eventually," Jack said. "How are you doing with the neck?"

"I'm about done. The hyoid is intact."

"Good! Why don't you get the brain out while I finish

up with the abdomen? We're making excellent time."
Jack glanced up at the wall clock. It was closing in on
eight p.m., and his stomach was growling. "Are you
going to take me up on the dinner offer?" he called to
Latasha, who was on her way back to the table.

"Let's see what time it is when we finish," she called
back over her shoulder.

Jack found a number of polyps throughout Patience's
large intestine. When he was finished with the gut, he
returned it to the abdominal cavity. "I do have to
give Harold Langley credit. His job with Patience Stanhope would have made an ancient Egyptian embalmer
proud."

"I don't have much experience with embalmed
bodies, but the condition of this one is better than I
expected," Latasha said as she plugged in the bone saw.
It was a vibrating device designed to cut through
hard bone but not soft tissue. She gave it a try. It produced a high-pitched whirring noise. She positioned
herself at the head of the table and went to work on
the cranium, which she had previously exposed by
reflecting Patience's scalp down over her face.

Relatively immune to the racket, Jack palpated the
liver, looking for metastases from the cancer in the colon.
Not finding any, he made a series of slices through the
organ, but it was seemingly clear. He knew that he might
find some microscopically, but that would have to be at
a later date.

Twenty minutes later, after the brain had been cleared
of gross abnormality and a number of specimens from
various organs were taken, the two pathologists turned
their attention to the heart. Jack had cut away the lungs,
so it was sitting in the pan by itself.

"It's like saving the best present for last," Jack said while gazing eagerly and intriguingly at the organ and wondering what secrets it was about to reveal. The size was about that of a large orange. The color of the muscle tissue was gray, but the greasy cap of adipose tissue was light tan.

"It's going to be like dessert," Latasha said with equal enthusiasm.

"Standing here looking at this heart reminds me of a case I did about half a year ago. It was a woman who collapsed in Bloomingdale's and whose heart couldn't be paced by an external pacemaker, just like Patience Stanhope."

"What did you find on that case?"

"A marked developmental narrowing of the posterior descending coronary artery. Apparently, a small thrombosis knocked out a good portion of the heart's conduction system in one fell swoop."

"Is that what you expect to find on this case?"

"It's high on my list," Jack said. "But I also think there is going to be some kind of septal defect causing a right-to-left shunt to account for the cyanosis." Then he added parenthetically, "What it's not going to tell us, I'm afraid, is why someone was so intent on us not finding out whatever it is we are about to learn."

"I think we're going to find widespread coronary disease and evidence of a number of previous small, asymptomatic heart attacks so that her conduction system was particularly at risk prior to the final event, but not compromised enough to show up on a standard ECG."

"That's an interesting thought," Jack said. He glanced across the table at Latasha, who continued to

stare at the exposed heart. His respect for her kept growing. He just wished she didn't look nineteen. It made
him feel over the hill.

"Remember, postmenopausal women have recently
been shown to have different symptomatology than
equivalent males when it comes to coronary heart disease! The case you just described is evidence of that."

"Stop making me feel ancient and uninformed," Jack
complained.

Latasha made a gesture of dismissal with her gloved
hand. "Yeah, sure!" she intoned with a chuckle.

"How about we make a little wager since neither one
of us is in our home office, where such activity is frowned
upon? I say it's going to be congenital and you say
degenerative. I'm willing to put up five bucks in support
of my idea."

"Whoa, big spender!" Latasha teased. "Five is a lot of
cash, but I'll double you to ten."

"You're on," Jack said. After turning the heart over,
he picked up a pair of fine forceps and scissors and went
to work. Latasha supported the organ as Jack carefully
traced and then opened the right coronary artery, concentrating on the posterior descending branch. When
he'd traced it as far as the instruments would allow, he
straightened up and stretched his back.

"No narrowing," he said with a combination of
surprise and disappointment. Although he usually maintained an open mind diagnostically, for fear of being
blinded by the positive finding, in this case he'd been
quite certain of the pathology he'd encounter. It was the
right coronary artery that supplied blood to most of
the heart's conduction system, which had been knocked
out by Patience Stanhope's heart attack.

"Don't despair yet," Latasha said. "The ten dollars is still in the balance. There's no narrowing, but I don't see any atheromatous deposits, either."

"You're right. It's perfectly clean," Jack agreed. He couldn't quite believe it. The entire vessel was grossly normal.

Jack turned his attention to the left coronary artery and its branches. But after a few minutes of dissection it was apparent the left was the same as the right. It was devoid of plaque and stricture. He was mystified and chagrined. After all he'd been through, it seemed a personal affront that there was no apparent coronary abnormality, either developmental or degenerative.

"The pathology has to be on the inside of the heart," Latasha said. "Maybe we'll see some vegetations on the mitral or aortic valve that could have thrown off a shower of thrombi that then cleared."

Jack nodded, but he was mulling over the probability of sudden cardiac death from a heart attack with no coronary artery disease. He thought it was extremely small, certainly less than ten percent, but obviously possible, as evidenced by the case in front of him. One thing about forensic pathology that he could always count on was seeing and learning something new.

Latasha handed Jack a long-bladed knife, waking him from a mini trance. "Come on! Let's see the interior."

Jack opened each of the heart's four chambers and made serial slices through the muscular walls. He and Latasha inspected the valves, the septa between the right and left sides of the heart, and the cut surfaces of the muscles. They worked silently, checking each structure individually and methodically. When they were finished, their eyes met across the table.

"The bright side is that neither of us is out ten dollars," Jack said, trying to salvage humor from the situation. "The dark side is that Patience Stanhope is keeping her secrets to herself. She was reputed to be less than cooperative in life, and she's staying in character in death."

"After hearing the history, I'm shocked that this heart appears so normal," Latasha said. "I've never seen this. I guess the answers are going to have to wait for the microscope. Maybe there was some kind of capillary disease process that involved only the smallest vessels of the coronary system."

"I've never heard of such a thing."

"Neither have I," Latasha admitted. "But she died of a heart attack that had to have been massive. We have to see pathology other than a small, asymptomatic colon cancer. Wait a second! What's that eponymous syndrome where the coronary arteries go into spasm?" She motioned to Jack as if she were playing charades, wanting him to come up with the name.

"I honestly have no idea. Now, don't spout some trivia that's going to make me feel inadequate."

"Prinzmetal! That's it." Latasha said triumphantly. "Prinzmetal angina."

"Never heard of it," Jack admitted. "Now you're reminding me of my brother-in-law, who's the victim in this disaster. He'd know it for sure. Can the spasm cause massive heart attacks? That's the question."

"It can't be Prinzmetal," Latasha said suddenly with a wave of dismissal. "Even in that syndrome, the spasm is associated with some stenoses of the vessel nearby, meaning there would be visible pathology, which we don't see."

"I'm relieved," Jack said.

"We have to figure this out one way or the other."

"That's my intention, but not seeing any cardiac pathology has me fooled and even embarrassed, considering all the fuss I've caused to do this autopsy."

"I have an idea," Latasha said. "Let's take all the samples back to my office. We can examine the heart under the stereo dissecting microscope and even do some frozen sections of the heart tissue to look at capillaries. The rest of the specimens will have to be processed normally."

"Maybe we should just go have some dinner," Jack said, suddenly wanting to wash his hands of the whole affair.

"I'll pick up some pizza on the way back to the office. Come on! We'll make it a party. There's one hell of a mystery here. Let's see if we can't solve it. We can even get a toxicology screen tonight. I happen to know the night supervisor at the lab at the university. He and I were an item a while back. Things didn't work out, but we're still acquaintances."

Jack's ears pricked up. "Run that by me again!" he said with disbelief. "We could get a toxicology screen done tonight?" Back in New York at the OCME, Jack was lucky to get one in a week.

"The answer is yes, but we'll have to wait until after eleven, when Allan Smitham begins his shift."

"Who's Allan Smitham?" Jack asked. The possibility of an immediate toxicology screen opened up another whole dimension of inquiry.

"We met in college. We took a lot of chem and bio classes together. Then I went to med school and he went to grad school. Now we work a few blocks apart."

"What about your beauty rest?"

"I'll worry about that tomorrow night. You have me hooked on this case. We have to save your brother-in-law from the evil lawyers."

CHAPTER TWENTY

Alexis answered on the fourth ring. Jack had called her number and put his phone on speaker before placing it on the rent-a-car's front passenger seat. He was on his way from the Langley-Peerson Funeral Home to the Newton Memorial Hospital. He'd decided to make a short visit before the three-to-eleven shift left for the day in hopes of catching Matt Gilbert and Georgina O'Keefe. It had been an impulsive decision when he and Latasha left the funeral home after finishing up with the autopsy. She had said she was going to stop at her apartment briefly to feed the dog, drop off the fluid samples at the toxicology lab with a message for Allan to call as soon as he got in, and pick up a couple of pizzas at an all-night joint before meeting him in the parking lot of the medical examiner's office. She had given Jack the opportunity to tag along, but the window of opportunity had made him decide to stop at the hospital instead.

"I was hoping it was you," Alexis said when she heard Jack's voice.

"Can you hear me okay?" Jack asked. "We're on my speaker phone."

"I can hear you fine. Where are you?"

"I'm always asking myself that same question," Jack

joked. His mood had flip-flopped from its nadir brought on by finding nothing relevant in Patience's autopsy to a near high. He had been energized by Latasha's enthusiasm and the prospect of getting the assistance of a toxicologist, and his mind had been picking up speed like an old-fashioned steam locomotive. Now ideas were flapping around inside his head like a flock of excited sparrows.

"You are in a rare mood. What's going on?"

"I'm in my rent-a-car on the way to the Newton Memorial."

"Are you all right?"

"I'm fine. I'm just going to duck in and ask a couple of questions to the ER people who handled Patience Stanhope."

"Did you do the exhumation and the autopsy?"

"I did."

"What did you find?"

"Other than a nonrelevant, from our perspective, cancer of the colon, I found nothing."

"Nothing?" Alexis questioned. The disappointment in her voice was apparent.

"I know what you are thinking, because I thought the same. I was depressed. But now I think it was an unexpected gift."

"How so?"

"If I'd found generic, garden-variety coronary disease, which is what I actually expected to find rather than something dramatic, which is what I'd hope to find, I would have left it at that. She had heart disease and had a heart attack. End of story. But the fact that she had no heart disease begs for an explanation. I mean, there is a slight chance that she had some fatal cardiac event that we're not going to be able to diagnose eight months after the fact, but now I believe the possibility is in our favor that there was something else involved, especially considering the resistance Fasano expressed about my doing the autopsy, and Franco trying to run me off the goddamn road, and, more significantly, the threat expressed to your children. How are they, by the way?"

"They're fine. They act very secure, and they're having a ball here at Grandma's. She's spoiling them as she always does. But back to your point: What are you really trying to say?"

"I don't know exactly. But here's some of my thoughts, whatever they are worth. Patience Stanhope's death and the resistance to my doing an autopsy could be two completely separate circumstances. Fasano and crew could be behind the threats, and purely for venal reasons. But somehow that doesn't make sense to me. Why would he go to the extent of breaking into your house and then blithely let me do the exhumation? It seems to me that the three events are separate and not connected. Fasano threatened me for the reasons he gave. Franco has this ego problem after I whacked him in the nuts, so my problems with Franco have nothing to do with Patience Stanhope. That leaves the break-in at your house unexplained."

"This is too complicated," Alexis complained. "If Tony Fasano wasn't behind terrorizing my children, then who was?"

"I have no idea. But I asked myself what the motivation might have been if it didn't involve Fasano and money. It's pretty clear that it would be an attempt to keep me from learning something, and what could be learned from an autopsy? One thing would be an overdose of medication or the wrong medication Patience Stanhope might have gotten at the hospital. Hospitals are big organizations with lots of stockholders, involving lots of money."

"That's crazy," Alexis said without hesitation. "The hospital wasn't behind my kids being victimized."

"Alexis, you wanted me to come up here to Boston and think out of the box, and that's what I'm doing."

"But the hospital?" she questioned with a whine. "Is that why you are on your way there now?"

"It is," Jack confessed. "I think of myself as a reasonable judge of character. I was impressed by the two ER people I spoke with Tuesday. They're forthright and devoid of artifice. I want to talk to them again."

"What are you going to do," Alexis asked scornfully, "ask them if they made some huge mistake that the hospital has to send people out to brutalize my children to try to cover up? That's ridiculous."

"When you put it that way, it does sound far-fetched. But I'm going to do it anyway. The autopsy is not over. I mean, the gross dissection is over, but we're now going to see what toxicology can come up with and also look at the microscopic. I also want to corroborate exactly what medication Patience Stanhope was given so I can tell the toxicologist."

"Well, that sounds more reasonable than accusing the hospital of some ridiculous cover-up."

"The thought of an overdose or wrong medication is not my only idea. Do you want to hear it?"

"I'm listening, but I hope this next idea is more sane than your first."

Jack thought of some witty, sarcastic comebacks, but he controlled himself. "The hospital idea was predicated

on Patience Stanhope's heart attack and the opposition
to the autopsy being two separate although related circumstances. What if both involved the same person?"

There was a deliberate pause while Jack let this comment sink in.

"I'm not sure I'm following you," Alexis said finally.
"Are you talking about someone causing Patience Stanhope's heart attack and then trying to prevent an autopsy
to keep from being discovered?"

"That's exactly what I'm suggesting."

"I don't know, Jack. That sounds almost as crazy. I
suppose you are talking about Jordan."

"Jordan is the first person that comes to mind. Craig
said Jordan and Patience were hardly a loving couple,
and Jordan is the big winner with her death. He certainly
didn't waste any time in mourning. For all we know, he
and his girlfriend were carrying on while Patience was
still in the picture."

"How can someone cause a heart attack in someone
on purpose?"

"Digitalis could do it."

"I don't know," Alexis said dubiously. "This seems
equally far-fetched. If Jordan was at all guilty, he certainly
wouldn't initiate a malpractice suit, and he absolutely
wouldn't have signed the exhumation authorization."

"I've thought of that," Jack said as he pulled into the
parking area for the Newton Memorial Hospital. "I
agree it doesn't seem rational, but maybe we're not dealing with a rational person. Maybe Jordan is getting a
charge out of all this, thinking it is showing how much
smarter he is than the rest of us. But this kind of supposition is jumping the gun. First, some kind of drug has

to be found by toxicology. If we find something, then we'll have to work backwards."

"That's the second time you've said 'we.' Are you just using that as a figure of speech or what?"

"One of the medical examiners from the Boston medical examiner's office is generously helping."

"I trust you've spoken to Laurie," Alexis said. "Is she okay with you still being here?"

"She's not the happiest camper, but she's doing okay."

"I can't believe you are getting married tomorrow."

"Nor can I," Jack said. He nosed into a parking space overlooking the pond. His headlights illuminated a flock of bobbing waterfowl. "What happened at the trial this afternoon?"

"Randolph called two expert witnesses, one from Yale and one from Columbia. Both were credible but hardly exciting. Best of all, they were not at all phased by Tony, who tried to rattle them. I think Tony was hoping Randolph would call Craig back on the stand, but Randolph wisely didn't. Instead, Randolph rested. That was it. Tomorrow morning will be the summations, with Randolph leading off."

"Has your intuition changed any about what you think the final outcome will be?"

"Not really. The defense witnesses were good, but they were from out of town. Since Boston is such a medical mecca, I don't think the fact that they came from distant universities resonated well with the jurors. Tony's experts had more of an impact."

"You probably have a point, I'm sorry to say."

"If by some slim chance you do discover some

criminality in regard to Patience Stanhope, it would probably save the day for Craig."

"Don't think for a moment that such a thought isn't in my mind. To be honest, it's my main motivation. How is Craig's mind-set?"

"Despondent, as usual. Maybe even a little worse. I worry a little with him home alone. When do you think you'll get back there?"

"I just don't know," Jack said, suddenly feeling guilty about not wanting to return to the Bowman home.

"Maybe you could check on him when you do. I don't like that alcohol–sleeping pill combination."

"Okay, I'll do that," Jack said. "I'm at the hospital now, and I have to run."

"No matter what happens, I truly appreciate all your efforts, Jack. You'll never know how much your support has meant to me these last few days."

"You still feel that way even though my meddling was responsible for what happened to the girls?"

"I don't hold that against you in the slightest."

After a few more sibling endearments that might have brought a tear to Jack's eye had they continued, they said good-bye. Jack flipped his phone closed and sat in the car for a minute, thinking about relationships and how they changed over time. It gave him a warm feeling to know that he and his sister were back to a semblance of their previous closeness, despite the years of separation while he'd struggled with his own despondency.

As Jack climbed out of the car, the zeal that Latasha had generated came back in a rush. Alexis's comments had been a bit of a downer, but he didn't need her to tell him his ideas were preposterous. He was, as he had explained, thinking out of the box with a bunch of facts that were themselves seemingly implausible.

In contrast to his first visit, the emergency room was hopping. The waiting room was full, with almost every seat taken. A few people were standing outside on the ambulance-receiving dock. It was a warm, humid, almost summer night.

Jack had to wait in line at the admitting desk behind a woman holding a feverish infant in her arms. The child stared at Jack over the mother's shoulder with glazed eyes and a blank expression. As Jack moved up to the counter and was about to ask for Dr. Matt Gilbert, the doctor appeared. He tossed a completed ER admission note attached to a clipboard onto the desk when he locked eyes with Jack.

"I know you," he said, pointing at Jack. He was obviously searching for the name.

"Dr. Jack Stapleton."

"Right! The medical examiner interested in the failed resuscitation case."

"Good memory," Jack commented.

"It's the main talent I picked up in medical school. What can we do for you?"

"I need two minutes of your time, hopefully with Georgina O'Keefe. Is she here tonight?"

"She runs the show," the admitting clerk said with a laugh. "She's here."

"I know this is not the best time," Jack said. "But we exhumed the body, and I just did an autopsy. I thought you might like to know what was found."

"Absolutely," Matt said. "And this isn't a bad time. We're busy, but it's all routine stuff that should have been seen in the outpatient clinic or a doctor's office.

There's no critical emergencies at the moment. Come on back into the lounge. I'll snare Georgina."

For a few minutes, Jack sat by himself. He used the time to look back over the two pages that constituted a record of Patience's ER visit. He'd pulled them from the case file while he'd been talking to Alexis.

"Welcome back," Georgina bubbled as she swept into the room. Matt came in after her. Both were dressed in white jackets over green scrub clothes.

"Matt said you dug up Mrs. Stanhope and did an autopsy. Cool! What did you find? I mean, no one has ever given us this kind of feedback."

"The interesting thing was that her heart appeared entirely normal. With no degenerative changes whatsoever."

Georgina thrust the backs of her hands onto her hips with her elbows out. Her mouth formed a disappointed, wry smile. "I thought we were going to hear something startling."

"It's startling in its own way," Jack said. "It's rare with sudden cardiac death not to find pathology."

"You came all the way over here to tell us you found nothing?" Georgina questioned with disbelief. She looked at Matt for support.

"Actually, I came to ask you if there was any chance she could have been given an overdose of any medication or maybe the wrong medication."

"What kind of medication are you talking about?" Georgina asked. Her smile faded, replaced by a wary confusion.

"Anything," Jack said. "Particularly any of the newer fibrinolytic or antithrombotic agents. I don't know; are you people involved in any randomized studies involving heart attack patients? I'm just curious. There's nothing like what I'm talking about on the order sheet." Jack handed the two pages over to Georgina, who glanced at them. Matt looked over her shoulder.

"Everything we gave her is on here," Georgina said, holding up the order sheet. She looked at Matt for confirmation.

"That's it," Matt agreed. "She was in extremis when she arrived, with practically a flatline on the cardiac monitor. All we tried to do was resuscitate her. We didn't try to treat her MI. What was the point?"

"She didn't get anything like digitalis?"

"No," Matt said. "We couldn't even get a heartbeat, even with dual-chamber sequential pacing. Her heart was completely unresponsive."

Jack looked from Georgina to Matt and back again. So much for the overdose or wrong medication idea! "The only laboratory reports on the ER notes are blood gases. Were any other tests done?"

"When we draw blood for blood gases, we routinely also order the usual blood count plus electrolytes. And with heart attacks, we order biomarkers."

"If they were ordered, how come there's no mention of it on the order sheet, and why aren't the results on the ER note? The blood gases are there."

Matt took the sheets from Georgina and quickly looked them over. He shrugged. "I don't know, maybe because they normally go in the hospital record, but since she died so quickly, she never got a hospital record." He shrugged again. "I suppose they are not on the order sheet because it's a standing order for all myocardial infarction suspects. I did mention sodium and potassium were normal in my note, so someone called the results to the ER desk."

"This isn't a big-city ER," Georgina explained. "It's rare to have a death here. Usually people get admitted, even those in bad shape."

"Could we call the lab and see if they could possibly locate the results?" Jack asked. He did not quite know what to make of this serendipitous discovery or whether it would have any meaning, but he felt obligated to see where the lead would take him.

"Sure," Matt said. "We'll have the clerk call up there. Meanwhile, we've got to get back to work. Thanks for coming by. It's strange you didn't find any pathology, but it's nice to know we didn't miss anything that could have saved her."

Five minutes later, Jack found himself in the tiny, windowless office of the evening laboratory supervisor. He was a large, heavyset man with heavily lidded eyes that gave him a sleep-deprived appearance. He was staring at his computer monitor with his head tilted back. His nametag read: "Hi, I'm Wayne Marsh."

"I don't see anything under *Patience Stanhope*," Wayne said. He had been very obliging when the ER had called, and invited Jack up to his office. He'd been impressed with Jack's credentials, and if he'd noticed the badge said New York rather than Massachusetts, he didn't mention it.

"I need a unit number," Wayne explained, "but if she wasn't admitted, then she didn't get one."

"What about through billing?" Jack suggested. "Somebody had to pay for the tests."

"Nobody's in billing at this hour," Wayne said, "but

didn't you mention you have a copy of the ER record. That will have an ER accession number. I can try that."

Jack handed over the ER notes. Wayne typed in the number. "Here we go," he said as a record flashed up on the screen. "Dr. Gilbert was right. We did a full blood count with platelets, electrolytes, and the usual cardiac biomarkers."

"Which ones?"

"We do CKMB and cardiac-specific troponin T on arrival at the ER with repeats at six hours postadmission and twelve hours postadmission."

"Was everything normal?"

"Depends on your definition of normal," Wayne said. He twisted his monitor screen in its base so Jack could see it. He pointed to the blood-count section. "There's a mild to moderate rise in the white count, which is expected with a heart attack." His finger then went to the electrolytes. "The potassium is at the upper edge of normal. Had she lived, we would have wanted to check that, for obvious reasons."

Jack inwardly shuddered at the mention of potassium. The frightening episode with Laurie's potassium during her ectopic pregnancy emergency was still fresh in his mind despite its being over a year ago. Then his eyes happened to notice the biomarker results. To his surprise, the tests were negative, and he immediately called it to Wayne's attention. Jack's pulse ratcheted up. Had he stumbled onto something significant?

"That's not unusual," Wayne said. "With improved response times to nine-one-one calls, we often get our heart attack victims into the ER within the three- to four-hour interval it takes for the biomarkers to rise. That's one of the reasons we routinely repeat the test at six hours. Jack nodded as he tried to sort out the discrepancy this new information provided. He didn't know whether he'd forgotten or never knew there was such a delay before biomarkers become positive. Not wishing to appear overly uninformed, he worded his next questions carefully. "Does it surprise you that an earlier bedside biomarker assay was positive?"

"Not really," Wayne said.

"Why not?"

"There are a lot of variables. First off, there's about a four percent false negative result as well as a three percent false positive. The tests are based on highly specific monoclonal antibodies, but they are not infallible. Secondly, the bedside kits are based on troponin I, not T, and there's a lot of bedside kits on the market. Was the bedside assay for troponin I alone or with myoglobin?"

"I don't know," Jack admitted. He tried to remember what was written on the box in Craig's doctor's bag, but he couldn't visualize it.

"That would be important. The myoglobin component becomes positive faster, often within as little as two hours. What's the time frame on this case?" He picked up the ER note and read aloud: "Patient's husband states chest pain and other symptoms developed between five and six p.m., probably closer to six." Wayne looked up at Jack. "She arrived in the ER close to eight, so the time frame is about right as far as our results are concerned, since it was less than four hours. Do you know when the bedside assay was done?"

"I don't," Jack said. "But if I had to guess, it would be somewhere around seven thirty."

"Well, that does seem marginal, but as I said, the bedside tests are made by a host of companies with widely differing sensitivities. The kits also should be carefully stored, and I believe there's an expiration date. Frankly, that's why we don't use them. We much prefer the troponin T, since it's made by only one company. We get very reproducible results with a short turnaround time. Would you like to see our Abbott analyzer? It's a beauty. It measures absorbance spectrophotometrically at four hundred fifty nanometers. It's right across the lab if you want to take a gander."

"Thank you, but I think I'll pass," Jack said. He was getting in technically way over his head, and his visit at the hospital had already been twice as long as he had planned. He certainly didn't want to keep Latasha waiting. He thanked Wayne for his help and returned quickly to the elevator. As he rode down to the first floor, he couldn't help but wonder if Craig's bedside biomarker assay kit had somehow been defective, either from improper storage or from being out of date, and had given a false positive. What if Patience Stanhope did not have a myocardial infarction? All at once, yet another dimension was opening up, particularly with the services of a toxicologist available. There were a lot more drugs that deleteriously affected the heart than those capable of simulating a heart attack.

Jack jumped into the car and quickly dialed Latasha's number. As he'd done with his call to Alexis, he put his phone on speaker and placed it on the passenger seat. By the time he was driving out of the hospital parking lot, Latasha answered.

"Where are you?" she asked. "I'm here in my office. I got two hot pizzas and two large Cokes. Where are you at?"

"I'm just leaving the hospital. I'm sorry it has taken

as long as it has, but I learned something possibly important. Patience Stanhope's biomarker test was negative when it was read by the hospital analyzer."

"But you told me it was positive."

"That was from a bedside biomarker kit," Jack said. He carefully explained what he'd learned from the lab supervisor.

"What it all comes down to," Latasha said when Jack was finished, "is that now we're not sure she had a heart attack, which would be consistent with what we found during the post."

"Precisely, and if that is the case, the toxicology is going to be key."

"I already dropped the samples off at the toxicology lab with a note for Allan to give me a call."

"Perfect," Jack said. He couldn't help but marvel at how lucky he was to have Latasha helping him. If it hadn't been for her, he might have given up after finding nothing in the heart.

"I guess this puts the mourning husband in the crosshairs," Latasha added.

"There are still some inconsistencies," Jack said, remembering Alexis's points against Jordan's being the bad guy, "but generally I agree, as trite and venal as it sounds."

"When will you be here?"

"As soon as I can. I'm coming up to Route Nine. You're probably a better judge than I. Why don't you start on the pizza while it's hot."

"I'll wait," Latasha said. "I've got myself busy making us some frozen sections of the heart."

"I'm not sure I'll be eating much," Jack said. "I've

gotten myself psyched. I feel like I've had ten cups of coffee."

When Jack flipped his phone shut, he checked the time. It was almost ten thirty, which meant Latasha's friend would soon be arriving at the toxicology lab. Jack hoped he'd have a lot of free time, since Jack could imagine keeping him busy most of the night. Jack had no illusions about the power of toxicology to detect poisons. It was not as easy a process as it was often portrayed in the popular media. For large concentrations of the usual drugs there usually was no problem, but for trace amounts of more toxic and lethal compounds that could kill a person in very small dosages, it was like finding the proverbial needle in a haystack.

Jack stopped at a traffic light and impatiently drummed his fingers on the steering wheel. The warm, soft, humid June air wafted in through the missing window. He was glad he'd taken the time to visit the hospital, although he now felt embarrassed about the idea of a hospital cover-up. Nonetheless he rationalized that the idea had indirectly led to his questioning whether Patience Stanhope had suffered a heart attack.

The light turned green, and he moved on. The problem was she still might have had a heart attack. Wayne had admitted that even with his vaunted absorbance analyzer, the rate of false negatives was higher than false positives. Jack sighed. There was nothing about this case that was simple and straightforward. Patience Stanhope was proving to be a problem patient even in death, which reminded him of his favorite lawyer joke: What's the difference between a lawyer and a prostitute? The prostitute stops screwing you when you die. From Jack's perspective, Patience was assuming some annoying lawyerlike qualities.

As Jack drove, he mulled over his promise to check in on Craig, who was probably at that time already in a deep, drug-and-alcohol-induced slumber. Jack wasn't excited about the idea and thought it unnecessary since, in his estimation, Craig was not suicidal in the slightest, and, as an intelligent physician, Craig was well aware of the power of the medications he was taking. On the other hand, the good side of making such a visit would be a chance for Jack to check what kind of biomarker kit Craig used and whether it was outdated. Until he had that information, he couldn't intelligently decide whether or not there was a higher than usual chance the result had been a false positive.

CHAPTER TWENTY-ONE

BOSTON, MASSACHUSETTS
Friday, June 9, 2006
1:30 a.m.

For almost five minutes Jack had watched the hands of the institutional wall clock as they implacably jumped staccato-fashion toward one thirty a.m. With the final leap of the minute hand, Jack took a breath. He hadn't realized he'd not been breathing for the final seconds, since the time was a mini-milestone. Exactly twelve hours hence he would be married, and all the years he'd avoided the issue would be history. It seemed inconceivable. Except for the relatively recent past, he'd practically institutionalized being by himself. Was he capable of marriage and thinking of two people instead of one? He didn't really know.

"Are you all right?" Latasha asked, yanking Jack back to reality by reaching out and briefly gripping his forearm.

"Fine. I'm fine!" Jack blurted. She'd startled him.

"I thought you were having an absence seizure. You didn't move a muscle for the last few minutes. You didn't even blink. What on earth were you thinking that had you so mesmerized?"

Despite being an intensely private person, Jack almost told Latasha what had been on his mind to get a fresh viewpoint. Such a reaction surprised him, even though he acknowledged having developed a strong affinity toward the woman. Except for his detour to the Newton Memorial Hospital, they had been closely working together for some six hours and had fallen into a natural familiarity. When Jack had arrived at the Boston medical examiner's office, they'd taken over what was supposed to be the library, but the shelves were mostly empty, in hope of future funding. The room's major asset was a large library table, onto which Jack had spread the contents of Craig's malpractice file and organized them so he'd be able to find anything in particular if there was a need. At the far end of the table were several open pizza boxes, paper plates, and large cups. Neither had eaten much. Both had been consumed by the conundrum of Patience Stanhope.

They had also carried in the dual-headed stereo-dissecting microscope and, sitting on opposite sides of the table, had spent several hours opening and tracing all the coronary arteries. Like their larger and more proximal brethren, all the distal vessels were normal and clear. Jack and Latasha had paid particular attention to those branches serving the heart's conduction system.

The last stage of examining the heart was to be the microscopic. They'd taken specimens from all areas of the heart but again concentrated in and around the conduction system. Before Jack had arrived, Latasha had made a series of frozen sections from a small sampling, and the very first thing they had done on his arrival was to stain them and then put them out to dry. At the moment, they were in the wings waiting for their cue.

Just after they'd finished staining the slides, Allan Smitham had called. He apparently had been pleased to hear from Latasha, at least it seemed so to Jack from the side of the rather personal conversation he was forced to hear even though he was trying not to. He felt uncomfortable that he was intruding, but the good news was that Allan was eager to help and would run the toxicology screen immediately.

"I didn't come up with any new ideas," Jack said in response to Latasha's question about what was on his mind. Back when his eyes had strayed to the clock and its staccato movement had hypnotized him into thoughts of his intimidatingly imminent marriage, he was supposed to have been trying to think up new theories about Patience. He'd related to Latasha all his old theories by essentially repeating what he'd told Alexis on the phone en route to the hospital. Throwing all pretenses of self-respect to the wind, he included the drug overdose/wrong drug idea even though in hindsight it sounded inane, almost dim-witted, and Latasha had responded appropriately.

"I didn't have any eureka moment, either," Latasha admitted. "I might have laughed at some of your ideas, but I have to give you credit for creativity. I can't come up with nothing, you know what I'm saying?"

Jack smiled. "Maybe if you combined what I've told you with some of this material, you would," Jack said. He gestured at the case-file material on the table. "There's quite a cast of characters. There's depositions here of four times the number of witnesses actually called."

"I'd be happy to read some if you could tell me which you think would be potentially the most helpful."

"If you were to read any, read Craig Bowman's and Jordan Stanhope's. As defendant and plaintiff, they occupy center stage. Actually, I want to reread both their recollections of Patience's symptoms. For sake of argument, if she had been poisoned as we're considering, subtle symptoms would be crucial. You know, as well as I, that some poisons are nigh impossible to find in the complicated soup of chemicals that make up a human being. More than likely, we'll have to tell Allan what to look for in order for him to find it."

"Where are Dr. Bowman's and Mr. Stanhope's depositions?"

Jack picked them up. He had placed them in their own stack. Both were thick. He reached across and gave them to Latasha.

"Holy shit!" she exclaimed, feeling their weight. "What is this, *War and Peace*? How many pages do we have here?"

"Craig Bowman's deposition went on for days. The court reporter has to take down every word."

"I'm not sure I'm up to this at nearly two a.m.," Latasha said. She let the volumes thump down on the table in front of her.

"It's all dialogue with lots of spacing. It's actually easy to breeze through them for the most part."

"What are these scientific reprints doing here?" Latasha said, picking up the small stack of scientific publications.

"Dr. Bowman is the lead author in most of them and a contributing author in the rest. Craig's lawyer had considered introducing them as supporting evidence of Craig's commitment to medicine as a way of blunting the plaintiff's stratagem of character assassination."

"I remember this one when it came out in the *Journal*," Latasha said, holding up Craig's seminal article in the *New England Journal of Medicine*.

Once again, Jack was duly impressed. "You find time to read such esoterica?"

"This isn't esoteric stuff," Latasha said with a disapproving chuckle. "Membrane physiology is key in just about every field of medicine these days, particularly pharmacology and immunology, even infectious disease and cancer."

"Okay, okay!" Jack said, holding up his hands as if to protect himself. "I take back what I said. My problem is that I went to medical school in the last century."

"That's a lame excuse," Latasha said. She flipped through the pages of Craig's paper. "Sodium channel function is the basis of muscle and nerve function. If they don't work, nothing works."

"All right already," Jack said. "You made your point. I'll bone up on it."

Latasha's cell phone suddenly sprang to life. In the silence, it made both of them jump.

Latasha snatched it up, glanced at the LCD screen, and then flipped it open. "What's happening?" she said without preamble, pressing the phone to her ear.

Jack tried to hear the voice on the other end but couldn't. He assumed and hoped it was Allan.

The conversation was pointedly short. Latasha merely said, "You got it," and flipped her phone shut. She stood up.

"Who was it?" Jack asked.

"Allan," Latasha said. "He wants us to pay him a visit in his lab, which is just around the corner. I believe it's worth the effort if we're thinking of keeping him busy with our stuff. Are you game?"

"Are you kidding?" Jack questioned rhetorically. He pushed his chair back and got to his feet.

Jack hadn't realized that the Boston medical examiner's office was on the periphery of the vast Boston City Hospital Medical Center complex. Despite the hour, they passed a number of medical-center employees, including several medical students, walking between various buildings. No one seemed in a hurry, despite the hour. Everyone was enjoying the warmth and silky texture of the air. Although technically still spring, it felt like a summer night.

The toxicology lab was a mere two short blocks' walk in a new, eight-story glass-and-steel structure.

In the elevator on the way up to the sixth floor, Jack looked over at Latasha. Her dark eyes were riveted on the floor indicator display, and her face was reflecting her rightful fatigue.

"I apologize in advance if I say anything inappropriate," Jack said, "but I have the sense that this special effort Allan Smitham is willing to devote to this case is because of unrequited feelings he has for you."

"Maybe," Latasha said equivocally.

"I hope that accepting his aid doesn't put you in an uncomfortable position."

"I think I can handle it," Latasha said in a tone that proclaimed: End of discussion.

The lab was state-of-the-art and almost deserted. In addition to Allan, there were only two other people there, both lab technicians who were busily engaged at the far side of the generous-sized room. There were three aisles of benches groaning under the weight of gleaming new equipment.

Allan was a striking-looking African American with a closely trimmed mustache and goatee that gave him an intimidatingly Mephistophelean air. Adding to his imposing appearance was a heavily muscular frame barely concealed by a white lab coat with rolled-up sleeves over a form-fitting black T-shirt. His skin was a burnished mahogany, a shade or two darker than Latasha's. His eyes were bright and fixated on his old college friend.

Latasha introduced Jack, who rated only a quick but firm handshake and a rapid, appraising glance. Allan was unabashedly interested in Latasha, whom he lavished with a broad smile filled with startlingly white teeth.

"You shouldn't make yourself such a stranger, girl," Allan said as he gestured toward his tiny, utilitarian office. He ended up sitting at his desk while Latasha and Jack took two straight chairs in his line of sight.

"You have an impressive lab," Jack said, hooking a thumb over his shoulder. "Seems lean on staff, though."

"Just for this shift," Allan said. He was still smiling at Latasha. "In terms of the number of employees, the difference between us and the day shift is like night and day." He laughed at his own joke. Jack had the feeling he wasn't lacking self-esteem or humor.

"What did you find with our samples?" Latasha asked, cutting to the chase.

"Ah, yes," Allan said, steepling his fingers while his elbows rested on the desk. "You gave me a little background in your note, which I'd like to go over to make sure I understand. The patient died of a heart attack approximately eight months ago. She was embalmed, interred, and recently exhumed. What you want to do is rule out drug involvement."

"Let's put it more succinctly," Latasha said. "Her manner of death was assumed to be natural. We want to be sure it wasn't homicide."

"Okay," Allan intoned as if mulling over what he wanted to say next.

"What was the result of the screen?" Latasha asked impatiently. "Why are you dragging this out?"

Jack inwardly cringed at Latasha's tone. It made him uncomfortable that she was being less than gracious with Allan, who was doing them an enormous favor. For Jack, it was becoming progressively clear there was something between them that he didn't know and didn't want to know.

"I want to be sure you interpret the findings correctly," Allan said defensively.

"We're both medical examiners," Latasha shot back. "I think we are relatively informed about the limitations of a toxicology screen."

"Informed enough to know the predictive value of a negative test is only about forty percent?" Allan questioned, eyebrows raised. "And that is with a recently deceased, not embalmed, corpse."

"So you are saying the toxicology screen was negative."

"I am," Allan said. "It was definitely negative."

"My God, it's like pulling teeth," Latasha complained. She rolled her eyes and flapped her arms impetuously.

"What drugs constitute your screen?" Jack asked. "Is digitalis included?"

"Digitalis is included," Allan said as he half-stood to hand Jack the lab's toxicology screen drug list.

Jack scanned the sheet. He was impressed with the number of drugs included. "What methods do you use?"

"We use a combination of chromatography and enzyme immunoassay for our screens."

"Do you have gas chromatography–mass spectrometry?" Jack asked.

"Bet your ass we got mass-spec," Allan said proudly. "But if you want me to use the artillery, you're going to have to give me an idea of what I'm looking for."

"We can give you only a general idea at the moment," Jack said. "According to the symptoms the patient was reported to have had if drugs or poisons were involved, we would be looking for something capable of producing a markedly slow heart rate unresponsive to all attempts at pacing and a respiratory depressant, since she was also described as being cyanotic."

"You're still talking about a shitload of potential drugs and poisons," Allan said. "Without more specifics, you're asking me for a miracle!"

"I know," Jack admitted. "But Latasha and I are going to go back and brainstorm to see if we can come up with some likely candidates."

"You'd better," Allan said. "Otherwise, this is probably going to be a fruitless exercise. First, I have to figure out what to ignore with all the embalming fluid on board."

"I know," Jack repeated.

"Why are you even considering homicide?" Allan asked. "If you don't mind my asking."

Jack and Latasha exchanged a glance, unsure of how much to say.

"We just did the post a few hours ago!" Latasha said. "We didn't find diddly-squat. There was no cardiac pathology, which doesn't make sense, considering the history."

"Interesting," Allan said pensively. He locked eyes with Latasha. "Let me get this straight. You want me to do all this work, take up my whole night, and do it on the sly to boot. Is that what you are saying?"

"Of course we want you to do it!" Latasha snapped. "What's the matter with you? Why else would we be sitting here?"

"I don't mean you and the doc here," Allan said, gesturing toward Jack. He then pointed at Latasha. "I mean you personally."

"Yeah, I want you to do it, okay," Latasha said. She stood up.

"Okay," Allan said. There was a trace of a satisfied smile on his face.

Latasha walked out of the office.

Surprised at the sudden ending of the meeting, Jack got up and fumbled for one of his cards. "Just in case you want to ask me something," he said as he put it on Allan's desk. He helped himself to one of Allan's from a small Plexiglas holder. "I appreciate your help. Thank you."

"No problem," Allan said. The lingering smirk was still apparent.

Jack caught up to Latasha at the elevator. He didn't say anything until they were on their way down.

"That was a rather precipitous ending," Jack said. He pretended not to look at Latasha by watching the floor indicator.

"Yeah, well, he was getting on my nerves. He's such a cocky bastard."

"I sensed he didn't have a self-esteem problem."

Latasha laughed and perceptively relaxed a degree.

They walked out into the night. It was going on three, but there were still people on the street. As they neared the medical examiner's office, Latasha spoke up: "I suppose you wondered why I appeared somewhat rude."

"It crossed my mind," Jack admitted.

"Allan and I were tight the last year of college, but then something happened that gave me insight into his personality that I didn't like." She keyed open the front door and waved to the security person. As they started up the single flight of stairs, she continued: "I got a scare that I was pregnant. When I told him, his response was to ditch me. I couldn't even get a call back, so I wrote him off. The irony is that I wasn't pregnant. During the last year or so when he found out I was here at the ME office, he's tried to get us to connect up, but I'm not interested. I'm sorry if it was uncomfortable back there in his office."

"No need to apologize," Jack said. "As I said on the way over, I hope accepting his help won't cause a problem."

"With as many years as there have been, I'd thought I'd handle myself better than I did. But just seeing him made me pissed about the episode all over again. You'd think I would have gotten over it."

They walked into the library. The clutter was exactly as they'd left it.

"How about we take a look at the slides we stained?" Latasha suggested.

"Maybe you should go home and get some shut-eye," Jack said. "There's no reason for you to pull an all-nighter. I mean I love the help and the company, but this is asking way too much."

"You're not getting rid of me that easy," Latasha said with a coy smile. "I learned back in medical school that for me, when it's this late, it's better to just stay up. Plus, I'd love to solve this case."

"Well, I think I'm going to take a drive out to Newton."

"Back to the hospital?"

"Nope. Back to the Bowmans' house. I told my sister I'd look in on her husband to make sure he's not in a coma. Thanks to his depression, he's been mixing alcohol in the form of a single-malt scotch with some sort of sleeping pill."

"Yikes!" Latasha said. "I've had to post several people like that."

"Truthfully, with him I don't think it's much of a worry," Jack said. "He thinks far too much of himself. I doubt I'd even go if checking on him was the only reason. What I'm also going to do is check the biomarker assay kit he used with Patience to see if there is any reasonable reason to suspect he got a false positive. If it were a false positive, the possibility goes way up that the manner of death was not natural."

"What about suicide?" Latasha questioned. "You've never mentioned suicide even as a wildly remote possibility. How come?"

Jack absently scratched the back of his head. It was true that he'd not thought about suicide, and he wondered why. He let out a small chuckle, remembering how many cases he'd been involved with over the years where the apparent manner of death was ultimately not the correct manner. The last such case had involved the wife of the Iranian diplomat that was supposed to be suicide but had been homicide.

"I don't know why I haven't given even a passing

thought about suicide," Jack said, "especially considering some of my other equally unlikely ideas."

"The little you've told me about the woman suggests she wasn't terribly happy."

"That's probably true," Jack admitted, "but that's the only thing the idea of suicide has going for it. We'll keep it in mind along with my hospital conspiracy idea. But now I'm going to head out to Newton. Of course, you're welcome to come, but I can't imagine why you'd want to."

"I'll stay," Latasha said. She pulled over Craig's and Jordan's deposition transcripts to a position in front of one of the chairs and sat down. "I'll do some background reading while you're gone. Where are the medical records?"

Jack reached for the correct pile and pushed it over against Craig's and Jordan's depositions.

Latasha picked up a short run of ECG that was sticking out of the stack. "What's this?"

"It's a recording Dr. Bowman made when he first got to Patience's house. Unfortunately, it's almost useless. He couldn't even remember the lead. He had to give up doing the ECG because she was in such dire straits and rapidly worsening."

"Has anyone looked at it?"

"All the experts looked at it, but without knowing the lead and not being able to figure it out, they couldn't say much. They all agreed the marked bradycardia suggested an AV block. With that and other suggestive conduction abnormalities, they all felt it was at least consistent with a heart attack someplace in the heart."

"Too bad there's not more," Latasha said.

"I'm out of here so I can get back," Jack said. "My

cell phone is on if you have a eureka moment or if Allan is able to pull off a miracle."

"See you when you get back," Latasha said. She was already speed-reading Craig's deposition.

At three o'clock in the morning, it was finally easy for Jack to drive in Boston. At some of the traffic lights on Massachusetts Avenue, Jack's Accent was the only vehicle waiting. On several occasions he debated ignoring the light when there also wasn't any cross-traffic, but he never did. Jack didn't have a problem breaking rules he judged ridiculous, but traffic lights didn't fall into that category.

The Massachusetts Turnpike was another story. It wasn't crowded, but there was more traffic than he expected, and it wasn't all trucks. It made him wonder with amazement what so many people were doing out and about at such an hour.

The short drive to Newton gave Jack a chance to calm down from the near mania Latasha had unleashed when she said she had access to a toxicologist just at the point Jack was ready to throw in the towel. In a more relaxed state of mind, he was able to think about the whole situation considerably more rationally, and when he did so, it was clear what the most probable outcome was going to be. First, he was going to decide from lack of proof to the contrary that Patience Stanhope most likely died of a massive heart attack despite there being no obvious pathology; and second, that Fasano et al. were most likely behind the despicable assault on Craig and Alexis's children for trite economic reasons. Fasano had been unambiguously clear about the rationale when he directly threatened Jack.

Jack's mild mania had devolved into a tepid despondency by the time he arrived at the Bowmans' house. He found himself again wondering if the reason he was still in Boston and imagining out-of-the-box conspiracies had more to do with half-conscious fears of getting married in ten hours than trying to help his sister and brother-in-law.

Jack climbed out of the car clutching the umbrella he had the presence of mind to rescue from the backseat. He was parked next to Craig's Lexus. Walking back to the street, he looked up and down for the police cruiser that had been there that morning. It was nowhere to be seen. So much for the surveillance. Turning back to the house, Jack trudged up the front walk. His fatigue was catching up to him.

The house was dark, save for a little light filtering through the sidelights bordering the front door. Tilting his head back as he approached the front stoop, Jack checked the second-floor dormer windows. They were as black as onyx, reflecting back the light from a distant streetlamp.

Being relatively quiet, Jack slipped the key into the lock. He wasn't trying to be secretive, but at the same time, he preferred not to wake Craig if at all possible. It was at that point Jack remembered the alarm system. With the key in the lock, he tried to remember the code. As tired as his mind was, it took him a minute to recall it. Then he wondered if he was supposed to hit another button after the code. He didn't know. When he was as prepared as possible, he turned the key. The mechanism seemed loud in the nighttime stillness.

Quickly stepping inside in a minor panic, Jack gazed at the alarm keypad. Luckily, the warning buzz he'd been expecting didn't sound, but he waited to be certain. The alarm was disarmed. A bright green dot of light suggested all was well. Jack closed the front door quietly. It was then that he became aware of the muted sound of the television coming from the direction of the great room. From the same direction came a small amount of light, spilling down the otherwise dark, main hallway.

Imagining that Craig might still be up or possibly asleep in front of the TV, Jack descended the corridor and walked into the great room. There was no Craig. The TV over the fireplace was turned to a cable news network, and the lights were on in that section, whereas the kitchen and the dining area were both dark.

On the coffee table in front of the couch stood Craig's nearly empty scotch bottle, an old-fashioned glass, and the TV remote. By force of habit, Jack walked over, picked up the remote, and turned the TV off. He then went back out in the hall. He looked up the stairs into the darkness and then down the length of the corridor to the study. A tiny bit of light was coming through the study's bow window from the streetlights, so it wasn't completely dark.

Jack debated what to do first: check Craig or check the biomarker assay kit. It wasn't a hard decision. When faced with a choice, Jack generally did the less desirable chore or errand first, and in this instance that was certainly the one involving Craig. It wasn't that he thought it would be difficult, but he knew by going to his room he risked waking the man, which he did not want to do for a variety of reasons. The most important one was that he was convinced Craig would not consider Jack's presence a favor. In fact, the implication of neediness would most likely offend and irritate him.

Jack looked back up into the darkness. He'd never been on the second floor and had no idea where the master bedroom would be. Not willing to turn on any lights, Jack retreated to the kitchen. It was his experience that most families had a gadget drawer, and most gadget drawers had flashlights.

As it turned out, he was half-right. There was a flashlight in the gadget drawer, but the Bowmans' gadget drawer was in the laundry, not the kitchen. In keeping with the rest of the house and its contents, the flashlight was an impressive foot-long Maglite that cast a serious and concentrated beam when Jack turned it on. Believing he could put his hand over the lens and vary the amount of light, Jack returned with it to the stairs and started up.

Reaching the top, Jack let enough light escape through his fingers to see down the upstairs hallway, first in one direction and then the other. Multiple doors led off the hall on both sides and, as luck would have it, most of them were closed. Trying to decide where to start, Jack checked both directions again and determined the right hallway was half the length of the left. Unsure of why, Jack started to his right. Picking a door at random, he silently opened it and pushed it ajar enough to step across the threshold. Slowly, he let light spread around the room. It certainly wasn't the master. It was one of the girls' bedrooms, and from the posters, photos, knick-knacks, and clothes strewn about, Jack could tell it was Tracy's. Back in the hall, Jack proceeded to the next door. He was about to open it when he noticed the doors at the very end of the hall facing him were double. Since all the other doors were single, it seemed a good bet that he'd found the master.

Keeping the flashlight mostly covered, Jack walked down to the double doors. He pressed the flashlight lens against his abdomen to block the light as he opened the right-hand door. It swung inward. As he slipped into the room, he could tell he was in the master suite for certain. He had stepped into deep-pile wall-to-wall carpet. For a moment, he didn't move. He strained to hear Craig's breathing, but the room was silent.

Slowly angling the flashlight, progressively more light extended deeper into the room. Out of the gloom emerged a king-size bed. Craig was lying on the side of the bed farthest from Jack.

For a moment Jack stood still, debating what he was going to do to make sure Craig was not comatose. Up until that moment, he hadn't given it much thought, but now that he was in the room, he had to. Although waking Craig would be definitive, it was not an option. Ultimately, Jack thought he'd just walk over and listen to Craig's breathing. If that sounded normal, Jack was willing to accept it as positive proof the man was okay, despite it being far from scientific.

Reducing the light again, Jack started across the room, moving more from memory than visually. A meager amount of ambient light was managing to finger its way through the dormer window from the street. It was enough to give Jack a vague outline of the larger pieces of furniture. Reaching the foot of the bed, Jack stopped and strained to hear the intermittent sibilant sounds of sleep. The room was deathly quiet. Jack felt a rush of adrenaline. To his horror, there was no sound of respiration. Craig was not breathing!

CHAPTER TWENTY-TWO

NEWTON, MASSACHUSETTS
Friday, June 9, 2006
3:25 a.m.

The next few seconds were a blur for Jack. The instant he realized his brother-in-law was not breathing, he lunged forward with the intention of rounding the corner of the bed to get to Craig's side in the shortest possible time. There he would whip back the covers, rapidly evaluate the man's status, and begin CPR if it was appropriate.

The sudden sideward movement possibly saved Jack's life. In the next instant Jack realized that he was not alone in the room. There was another figure, clad in black, making him all but invisible, who streaked out of the open bathroom doorway. The individual was brandishing a large club that he swung in a wide arc at the spot where Jack's head had been.

Although the blow missed Jack's head, it did hit his left shoulder. Luckily, it was a glancing blow that did not impact with its full force. Still, it sent a shooting, searing pain into the core of Jack's body, weakening his knees in the process.

Jack was still clutching the flashlight, the beam of which raced haphazardly around the room as he scrambled past the end of the bed, avoiding going alongside it. He did not want to be trapped by the intruder. More

by instinct than vision, he knew that another blow with
the club was coming as the figure leapt at him in pursuit.
Jack ducked down low to the floor and, believing offense
the best defense, threw himself forward, meeting his
attacker with the point of his right shoulder as if he
intended to tackle him. Jack had the man around the
upper thighs and with continued pumping of his legs
strengthened by all his bicycle riding, he was able to drive
the man backward before both fell to the floor.

In close proximity, Jack felt he had the advantage by
using the foot-long, heavy Maglite as a weapon. The
longer club, wielded by the attacker, was at a distinct disadvantage. Letting go of the man's thighs, Jack grabbed
a handful of shirt and rapidly lifted the flashlight alongside his head with full intention of striking the man's
forehead. But as he raised the flashlight, its beam had
illuminated the man's face. Luckily, before Jack struck,
his mind quickly fired the right neurons and recognized
the man. It was Craig.

"Craig?" Jack shouted in disbelief. He swiftly brought
the light down from its threatening position and shined
it on Craig's face just to be certain.

"Jack?" Craig sputtered in return. He raised his free
hand to shield his eyes from the blinding light.

"Good God!" Jack voiced. He let go of Craig's shirt,
directed the flashlight away from Craig's face, and got to
his feet.

Craig got to his feet as well. He went to a wall switch
and turned on the light. "What the hell are you doing
here, sneaking around in my house at whatever the hell
time it is?" He looked over at the bedside clock. "Three
thirty in the goddamn morning!"

"I can explain," Jack said. He winced at a stab of

shoulder pain. Tentatively, he touched the area, finding a point of tenderness at the juncture of his collarbone and shoulder.

"Good grief," Craig complained. He tossed what turned out to be a baseball bat onto the bed. He came over to Jack. "God, I'm sorry I freakin' hit you. I could have killed you. Are you all right?"

"I've had worse," Jack said. He glanced over at the bed. What he'd thought had been Craig was merely pillows and bedcovers. "Can I check it?" Craig asked solicitously.

"Sure, I guess."

Craig took hold of Jack's arm and gently put his hand on Jack's shoulder. He rotated Jack's arm in its shoulder socket, then raised it slowly. "Any pain?"

"A little, but the movement doesn't make it worse."

"I don't think anything is broken, but an X-ray wouldn't hurt. I could drive you over to the Newton Memorial if you'd like."

"I think I'll put some ice on it for now," Jack said.

"Good idea! Come on down to the kitchen. I'll put some ice in a Ziploc bag."

As they walked along the upper hallway, Craig said: "My heart is going a mile a minute. I thought you were one of these guys who'd broken in and manhandled my daughters, who was back to carry out his threat. I was ready to knock you into the next county."

"I suppose I thought you were one of those guys as well," Jack said. He noticed that Craig was wearing a dark-colored bathrobe and not the black ninja outfit Jack had creatively imagined. He also felt the gun in his jacket pocket knocking against him. He'd not thought of it in the fury of the moment, and it was a good thing.

Craig got Jack set up with an ice bag. Jack was sitting at one end of the couch, holding the cold pack against the point of his shoulder. Craig collapsed at the other end, holding a hand against his forehead.

"I'll get out of here so you can get back to sleep," Jack said. "But I owe you an explanation."

"I'm listening," Craig said. "Before I went to bed, I went downstairs to check the apartment. You'd pulled the linens off the bed. I certainly didn't expect you, and especially at this hour, and especially not sneaking around upstairs."

"I promised Alexis I'd check on you."

"Did you talk with her tonight?"

"I did, but not until quite late. Frankly, she's worried about your mixing alcohol and sleeping pills, and she should be worried. I've autopsied a few people, thanks to that combination."

"I don't need your advice."

"Fair enough," Jack said. "Nonetheless, she asked me to check on you. To be honest, I didn't think it was necessary. The reason I was seemingly sneaking was because I was afraid to wake you for fear you'd be angry I was there."

Craig took his hand away from his face and gazed at Jack. "You're right about that."

"I'm sorry if I offended you. I did it for Alexis. She was afraid you might be more upset than usual after what happened at the trial."

"At least you're honest," Craig said. "I suppose I should see it as a favor. It's just hard with what's going on. I'm being forced to see myself in an unflatteringly different light. I was a miserable, ridiculous, self-defeating witness today. When I think about it in retrospect, I'm embarrassed."

"How do you think the afternoon went with the defense experts?"

"It was reasonable. It was nice to hear some positive words for a change, but I don't think it was enough. Unless Randolph pulls off an Oscar-winning performance with his summation tomorrow, which I personally believe he's incapable of, I think the jury is going to find for that bastard, Jordan." Craig sighed despondently. He was staring at the blank TV screen.

"I had another reason for coming out here at this late hour," Jack said.

"Oh! And what was that?" Craig asked. He turned to look at Jack. His eyes were glazed, as if he was ready to cry but too embarrassed to do so. "You haven't told me about the autopsy. Did you do it?"

"I did," Jack said. He went on to tell Craig a truncated version of the day's events, starting with the exhumation and ending with the meeting with the toxicologist. He didn't tell Craig as much as he'd told Alexis, but the gist was the same.

As Jack spoke, Craig became progressively riveted, especially about the toxicologist and the possibility of the involvement of criminality. "If the toxicologist could find some drug or poison, it would be the end of this malpractice nonsense," Craig said. He sat up straighter.

"No doubt," Jack said. "But it is a very, very long shot, as I explained. Yet if Patience did not have a heart attack, it opens up the possibility of many more potential agents. The other reason I came out here tonight was to look at the box of bedside biomarker assay devices in your doctor's bag. Is there any reason you can think of that your result could have been a false positive?"

Craig raised his eyebrows for a moment while he mulled the question. "I can't think of any," he said at length. "I wish I could, but I can't."

"The lab supervisor at the hospital asked me if the one you used tested for both troponin I and myoglobin or just troponin I."

"It's the one with the myoglobin. I chose to stock that one for the reason the lab supervisor mentioned—namely, it gives a result in as little as two hours."

"Is there a shelf life for those devices?"

"Not that I know of."

"Then I guess we'll just have to limit the possible agents to those capable of causing a heart attack."

"What about digitalis?" Craig suggested.

"I thought of digitalis, for sure, and it was part of the screen. So digitalis was not involved."

"I wish I could help more," Craig said. "One of the worst parts of being sued is you feel so helpless."

"You could help if you could think of any cardiotoxic drugs Patience or Jordan might have had access to."

"She had quite a pharmacopoeia in her medicine cabinet, thanks to my absent partner, Ethan Cohen. But all those records were turned over in discovery."

"I've been through those," Jack said. He got to his feet. Relaxing for a few minutes seemed to make his legs feel heavy and sluggish. It was obvious he was going to need some coffee before the night was over. "I better get back and see if the toxicologist has had any luck, and you better get back to bed." He started for the door.

"Are you going to work all night?" Craig asked, accompanying Jack.

"It looks like that," Jack said. "After everything that's happened, I wish I could be certain of some positive result, but it's not looking likely."

"I don't know what to say other than thanks for all your effort."

"You're welcome," Jack said. "And it's been positive despite the problems I've caused and the whacks I've taken. It has been nice to hook back up with Alexis."

They reached the front door. Craig pointed down toward the study. "Should I run and grab my doctor's bag so you can look at the biomarker assay box? I'm sure it's the same box. After this fiasco, I'm not making many house calls."

Jack shook his head. "I'm good. You told me what I needed to know."

"Will we see you in court tomorrow?"

"I don't think so. I've got some pressing personal plans that are dictating I take the first shuttle back to the Big Apple. So let me say, good luck!"

Jack and Craig shook hands, having become, if not friends, a bit more knowledgeable and appreciative of each other.

The ride back into the city a little after four a.m. was a mirror of the ride out. There was traffic on the Mass Pike but very little once in the city along Mass Ave. It took Jack less than twenty minutes to get all the way to the medical examiner's office. He parked right on the side of the building in a reserved space, but since he would be leaving at such an early hour, he didn't think it would matter.

Security recognized him and let him in. As he

climbed the stairs, he looked at his watch. It was coming down to the wire. In less than two hours he'd be on the plane, taxiing away from the terminal.

Walking into the library, Jack did a double take. The place was in considerably greater disarray than when he had left. Latasha looked as if she were cramming to take her medical specialty boards. There were numerous large books that she'd gathered from around the office lying open on the tabletop. Jack recognized most. They included standard internal-medicine textbooks, physiology books, toxicology books, and pharmacology books. The case file material that Jack had organized was now randomly spread out, at least according to his eye.

"What the hell?" Jack questioned with a laugh.

Latasha's head popped up from an open textbook. "Welcome back, stranger!"

Jack flipped the covers back on a couple of the books he didn't recognize. After he saw the titles, he reopened the books to where Latasha had them. He took a seat opposite her.

"What happened to your shoulder?"

Jack was continuing to press the Ziploc bag against his bruise. By now the bag contained mostly water, but it was still cool enough to be of some benefit. He told her what had happened, and she was appropriately sympathetic for him and inappropriately critical of Craig.

"It wasn't his fault," Jack insisted. "I've been so consumed by this case for a variety of reasons that I never stopped to think of what a harebrained idea it was for me to go sneaking into his house. I mean, this is after someone else had broken into it and terrorized his kids to give him a message that they'd be back if I did an autopsy. And I just did the autopsy, for chrissake. What was I thinking?"

"But you were a houseguest. You'd think he'd make sure who he was hitting with a baseball bat."

"I wasn't a houseguest any longer. But let's drop it. Thank God no one got hurt any more than a shoulder contusion. At least I think it is just a contusion. I might have to get my clavicle x-rayed."

"Look on the positive side," Latasha said. "You certainly made sure he wasn't comatose, you know what I'm saying?"

Jack had to smile in spite of himself.

"What about the biomarker assay kit? Did you find out anything?"

"Nothing that raised the possibility he'd gotten a false positive. I think we have to assume it was a legitimate result."

"I suppose that's good," Latasha said. "It eliminates a lot of potential lethal agents." Her eyes swept over the books she had arranged around her.

"It looks like you've been busy."

"You have no idea. I got my second wind with the help of a few Diet Cokes. It's been like a great review course in toxicology. I haven't studied this stuff since forensic boards."

"What about Allan? Has he called you?"

"Several times, to be exact. But it's good. The more I hear his voice, the easier it is not to drag up old memories and get pissed."

"Has he had any luck?"

"Nope. Not at all. Apparently, he's trying to impress me, and you know something? He's not doing such a bad job. I mean, I knew he was smart and all back in college with his majoring in chem, math, and physics, but I didn't know he'd gone on to get a Ph.D. at MIT. I know that takes a few more brains than medical school, where perseverance is the major requirement."

"Did he say what kinds of things he's ruled out?"

"Most of the more common cardiotoxic agents that were not on the screen. He also explained to me some of the tricks he's using. The embalming chemicals are making it much harder with the tissue samples, like from the heart and liver, so he's concentrating on the fluids, where there's been less contamination."

"So what's with all these textbooks?"

"I started by reviewing cardiotoxic agents, a lot of which, I learned, could cause heart attacks or at least enough damage to the cardiac muscle so that clinically it would present as one even though there was no occlusion of cardiac vessels. I mean, that's what we've found from the autopsy. It's also what I found on the frozen sections we stained. I took a peek at a couple of the slides while you were gone. The capillaries look normal. I left the slide in the microscope in my office, if you'd like to take a peek."

"I'll take your word for it," Jack said. "I didn't expect we'd see anything as clear as the gross was."

"Now I've expanded from purely cardiotoxic agents to neurotoxic agents, since a lot of them do both. I tell you, it's fascinating stuff, especially how it dovetails with bioterrorism."

"Did you read the depositions?" Jack asked. He wanted to keep the conversation on track.

"Hey, you weren't gone that long. I think I've gotten a lot done. Give me a break!"

"We are running out of time. We have to stay focused."

"I'm focused, man," Latasha scoffed. "I'm not out

driving around, learning something I essentially already knew, and getting beat on in the process."

Jack rubbed his face briskly with both hands in an attempt to dispel the cobwebs of fatigue that were interfering with his cognition and emotion. Being at all critical of Latasha was surely not his intent. "Where are those Diet Cokes? I could use a blast of caffeine."

Latasha pointed toward the door to the hall. "There's a vending machine in the lunchroom down on the left."

When the can of soda thudded down into the vending machine's opening, it was loud enough in the building's silence to make Jack jump. He was tired, but he was also tense, and he wasn't entirely sure why. It could have been because time was running out as far as the case was concerned, but it also could have been anxiety about returning to New York and all that it entailed. After flipping open the can of soda, Jack hesitated. Was caffeine advisable if he was already mildly uptight? Throwing caution to the wind, he downed the can, then burped. He rationalized that he needed his wits to be sharp, and for that, caffeine was what the doctor ordered.

Feeling a slight buzz since caffeine was not one of his vices, Jack reclaimed the seat across from Latasha and cherry-picked Craig's and Jordan's deposition transcripts from the debris around Latasha.

"I didn't read those depositions cover to cover," Latasha said. "But I did kinda breeze through them to make a list of Patience's symptoms."

"Really?" Jack questioned with interest. "That's what I was just about to do."

"I guessed as much, since that's what you suggested before your ill-fated drive out to the suburbs."

"Where is it?" Jack asked.

Latasha scrunched up her features in concentration while she riffled through some of the material in front of her. Eventually, she came up with a yellow legal pad. She handed it across to Jack.

Jack settled back in his chair. There was no order to the symptoms other than their being divided into two major groups: the morning of September eighth, and the late afternoon and early evening. The morning group included abdominal pain, increased productive cough, hot flashes, nasal congestion, insomnia, headache, flatulence, and general anxiety. The late afternoon/early evening group comprised chest pain, cyanosis, inability to talk, headache, difficulty walking, difficulty sitting up, numbness, a sensation of floating, nausea with a little vomiting, and generalized weakness.

"Is this all?" Jack asked, waving the pad in the air.

"You don't think that's enough? She sounds like most of my patients in third-year medical school."

"I just wanted to make sure it's all the symptoms mentioned in the depositions."

"It's all the ones I could find."

"Did you find any mention of diaphoresis?"

"No, I didn't, and I looked for it specifically."

"I did, too," Jack said. "Sweating is so typical of a heart attack, I couldn't believe it when I didn't see it on my first reading. I'm glad you didn't see it, either, because I thought maybe I'd just missed it."

Jack glanced back at the list. The trouble was that most of the entries had no modifiers, and the ones that did had modifiers that were too general and not descriptive enough. It was as if all the symptoms were equally important, which made it difficult to weigh each symptom's contribution to Patience's clinical state. Numbness, for instance, had little meaning without a description of location, extent, and duration, and whether it meant no feeling whatsoever or paresthesia, more commonly known as *pins and needles*. In such a circumstance, it was impossible for Jack to decide if the numbness was of neural or cardiovascular origin.

"You know what I find most interesting about this toxicology stuff?" Latasha said, looking up from a large textbook.

"No! What?" Jack said vaguely. He was preoccupied in deciding he would need to go back through the depositions himself and see what qualifiers existed for the symptoms mentioned.

"Reptiles," Latasha said. "It's a wonder how all their venoms evolved, and why there is such a difference in potency."

"It is curious," Jack said as he opened Jordan's deposition and began rapidly flipping through the pages to get to the section involving the events of September eighth.

"There are a couple of snakes whose venom contains a powerful specific cardiotoxin capable of causing direct myocardial necrosis. Can you imagine what that would do to the level of cardiac biomarkers?"

"Really?" Jack questioned with sudden interest. "What kind of snakes?"

Latasha cleared a trench through the material on the desk, and, after turning the textbook around, she pushed it over in front of Jack. She used her index finger to point to the names of two types of snakes on a table comparing snake venom virulence. "The Mojave rattlesnake and the Southern Pacific rattlesnake."

Jack glanced at the table. The two snakes she pointed out were among the most poisonous of those listed. "Very interesting," Jack said. His interest faded as quickly as it had arisen. He pushed the book back. "However, we are not dealing with an envenomation. Patience wasn't bitten by a rattlesnake."

"I know," Latasha said, taking the book back. "I'm only reading about venom to get ideas for various classes of compounds to consider. I mean, we are looking for a cardiotoxin."

"Uh-huh," Jack said. He had already gone back to the deposition and found the part he was looking for. He began to read more closely.

"Actually, the most interesting venomous animals are a group of amphibians, of all things," Latasha said.

"Really," Jack said without actually hearing. He'd come across the mention of abdominal pain in the deposition. Jordan testified it was "lower" abdominal pain, more on the left than the right. Jack amended Latasha's entry on the yellow legal pad.

"It's the Colombian poison dart frogs that take the cake," Latasha said, flipping the pages in the textbook until she came to the right section.

"Really," Jack repeated. He skipped ahead in Jordan's deposition until he got to where Jordan was talking about the evening symptoms. Jack was particularly looking for the section where Jordan talked about the numbness Patience had experienced.

"Their skin secretions contain some of the most toxic substances known to man," Latasha said. "And they have an immediate toxic effect on heart muscle. Are you familiar with batrachotoxin?"

"Vaguely," Jack said. He found the reference to

numbness, and it was apparent from Jordan's description that it was paresthesia, not the absence of feeling, and it involved her arms and legs. Jack wrote the information on the yellow pad.

"It is the worst toxin of all. When batrachotoxin comes in contact with heart muscle, it stops all activity immediately." Latasha snapped her fingers. "In vitro, one minute cardiac myocytes are pumping away, and the next instant, after exposure to a few molecules of batrachotoxin, they are completely stopped. Can you believe that?"

"It's hard to believe," Jack agreed. He found Jordan's reference to floating and, interestingly, it was associated with the paresthesia and had nothing to do with being in liquid. It was a sensation of not being grounded and floating in air. Jack wrote the information on the yellow pad.

"The poison is a steroidal alkaloid rather than a polypeptide, for whatever that's worth. It's found in several frog species, but the one that has the highest concentration is called *Phyllobates terribilis*. It's aptly named, since one tiny frog has enough batrachotoxin to kill a hundred people. It's mind-boggling."

Jack found the section where Jordan discussed Patience's weakness, which, it turns out, didn't refer to a diminution of any particular muscle group. Rather, the weakness was a more global problem. It started with difficulty walking and progressed to difficulty sitting up in short order. Jack added the information to the yellow pad.

"There's something else you should know about batrachotoxin if you don't already. Its molecular mode of action is to depolarize electrical membranes like heart muscle and nerves. And do you know how it does it? It does it by affecting sodium transport, something you thought was esoterica. Remember?"

"What was that about sodium?" Jack asked as Latasha's comments penetrated his concentration. When Jack was thinking hard about something, he often could be oblivious to his surroundings, as Latasha had experienced.

"Batrachotoxin latches onto nerve and muscle cells and causes the sodium ion channels to lock in the open position, meaning the involved nerves and muscles stop functioning."

"Sodium," Jack repeated, as if in a daze.

"Yes," Latasha said. "Remember we were speaking . . ."

All of a sudden, Jack leaped to his feet and scrabbled madly through the litter spread around the table. "Where are those papers?" he demanded in a minor frenzy.

"What papers?" Latasha questioned. She had stopped speaking in mid-sentence and had leaned back in her chair, surprised by Jack's abrupt impetuosity. In his haste, he was knocking deposition transcripts off the table.

"You know!" he blurted, struggling to come up with the right word. "Those . . . those papers!"

"We've got a lot of papers here, big guy. God! How many Diet Cokes did you drink anyway?"

"Screw it!" Jack sputtered. He gave up on his search. Instead, he reached out toward Latasha. "Let me see that toxicology text!" he demanded.

"Sure," Latasha said, mystified at his transformation. She watched as he riffled through the pages of the massive tome to get to the index. Once there, he hastily ran his fingers down the columns until he found what he was looking for. Then he went back to rapidly leafing through the book so fast that Latasha had a fear for its integrity. He found the correct page and was silent.

"Would it be asking too much for you to tell me what you are doing?" Latasha scoffed.

"I think I've had what you would call a eureka moment and I would call an epiphany," Jack muttered while continuing to read. "Yes!" he cried after a few moments, raising a triumphant fist in the air. He slammed the book closed and looked across the table at Latasha. "I have an idea of what to ask Allan to look for! It's weird, and if it is present, it might not fit all the facts as we know them, but it fits some of the most important ones, and it would prove Craig Bowman did not commit medical negligence."

"Like what?" Latasha demanded. She couldn't help but feel some irritation that Jack was being so coy. She was in no mood for games at almost five o'clock in the morning.

"Check out this strange symptom you wrote," Jack said. He reached over with the yellow pad and pointed to the notation "sensation of floating." "Now, that's not your run-of-the-mill complaint of even the most dedicated hypochondriac. That suggests something truly weird was going on, and if Allan is able to find what I'm thinking, there would be the suggestion that Patience Stanhope was either a die-hard sushi fan or a crazed devotee of Haitian voodoo, but we're going to know differently."

"Jack!" Latasha said irritably. "I'm too tired for this kind of joking."

"I'm sorry," Jack said. "This apparent teasing is because I'm afraid I might be right. This is one of those situations, despite the effort involved, where I'd rather be wrong." He reached out for her. "Come on! I'll tell it to you straight while we hurry over to Allan's lab. This is going to go right down to the wire."

CHAPTER TWENTY-THREE

Jack nosed his worse-for-wear Hyundai to the curb behind a brown UPS truck. It was a loading area on busy Cambridge Street in front of a long, arcaded, curved building facing Boston City Hall. Jack thought the chances of getting a parking ticket, even though he was planning on being as fast as he could, were close to one hundred percent. He was hoping the car wouldn't be towed, but in case it was, he took his carry-on bag with him along with a large envelope with the return address of the Office of the Chief Medical Examiner printed in the upper-left-hand corner.

He charged up a flight of stairs that penetrated the building and emerged into the courtyard fronting the Suffolk County Superior Court. Wasting no time, Jack sprinted over to the entrance. He was slowed down by security and the need for his carry-on, envelope, and cell phone to go through the X-ray machine. At the elevators, he made sure he pushed into the very next car.

As the elevator rose, Jack managed to glance at his watch. The fact that he was to be married in four hours wasn't lost on him, and the fact that he was in the wrong city gave him considerable anxiety. When the elevator arrived on the third floor, Jack tried to be as polite as he could as he struggled to get off. If he didn't know better, he would have thought the other passengers were deliberately impeding him.

Although on previous occasions, Jack had tried to be as quiet as possible while entering the courtroom, on this day he just burst in. His feeling was the more of a scene he created, the better. As he walked deliberately down the aisle toward the gate separating the bar area from the spectator area, most of the spectators turned to look at him, including Alexis in the first row. Jack nodded to her. The court officer was in his box, reading something out of sight on his desktop, and did not look up. The jury was in the jury box, as impassive as ever, and was focusing on Randolph, who was at the podium, apparently just beginning his closing statement. The judge was at his bench, looking at papers on his desktop. Both the court reporter and the clerk were busy at their stations. At the defense table, Jack saw the back of Craig's head and that of Randolph's assistant. At the plaintiff's table, Jack could see the backs of the heads of Tony, Jordan, and Tony's assistant. All was in order; like an old-fashioned steam locomotive, the wheels of justice were slowly, implacably picking up speed and rolling to a conclusion.

It was Jack's intention to hijack the train. He didn't want to derail it, but wanted to stop it and let it take a different track. He reached the bar and stopped. He could see the jurors' eyes swing toward him without so much as a dent in their acquired impassivity. Randolph was continuing to speak in his cultured, mellifluous voice. His words were golden like the shafts of late-spring sunlight that skirted the blinds on the high windows and knifed down through the mote-filled air.

"Excuse me!" Jack said. "Excuse me!" he said louder when Randolph had continued to speak. Jack was not in his line of sight, but Randolph turned in Jack's direction when Jack called out the second time. His arctic-blue eyes reflected a mixture of confusion and vexation. The court officer, who had also missed Jack's first utterance, definitely heard the second. He got to his feet. Security in the courtroom was his bailiwick.

"I need to talk with you this very instant," Jack said, loud enough for everyone in the otherwise-silent courtroom to hear. "I know it's rather inconvenient, but it is of vital importance if you are interested in avoiding a miscarriage of justice."

"Counselor, what the devil is going on?" Judge Davidson demanded. He was tipping his head down to see over the top of his half-glasses. He motioned for the court officer to stay in his box.

Still bewildered but calling on years of litigation experience, Randolph quickly reverted to his signature refined neutrality. He cast a glance in the judge's direction before redirecting his attention to Jack.

"I wouldn't be doing this if it weren't crucial," Jack added, lowering his voice. He could see that the occupants of both the defense and plaintiff's tables had swung around in Jack's direction. Jack was interested in only two: Craig and Jordan. Of the two, Jordan was the more surprised and seemingly disturbed at Jack's disruptive arrival.

Randolph turned to the judge. "Your Honor, may I indulge the court's patience for just a moment?"

"Two minutes!" Judge Davidson said petulantly. He would allow Randolph to speak with Jack but only to get rid of him. It was painfully clear that the judge was unhappy with an interruption in his courtroom.

Randolph moved over to the bar and gave Jack an imperious glance. He spoke sotto voce: "This is highly irregular."

"I do this all the time," Jack whispered, reverting to his old sarcastic style. "You have to put me on the stand!"

"I cannot put you on the stand. I've already explained why, and I'm giving my closing statement, for heaven's sake."

"I did the autopsy, and I can provide evidence corroborated by affidavits from a Massachusetts medical examiner and a Massachusetts toxicologist that Dr. Bowman did not commit medical negligence."

For the first time, Jack detected a tiny crack in the shell of equanimity within which Randolph operated. It was his eyes that betrayed him as they rapidly and nervously flicked back and forth between the judge and Jack. There was little time for reflection, much less debate.

"Mr. Bingham!" Judge Davidson called out impatiently. "Your two minutes are up."

"I'll see what I can do," Randolph whispered to Jack before returning to the podium. "Your Honor, may I approach the bench?"

"If you must," Judge Davidson said, none too pleased.

Tony leaped his feet and joined Randolph at the sidebar.

"What in tarnation is going on?" Judge Davidson whispered forcibly. "Who is this man?" His eyes briefly whipped over to Jack, standing at the gate like a supplicant. Although Jack had put down his carry-on, he was still holding the envelope.

"His name is Dr. Jack Stapleton," Randolph said. "He is a board-certified medical examiner from the Office of the Chief Medical Examiner in New York. I've been informed he is very well regarded professionally."

Judge Davidson looked at Tony. "Do you know him?"

"I've met him," Tony admitted without elaboration.

"What the hell does he want, barging in here like this? This is highly irregular, to say the least."

"I expressed the same sentiments," Randolph reported. "He wants to be put on the stand."

"He can't be put on the stand!" Tony snapped. "He's not been on a witness list, and he's not been deposed. This is an outrageous suggestion."

"Tame your indignation!" Judge Davidson said to Tony, as if he were speaking to an unruly child. "And why is he asking to be put on the stand?"

"He claims he can offer exculpatory testimony that proves Dr. Bowman did not commit medical malpractice. He further claims he has corroboration in the form of affidavits by a Massachusetts medical examiner and a Massachusetts toxicologist."

"This is insane!" Tony sputtered. "The defense cannot bring in a last-minute surprise witness. It violates every rule in the book since the signing of the Magna Carta."

"Stop your moaning and groaning, counselor!" Judge Davidson barked.

Tony controlled himself with effort, but his suppressed ire and frustration were clearly evident when his heavy-lipped mouth formed an inverted U.

"Do you have any idea of how he has come across the information he's willing to testify to?"

"He mentioned that he autopsied Patience Stanhope."

"If this autopsy is potentially exculpatory, why wasn't it done sooner so that it could have been a subject of proper discovery?"

"There was no reason to suspect that an autopsy would have any probative value. I'm certain Mr. Fasano would agree. The clinical facts in this case have never been in dispute."

"Mr. Fasano, did you know about this autopsy?"

"Only to the extent it was being considered."

"Damn!" Judge Davidson intoned. "This puts me between a rock and a hard place."

"Your Honor," Tony said, unable to keep still. "If he's allowed to testify, I will—"

"I don't want to hear your threats, counselor. I'm perfectly aware Dr. Stapleton cannot waltz in here and take the stand. That's not on the table. I suppose I could order a continuance, and Dr. Stapleton and his findings could be subjected to normal discovery, but the trouble with that is that it shoots my calendar to hell. I hate to do that, but I also hate to have my cases reversed on appeal, and if this testimony is as dramatic as Dr. Stapleton seems to feel, it makes such a reversal a real possibility."

"What about you hearing the evidence Dr. Stapleton has?" Randolph suggested. "That would make your decision-making considerably easier."

Judge Davidson nodded as he contemplated the idea.

"To save time, you could do it in your chambers," Randolph said.

"Taking a witness into my chambers is in itself irregular."

"But not unheard of," Randolph offered.

"But the witness could go to the papers and claim whatever. I don't like that idea."

"Take in the court reporter," Randolph said. "Let it be part of the record. The point is that the jury will not hear it. If you decide it's not relevant and material, I can just restart my summation. If you decide it is relevant and material, you'll have more information to help you make a decision about how to proceed."

Judge Davidson mulled over the idea. He nodded his head. "I like it. I'll call a short recess, but I'll keep the jury where they are. We'll make this fast. Are you all right with this plan, Mr. Fasano?"

"I think it sucks," Tony growled.

"Do you have an alternative suggestion?" Judge Davidson asked.

Tony shook his head. He was furious. He was counting on winning his first malpractice case, and now, within hours of the goal, a major screwup was brewing, despite everything he'd done. He walked back to the plaintiff's table and poured himself a glass of water. His mouth was dry and his throat was parched.

Randolph went back to Jack and opened the gate for him to step into the bar area. "You can't take the stand," Randolph whispered. "But it is arranged for you essentially to testify for the judge, which will determine if you get to testify in front of the jury at a later date. It will take place in the judge's chambers. He's willing to give you only a few minutes, so you'd best be concise and to the point. Understood?"

Jack nodded. He was tempted to tell Randolph he had only a few minutes to offer, but he refrained. He looked at Jordan, who was nervously trying to get Tony to explain what was happening, since the judge had announced there was to be a short recess although he wanted the jury to stay put. Among the spectators, there was a general buzz as people tried to figure out what was happening and who Jack was. Jack looked over at Craig, and Craig smiled. Jack nodded in return.

"All rise!" the court officer called out as the judge got to his feet and swiftly descended from the bench. In a blink of the eye, he was through the paneled door and out of sight, although he left the door invitingly ajar behind him. The court reporter followed a few steps behind.

"Are you ready?" Randolph asked Jack.

Jack nodded again, and as he did so, he happened to lock eyes with Tony. *If looks could kill, I'd be dead*, Jack thought. The man was plainly incensed.

Jack followed Randolph, and Tony joined them as they walked past the empty witness stand and the clerk's desk. Jack inwardly smiled as he wondered what Tony's reaction would be if Jack inquired about Franco's well-being, since Franco was nowhere to be seen.

Jack was disappointed in the judge's chambers. He'd conjured up an image of highly polished dark wood, leather furniture, and the aroma of expensive cigars, like an exclusive men's club. Instead, it was decidedly seedy, with walls in need of paint and government-issue furniture. Over all hung a miasma of cigarette smoke. The only high point was a massive Victorian-style desk, behind which Judge Davidson sat in a high-backed chair. He was leaning back with his hands clasped behind his head in relative repose.

Jack, Randolph, and Tony sat in low-slung vinyl-covered chairs such that their line of sight was well below that of Judge Davidson. Jack assumed it was a deliberate ploy on the part of the judge, who liked to keep himself on a higher plane. The court reporter sat at a small table off to the side.

"Dr. Stapleton," Judge Davidson began after a brief introduction. "Mr. Bingham tells me you have in this eleventh hour exculpatory evidence in the defendant's favor."

"That is not entirely true," Jack said. "My words were that I can provide corroborated evidence that proves Dr. Bowman did not commit medical malpractice as defined by statute. There was no negligence."

"Is that not exculpatory? Are we playing some sort of word game here?"

"Hardly a game," Jack said. "In this circumstance, it is exculpatory on one hand and incriminating on the other."

"I think you'd better explain," Judge Davidson said. He brought his hands down onto his desktop and leaned forward. Jack had captured his full attention.

Getting his finger under the flap of his envelope, Jack opened it and extracted three documents. He leaned forward and slid the top one across the desk to the judge. "This first affidavit is signed by a licensed Massachusetts undertaker, and it affirms that the body autopsied was indeed the late Patience Stanhope." Jack slid the second paper across. "This affidavit confirms that Dr. Latasha Wylie, a licensed Massachusetts medical examiner, participated in the autopsy, aided in obtaining all specimens, and transported the specimens to the University toxicology laboratory, where she duly transferred them to Dr. Allan Smitham."

Judge Davidson had picked up each affidavit and

scanned it. "I'd say this is a commendable chain of custody," he said. He looked up. "And what's the final affidavit?"

"This is what Dr. Smitham found," Jack said. "Are you familiar with fugu poisoning?"

Judge Davidson treated his guests to a brief, wry smile. "I think you better get to the point, son," he said patronizingly. "I've got a jury out there twiddling their thumbs and eager to haul ass."

"It's a kind of often-lethal poisoning people get from eating sushi made from puffer fish. Understandably, it is seen almost exclusively in Japan."

"Don't tell me you are suggesting Patience Stanhope died from eating sushi," Judge Davidson said.

"I wish that were the case," Jack responded. "The poison involved is called tetrodotoxin, and it is an extremely interesting compound. It is extraordinarily toxic. To give you an idea, it is up to one hundred times more lethal than black widow spider venom and ten times more deadly than the venom of the many-banded krait, one of the most venomous snakes of Southeast Asia. A microscopic amount taken by mouth will cause rapid death." Jack leaned forward and slid the final paper toward the judge. "This last affidavit, signed by Dr. Allan Smitham, explains that tetrodotoxin was found in all of the specimens obtained from Patience Stanhope that he tested, at levels suggesting her initial dose was a hundred times greater than what would have been adequate to kill her."

Judge Davidson scanned the document, then extended it to Randolph.

"You might ask: How reliable are the tests for tetrodotoxin?" Jack continued. "The answer is extremely reliable. The chance of a false positive is close to zero, especially since Dr. Smitham used two entirely separate methods. One was high-pressure liquid chromatography followed by mass spectrometry. The other was radioimmunoassay using a specific antibody to the tetrodotoxin molecule. The results are conclusive and reproducible."

Randolph offered the affidavit to Tony, who snatched it away irritably. He was well aware of its implication.

"So are you saying the deceased did not die of a heart attack?" Judge Davidson said.

"She did not die of a heart attack. She died of overwhelming tetrodotoxin poisoning. Since there is no treatment available, the time of her arrival at the hospital was entirely immaterial. Essentially, from the moment she swallowed the poison she was doomed."

A loud knock on the judge's door reverberated around the room. The judge bellowed for whoever it was to enter. The court officer poked his head in and said, "The jury is requesting a coffee break. What should I tell them?"

"Let them have their coffee break," the judge said with a wave of dismissal. He drilled Jack with his dark, gun-barrel eyes. "So that's the exculpatory part. What's the incriminating part?"

Jack sat back in his chair. This was the part he found the most troubling. "Because of its striking toxicity, tetrodotoxin is a highly controlled substance, especially in this day and age. But the compound has a curious redeeming quality. The same molecular mechanism responsible for its toxicity makes it an outstanding tool to study sodium channels in nerve and muscle."

"How does that impact the case at hand?"

"Dr. Craig Bowman's published and ongoing research

concerns the study of sodium channels. He uses tetrodotoxin extensively."

A heavy silence hung over the room as Jack and Judge Davidson stared at one another across the judge's desk. The other two men looked on. For a full minute no one spoke. Finally, the judge cleared his throat and said, "Other than this circumstantial evidence of access to the toxin, is there anything else that associates Dr. Bowman with the actual act?"

"There is," Jack said reluctantly. "The moment tetrodotoxin was determined to be present, I returned to the Bowman residence, where I had been a house-guest. I had known there was a small vial of pills Dr. Bowman had given to the deceased the day she died. I took the vial back to the toxicology lab. Dr. Smitham did a rapid check, and the interior of the vial was positive for tetrodotoxin. He is doing the full, definitive test as we speak."

"Okay!" Judge Davidson said. He rubbed his hands together briskly and looked over at the court reporter. "Hold up on the record until we get back into the court-room." He then sat back, causing his aged chair to squeak. He'd assumed a grim but thoughtful expression. "I could order a continuance of this trial so all this new information could go through the discovery process, but there is not much point. This is not civil negligence, it is murder. I'll tell you what I'm going to do, gentlemen. I'm going to declare a mistrial. This case needs to be turned over to the district attorney. Any questions?" He looked over his audience, stopping at Tony. "Don't look so glum, counselor. You can bask in the realization that justice prevails and your client can still sue for wrongful death."

"The trouble is the insurance company will be off the hook." Tony snorted.

The judge looked at Jack. "That was an admirable investigation, doctor."

Jack merely nodded to acknowledge the compliment. But he didn't feel deserving. Having to report the shocking findings caused him anguish for what it was going to do to Alexis and her girls. They would now have to suffer through a protracted investigation and a new trial with horrific consequences. It was a tragedy for everyone concerned, especially Craig. Jack was shocked at the depth of the man's narcissism and apparent lack of conscience. Yet at the same time he sensed that Craig had been victimized by the highly competitive academic medical system that touted altruism and compassion yet rewarded the opposite; one never became chief resident by being kind and sympathetic to patients. With Craig's perennial necessity of gainful employment during the early portion of his medical training, he had been denied the normal social interaction that would have blunted such a contradictory message.

"All right, gentlemen," Judge Davidson said. "Let's wrap up this fiasco." He stood, and the others did as well. He then skirted around his desk and headed for the door. Jack followed behind the two lawyers, and the court reporter came behind Jack. Ahead, within the courtroom, Jack heard the court officer yell for everyone to rise.

When Jack emerged from the judge's chambers, the judge was taking his seat on the bench while Randolph and Tony were approaching their respective tables. Jack noticed that Craig was momentarily not present, and Jack shuddered to think what the man's reaction was going to be when he learned that his secret had been unraveled.

Jack quietly crossed the well. Behind him he heard the judge ask the court officer to bring back the jury. Jack opened the gate. He caught Alexis's eye. She was looking at him with an understandably questioning, confused yet hopeful expression. Jack politely worked his way toward her and took the neighboring seat. He squeezed her hand. He noticed she had rescued his carry-on bag that he'd left at the gate before going into the judge's chambers.

"Mr. Bingham," Judge Davidson called out. "I notice the defendant is not presently at the defendant's table."

"My assistant, Mr. Cavendish, tells me he requested to use the men's room," Randolph said, partially rising out of his chair.

"I see," Judge Davidson responded.

The jury was then led into the courtroom, and they filed into the jury box.

"What's going on?" Alexis questioned. "Did you find something criminal?"

"I found more than I bargained for," Jack confessed.

"Perhaps someone should let Dr. Bowman know we are back in session," Judge Davidson said. "It is important for him to witness these proceedings."

Jack gave Alexis's hand another squeeze before getting to his feet. "I'll get Dr. Bowman," he said. As he moved back down the aisle, he motioned to Randolph's assistant, who'd gotten up, presumably to get Craig, that he would fetch the defendant.

Jack pushed out through the door to the hall. There were the usual clumps of people engaging in hushed conversations sprinkled around the hallway and the elevator lobby. Jack made a beeline for the men's room. He glanced at his watch. It was a quarter past ten. He yanked open the door and entered. A man of Asian ancestry was washing his hands at the sink. The area around the urinals was empty. Jack continued to the stalls and bent down at the waist to look under the walls. Only the last stall was occupied. Jack walked down to the door and debated whether to wait or call out. As late as it was, he decided to call out.

"Craig?" Jack questioned.

The toilet flushed, and a moment later the locking mechanism of the door clicked. The door opened inwardly, and a young Hispanic man emerged. He gave Jack a quizzical look before brushing past on his way to the sink. Surprised at not having had to face Craig after building up his courage to do so, Jack bent over again to make sure all the stalls were empty, and they were. Except for the two men at the sink, there was no one else in the bathroom. Craig was nowhere to be seen. Intuitively, Jack knew he was gone.

CHAPTER TWENTY-FOUR

After returning to the courtroom, where Craig had failed to reappear, Jack had taken Alexis aside. As quickly and humanely as possible, he had related everything that had happened since he'd spoken with her the night before. She had listened with initial disbelief and consternation until she learned the extent of the proof of Craig's apparent guilt. At that point, she'd allowed her professional persona to take over, enabling her to analyze the situation clinically. In that frame of mind, she, not Jack, had been the one to bring up the time issue and that Jack had to make tracks if he hoped to get to the church on time. With a promise to call that afternoon, Jack had grabbed his carry-on and dashed for the elevators.

Running headlong, Jack traversed the courtyard in front of the courthouse and descended the two short flights of steps to the street. To his relief, the battered Accent was where he'd left it, although a parking ticket was stuck beneath the windshield wiper. The first order of business was to get the paper bag containing the gun from the trunk. Anticipating needing to return the firearm on his way to the airport, Jack had gotten the directions to police headquarters that morning from Latasha.

The police station was right around the corner from

where Jack was parked, although it required him to do a U-turn over a median. Jack looked in his rearview mirror for pursuing squad cars after pulling off the stunt. Jack had learned from sore experience that when you missed your turn while driving in Boston, it was frequently impossible to loop back.

The stop at the police station was accomplished expeditiously. The bag had Liam Flanagan's name on it, and the duty officer was willing to accept it with no comment whatsoever. Glad that chore was out of the way, Jack ran out to the car, which was double-parked with the engine running.

The signage to the airport was superior to the signage in the rest of the city, and Jack soon found himself in a tunnel. Thankfully, the distance from downtown Boston to the airport was short, and Jack got there surprisingly quickly. Following the signs for the rent-a-car company, he drove onto the Hertz lot a few minutes later.

Jack pulled into one of the car-return lanes. There were some instructions of what to do when dropping off a vehicle, but Jack just ignored them as he ignored the agents who were roaming around assisting customers. The last thing Jack wanted to do was get into an extended discussion about the damaged vehicle. He was confident he'd hear from Hertz. He grabbed his carry-on and ran for the bus to the terminal.

When he boarded the bus, he thought it was about to leave, but instead it sat there with its motor idling and no driver. Jack nervously eyed the time. It was a little after eleven. He knew he had to catch the eleven thirty Delta shuttle or all was lost.

Finally, the driver appeared. He cracked a few jokes as

he asked which terminals people wanted. Jack was happy
to learn that Delta was the first stop.

The next aggravation was getting a ticket. Luckily, the
shuttle had its own section. After that came the security
line, but even that was not too problematic. It was eleven
twenty when Jack shoved his feet back into his shoes and
sprinted down the concourse toward the shuttle gate.

Jack was not the last person on board, but it was close.
The plane's door was closed behind the individual who'd
boarded right after him. Jack took the first seat available
to facilitate deplaning in New York. Unfortunately, it was
a middle seat between a scruffy student with an iPod so
loud Jack could hear every note and a pin-striped businessman with a laptop and a Blackberry. The businessman
treated Jack to a disapproving glare when Jack indicated
he wanted to occupy the middle seat. It required the
businessman to move his carry-on from where he'd
stowed it and to pick up his jacket and briefcase, which
he'd placed on the seat.

Once seated with his carry-on at his feet, Jack put his
head back against the headrest and closed his eyes.
Despite his bone-weary exhaustion, there was no chance
he could fall asleep, and not just because of his neigh-
bor's iPod. He kept replaying the too short and
unsatisfactory conversation he'd had with Alexis, and the
belated realization that he'd not apologized for being the
one who had uncovered Craig's perfidy, not only to the
profession but also to his family. Even the rationalization
that Alexis and the children might be better off knowing
the truth did not make Jack feel any better. The chances
of the family hanging together in the face of what was
coming were unfortunately slim, and that thought
underlined for Jack how deceptive appearances could be.

From the outside, the Bowmans seemingly had it all: professional parents, beautiful children, and a storybook house. Yet on the inside there was a kind of cancer undermining it all.

"May I have your attention please," a voice cracked over the plane's intercom. "This is the captain speaking. We've just been informed from ground control that we have a gate hold situation. There's a thunderstorm passing through the New York area. We are hoping this will not be long, and we will keep you informed."

"Shit!" Jack exclaimed to himself. He gripped his forehead with his right hand, using the balls of his fingers to massage his temples. The anxiety and lack of sleep were conspiring to give him a headache. As a realist, he began to contemplate what would happen if he did not make the wedding. Laurie had given him more than a hint. She'd said she'd never forgive him, and he believed her. Laurie was frugal with promises, and when she made one, she kept it. Knowing that, again begged the question in Jack's mind whether he'd stayed in Boston as long as he had more from an unconscious wish to avoid getting married than to solve the Patience Stanhope mystery. Jack took a deep breath. He didn't believe that was true, nor did he want it to be true, but he didn't know for sure. What he did know was that he wanted to get to the church on time.

Then, as if in response to his thoughts, the intercom came back to life. "This is the captain again. Ground control has reversed themselves. We are ready to push back. We should have you at the gate in New York on schedule."

The next thing Jack knew was that he was jarred awake by the plane's wheels touching down at LaGuardia

Airport. To his utter surprise, he had fallen asleep despite his anxiety, and to his embarrassment, he had drooled a little. He wiped his mouth with the back of his hand, scraping against the stubble on his chin in the process. With the same hand, he felt the rest of his face. He was in need of a shave and even worse for a shower, but a glance at his watch suggested that neither was possible. It was twenty-five after twelve.

Shaking himself like a dog to get his circulation going, Jack ran his hands through his hair. This activity evoked a questioning expression from the businessman, who was plainly leaning into the aisle away from Jack. Jack wondered if that was ostensibly additional evidence of his need for a shower. Although he'd donned Tyvek protective coveralls, Jack was aware he'd not showered since he'd done an autopsy on an eight-month-old corpse.

Jack suddenly realized that he'd been tapping his foot at a frenzied frequency. Even when he put his hand on his knee, it was hard to keep his leg still. Jack could not remember ever being quite so agitated. What made it difficult was having to sit still. He would have preferred to be out on the tarmac, running alongside the plane.

It seemed to take forever for the plane to taxi to the terminal and then agonizingly slowly ease into the gate. When the chime sounded, Jack was up out of his seat. Pushing past the businessman, who was getting a bag from the overhead bin, garnered Jack yet another disapproving scowl. Jack couldn't have cared less. Excusing himself, he managed to worm up to the front of the plane. When the door finally opened after what seemed like an interminable wait, he was the third one off.

Jack ran up the jetway, pushing past the two people who'd deplaned before him. Once in the terminal, he ran toward baggage claim and out on to the street, which was steaming from a recent downpour. By being the first passenger from the Boston–New York shuttle, he'd hoped the taxi line would be nonexistent. Unfortunately, that was not the case. The Washington, D.C.–New York shuttle had landed ten minutes earlier, and a portion of its passengers were waiting for cabs.

Unabashed at his assertiveness, he cut to the front of the line. "I'm a medical doctor, and I'm in an emergency," Jack called out, rationalizing that both were true, just not related. The people in the line wordlessly regarded him with a touch of irritation, but no one offered any challenge. Jack jumped into the first cab.

The driver was from India or Pakistan, Jack couldn't tell which, and was on his cell phone. Jack barked out his address on 106th Street, and the taxi accelerated away from the curb.

Jack checked his watch. It was now eighteen minutes before one o'clock, meaning he had only forty-eight minutes before he was due at the Riverside Church. He sat back and tried vainly to relax, but it was impossible. To make things worse, they hit every traffic light just getting out of the airport. Jack looked at his watch again. It seemed to him unfair that the second hand was sweeping around the dial more quickly than usual. It was already a quarter before the hour.

Jack began to question nervously if he should go directly to the church and forgo the pit stop at home. The benefit would be he'd be on time; the disadvantage was that he was dressed a step below casual and needed a shave and a shower.

When the taxi driver was finally finished with his cell phone call and before he made another, Jack leaned forward. "I don't know whether it would make much difference, but I'm in a hurry," he said. Then he added, "If you would be willing to wait at the address I gave you, there would be an extra twenty-dollar tip."

"I'll wait if you'd like," the driver said agreeably, with the typical charming Indian subcontinent accent.

Jack sat back and reattached his seat belt. It was now ten minutes before one.

The next bottleneck was the toll on the Triborough Bridge. Apparently, someone without a fast lane pass was in the fast lane and couldn't back up because of the line of cars behind him. After a horrendous cacophony of car horns and shouted expletives, the problem was sorted out, but not before another five minutes was lost. By the time Jack reached the island of Manhattan, it was one o'clock.

The only benefit from Jack's mounting anxiety was that it effectively stopped his obsessing about Alexis and Craig and the disaster that was about to begin. A malpractice trial was bad; a murder trial was god-awful. It was going to put the entire family in an unrelenting, many-year-long torment with little possibility of a happy outcome.

To the driver's credit, he managed to get across town rapidly by knowing a relatively quiet street through Harlem. When he pulled up in front of Jack's building, it was quarter after one. Jack had the taxi door open before the vehicle came to a complete stop.

Jack ran up the front steps and dashed through the front door, surprising some workmen. With the building under total renovation, the dust was an unmitigated disaster. As Jack ran down the hall to the apartment he and Laurie were temporarily occupying during the construction, billows of it rose from the debris-strewn floor.

Jack keyed open his apartment door and was about to enter when the construction supervisor caught sight of him from several floors above and yelled that he needed to talk about a plumbing problem. Jack yelled back that he couldn't at the moment. Once inside, Jack tossed his carry-on onto the couch and began stripping off his clothes. He left a trail of apparel en route to the bathroom.

First he took a glimpse of himself in the mirror and winced. Heavy stubble blackened his cheeks and chin like smudges of soot, and his eyes were red-rimmed and sunken. After a quick, internal debate of a shave or a shower, since he hardly had time for both, he decided on the shower. Leaning into the tub, he turned on both faucets full-blast. Unfortunately, only a few drips emerged: The plumbing problem was obviously global to the building.

Jack turned off the faucets and, after splashing himself liberally with cologne, ran out of the bathroom and into the bedroom. He pulled on underwear, then put on his formal shirt. Next came the tuxedo pants and jacket. He grabbed the studs and cuff links and jammed them into his pants pocket. The black pre-tied bow tie went into the other pocket. After jamming his feet into formal shoes, his wallet into his back pants pocket, and his cell phone into his jacket pocket, he ran back out into the hall.

Slowing enough to keep the dust to a minimum, he was again spotted by the construction supervisor, who again yelled that it was critical for them to talk. Jack didn't even bother to answer. Outside, the taxi was still waiting. Jack crossed the street and jumped in.

"Riverside Church!" Jack yelled.

"Do you know what cross street?" the driver asked, looking at Jack in the rearview mirror.

"One hundred twenty-second," Jack clipped. He began struggling with his studs, dropping one on the seat, where it quickly disappeared into a black hole between the seat and the seat back. Jack tried to get his hand into the crack but couldn't and quickly gave up. Instead, he used the studs he had, leaving the lowest buttonhole empty.

"Are you getting married?" the driver asked, continuing to glimpse at Jack in the mirror.

"I hope so," Jack said. He then turned to the cuff-link challenge. He tried to recall the last time he had donned a tux as he finished with the first cuff link and began on the second. He couldn't remember, although it had to have been back in his previous life, when he was an ophthalmologist. After the cuff links, Jack bent down and tied his shoes and dusted himself. The final job was buttoning the top button of his shirt and hooking the bow tie behind his neck.

"You look fine," the driver said with a broad smile.

"I'll bet," Jack said with his usual sarcasm. He leaned forward and extracted his wallet. Looking at the taxi meter, he got out enough twenty dollar bills to cover it, plus two extra. He dumped the money into the front seat through the Plexiglas partition as the driver turned onto Riverside Drive.

Ahead, the Riverside Church's sand-colored belfry came into view. It towered over its neighboring structures and stood out with its Gothic architecture. In front

of the church were several black limousines. Except for
the drivers, who were out of their vehicles leaning against
the sides, there were no people. Jack looked at his watch.
It was one thirty-three. He was three minutes late.

Jack again had the taxi door open before the car was
completely stopped. He yelled a thank-you to the driver
over his shoulder as he leaped out into the street. Buttoning his jacket, he took the church's front steps two at
a time. Ahead in the open doorway, Laurie suddenly
appeared like a mirage. She was gowned magnificently in
a white wedding dress. From behind her issued forth
powerful organ music.

Jack stopped to take in the scene. He had to admit she
looked more lovely than ever, truly radiant. The only
slight detraction was her hands, which were balled into
fists and planted defiantly on her hips. There was also her
father, Dr. Montgomery, who looked regal but not
amused.

"Jack!" Laurie intoned in a voice hovering between
anger and relief. "You are late!"

"Hey," Jack called back spreading his hands. "At least
I'm here."

Laurie broke into a smile in spite of herself. "Get
yourself into the church," she ordered playfully.

Jack climbed the rest of the way up the stairs. Laurie
reached out with her hand, and Jack took it. She then
leaned close and looked at him appraisingly with a touch
of concern.

"God, you look awful."

"You shouldn't flatter me so," Jack said with feigned
bashfulness.

"You haven't even shaved."

"There are worse secrets," he confessed, hoping she

couldn't tell he'd not showered for more than thirty hours.

"I don't know what I'm getting myself into," Laurie said with her smile returning. "My mother's friends are going to be appalled."

"And indeed they should be."

Laurie smiled wryly at Jack's humor. "You are never going to change."

"I disagree. I can tell I've changed. I might be a tad late, but I'm glad I'm here. Will you marry me?"

Laurie's smile broadened. "Yes, of course. That's been my intention for more years than I care to admit."

"I can't tell you how thankful I am that you were willing to wait."

"I suppose you have some elaborate explanation for this anxious, down-to-the-wire arrival."

"I'm looking forward to telling you. Frankly, the denouement in Boston has me stunned. It's a story you are not going to believe."

"I'm looking forward to hearing it," Laurie said. "But now you'd better get into the church and up onto that altar. Your best man, Warren, is fit to be tied. Fifteen minutes ago, he was out here and said he was, quote, 'going to whip your ass.' "

Laurie propelled Jack forward into the interior of the church, where he was engulfed by the organ music. For a moment he hesitated, looking down the length of the impressive nave. He was overwhelmingly intimidated. The right side of the church was packed, with hardly a seat available, whereas the left was nearly empty, although Jack saw Lou Soldano and Chet. Ahead at the altar stood the priest, or reverend, or pastor, or rabbi, or imam: Jack didn't know and didn't care. He was not thrilled by organized religion and did not feel one was any better than another. Next to the clergyman stood Warren, and even from a distance, he looked impressive in his tuxedo. Jack took a deep breath for fortitude and started forward into a whole new life.

The rest of the ceremony was a blur for Jack. He had to be pushed and nudged in this direction or that or whispered to in an attempt to get him to do what was required. Because of his being in Boston, he'd missed the rehearsal, so from his perspective, it was all ad lib.

The part he liked the best was running out of the church, because it meant the ordeal was over. Once in the car, he had a rest, but it was much too short. The drive from the church to Tavern on the Green and the reception was only a quarter of an hour.

The reception was less intimidating than the wedding, and in different circumstances of being less exhausted, he almost would have found it enjoyable. Particularly after a heavy meal including wine and some obligatory dancing, Jack was beginning to fade. But before he did so, he needed to make a call. Excusing himself from his table, he found a relatively quiet spot at the restaurant's entrance. He punched in Alexis's cell phone number and was pleased when she answered.

"Are you married?" Alexis asked as soon as she knew it was Jack.

"I am."

"Congratulations! I think it's wonderful and I'm very happy for you."

"Thank you, sister," Jack said. "I particularly wanted to call to apologize for my role in creating more turmoil in your life. You invited me to Boston to help Craig and thereby help you, and I ended up doing the opposite. I'm terribly sorry. I feel complicit."

"Thank you for apologizing," Alexis said. "I surely don't hold you responsible for Craig's behavior and for it being exposed. I truly believe it would have been eventually. And to be entirely honest, I'm glad to know. It will make my decision-making much easier."

"Did Craig reappear in court?"

"No, he didn't, and I still have no idea where he is. There is a warrant for his arrest, and the police have already appeared at the house with a search warrant. They have confiscated all his papers, including his passport, so he's not going far. Wherever he is, he's just putting off the inevitable."

"Surprisingly enough, I feel sorry for him," Jack said.

"I feel sorry for him as well."

"Has he tried to see the children or call?"

"No, he hasn't, although that doesn't surprise me. He's never been close to the children."

"I don't think he's ever been close to anyone, except maybe you."

"In retrospect, I don't think he was even close to me. It's a tragedy, and I personally believe his father shares a portion of the blame."

"Please keep me posted!" Jack said. "We're heading out on our honeymoon, but I'll have my cell phone."

"I did learn something else disturbing this afternoon. A week ago, Craig had refinanced our house, taking out several million dollars."

"Could he do that without your signature?"

"He could. Back when we bought the house, he insisted it be in his name only. He gave me some excuse about taxes and insurance, but at the time I didn't care."

"Did he take it in cash?" Jack questioned.

"No, I've been told it was wired to a numbered off-shore account."

"If you need cash, let me know. I have more than I've ever had, thanks to not spending even a pittance of my salary for the last decade."

"Thank you, brother. I'll keep that in mind. We'll make out fine, although I might have to augment my salary with some private practice."

After a few endearments, Jack disconnected. He did not return to the party immediately. Instead, he thought about the unfairness and capriciousness of life. While he was looking forward to a honeymoon with Laurie and a promising future, Alexis and the children were staring at uncertainty and emotional pain. It was enough, Jack thought, to make someone an epicurean or very religious, one extreme or the other.

Jack stood up. He opted for the former and was interested in getting Laurie home.

`EPILOGUE

HAVANA, CUBA
Monday, June 12, 2006
2:15 p.m.

Jack had wanted to take Laurie to someplace unique and off the beaten path for their honeymoon. He'd thought of someplace in Africa, but decided it was too far. He'd thought of India, but that was worse, as far as distance was concerned. Then someone suggested Cuba. At first Jack had dismissed the idea because he thought it couldn't be done, but going on the Internet, he soon learned he was wrong. A number of people, but not too many, were going to Cuba either through Canada, Mexico, or the Bahamas. Jack had chosen the Bahamas.

The flight from New York to Nassau on Saturday, the day after the wedding, had been ho-hum, but the one from Nassau to Havana on Cubana Airlines had been livelier and entertaining, and had given them an early taste of the Cuban mentality. Jack had arranged for a suite in the Hotel Nacional de Cuba, sensing it would have a hint of old Cuban charm. They hadn't been disappointed. It was sited on the Malecón in the Vedado section of old Havana. Although some of the amenities were dated, the original Art Deco splendor shone through. Best of all, the service was a joy. Contrary to what Jack might have thought, the Cubans were a happy people.

Thankfully, Laurie had yet to insist on more sightseeing than relaxing walks through the old, central section of Havana, which had been restored for the most part. Several of their strolls had taken them beyond the restored area and into sections where the buildings were in a sad state of disrepair yet still with a vague hint of their original grandeur.

For the most part, both Jack and Laurie had been content to sleep and eat and lie in the sun. Such a schedule had given Jack adequate time to tell Laurie the details of what had happened in Boston as well as to discuss the situation at length. Laurie was sympathetic to everyone, including Jack. She'd called it an American medical tragedy. He'd agreed.

"How about we arrange for a tour into the countryside," Laurie suggested suddenly, breaking into Jack's rejuvenating, mindless repose.

Jack shielded his eyes from the sun and turned to look at his new wife. Both were reclining poolside on white lounge chairs. Both were clad in bathing suits and mutually slathered in SPF forty-five sunblock. Laurie was regarding him with eyebrows raised. He could just see them over the top of her sunglasses.

"Do you really want to sacrifice this wonderfully indolent life?" Jack questioned. "If it's this hot seaside, it will be like an oven in the countryside."

"I'm not saying we have to do it today or even tomorrow, just someday before we leave. It would be a shame to come all this way and not get a flavor of the island outside of this touristy area."

"I suppose," Jack said without a lot of enthusiasm. Just thinking about the heat of the island's interior made

him feel thirsty. He sat up. "I'm going to get something
to drink. Want me to bring you back something?"

"Are you going to have one of those mojitos?"

"I'm tempted," Jack said.

"You really are on vacation," Laurie said. "All right.
If you're game, I am, too. I just might have to nap this
afternoon."

"Nothing wrong with that," Jack said. He got to his
feet and stretched. What he really needed to do was rent
a bike and go for a serious ride, but that thought stayed
with him only halfway to the bar. Lazily, he decided he'd
look into it tomorrow.

Catching the eye of one of the bartenders, Jack
ordered the two drinks. It was exceptional for him to
drink at all, much less in the afternoon, but he'd been
encouraged to try it the day before, and he'd enjoyed the
utterly relaxed feeling the alcohol had given him.

While he waited, Jack's eyes wandered around the
pool area. There were a few women with world-class
figures that encouraged a brief appreciative glance. His
eyes then wandered out to the broad expanse of the
Caribbean Sea. There was a slight, silky breeze.

"Your drinks, sir," the bartender said, catching Jack's
attention. Jack signed the check and picked up his drinks.
As he started to turn back toward the pool, his eyes
caught the face of a man across the peninsula-shaped
bar. Jack did a double take. He leaned forward and
unabashedly stared. The man's eyes briefly engaged
Jack's but without recognition and were soon redirected
to the handsome Latin woman sitting next to him. Jack
watched him laugh with easy grace.

Jack shrugged, turned again, and started back to his
lounge chair, but he got only a few steps before he

turned again. Making up his mind to get a closer look, Jack walked around the bar and approached the man from the rear. He advanced until he was directly behind the individual. He could hear him speaking. It was passable Spanish, certainly better than Jack could muster.

"Craig?" Jack said, loud enough for the man to hear, but the individual did not turn around. "Craig Bowman," Jack said a tad louder. Still there was no response. Jack looked down at the two drinks he was holding, which were restricting his options. After another short debate, Jack leaned into the bar on the side of the man opposite his companion. Jack put one of the drinks on the bar and tapped the man on the shoulder. The man swung around and met Jack's gaze. There was no recognition, only a question with eyebrows raised and forehead furrowed.

"Can I help you?" the man questioned in English.

"Craig?" Jack questioned, watching the man's eyes. As a former ophthalmologist, Jack tended to look at people's eyes. The same way they often gave hints of general illness, they could give hints of emotion. Jack saw no change. The pupils remained exactly the same size.

"I believe you have me confused with someone else. My name is Ralph Landrum."

"Sorry," Jack said. "I didn't mean to be a pest."

"No problem," Ralph said. "What's your name?"

"Jack Stapleton. Where are you from?"

"Boston originally. How about yourself?"

"New York City," Jack said. "Are you staying here at the Nacional?"

"No," Ralph said. "I've rented a house just out of town. I'm involved in the cigar business. How about yourself?"

"I'm a medical doctor."

Ralph leaned back so Jack could see his lady friend. "This is Toya."

Jack shook hands with Toya across the front of Ralph.

"Nice to meet you both," Jack said after stumbling through a little Spanish for Toya's benefit. He picked up his drink. "Sorry to be intrusive."

"Hey, no problem," Ralph said. "This is Cuba. People expect you to talk with them."

With a final nod, Jack took his leave. He skirted the bar and returned to Laurie. She pushed herself up on one elbow and took one of the drinks. "It took you long enough," she said jokingly.

Jack sat down on his lounge chair and shook his head. "Have you ever run across someone, and you are sure they are someone you know?"

"A few times," Laurie said, taking a sip of her drink. "Why do you ask?"

"Because it just happened to me," Jack said. "Can you see that man talking with that buxom woman in red on the other side of the bar?" Jack pointed toward the couple.

Laurie pulled her feet around, sat up, and looked. "Yeah, I can see them."

"I was sure that was Craig Bowman," Jack said with a short laugh. "He looks enough like him to be his twin."

"I thought you said Craig Bowman had sandy-colored hair similar to yours. That fellow has dark hair."

"Well, except for the hair," Jack said. "It's incredible. It makes me question my impressions."

Laurie turned back to Jack. "Why is it so incredible? Cuba would be a good place for someone like Craig to go. There is certainly no extradition treaty with the United States. Maybe it is Craig Bowman."

"No, it's not," Jack said. "I had the nerve to ask him and watch his response."

"Well, don't let it worry you," Laurie said. She regained her reclining position, drink in hand.

"It's not going to worry me," Jack said. He, too, lay back on his chair. But he couldn't get the coincidence out of his mind. All at once, he had an idea. Sitting up, he fumbled in the pocket of his robe and pulled out his cell phone.

Laurie had sensed his sudden motion and opened one eye. "Who are you calling?"

"Alexis," Jack said. She answered but told Jack she couldn't talk and that she was between sessions.

"I just have a quick question," Jack said. "Do you by any chance know a Ralph Landrum from Boston?"

"I did," Alexis said. "Listen, Jack, I really have to go. I'll call you in a couple of hours."

"Why did you put it in the past tense?" Jack asked.

"Because he died," Alexis said. "He was one of Craig's patients who died of a lymphoma about a year ago."

AUTHOR'S NOTE

Concierge medicine (also known as retainer medicine or boutique medicine or luxury primary care) is a relatively new phenomenon that first appeared in Seattle. As described in *Crisis,* it is a style of primary-care medical practice that requires an annual membership fee that varies from hundreds to many thousands of dollars per person (the median being about $1,500 and the maximum about $20,000). In order for this fee not to be construed as a health-insurance premium, which would be against regulations, the patient is offered a laundry list of specified medical attention or services not covered by health insurance, for example, elaborate yearly physicals, preventive care, nutrition counseling, and individually tailored wellness programs to name a few. But the real perk stems from the physician's guarantee to limit enrollment in the practice to a number far less than usual, making possible special amenities and special access to standard medical services (but not payment, which remains the responsibility of the patient either through health insurance or out of pocket).

The amenities might include: a very personal doctor–patient relationship, unhurried appointments that are as long as needed, nicer and uncrowded reception areas (not called *waiting rooms* since as an amenity waiting is to be avoided), house calls or patient office visits if appropriate and desirable, facilitation of appointments to needed specialists and immediate consultation, and even possible travel by the doctor to distant locales if the patient becomes ill or injured on a trip. Special access includes same-day appointments if needed or certainly within just a day or so, and twenty-four-hour doctor accessibility with the doctor's cell phone, home phone, and e-mail address.

There have been a few articles about concierge medicine in professional journals as well as in *The New York Times* and other mass media publications, but, for the most part, the slowly burgeoning practice style has gone unnoticed by the vast majority of the public. I believe this will and should change, because concierge medicine is yet another subtle but significant symptom of a healthcare system that is out of whack since good, patient-oriented medicine used to be available, and should be available, without a considerable up-front fee. More important it is common knowledge there are already significant inequities involving healthcare access worldwide, and one doesn't have to be the proverbial "rocket scientist" to understand that concierge medicine will make a bad situation only that much worse: Those doctors practicing in this style will, by definition, see far fewer patients, and all those patients who do not come up with the retainer fee for whatever reason will face less choice in a further constrained system. Indeed, a handful of U.S. senators officially complained to the Department of Health and Human Services about the phenomenon's potential impact on limiting the ability of Medicare recipients to find a primary-care physician. In response, the Government Accountability Office issued a report in August of 2005 suggesting that concierge medicine was not yet a problem, but that the trend would be monitored. The implication was that there will be a problem as the practice style mushrooms. Unfortunately, I can personally attest that it has already reached this situation in Naples, Florida, where concierge medicine has taken root. Currently in Naples, it is difficult for a new Medicare patient to find a physician without anteing up the requisite concierge retainer, or paying an exorbitant, out-of-pocket yearly physical fee, or opting out of Medicare altogether. Although Naples is admittedly a unique community economically, I believe it is a harbinger of what is to come in other communities both in the U.S. and internationally as well.

Although there have been articles about concierge medicine, none that I have read have truly addressed the question of why this phenomenon has emerged at this particular time. What is usually offered are economic explanations revolving around the idea that concierge medicine makes sense from a marketing perspective. After all, provided he or she can afford it, who wouldn't want the promised amenities, considering what the experience of going to the doctor is like all too often in today's world, and what physician wouldn't prefer to have financial security right out of the starting gate and to be able to practice the unhurried medicine they learned in medical school? Unfortunately, this superficial answer doesn't explain why the phenomenon makes sense now and didn't, say, twenty years ago. It is my belief that the real answer is that concierge medicine is a direct result of the dire, unprecedented state of disarray in current healthcare on a worldwide basis. In fact, there are those who evoke the metaphor of the perfect storm to describe the current situation, particularly in the United States.

There have been a number of problems plaguing medical practice over the last quarter-century or so, but never have there been so many all converging at the same time. Concurrently, we are seeing aggressive medical cost containment; personnel and equipment shortages; expanding technology; strenuous and appropriate efforts at medical error reduction; soaring litigiousness and settlement awards; rising ancillary costs; a bewildering multiplication of health-insurance products, including managed care with its associated intrusion into medical decision-making; and even the changing role of hospitals. All of these forces have contributed to making the bedrock of medicine—the practice of primary care—a nightmare, if not impossible. For a primary-care physician to stay in business, meaning earning enough to keep the doors open and the lights on (or staying employed in a managed-care environment), he or she must see patients at an extraordinary rate with an entirely predictable result: dissatisfaction on the part of both the doctor and the patient, and, ironically enough, increased utilization and cost and rising litigation.

Consider the following example: A patient with some mild ongoing medical conditions (for example, high blood pressure and elevated cholesterol) visits his primary-care physician with new complaints of shoulder pain and abdominal discomfort. In the current practice environment, the doctor has a mere fifteen minutes to deal with everything, including basic social civilities. Understandably, the conditions the doctor had previously taken responsibility for would take precedence (the high blood pressure and cholesterol level). Only then would the new symptoms be addressed. With the clock ticking and a waiting room full of disgruntled patients because the schedule was thrown off by an earlier minor emergency (an almost daily occurrence), the doctor resorts to the most expeditious approach: for example, ordering an MRI or a CAT scan for the shoulder and referring the patient to a gastroenterologist for the abdominal discomfort. With the pressure to meet the practice overhead, there is no time for the doctor to investigate each complaint properly with a careful history and examination. The result is a tendency for overutilization and inconvenience for the patient, much higher cost, and less than satisfaction for both the patient and the doctor. The doctor is forced by circumstance to function more like a triage assistant than a fully trained physician. This is especially true if the doctor is a board-certified internist, many of whom practice primary care.

Getting back to the question of why concierge medicine has evolved now and not in the past, it is my belief that it is a direct result of the "perfect storm" in healthcare and the resultant physician disillusionment and dissatisfaction with medical practice, which is reaching epidemic proportions as indicated by numerous polls. Doctors are unhappy, particularly primary-care doctors. In this light, concierge medicine is a reactionary movement rather than a mere marketing stratagem. It is an attempt to rectify the disconnects physicians have come to face between the medicine they learned in the academic setting and had hoped to practice and the medicine they are forced to practice, whether constrained by bureaucracy (government or managed care) or poverty (no equipment or facilities), and between the expectations of patients and the reality of what the physicians are actually providing[1]. Concierge medicine has started in the United States, but because current physician disillusionment and dissatisfaction is a worldwide phenomenon, it will spread, if it hasn't already, to other countries.

Intellectually, I have trouble with the concept of concierge medicine for the same reasons Dr. Herman

Brown offers during his testimony for the plaintiff in *Crisis*. In short, concierge medicine flies in the face of traditional concepts of altruistic medicine. Indeed, it is a direct violation of the principle of social justice, which is one of the three underpinnings of the newly defined medical professionalism, requiring physicians "to work to eliminate discrimination in healthcare, whether based on race, gender, *socioeconomic status* [italics mine], ethnicity, religion, or any other social category"[2].

But there is a problem. At the same time that I am philosophically against concierge medicine, I am also for it, which makes me feel decidedly hypocritical. I fully admit that if I were a practicing primary-care physician in today's world, I would certainly want to have a concierge practice rather than a standard practice. My excuse would be that I would prefer to take care of one person well rather than ten people poorly. Unfortunately, it would be a rationalization and a rather poor one. Instead, perhaps I'd say I have a right to practice medicine the way I want to practice medicine. Unfortunately, that would be denying the fact that a lot of public money is spent training all doctors, including me, which comes with an obligation to take care of all comers, not just those capable of up-front fees. Maybe then I'd say that concierge medicine is akin to private school and that patients with means have the right to pay for more service. Unfortunately, that misses the point that those people who send their kids to private school also have to pay for public school through their taxes. It also misses the point that medical service, even basic medical service, is inequitably distributed, and I'd be adding to that inequality. Ultimately, I'd have to admit to myself that the reason I wanted to practice concierge medicine was probably more because it provided me with day-to-day professional satisfaction, even though deep down I'd lament that I'd become a doctor different from the one I had started out to be. Such an admission means that I don't fault M.D.s practicing concierge medicine but rather the system that has forced them to do so.

It is always easier to be a critic than a problem solver. Yet, in regard to concierge medicine, I do think there is a solution to limit its growth, and it's a rather simple one. It involves merely changing the mechanism of reimbursement for primary care, which today is based on a simple, flat rate of slightly more than fifty dollars per visit as determined by Medicare (Medicare serves as the de facto trendsetter for health policy). Primary care is, as I have mentioned, the bedrock of healthcare, and accordingly this low, flat-rate reimbursement is counterintuitive, as evidenced by the example I gave. Patients and illnesses vary considerably, and if the patient needs fifteen minutes, thirty minutes, forty minutes, or even an hour, the physician should be paid accordingly. In other words, the reimbursement for primary care should be predicated on time and should include phone and e-mail time. It should also be on a sliding scale, depending on the level of training of the physician. It is only reasonable.

If primary care was reimbursed in such a rational fashion, quality care would be encouraged, significant autonomy would be appropriately returned to the primary-care physician, and satisfaction of both the physician and patient would go up. As a corollary, the impetus toward concierge medicine would go down. I also believe such a reimbursement scheme would have the paradoxical effect of lowering overall healthcare costs by lowering utilization of subspecialty services. To help in this regard, reimbursement should be tipped away from procedure-based specialty care, which is the case today, and toward primary care.

Some people might worry that basing reimbursement on *time* would throw open the door to the kind of abuse that is seen in those professions where charges are based on time, but I disagree. I think abuse would be the exception rather than the rule, especially with the strong movement afoot to reassert medical professionalism with the newly promulgated Physician Charter.

On a final note, I want to say something about medical malpractice. When I finished my long medical training in the 1970s and opened a small private practice, I was welcomed into the throes of the first medical malpractice crisis, which had been provoked by a surge in litigation and plaintiff victories. What I experienced, like many other physicians, was a difficulty in obtaining coverage, since a number of the major malpractice insurers suddenly abandoned the market. Luckily, things settled down with the creation of alternative methods for physicians to find malpractice insurance, and everything was fine until the 1980s, when a second medical malpractice crisis loomed. Again, there was a sudden upswing in malpractice suits as well as a marked increase in the size of awards, resulting in a sharp and unsettling increase in insurance premiums.

During these two crises, the healthcare system was resilient enough to absorb the increased costs, mainly by ultimately passing them on to patients and the government through Medicare. As a result, the system didn't suffer any huge disruption other than a marked hardening of the medical profession's dislike for the legal profession, particularly what they considered the "greedy" malpractice plaintiff attorneys. I can remember the time well, and I shared the feelings. With my close association with academic medicine, it seemed to me that only the good doctors who were willing to take on the difficult cases got sued. Consequently, I was fervently behind what most doctors thought was the solution, namely tort reform, such as capping noneconomic rewards, capping attorneys' fees, adjusting certain statutes of limitations, and eliminating joint and several liability.

Unfortunately, there is now a new malpractice crisis, and although its origins are similar—namely, another significant bump in litigation with even higher awards—it is different from the two previous crises and far worse. The new crisis involves both problems of coverage and soaring premiums, but more important, it is occurring during the "perfect storm" that is racking the healthcare system. Indeed, it is one of its causes. Secondary to a number of factors, some of which I have mentioned, the increased costs the crisis is engendering cannot be passed on. Beleaguered physicians are weathering the full force of the gale, adding immeasurably to their dissatisfaction and disillusionment. Consequently, it is affecting access to healthcare in certain areas, with doctors moving or leaving practice and various high-risk services being curtailed. Beyond the economic woes, being sued is a terrible experience for a doctor, as *Crisis* clearly illustrates, even if the doctor is ultimately vindicated, which most are.

Since this new medical malpractice crisis is occurring despite a number of states having passed elements of tort reform, and because new information about the extent of iatrogenic injury has surfaced, I have changed my position. I no longer see tort reform as the solution. Also, I no longer myopically see the problem as a confrontation between the "good guys" and the "bad guys," with altruistic doctors pitted against greedy lawyers. As the storyline of *Crisis* suggests, I'm now convinced there's blame on both sides of the equation, with good and bad in both camps such that I am embarrassed about my original, naive assessment. Global issues of patient safety and appropriate compensation for all patients who suffer adverse outcomes are more important than assigning blame and more important than providing windfall settlements in a kind of lawsuit lottery for a few patients. There are better ways of dealing with the problem, and the public should demand it over the objections of the current shareholders: organized medicine and the personal-injury malpractice trial bar.

The fact is that the tort approach to medical malpractice is not working. Studies have shown that in the current system the vast majority of claims are not meritorious, the vast majority of cases that are meritorious are not filed, and payments are often made with little evidence of substandard care. Such an outcome is hardly a commendable record. In short, the present method of dealing with malpractice is failing in its supposed dual goals of compensating patients with adverse outcomes and providing effective deterrence to medical negligence. On the positive side, there is plenty of money available for a better stratagem with malpractice premiums doctors and hospitals are forced to pay. Currently, very little of this money ends up in the hands of patients, and those who do get some all too frequently don't get it until far down the road after a bitter struggle. We need a system that takes the money and gives it to injured patients without delay while, at the same time, openly investigates the reason for the injury to ensure that it doesn't happen to the next patient. There have been many suggestions for such a system, ranging from a kind of no-fault insurance to something akin to workers' compensation to methods of arbitration/mediation. The time for an alternative approach is now.

1. Zuger, A. 2004. "Dissatisfaction with Medical Practice." *NEJM* 350:69–75.
2. "A Physician Charter." 2005. American Board of Internal Medicine Foundation, American College of Physicians Foundation, European Federation of Internal Medicine.

FOR FURTHER READING

Brennan, T. A. 2002. "Luxury Primary Care—Market Innovation or Threat to Access." *NEJM* 346:1165–68.

Brennan et al. 1991. "Incidence of Adverse Events and Negligence in Hospitalized Patients: Results of Harvard Medical Practice Study." *NEJM* 324:370–76.

Brennan et al. 1996. "Relation Between Negligent Adverse Events and the Outcomes of Medical Malpractice Litigation." *NEJM* 335:1963–67.

Kassirer, J. P. 1998. "Doctor Discontent." *NEJM* 348:1543–45.

Melo et al. 2003. "The New Medical Malpractice Crisis." *NEJM* 348:2281–84.

Studdert et al. 2004. "Medical Malpractice." *NEJM* 350:283–92.

Zipkin, A. "The Concierge Doctor Is Available (At a Price)." *NYT.* 31 July 2005.

Visit **www.panmacmillan.com** to read more about all our books and to buy them. You will also find features, author interviews and news of any author events, and you can sign up for e-newsletters so that you're always first to hear about our new releases.

www.panmacmillan.com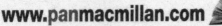

GIFT SELECTOR
YOUR ACCOUNT
WISH LIST
WAITING LIST

HOME | ABOUT US | IMPRINTS | TRADE/MEDIA | CONTACT US | ADVANCED SEARCH | SEARCH | GO

BOOK CATEGORIES | WHAT'S NEW | AUTHORS/ILLUSTRATORS | BESTSELLERS | READING GROUPS

Coming Soon...

Reading Groups

Competitions
Feeling Lucky?

Extracts
Sneak Previews

Interviews

Events
Meet Our Stars

Reviews
What The Critics Say

News & Awards

Editor's Choice
What We're Reading